A BOND UNDONE

Legends of the
Condor Heroes II

JIN YONG

Legends of the Condor Heroes II

A BOND UNDONE

Translated from the Chinese by
Gigi Chang

MACLEHOSE PRESS
QUERCUS · LONDON

First published in the Chinese language as
Shediao Yingxiong Zhuan (2) in 1959; revised in 1976, 2003

First published in Great Britain in 2019 by MacLehose Press
This paperback edition published in 2019 by

MacLehose Press
An imprint of Quercus Publishing Ltd
Carmelite House
50 Victoria Embankment
London EC4Y oDZ

An Hachette UK company

A CIP catalogue record for this book is
available from the British Library.

ISBN (MMP) 978 1 78429 958 3
ISBN (Ebook) 978 0 85705 460 9

1 3 5 7 9 10 8 6 4 2

Designed and typeset in Columbus MT by Patty Rennie
Printed and bound in Great Britain by Elcograf S.p.A.

CONTENTS

CHARACTERS

As they appear in this, the second volume of
Legends of the Condor Heroes: A Bond Undone

MAIN CHARACTERS

Guo Jing, son of Skyfury Guo and Lily Li. He grows up with his mother in Mongolia and they are looked after by Genghis Khan. He is now on his first journey to the Central Plains, the native land of his parents.

Lotus Huang, witty and mischievous, a skilled martial artist and extremely fast learner. She becomes a friend of Guo Jing early on in his travels, and they now journey together and share many adventures.

THE JIN EMPIRE

Wanyan Honglie, Sixth Prince, also known as **Prince of Zhao**, has made conquering the Song his personal mission, in order to secure his reputation and legacy among his own people. He is an astute tactician, using rivalries and jealousies within the Song court and the *wulin* to his own advantage.

Wanyan Kang, son of the Sixth Prince, is arrogant and entitled, but possesses considerable martial skill. He fights Guo Jing after refusing to honour his prize when he wins the Duel for a Maiden.

Consort to the Sixth Prince, mother of Wanyan Kang.

FOLLOWERS OF THE SIXTH PRINCE OF THE JIN EMPIRE

Gallant Ouyang, Master of White Camel Mount in the Kunlun Range, nephew to one of the Five Greats, Viper Ouyang, Venom of the West.

The Dragon King Hector Sha controls the Yellow River with his four rather more useless apprentices, whose lack of skill infuriates their Master, despite the fact that it is most likely his foul temper that has prevented them from learning anything more than their rather basic moves.

The Four Daemons of the Yellow River

> **Shen Qinggang the Strong**, whose weapon is a sabre called the Spirit Cleaver.

> **Wu Qinglie the Bold** fights with a spear called the Dispatcher.

> **Ma Qingxiong the Valiant** is known for his Soul Snatcher whip.

> **Qian Qingjian the Hardy** is armed with a pair of axes known as the Great Reapers.

Browbeater Hou, the Three-Horned Dragon, so named for the three cysts on his forehead.

Greybeard Liang, also known as **Old Liang**, the **Ginseng Immortal** and, more disparagingly, the **Ginseng Codger**. He comes from the Mount of Eternal Snow (Changbai Mountains) up in the north-east, close to the current border with Korea, where he has practised kung fu for many years as a hermit, as well as mixing special medicinal concoctions with the aim of prolonging life and gaining strength.

Lama Supreme Wisdom Lobsang Choden Rinpoche, from Kokonor, now known as Qinghai. He is famed for his Five Finger Blade kung fu.

Tiger Peng the Outlaw, Butcher of a Thousand Hands, has command of much of the mountainous region surrounding the Jin capital Zhongdu, which would later become Peking.

SUBJECTS OF THE SONG EMPIRE

Ironheart Yang, descendent of Triumph Yang, one-time rebel turned patriot who served under General Yue Fei. He practises the Yang Family Spear, a technique passed from father to son.

Married to **Charity Bao**, daughter of a country scholar from Red Plum Village.

Yang Kang, son of Ironheart Yang and Charity Bao, sworn as brother to Guo Jing while both are still in their mothers' bellies.

Mercy Mu, god-daughter of Ironheart Yang, takes part in martial contests her godfather stages to find her a suitable husband and is defeated by Wanyan Kang.

Justice Duan, a government official of the Song who, in actual fact, works for the Jin.

THE MONGOLIANS

Tolui, fourth son of Genghis Khan Temujin, and Guo Jing's sworn brother.

Khojin, one of Genghis Khan's many daughters whose names are mostly lost to history, betrothed by her father to Guo Jing.

Jebe, whose name means "arrow" and "Divine Archer" in Mongolian, is a general under Genghis Khan and known for his great skill with the bow and arrow. He has taught Guo Jing archery and wrestling.

Boroqul, one of Genghis Khan's Four Great Generals.

THE SEVEN FREAKS OF THE SOUTH

Also known as the Seven Heroes of the South when being addressed respectfully by other characters. They refer to themselves as a martial family, despite being of no blood relation. After the death of one of their group, they are sometimes called the Six Freaks of the South.

Ke Zhen'e, Suppressor of Evil, also known as **Flying Bat**. The oldest of the Freaks, he is often referred to as Big Brother. Blinded in a fight, his preferred weapon is his flying devilnuts, iron projectiles made in the shape of a kind of water chestnut native to China.

Quick Hands Zhu Cong the Intelligent is known for his quick thinking and even quicker sleight of hand. His dirty scholar's dress and broken oilpaper fan, really made from iron, belie his real martial skill. He is particularly knowledgeable in acupressure points, using them to disable his opponents in a fight.

Ryder Han, Protector of the Steeds, only three foot in height but a formidable fighter and an expert horseman. His weapon of choice is a whip.

Woodcutter Nan the Merciful, known for his kind, if not shy, nature, fights with an iron-tipped shoulder pole.

Zhang Asheng, also known as the **Laughing Buddha**, is a burly man dressed as a butcher, whose preferred weapon is the butcher's knife. He is secretly in love with Jade Han.

Gilden Quan the Prosperous, Cloaked Master of the Market, is a master of the rules of the marketplace and always looking for a good deal. He fights with a set of scales.

Jade Han, Maiden of the Yue Sword, is the youngest of the group and the only female. She is trained in the Yue Sword, a technique particular to the region surrounding Jiaxing and developed when the Kingdom of Yue was at war with the Kingdom of Wu in the fifth century B.C.

THE FIVE GREATS

Considered the five greatest martial artists after a contest was held on Mount Hua. Four are mentioned in this second book in the series:

The Eastern Heretic Apothecary Huang, a loner and radical who practises his unorthodox martial arts on Peach Blossom Island along with his wife and six students. He holds traditions and their accompanying morals in contempt and believes only in true love and honour. His eccentricity and heretical views make others suspicious of him, an image he himself cultivates.

Double Sun Wang Chongyang, also known as **Central Divinity**, is the founder of the Quanzhen Sect in the Zhongnan Mountains, with the aim of training Taoists in the martial arts so that they might defend the Song against the Jurchen invasion. A real historical figure, he lived from A.D. 1113 to 1170.

The Northern Beggar Count Seven Hong, sometimes referred to as the **Divine Vagrant Nine Fingers**, is the Chief of the Beggar Clan and commands all the beggars in the Song and Jin Empires. He is respected for his sense of righteousness, but few know his whereabouts as he likes to roam the *jianghu* alone. He is also known for his great love for exceptional cooking.

The Western Venom Viper Ouyang, uncle to Gallant Ouyang, is a master in taming venomous snakes and using poison. He draws inspiration from the deadly creatures he keeps in his martial practice and rarely sets foot in the Central Plains.

PEACH BLOSSOM ISLAND

Twice Foul Dark Wind were apprentices of Apothecary Huang, who fled Peach Blossom Island and eloped after stealing the Nine Yin Manual. Husband **Hurricane Chen**, known as **Copper Corpse**, and wife, **Iron Corpse Cyclone Mei**, are masters of the Nine Yin Skeleton Claw. They killed Ke Zhen'e's brother, Ke Bixie the Talisman.

They have four martial siblings: an elder martial brother, **Tempest Qu**, and three younger martial brothers, **Zephyr Lu**, **Galeforce Wu** and **Doldrum Feng**.

THE QUANZHEN TAOIST SECT

A real branch of Taoism, whose name means "Way of Complete Perfection".

The Seven Immortals, students of Wang Chongyang

Only three of the Immortals make their appearance in this second book of the series:

Scarlet Sun Ma Yu, the oldest of the Immortals, teaches internal kung fu, based on breathing techniques.

Eternal Spring Qiu Chuji befriends Ironheart Yang and Skyfury Guo at the beginning of the series and vows to protect their unborn offspring. To this end, he devises a martial contest with the Seven Freaks of the South. He becomes teacher to Yang Kang.

Jade Sun Wang Chuyi, the Iron Foot Immortal, befriends Guo Jing after hearing of Qiu Chuji's contest with the Seven Freaks of the South.

Zhou Botong the Hoary Urchin, sworn brother and student of Wang Chongyang, martial uncle to the Seven Immortals and a lay member of the Quanzhen Sect. He has not been seen in the *wulin* for fifteen years at the start of this volume.

ROAMING CLOUD MANOR

On the shore of Lake Tai is Roaming Cloud Manor, a grand estate with an unusual layout. Its master is **Squire Lu**, a cultured man who has lost the use of his legs, and his son **Laurel Lu** is in charge of the everyday running of the household.

IRON PALM GANG

The Iron Palm Gang wields great influence over Hunan and Sichuan in the south and south-west of China, and its leader is **Qiu Qianren the Iron Palm Water Glider**.

CHAPTER ONE

SMOKE OF THE PAST

I

"I WON!" GIGGLING AND TRIUMPHANT, LOTUS HUANG HEADED
for the doors.

"You are a disciple of Twice Foul Dark Wind." Tiger Peng leapt
over to block her. "I won't make trouble with you. But you cannot
leave until you've explained why your *shifus* sent you here."

"You promised to let me go if you couldn't name the school of my
kung fu within ten moves. Surely a martial master like you would not
go back on your word?" Lotus smiled sweetly.

"Your last move, Hallowed Turtle Steps, is part of Twice Foul
Dark Wind's repertoire. Who else could have taught you that?" Tiger
Peng snapped.

"Do you truly think their paltry skills are worthy of my attention?
I have never met Twice Foul Dark Wind—"

"We won't be fooled by your lies!"

"But I know them by reputation," Lotus went on, ignoring the
interruption. "I know they don't shy from evil deeds. I know they are
disloyal to their Master. I know they are cruel and savage in all their
dealings. I know they are the most depraved characters of the whole

wulin. How could Master Peng think that I am associated with such scoundrels?"

Tiger Peng looked over to his companions. He could tell they were also convinced that she had learned her kung fu from Twice Foul Dark Wind. But no student of the martial arts would heap such insults on their teacher. It would be an irreparable breach of every moral code.

"Young lady, you have won this time. I am most impressed by your skill." He stepped aside. "May I ask your name?"

"Why, thank you. I am Lotus."

"And your family name?"

"Let's just say it's not Peng."

Of the five men of martial learning in the banqueting hall, Lotus Huang had defeated three: Browbeater Hou, the Three-Horned Dragon; his martial brother Hector Sha, Dragon King of the Daemon Sect; and now their friend Tiger Peng the Outlaw, Butcher of a Thousand Hands. The fourth Master, Lama Supreme Wisdom, had suffered an injury from the previous evening when he fought the Taoist monk Jade Sun Wang Chuyi, and was currently confined to his seat.

All eyes were now on the last of their number, Gallant Ouyang. He was their only hope of finding out why this young girl had broken into the palace of the Sixth Prince of the Jin Empire and why she was spying on them.

Dressed head-to-toe in a pure white scholar's outfit, Gallant Ouyang cut a dashing figure among the bulky, bellicose men. He flashed his most winning smile and stepped forward. "I should like to sample a few of my lady's kung fu moves."

Known as the Master of White Camel Mount, he prided himself as a connoisseur of beauty as well as of the martial arts. Together with his uncle, Viper Ouyang, who was one of the greatest martial masters of the age, he was a formidable figure in the Western Regions. Over the years, he had collected – often by force – many pretty girls to serve as his concubines and had taught them kung fu in his spare time. He was in the habit of taking them with him on his travels. On this trip to the Central Plains as a guest of the Sixth Prince Wanyan Honglie, twenty-four of these concubines had come with him, though four had met their end on the journey. The women rode camels and disguised themselves as young men, donning all-white robes.

Lotus looked him up and down. "The girls in white, outside, came here with you, didn't they?"

"The sum of their beauty is less than half of your charm," Gallant Ouyang gushed.

The compliment brought a tinge of pink to Lotus's cheeks. "You seem more reasonable than the old uncles, here."

Gallant Ouyang was sure that he had a collection of beauties to rival the imperial harems of the Jin or Song Empires. Yet the exceptional grace of this teenage intruder eclipsed all his concubines. They now appeared common and repulsive in comparison. Despite her tender age, Gallant Ouyang had been smitten from the moment he caught sight of her. And now she had turned her eyes on him, addressing him with her gentle, soft voice, he could feel the urge to possess her weakening his whole being, and his usual eloquence vanished without a trace.

"I'm leaving now," Lotus said to Gallant Ouyang. "If they try to stop me again, you'll help me, won't you?"

"Of course, but in return you must call me *shifu* and stay with me always." He found his voice at last.

"Not always, surely?"

"My disciples are unlike any others. Not only are they all female, they are also always by my side, and they all come at once when I call."

"I don't believe you."

Gallant Ouyang whistled and a flutter of white robes appeared. Twenty women filed in and took their place in a line behind their *shifu*. Some were tall, some short, some slim, some buxom. They were dressed the same, but each was dazzling in her own way. They had been standing at attention near the Hall of Perfumed Snow since the start of the banquet, in case their master needed them.

This was the first time Tiger Peng and the others in the room had clapped eyes on all of Gallant Ouyang's women and they were instantly beside themselves with envy.

Lotus had hoped that the women's entrance would be enough of a distraction to allow her to escape, but Gallant Ouyang was too quick for her, planting himself by the doorway.

Fanning himself idly with his gentleman's folding fan, the leering dandy let his gaze rest on Lotus as his concubines regrouped. They now flanked him protectively, blocking the way out like two screens. Their eyes fixed on Lotus with sadness and jealousy. They knew they were about to lose favour with their fickle master.

Knowing she would not stand a chance against this human blockade, Lotus said, "If your kung fu proved worthy of the title *shifu*, I'd happily call you that so no-one could trouble me again."

"You wish to try my skills?"

"Indeed."

"It would be my pleasure. I promise I won't raise a hand against you."

"You think you can win without using your hands?"

"You can't imagine the thrill our encounter has given me. How could I lift a finger against you?"

The men sniggered at Gallant Ouyang's suggestive reply — though, having seen her martial skills, they all doubted his claim. Unless he used sorcery, surely there was no earthly way he could defeat her without taking the offensive.

"I don't trust you. You must tie your hands."

Gallant Ouyang obliged, removing his belt and holding it out for Lotus. She took it with a smile, but his confidence made her uneasy.

I'll just have to take it one step at a time, she said to herself as she summoned her internal strength and tugged the belt to test how strong the fabric was. To her surprise, it did not give. Could it be woven from metal threads?

By now, Gallant Ouyang had folded his hands behind his back, waiting for her to bind them.

Lotus wound the belt around his wrists and secured it with a tight double knot. "So, how do I win?"

Extending his right leg, Gallant Ouyang placed the tip of his foot on the ground, three foot from his body. Then, suddenly, he pivoted on his left, quickly scoring a perfect circle, half an inch deep, into the stone floor. His extraordinary control and internal strength was evident to all.

"The first to be pushed beyond the perimeter loses this fight," Gallant Ouyang explained.

"What if we both end up outside?"

"Well, then I lose."

"And, if you lose, you promise you won't stop me from leaving and you won't come after me."

"Of course. But, if you lose, you must come with me without a word. The Masters here will be our judges."

"Alright!" Lotus stepped inside the ring and immediately launched two palm strikes, Willow in the Wind and Stars in the Sky. Balancing supple strength in her left hand with vigorous force in her right, she sliced at his shoulder and his back.

Gallant Ouyang adjusted his stance slightly, but, staying true to his word, did not lift a hand. He simply tilted a little to the side and let the blows fall on him.

Lotus immediately realised her mistake. His superior *neigong* internal-strength training bounced the force of her blows back at her. She was being attacked by her own inner energy! The impact nearly sent her reeling out of the circle. Fighting him was no longer an option.

She paced along the perimeter, turning ideas over in her head. After a few laps, she announced, "I'm stepping outside this circle now by my own choice, not because I was pushed out by you. You said that if we both cross this line, then you lose. And you also promised that, if you lost, you wouldn't stop me from leaving and you wouldn't come after me." She ambled out of the ring, then quickened her stride in case the men found another excuse to detain her.

Gallant Ouyang cursed himself, but it would be ungentlemanly to break his own rules. All he could do was watch the glittering golden loops bobbing in her hair as she walked away.

Raucous laughter broke out from Tiger Peng. Though he was none the wiser as to why this girl was eavesdropping on them, it gave him great pleasure to see her outwitting Gallant Ouyang.

Just as Lotus was reaching the doorway, she felt a gust of air sweeping overhead and something enormous fell in front of her. She twirled sideways to avoid being crushed. As she found her footing, she was greeted by the sight of the wooden armchair containing Lama Supreme Wisdom, who was half a head taller than her even when sitting down.

The lama pulled out a pair of copper cymbals from his crimson vestment and struck them together before Lotus could say a word.

Clang!

Lotus's ears rang painfully, and she was dimly aware that the noise did not match the cymbals' appearance. They must be made of steel rather than copper.

The harsh sound was followed by a flash. The cymbals were now flying horizontally at her. Their edges glistened with the chill of sharp blades.

They'll cut me in three!

Instead of ducking, Lotus leapt and dived straight at the airborne cymbals. She squeezed between them with a push from her right hand and a tap from her left foot, but the desperate move propelled her headlong into the seated lama. Unable to halt her momentum as she landed, she slammed into the monk's waiting palm, which was raised in his deadliest kung fu, the Five Finger Blade.

"No!" Gallant Ouyang shouted as gasps of shock echoed around the banqueting hall. He lunged, but he was too far away to intervene. He watched the lama's monstrously large hand slap against Lotus's dainty back. The bones of this delicate flower would surely be crushed. Then a shriek tore at his ears and, at the same time, he noticed Lotus flying through the doorway as Lama Supreme Wisdom jerked his hand back.

The monk howled. A peal of laughter from beyond the hall came as the reply.

She didn't sound like she was hurt. The thought was quickly chased away by a torrent of questions in Gallant Ouyang's mind. How had she managed to stay unharmed by such a powerful strike? Did he pull his hand away before channelling his inner strength? But why would he do that?

Lama Supreme Wisdom held up his right palm. It was a grisly sight. The flesh was pierced and torn with dozens of small wounds. He stared at his mutilated hand as he declared in a voice laced with pain and terror: "Hedgehog Chainmail."

"That's the most coveted treasure from the armoury of Peach Blossom Island in the Eastern Sea!" Tiger Peng could not believe his ears.

More interested in Lotus than her attire, Gallant Ouyang slipped outside. The dark night had long engulfed her retreating form, but he was secretly pleased that was the case. If she could get away, that meant she wasn't hurt. I shall hold that heavenly creature in these arms, he promised himself as he whistled to gather his concubines. Together, they headed into the palace grounds to find the beguiling young woman.

"How did the little girl get her hands on something like that?" Hector Sha wondered aloud.

"What is Hedgehog Chainmail, brother?" Browbeater Hou asked.

"You've seen a hedgehog, right?" Tiger Peng answered for Hector Sha.

"Of course."

"She wears this steel shirt under her dress. No weapon, blade or spear can cut through it. And it's covered in short spikes. Like a hedgehog."

Browbeater Hou stuck his tongue out. "Thank the heavens I never tried to punch her."

"I'll bring her back here!" Hector Sha declared.

"Watch out for the chainmail, brother!" Browbeater Hou said.

"Of course! I'll drag her by the hair!" Hector Sha rushed out with Tiger Peng, leaving his martial brother Browbeater Hou scrambling after them.

The Sixth Prince Wanyan Honglie had much enjoyed the diversion. It had granted him further insight into the skills and personality of his *wulin* guests. But, at that moment, his son Wanyan Kang ran into the hall with the news of his Consort's abduction.

The palace was thrown into a tumult. The Princes organised the search parties, and the lanterns and torches made the black sky as bright as day. The sound of marching soldiers and whinnying horses broke the silence of the night.

2

GUO JING RAN.

He did not care where he was going. He just wanted to get away from the old man who was chasing him. He chose the darkest path at every turn, using his fastest lightness *qinggong* technique.

Soon, he lost sight of the lanterns from the palace buildings. He had also lost his bearings. He seemed to be in an untended part of the garden, caught among clumps of thorns and strange rocks that jabbed into the earth like swords. His skin was prickled and torn, but he had avoided a worse fate. The old man wanted to drink his blood! The memory of bare teeth snapping at his throat drove Guo Jing through the barbed shrubs.

Aiiiyaaaaaaa! The ground had given away. He plummeted for four, maybe five metres.

Guo Jing summoned his *qi* to cushion the fall, but his feet found no flat surface on which to land.

Thud! He made contact with something. Round objects. His feet rolled, sending him crashing onto his backside. He tried to push himself up, but everywhere he put his hands he found more of the same curious orbs.

Skulls? A chill ran through Guo Jing. This is where they dump dead bodies in the palace!

"Come out, boy!" the old man shouted.

Never! Why would I let you drink my blood? Guo Jing retorted, to himself. He felt around, seeking somewhere to hide in case the man jumped down. Finding a cavity behind him, he retreated a few steps.

The man raved and cursed, but of course it was of little use. "I'll catch you, even if you have descended into the underworld!" he cried, and leapt into the pit.

Guo Jing realised that he was actually standing at the mouth of a tunnel. He spun around and clambered inside.

The old man followed the noise of Guo Jing groping in the dark. It was pitch black, but he was so confident of his superior kung fu that he had no fear of being ambushed by the young man.

It's like catching a turtle in a tank. You can't run from me! He congratulated himself on having cornered the thief, and hurried after his prey.

Guo Jing soon realised the hopelessness of his situation. When this tunnel comes to an end, I'll be trapped. But what else could he do but push forward?

The old man threw his arms wide, touching the sides of the tunnel as he prowled on through the dark. A single thought circled in his mind: You killed my precious snake and drank its blood. I will claim what's mine and suck your blood dry!

Guo Jing fumbled on for another dozen paces. Suddenly, the tunnel opened up into a chamber, but he could also sense the old man closing in quickly.

Now that his prey was within reach, the man crowed, "You have nowhere to run, boy!"

"Who dares make trouble here?"

An icy voice emanated from the left side of the chamber. These words were spoken softly, but they knocked on their eardrums like bolts of thunder.

Guo Jing's heart thumped loudly, and the old man shivered. Neither had expected to find company in such a place.

"No-one comes out of this pit alive." A ghostly voice. But the shallow breathing made it human.

She sounds sickly, Guo Jing thought, his fear subsiding somewhat.

"I fell into this pit. I was running from—"

The old man now knew where Guo Jing was and he ran forward, his arms flailing. Guo Jing, in turn, was alerted by the sound of shuffling footsteps and he tried to duck out of the way.

The man grabbed Guo Jing's sleeve and the fabric tore with a *rip!*

"Who comes down here to fight?"

"You don't scare me." The old man's response was not entirely truthful.

"Young man, come here," the strange voice said.

I'd rather put my life into the hands of this— Before Guo Jing could finish the thought, five icy fingers closed around his wrist. An energy of exceptional potency flowed through them. The fingers tugged him from the old man's grip and he lurched, face first, into a bale of straw.

"Grappling technique." The strange voice addressed the old man. "You come from beyond the border?" Her breathing became a wheeze.

It's pitch black down here. How could she tell what kung fu I used? The old man knew he needed to tread carefully.

"I am merely a ginseng picker from the north-eastern borderlands. I go by the surname Liang." He projected his words with internal strength to demonstrate his kung fu. "This boy has taken a valued possession from me. I trust Madam would not interfere in this personal matter."

"Ah, Greybeard Liang, the Ginseng Immortal," she gasped, as if in pain. "For a nobody to stumble into my cave is already an unforgiveable crime. You are a master of the *wulin*. You should know the rules that govern our martial world. You of all people should realise that your presence here is an inexcusable affront."

Taken aback by how much this woman knew about him, Old Liang said, "May I ask Madam's name?"

The hand clutching onto Guo Jing's wrist shook violently at this innocent question. She spluttered, but no answer came. Then her grip loosened for a moment as she struggled to suppress the groan rising in her body.

She must be in a lot of pain, Guo Jing thought. "Are you unwell?" he asked, with genuine concern.

The Ginseng Immortal, meanwhile, felt less nervous. She might be a kung fu master, but she was either ill or injured. Not a threat, in this state. Safe in that assumption, he gathered his inner strength into his arms and lunged at Guo Jing.

Just as he made contact with the front of Guo Jing's shirt, Old Liang felt a great energy drawing his wrists to the left. He twirled his left hand around to grab the offender.

"Shoo!" The woman struck Greybeard Liang in the back.

The unexpected blow made the old man stumble a few steps, but, using his inner strength, he recovered quickly. Once out of her reach, he called, "Come and get me, crone!" – and waited.

Panting.

And that was it. No sound of any movement. Greybeard Liang knew he was right. The woman could not walk. Guided by her loud, ragged breathing, he edged closer. Then pounced. Suddenly, he sensed something strike his ankle and coil around it.

A whip?

It had come without warning, the air still and silent. Yet the Ginseng Immortal's reaction, honed through decades of combat, was quick as lightning. As the whip curled upwards, he lifted his body and went with it. Then he lashed out with a right-footed kick.

For twenty long years, this kick had never failed him. It was what had made his name. One sweep was enough to annihilate any martial master on the receiving end.

As the tip of his foot hit its target, Greybeard Liang's head smacked into the earthen wall of the narrow underground chamber.

The beginnings of a numbing sensation spread through the top of his foot, five inches from his big toe: his Surging Yang pressure point. If she were to strike it harder, he would lose all movement in his leg.

He wrenched his foot away in a panic and flipped into a somersault to escape.

How could her aim be so precise? It was as if she was fighting him in broad daylight. Was she even human? Her movements were almost otherworldly.

Once Greybeard Liang had found his footing, he swung to face the ghostly woman, guided by her gasping, and thrust out his palm with all his inner *neigong* power. Though his knee and his head throbbed with pain, he was certain that an opponent who was struggling to breathe would not have the internal strength to counter this blow.

Just then, the sound of joints cracking echoed around the underground chamber. To the Ginseng Immortal's horror, he found her fingertips digging into his shoulder.

Did she just extend the length of her arm?

He lifted his arm to bat away the attacking hand. Her wrist had a frosty chill not born of flesh and blood.

Greybeard Liang had no desire to fight this thing. He dived into a front roll and made for the tunnel, scampering along the passageway. He heaved with relief as he emerged into the night, dumbstruck by the encounter.

Was she human? Was she a spectre? He had never experienced anything like it in all his decades. Now she had the boy, and the precious python blood he had spent so many years cultivating, she would surely drain him dry for her own gain. Was he destined to fail again in his search for immortality?

Just then, it struck him. The Sixth Prince must know about her . . .

At that thought, he hurried back to the Hall of Perfumed Snow to seek answers.

3

"THANK YOU, MASTER, FOR SAVING MY LIFE." GUO JING CAST himself on the ground and kowtowed. Greybeard Liang's footsteps had faded into the distance.

The exertion of the scuffle had turned the woman's wheezing into a hacking cough. It was some time before she was able to speak. "Why did he try to kill you?"

"I came here to find herbs to cure Elder Wang's injury . . ." It dawned on Guo Jing that she was probably yet another martial master in the pay of the Jin Prince Wanyan Honglie.

"Greybeard Liang is famous for his knowledge of medicinal herbs. You must have stolen something very precious."

"I only took some remedies, things that are good for internal injuries. Does Master suffer a similar problem? I have plenty of herbs here. Cinnibar, resina draconis, notoginseng, bear's gall bladder and myrrh. Elder Wang won't need them all. If Master—"

"I am fine! I don't need your help."

Guo Jing mumbled something, but he could not stay silent for long, listening to her pained breathing. "If Master has trouble walking, I am happy to carry my senior out—"

"Senior? What makes you think I'm old?"

Snubbed once more, Guo Jing held his tongue. He wanted to leave, but felt bad deserting her in this dark and horrible place. After a moment, he offered timidly, "If Master requires anything, please allow me to fetch it."

"You are tiresome . . . but you have heart . . ."

Guo Jing felt an icy hand grab him by the shoulder and drag him closer. The grip was so firm it sent a sharp pain down his spine. Then he felt a chill around his neck. She had him in a headlock.

"Carry me out."

I offered to do just that! Grumbling silently to himself, he bent down and lifted her onto his back.

"Remember, I made you do this," the woman clarified as Guo Jing felt his way out of the tunnel. "I don't accept kindness from anyone."

What a strange, proud lady, Guo Jing said to himself. Lotus won't believe me when I tell her what I've just been through.

Emerging from the dark tunnel, he could now see the clear night sky beyond the mouth of the pit. The ascent was steep, but he had climbed cliffs more treacherous than this nightly in Mongolia as part of his training.

"Who taught you lightness kung fu?" Her fingers tightened around Guo Jing's throat.

Gasping for air, Guo Jing summoned his internal strength to push back. The woman dug her fingers in harder. She wanted to make him reveal the depth of his training.

"You practise orthodox *neigong* technique." She loosened her grip somewhat. "You said this Elder Wang was injured. Tell me his full name."

"His name is Wang Chuyi. He is known as Jade Sun."

Guo Jing answered out of respect for her seniority, but inside he felt rather mistreated. You saved my life; I'd have told you the truth anyway. You didn't have to use force.

A shudder ran through the woman. "You are a disciple of the Quanzhen Sect? That's . . . wonderful."

Guo Jing wondered what had softened her tone. She sounded almost pleased.

"Why do you call Wang Chuyi 'elder' instead of 'teacher' or 'martial uncle'?"

"I am not a disciple of the Quanzhen Sect. But Elder Ma Yu the Scarlet Sun did teach me some breathing techniques."

"So you were trained in Quanzhen internal-strength kung fu? Very good . . . Who is your Master, then?"

"I have seven mentors. They are known as the Seven Heroes of the South. My First *Shifu* is Flying Bat Ke, the Suppressor of Evil."

A violent fit of coughing overcame the woman. When she recovered, she spat the name out like a bad taste in the mouth: "Ke Zhen'e!"

"That's right."

"You came from Mongolia?"

"Yes."

How does she know? Guo Jing wondered.

"Your name is Yang Kang, is it not?" She was now speaking slowly and deliberately. The chill had returned to her voice. In fact, she sounded more menacing than before.

"No, Guo Jing is my name."

The woman pondered his answer. "Sit down."

Guo Jing obeyed without a word as she took an object from inside her shirt and put it on the ground. It gleamed under the stars.

Guo Jing picked it up. It was the dagger he had kept since he was a boy. A gift from his mother.

Twelve years had passed since he last held it. He remembered that night very well. Climbing up the mountain on the Mongolian steppe, hoping to learn kung fu from the seven strangers he had met that morning. As he reached the top, he got caught up in a bloody fight between his future *shifus*, the Seven Freaks of the South, and the terror of the martial world, Twice Foul Dark Wind. He pulled out the knife to defend himself – and the seven strangers who were so kind to him that morning – and buried it in the stomach of the man who had caused the carnage, the man who killed the Fifth *Shifu* he never got to know. That man was Copper Corpse Hurricane Chen, one half of Twice Foul Dark Wind.

But Guo Jing did not know the story behind the dagger. He had not yet learned to read, when the blade was his. He did not recognise the characters carved into the hilt as a name. Yang Kang. Vitality Yang. He did not realise his fate had been entwined with that of this Yang Kang even before he was born. He had no idea the knife was one of a pair given to his father and his father's best friend by a Taoist monk when his mother was with child. Or that his father and his friend exchanged these little swords to seal a pact of marriage if one had a boy and the other a girl, or of brotherhood if their children were of the same sex. That was how the dagger with the name Yang Kang had ended up in Guo Jing's possession.

The young man was also not aware that he had in fact met this Yang Kang in combat not two days before, or that he had already come face to face with Yang Kang's mother and father, as well as the man Yang Kang thought was his sire.

And yet, he had heard the name Yang Kang before. Indeed, it had been uttered this very evening in the palace – by the Prince's Consort.

The woman snatched the knife back. "You know this dagger, don't you?"

"Yes," he answered, unaware of the bile evident in her voice.

Guo Jing, by nature, was a trusting, artless creature. This aspect of his character had only been amplified by growing up among the straight-talking, hospitable men of Mongolia. Because she had saved his life, he had made up his mind that this sickly woman on his back must be kind-hearted and that he must repay her with honesty. Even when she spoke in such an alarming tone, it did not occur to him to turn and look at her face.

He then added, "I stabbed an evil man with this dagger when I was a child. He disappeared, along with—"

The hand tightened over Guo Jing's windpipe, squeezing hard. He thrust back with his elbow, but, instead of freeing himself, all he managed to do was to offer her his wrist, which she locked in an iron grip between her fingers.

Now the woman took her hand off his throat and slid down from his back. Once settled on the ground, she barked, "Look at me!"

Then she crushed her fingers together.

The pain from his wrist sent a firework of stars across Guo Jing's eyes. He fought to focus. Long, unkempt hair. Skin pale as paper. He knew her. Iron Corpse Cyclone Mei. The other half of Twice Foul Dark Wind.

He struggled with all his might to wrench free, but she dug her claws deeper into his flesh.

How can it be? I was saved by Cyclone Mei? Impossible! But it is her! The absurdity of the situation cut through the fear, panic and pain that seized Guo Jing.

The irony of this encounter was not lost on Cyclone Mei either. But was it fortuitous? She began to wonder. She had searched and searched, without luck, for more than ten years for the owner of this dagger. And now he had come to her.

Seeing the recognition in the young man's eyes, she locked him by the throat again. However, her fingers stayed slack as her focus started to drift from the here and now.

Sweet bastard husband, did you deliver your murderer to me? Dearest filthy dog, do you think of me from the underworld? Do you know revenge has been the only thing on my mind since that horrible, horrible night?

She threw her head back to look at the stars, but her eyes were cloaked by an unceasing blackness. She tried to stand up, yet the lower half of her body stayed limp and motionless.

My internal-energy flow must have taken a wrong turn. If *Shifu* was here, he'd point me in the right direction, and I'd be able to walk again. If *Shifu* was here, he'd teach me, he'd explain patiently. Even if I had a thousand, ten thousand questions. *Shifu* . . . *Shifu*, I wish I could hold your hand once more. Would you . . . Would you teach me again?

Waves of memories and emotions long suppressed surged through Cyclone Mei, lapping at the fringes of her mind.

4

FLORA MEI.

That was the name my doting parents gave me. I spent my days playing and did not have a care in the world. Then they left me to fend for myself in this world.

My father's brother and his wife took me in. When I turned

eleven, they sold me for fifty *taels* of silver to a wealthy family, the Jiangs of Jiang Village in Shangyu County.

I became a maidservant.

Master Jiang was kind at first, but the mistress was always cruel.

And soon I turned twelve.

I was doing laundry by the well and Master Jiang approached me, a smirk on his face.

"The little lady is growing prettier by the day." He stroked my cheek. "You'll be a great beauty before you turn sixteen."

I turned away from his touch and ignored him. Then his hand crept down to my bosom. I shoved him aside. I had been doing laundry, so my hands were covered with soap bubbles and they stuck to his beard. It was an absurd sight and I could not help but laugh.

Thump! My head split with pain. I almost fainted.

"Little vixen! Are you seducing my husband already?" The mistress struck me over the head again and again with a wooden staff.

I fled. But she quickly caught up with me and pulled my hair, yanking my head back.

"Strumpet! I'll smash your face! I'll pluck out your eyes!" She swung the staff at my face and jabbed at my eyes with her pointy nails.

I shrieked and pushed her back. She fell on her backside and that made her blind with rage. She screamed and yelled. Three older maidservants rushed over, grabbed hold of my arms and legs and dragged me into the kitchen. She had them press me down on the floor and made a show of heating the fire tongs in the stove until they were red hot.

"I'll brand your face. I'll sear your eyes. I'll make you blind and ugly!"

"No! My lady! Please!"

I fought, but I could not break free. I screwed my eyes shut. The heat was inching closer and closer.

Suddenly, a clatter.

"Have you no shame?!"

The searing heat melted away. The pressure on my limbs vanished. I scrabbled to pull myself up.

A man in a light green robe hoisted the mistress by the back of her collar. Her whole person was lifted from the ground. He held the fire tongs in his right hand, inches from her face.

"Help! Help! Bandit! Murder!" Mistress Jiang screeched like a pig at the slaughter.

Several male servants came running in, armed with batons and pitchforks. The man extended his leg and flicked his foot. One by one, they flew out of the kitchen and into the courtyard.

"Sir! Have mercy!" The mistress changed tactic.

"Dare you do this again?"

"Never! Sir can come by to check."

"You think I have nothing better to do? Let me gouge out your eyes first."

"No, sir, please! Take the maid. A gift – for my trespasses."

He let her go and the mistress collapsed in a heap. She scrambled onto her knees and knocked her head loudly against the floor in a great show of submission and gratitude.

"Thank you, merciful sir! This girl is yours. We paid fifty *taels* of silver for her. But she is yours for free."

"I don't want a gift. You would have killed her if I hadn't stepped in." The man took a large *sycee* ingot of silver from his robe and threw it on the floor. "That's a hundred *taels*. Put it in writing that she is free."

The mistress ran into the house, dripping tears and snot. She soon returned with the note of my freedom, as well as Master Jiang. His cheeks were red and swollen. She must have slapped him very hard.

I kowtowed to thank my saviour.

"Stand up and come with me." He was so slender and his face so serious.

"I shall give my whole being to serving Master," I promised as I bowed on my knees.

"You shall never be in servitude again. You are to become my disciple." A smile tugged lightly at the man's lips.

He was Apothecary Huang, Lord of Peach Blossom Island. He became my *shifu*. He had already taken five protégés by that time, the most senior being Tempest Qu, followed by Hurricane Chen. The remaining three – Zephyr Lu, Galeforce Wu and Doldrum Feng – were a little younger than me.

Shifu gave me a new name: Cyclone Mei.

SHIFU TAUGHT me kung fu. He also taught me how to read and write. When *Shifu* was busy, he had Brother Tempest Qu look after me. He was our eldest martial brother and learned in both the martial and the literary arts. He was also a painter. He enjoyed discussing poetry and lyrics with me, explaining their meanings and nuances.

In no time at all, I had turned fifteen.

I was now much taller and my hair had grown lush and long. When I caught my reflection in the water, I had to admit that I had grown quite pretty.

From time to time, I would catch Brother Qu's eyes lingering on me. I felt shy under his gaze. He was thirty – twice my age. Tall and thin, like *Shifu*. He had the same melancholic air, too. Always frowning, never happy. But he did sometimes crack jokes when I was around, to make me laugh. He also liked to tell me about the ancient poems *Shifu* copied in his precise calligraphy.

One day, Brother Qu silently put one of *Shifu*'s manuscripts on my desk while I was doing my daily penmanship practice.

> *One playing a game with coins on the stairs,*
> *One passing by the bottom of these steps.*
> *Our encounter was lodged in my heart then,*
> *And ever more so now.*

Written in black ink, on white notepaper, in *Shifu*'s hand – gallant, wiry and angular. I looked up. Tempest did not seem to be his usual self. There was a strange glint in his eyes.

"Did our *shifu* write this?"

He nodded and laid another sheet of paper over the one he had just placed on my desk. Also in the same dashing handwriting.

> *Southern willow,*
> *Its tender leaves yet to grow lush.*
> *Fourteen, fifteen,*
> *Idly with the pipa lute in hand, searching.*
> *Our encounter was lodged in my heart then,*
> *And ever more so now.*

I could tell something was not right, but I could not put my finger on it. I felt my cheeks grow hot, my heart beat faster. I wanted to stand up, to step away.

"Little sister, do sit down."

"Is this also by *Shifu*?" My voice sounded feeble.

"It is his handwriting. Ouyang Xiu wrote the poem."

I heaved a sigh. My body relaxed.

"In this lyrical poem, Ouyang Xiu revealed the feelings he had developed for his niece. When she was twelve or thirteen, he saw her playing a game of coins with her friend, laughing and running around the courtyard. He was struck by her beauty, the pureness of her energy. She was even more beautiful by the age of fourteen or fifteen, but Ouyang Xiu was an old fellow in his fifties, and he could only 'lodge the feelings in his heart' and pour them out again in his writing.

"This personal verse actually caused quite a stir when it was somehow circulated. Ouyang Xiu was an important government official and greatly admired for his morality. But this composition led to criticism and a backlash at court. To be honest, nothing in the poem breaks the bounds of any ethical codes. He was stirred by her beauty and youth and put his feelings into words, but he never acted on his compulsions. There was nothing to make a fuss about. Do you know why *Shifu* likes this poem so much?"

Tempest waved a wad of paper. Each inscribed with the same verse:

> *Our encounter was lodged in my heart then,*
> *And ever more so now.*

"Do you see, now?"

I shook my head.

He leaned in. "You don't?"

I shook my head again.

"Then why are you blushing?"

"I'll tell *Shifu*."

The blood drained from his face. "Please don't! Don't say anything to him. He'll break my legs."

His voice was unsteady. He must have been really frightened. But then we were all a little afraid of *Shifu* in our own way.

"Of course I won't! I'm not a fool – I don't go asking for trouble."

"Has *Shifu* ever raised his voice at you?"

NO, HE hadn't. *Shifu* had never once raised his voice at me.

But he would raise his hand at Hurricane when Brother Chen's rough speech riled him. Hurricane could tell when *Shifu* was about to hit him, and he would dart and dodge, beautifully agile in his superb lightness kung fu. But *Shifu* was always faster, smacking him on the top of his head, ever so lightly.

Shifu would also ignore Galeforce for days when his headstrong student got too argumentative. It troubled Brother Wu so much that he sank to his knees and knocked his head against the ground to beg for forgiveness. In response, *Shifu* would flick a sleeve and send him flying in a somersault. Galeforce always made sure to make a clumsy spectacle of his fall, dust and earth all over his face. The display would make *Shifu* chuckle and all would be well again.

Whereas *Shifu* was always kind to me. He never even darkened his countenance on my account, though sometimes his brow would furrow as though something were troubling him.

And I always knew what to say to cheer him up.

"*Shifu*, why are you upset? Is it something Brother Chen or Brother Wu has done?"

"I wish it were them. I'm angry at the heavens."

"Why?"

"You won't understand."

I would take his hand, then, swinging it back and forth lightly. "Please, *Shifu*. Tell me. If you explain, then I'll understand."

It always worked.

Shifu would smile, go to his study and come back with a few sheets of poetry written in his calligraphy.

But, after that exchange with Brother Qu, I grew wary whenever *Shifu* brought out his poems. I would blush and avert my gaze. I feared reading those lines again.

Thankfully, it was something else:

Verses by Zhu Xizhen
Copied by Old Heretic Huang

Men aged, things changed.
No desire to drink amid flowers as tears stain my clothes.
Now I but wish for sleep with the door shut,
Let plum blossoms fly like snow.

An old man can never regain the joy of youth,
Resentful of wine and tired of music.
With the twilight once more comes storm and rain,
Outside the wind chimes strike a broken tune.

The poet has aged,
He cares not if the peach blossoms still smile as old.
The east wind blows ten thousand li,
The realm red and broken under the setting sun.

Things bygone, hero's tears, wrinkled face.
Bemoan the westward dusk,
Rue the night tide's return.

"*Shifu*, why do you always write about being old? You're not old," I said, commenting on the inscription. "You're in your prime and your martial skills are incomparable. None of my brothers is as strong as you."

"Everyone grows old. You are in the blossom of youth, but decay is the only prospect for me.

Grief for the grey hair reflected in the mirror,
Silken black at dawn, snowy white at dusk."

"*Shifu*, come, sit down. Let me pluck out those pesky greys." I pulled one from his temple and showed it to him. He blew at it. A deep, powerful exhalation. I let go. The strand flew out of the window and high up into the sky.

"A feather of lofty heights among ancient clouds," I said, trying my hand at poetry. "*Shifu*, someone as knowledgeable as you only comes along once in a thousand years."

"Cyclone, you know how to make me smile. But no knowledge can keep me from growing old, or keep you from growing up. One day, you will leave your *shifu*."

"*Shifu*, I won't grow up!" I took his hand and made a promise. "I will stay with you and learn from you all my life."

"That's child's talk." A rueful smile. "Ouyang Xiu said it well in the lyrics set to the tune of 'Settling Wind and Waves':

Sitting by the blossoms, wine in hand, I wish to ask my gentle friend,
Is there a way to hold on to spring?
If only spring could be persuaded to stay.

Empty words,
Flowers, which care not for sentiment, look on men of feeling.
All that blooms must one day wilt.
Since time bygone,
How oft would that face of rouge blossom anew?

"You will grow up, Cyclone, and no internal kung fu can defy the heavens. If *he* wants us to grow old, we will."

"I will learn from you all my life, *Shifu*. I will wait on you until you are a hundred years old – two hundred years old!"

"That's sweet of you." *Shifu* shook his head and returned to the security of verse:

"*Treasure spring when it comes,*
Precious,
Realise flowers will not bloom forever.
Waking after drinking, my gentle friend is gone.
A thousand times,
Whether wind or water, the current carries you away."

"*Shifu*, come wind or water, Cyclone Mei won't be carried away! I will stay here and focus on learning the Divine Flick."

"You do know how to take my mind off my troubles. I shall teach you that kung fu tomorrow."

I RECALL asking Brother Qu a question once: "Why does *Shifu* call himself Old Heretic Huang? It's such a horrible name. He's only a decade or so older than you. He's neither old nor a heretic."

"He'd be so pleased to hear that." Tempest broke out one of his rare smiles and told me *Shifu*'s story in great detail.

"*Shifu* came from a literati family of great power and influence in the Zhejiang area, not far from our capital, Lin'an, today. His ancestors served our founding Emperor and performed great deeds, so, for generations after, they were granted noble titles and held important positions at court.

"*Shifu*'s grandfather was the Censor-in-Chief during the reign of the Gaozong Emperor, in charge of uncovering misdeeds and corruption among the Empire's officials. When the villainous Chancellor Qin Hui imprisoned General Yue Fei, *Shifu*'s grandfather petitioned again and again for the General's release. His persistence enraged the Emperor and Qin Hui; he was removed from his post and demoted. He continued to petition for the patriotic General even though he had been barred from court, inciting officials and the common people to rise up in support of Yue Fei. For that, Qin Hui had *Shifu*'s grandfather executed, and exiled his family far into the south-west borderlands to serve in the army. That is why our *shifu* was born in Jang Satam.

"*Shifu* grew up receiving training in both the martial and the literary arts. When he was a boy, he vowed to avenge General Yue and his grandfather by bringing down the Song court and assassinating the Emperor and his corrupt officials. But the culprit, Qiu Hui, was long dead, and Emperor Gaozong had grown even more muddled with age. *Shifu*'s father tried to rein him in with the way of the sages – loyalty to the rulers and deference to the family – but he refused to obey blindly and always argued back.

"Eventually, after one particularly heated disagreement, his father threw him out. *Shifu* travelled all the way back to his homeland, Zhejiang – not to Lin'an, to take the imperial examination, but to Qingyuan prefecture, to vandalise the Hall of Ethics at the Confucius Temple. He also posted notices inside the Imperial Palace and outside the Chancellor's Office and the Ministry of War, in Lin'an. He even went to Quzhou to nail protest letters to the doors of Confucius's descendants who had retreated south with the Song Empire after the Jurchen invasion. These inflammatory, iconoclastic statements pointed the finger at the corrupt court and refuted Confucian teachings, proclaiming that a campaign to recover lost territories in the north was the only just course of action.

"The court sent soldiers and cavalrymen in their hundreds to hunt him down, but how could they ever subdue our *shifu*? His supreme kung fu, his open apostasy, together with his utter contempt for authority, earned him the name the Heroic Heretic in the *jianghu*, across the rivers and lakes of his native land. He gave voice to thoughts the people were too frightened to say out loud.

"Some years ago, a long-forgotten text known as the Nine Yin Manual was discovered and the scramble over its ownership led to great carnage in the martial world. It was an anthology of the most profound and powerful kung fu from every martial branch under the heavens, with detailed instructions for attaining these skills. Whoever had possession of the book would hold immense power and knowledge, making them invincible in the *wulin*.

"The Quanzhen Sect leader Double Sun Wang Chongyang sought to end the senseless killing, and organised a melee, stating that whoever could demonstrate the finest martial skills would be the work's custodian. He invited the greatest to this tournament. Five men took part in what we now call the Contest of Mount Hua – our *shifu*, Heretic of the East, together with Venom of the West, King of the South, Beggar of the North and Central Divinity Double Sun Wang Chongyang.

"It was a fierce competition, but ultimately they all agreed that Central Divinity was the strongest and most deserving. A Taoist monk, he was upright, fair and kind. His pursuit of celestial enlightenment meant he had little concern for earthly reputation. Most importantly, Wang Chongyang was not interested in using the power conferred on him by the Manual to suppress others."

For all of us on Peach Blossom Island, it was hard to imagine someone more skilled than our *shifu*, but that was the way of martial training. As Brother Qu put it, "Above the sky is a loftier heaven, beyond the man a mightier body."

∽

Waking after drinking, my gentle friend is gone.
Whether wind or water, the current carries you away.

And then, one day, the verse *Shifu* quoted came true.

One morning, *Shifu* woke up and I was gone. Carried away by my second-eldest martial brother, Hurricane Chen.

His thick eyebrows, his intense eyes, Hurricane was a man of few words. He did not talk to me much, but his eyes were always on me. He looked at me so intently – it makes me blush to think of it – I had to turn away.

When the peaches ripened on Peach Blossom Island, he always left the biggest, juiciest ones in my room. He put them on my table and left without saying a word.

We were almost the same age. He was just a little bit older. Tempest was more than a decade our senior, Zephyr was a couple of years younger, whereas Galeforce and Doldrum were little boys in my eyes.

Hurricane's manners were as rough as his sinewy physique.

"Dainty thief, let's pinch a few peaches." He grabbed my hand.

I waved him away. "What did you call me?"

"We're stealing peaches. What does that make us? Thieves. And the next rosy peach this burly rogue will take is his dainty thief."

I pretended to ignore him, but a sweet giddiness I had never known spread inside me.

He led me to the orchard after nightfall. We picked many, many peaches and carried them back to my room. He set them down on the table in the dark and wrapped his arms around me. I squirmed and struggled, but, the moment he whispered into my ear, I lost all my powers of resistance.

"I want you to be my dainty thief always."

I felt myself melting into him.

A FLUSH of crimson warmed Cyclone Mei's cheeks and her wheezing suddenly sounded worse.

Guo Jing could pick out gasps and sighs and snatches of words as she heaved air into her lungs.

"Why?" she rasped. "Why?"

They were still sitting on the ground, not far from the pit. Her fingers were still around his neck.

"Why break his legs? Why banish him?"

Cyclone Mei held revenge literally in her hand, yet her grip seemed to be loosening.

BY THE time I was eighteen, I understood why Tempest looked at me that way. I knew what it meant. He was a widower with a young daughter and I had been swept away by my Hurricane. I needed to avoid his eyes.

One night, when my burly rogue was holding me, in bed, someone shouted outside my window.

"Hurricane Chen, come out, you bastard!"

Brother Qu.

Hurricane pulled on his clothes and rushed out. Immediately, a gust of wind rustled the paper in the wooden window frame. They were fighting!

"Tempest, please, forgive us!" I implored from inside.

"Forgive you? 'Our encounter was lodged in my heart then, and ever more so now.' Who wrote those words? I can forgive you, but I doubt *Shifu* will."

Thwack! Someone had taken a heavy blow.

"You intend to kill me?" It was my storm speaking.

"Cyclone, you said you'd learn kung fu from *Shifu* all your life. You said you'd serve him forever. You lied!" Tempest had never been so angry with me.

"Why does it bother you?" Hurricane would not let anyone speak rough to me. "You're jealous, aren't you?"

Shadows flitted and swirled. My kung fu was not good enough to catch what was happening.

Then Hurricane's body flew up and hit the ground with a *thud!*

"I am not jealous. I'm doing this for *Shifu*. You will pay with your life today, you ungrateful dog!"

I leapt through the window and shielded him with my body.

"Brother, have mercy!"

Tempest took one look at me, sighed, and walked away.

IN THE morning, *Shifu* summoned the three of us. I was too scared to look at him and kept my eyes on the ground, but I could sense the sadness that was engulfing him.

"Why?" *Shifu*'s voice was almost tearful. "Why?"

Hurricane decided to answer for us all.

"Brother Qu is jealous. He wants to kill me because Sister Mei and I are together."

"Tempest, it's futile." *Shifu* shook his head and sighed. "This is fate."

I fell on my knees in tears. "*Shifu*, it is my fault! Please don't blame Brother Qu."

"Why did you recite that poem, Tempest? Why did you say Cyclone lied to me? Why did you say she broke her promise of waiting on me for a lifetime? Why did you eavesdrop on us? Do you think I didn't know you were listening? Well, you've grossly underestimated me. And what grievances have I got? If I had any, do you think I would need another to act on my behalf? If I ordered you to confront them, then, yes, you could assume that I was jealous, but I never sent you to do what you did. Hurricane, Cyclone, out!"

A swing of the wooden staff and the bones in Brother Qu's legs were shattered. *Shifu* then announced, "Tempest Qu broke the rules of our house. A disciple of Peach Blossom Island he shall no longer be." Then he ordered the servants to take Brother Qu to Lin'an.

From that day forward, *Shifu* would not speak to Hurricane or to me. He also stopped teaching us kung fu and left the island soon after. He travelled to Qingyuan and then Lin'an. When he came back, it was two years later, and he was married.

Shifu's wife was very young. She and I were born in the same year, the Year of the Monkey. Her birthday was in the tenth month, so she was actually a couple of months younger than me. She was beautiful, her skin unblemished and smooth like milk. No wonder *Shifu* was so enamoured, taking her on all his travels. *Shimu* was not trained in the martial arts, but, like *Shifu*, she had a great love for literature and calligraphy.

One day, *Shimu* said to me, "*Shifu* has told me many times how good you are, how loyal you are to him. He also says that you had a difficult start in life and bids me again and again to treat you well. He doesn't understand anything about our sex, but he is very remorseful that he wasn't able to look after you better as you were growing up on this island. I want you to know that, if there is anything I can help you with, you can come to me."

I was moved to tears. "*Shifu* couldn't be more kind. He couldn't have looked after me better. We're all very pleased to see how happy he is now that he has found you."

"I know *Shifu* hasn't been teaching you kung fu; rest assured, it has nothing to do with you. *Shifu* and I came across a martial-arts tract called the Nine Yin Manual on our last trip. Inside, there was a strange passage that makes no sense. You know how fond he is of deciphering codes and riddles, and how he never lets anything beat him. We've been working on this text since our return and we still can't make head nor tail of it. You know what he's like. He's now refusing to do anything else until he's figured it out. That's why he has been keeping to himself."

She pointed at two volumes on her desk. "There it is. I don't know why he's so interested in someone else's martial secrets when Peach Blossom Island already possesses skills that are unrivalled in the heavens and on earth. But then I guess I share the same sentiment when I see an exceptional verse; I won't rest until I've learned it by heart and understood its craft inside out."

ONE MOON Festival, *Shimu* prepared a banquet to celebrate with all of us, and *Shifu* drank heavily throughout the meal. When she went to the kitchen to prepare the soup course, *Shifu* mumbled to himself, "Now, no-one can say Old Heretic Huang wanted to marry his own disciple . . . How is Tempest? I bear no grudges. How are his legs?"

Those words affected Hurricane. A while later, he said to me, "Do you recall *Shifu*'s words on Moon Festival? He let slip his feelings about Tempest. If Brother Qu returns, he won't let me live. Dainty thief, let's live up to our names and steal that Nine Yin Manual." He reminded me of the conversation I'd had with *Shimu* about the Manual. "Once we've learned its powerful kung fu, we can bring the book back to *Shifu*. By then, we'll be afraid of no-one – not *Shifu*, nor Tempest Qu."

I begged him to banish the thought. I threatened to tell *Shifu*. But my storm was fearless. He put his words into action that very night.

IN THOSE days, *Shifu* was always preoccupied. His fingers were never still, always counting, but it did not look like he was working out a rhyme or fitting lyrics to a tune. He did not teach us kung fu and hardly spoke to anyone. His hair was turning greyer by the day and the sight broke my heart.

When I mentioned this to Hurricane, he was certain that *Shifu* was thinking about the kung fu in the Nine Yin Manual.

That night, Hurricane came across *Shifu* heading to the Sword Trial Pavilion with one volume of the Manual in his hand. He told me *Shifu*'s eyes were fixed at the sky and nonsensical mutterings were coming out of his mouth. He greeted *Shifu* loudly, but he just walked on, oblivious.

Hurricane saw his chance and sneaked into *Shifu*'s study. There, on the desk, was the other volume of the Manual.

Yet Hurricane was not content. He could not stop thinking about the one in *Shifu*'s hand. He convinced himself he needed it too, but I would not let him take anything else.

Stealing one volume from *Shifu* was bad enough. If we took both, we would be worse than animals. *Shifu* had always been kind to us. It would be a betrayal too far.

"Of course he's kind to you, but to me?"

"Don't do it! I will scream and shout!"

"*SHIFU!*" CYCLONE Mei croaked. "Someone has come to take the Nine Yin Manual! *Shifu!*"

"Huh?" Guo Jing was confused.

"Mind your own business."

She caught the scent of plum blossoms in the night air. The Peach Blossom Island of her memory smelt just as sweet.

WE FLED Peach Blossom Island that night. We found a boat to take us to Mount Salvation and hid in a cave by the shoreline. We had with us the second volume of the Manual. Hurricane spent the next days poring over the text written in *Shimu*'s hand, his brow locked in a frown.

"Maybe we should make a copy and return this to *Shifu*. But how?" He was talking more to himself than to me.

"Let's go back!"

"Do you think we can set foot on that island again and come out alive?"

We stayed on Mount Salvation for one month, but it was too close to Peach Blossom Island, so we sailed to the mainland. We spent the next few months flitting between towns like Qingyuan, Shangyu, Baiguan, Yuyao, then we moved inland to Lin'an, Jiaxing, Huzhou, Pingjiang, lying low in the myriad waterways that criss-crossed these cities. We shut ourselves in our boat during the day to avoid being seen – in case *Shifu* or our martial brothers were seeking us – and the incessant river traffic kept us well concealed.

WE STUDIED the Manual together. It was indeed full of powerful martial skills. Our volume opened with the Nine Yin Skeleton Claw and the Heartbreaker Palm, how to master and overcome each move: *These skills can be acquired through external training and do not require a foundation in inner strength. By these methods, my younger brother and sister were slain. The verse "Silently slaughter with the ease of cutting grass" aptly describes their effect.*

This was perfect, and so our training began. We needed to practise on living human beings, so I suggested Jiang Village in Shangyu. We could start with the malicious Mistress Jiang, then reduce all the men and women in the village – old and young – to piles of skulls and bones.

But the place also reminded me of the day *Shifu* rescued me, the new lease of life he granted me. What did I do to requite him? This! The thought broke my heart. When I mentioned it to Hurricane, he became wild with jealousy and berated me for thinking about *Shifu*.

Before long, we reached an impasse. The remaining martial techniques required a basis of internal strength. The *neigong* principles were explained in the first volume – the one we did not have. To complicate matters, the skills were all rooted in the Taoist tradition, a completely different branch of kung fu from that of *Shifu*.

But, each time we became stuck, Hurricane would say, "He who aspires shall achieve great deeds."

He believed it with all his heart. With time, he developed his own interpretation and devised a way to learn the skills described within the Manual, which he also taught me. He focused on palm strikes and I worked on the White Python Whip.

He had a whip made especially for me, gilded with silver. He said that, as he had not given me a love token to mark our nuptials, he would make it up to me with this opulent weapon.

We might have been in hiding from *Shifu* and our martial brothers, but we had plenty of gold and silver. With our kung fu skills, we took whatever we wanted, whenever we felt the urge. Wealthy households, government treasuries – we plundered them with ease. No-one could stop us.

FEELING A breeze ruffling her hair, Cyclone Mei tilted her head back. "Are there stars tonight?"

"Many," Guo Jing replied.

"Can you see the Silver Stream?"

"Yes."

"Is it separating the Weaver Girl from the Cowherd?"

"It is."

"What about the Northern Dipper?"

"Huh?"

"What an idiot! Look to the north. Seven bright stars. Aligned in the shape of a ladle."

Guo Jing scanned the sky, following the description, until eventually he exclaimed, "I can see them!"

"What is the Gathering of Seven Stars?"

"I don't know."

"Didn't Ma Yu teach you?" Mei tightened her grip.

"The Elder only taught me how to breathe lying on my back."

"How?"

"My belly pushes out when I breathe in and then is sucked into my back when I breathe out."

We did the opposite, she said to herself. Perhaps this is the Taoist secret.

EACH TIME my burly rogue reached a plateau in his training, he would talk about stealing the first volume. I told him I would not mind going back to Peach Blossom Island, but, whatever we decided to do, we must first return this second volume to *Shifu* and *Shimu*.

"But we haven't mastered the rest of the kung fu yet! We can skip those marked 'Attainment Five Years', 'Attainment Seven Years' and 'Basics Grasped in Ten Years'. But we must first learn the martial techniques we can assimilate quickly before we go back to the island. The Nine Yin Skeleton Claw, Heartbreaker Palm and White Python Whip are said to be achievable in a short time without *neigong*. How's your White Python Whip?"

"It will be another year before I can use it in combat."

WE RUFFLED a lot of feathers learning this kung fu. It became difficult to stay in one place for long because those self-righteous dogs of the martial world would not leave us alone. They kept coming after us in groups and gangs, but that only pushed us to train harder, killing more in the process.

They called our kung fu "infernal" and gave us the name Twice Foul Dark Wind. It made us sound so horrible! We should have been called something graceful, like Peach Blossom Duet.

They claimed they had to stop us from murdering innocent people, but I knew they just wanted to lay their greedy paws on the Manual.

What we had learned from *Shifu* was more than enough to send these yelping dogs fleeing with their tails between their legs. But such pests just kept coming out of the woodwork, and they were growing stronger. We were finding it harder and harder to escape. We were not allowed a moment of peace for two whole years.

If I had known it would turn out like this, I would not have had anything to do with that dreadful Manual. I thought about it often, how I could have lived in peace on Peach Blossom Island. But *Shifu* knew about Hurricane and me. My shame would have chased us off the island eventually, and we were also worried about Tempest's return.

It was around this time that news of *Shifu*'s fit of fury after we ran away with the Nine Yin Manual reached us. Zephyr and Galeforce had tried to calm him, but their words only angered him further and he broke their legs in a rage. Doldrum later suffered the same fate. Apparently, he had tried to reason with *Shifu*: "The two ingrates are Hurricane Chen and Cyclone Mei. They alone betrayed you, *Shifu*. We are loyal and devoted. There was no cause to turn your wrath on Brother Qu, Brother Lu and Brother Wu."

"You shall be next! I spent years teaching the six of you, and all I got in return was betrayal and ingratitude. I might as well not have lived!" A swing of the wooden staff and Brother Feng's legs were shattered too.

After our three little brothers were cast off the island, the *jianghu* was sizzling with cruel gossip about *Shifu*. They said Old Heretic Huang had truly lived up to his pernicious reputation. Such words were daggers to my heart. How I wanted to kneel before *Shifu* and *Shimu* and confess my crimes. How I wished *Shifu* would absolve my sins by granting me the punishment of death.

I desired nothing more than to catch a glimpse of *Shifu* again.

So, when Hurricane told me he wanted to go back to Peach

Blossom Island, I voiced no objection. His reasoning was that the curs of the *wulin* would lead *Shifu* onto our tracks before long and our fate would be sealed. But, if we had the first volume of the Manual, we could move to Mongolia, to Tangut, somewhere tens of thousands of *li* west of our troubles. Somewhere so far away that no-one could find us.

I succumbed to his logic. Sooner or later, this life would no longer be mine. The thought that *Shifu* might be the one to take it actually gave me some comfort.

ONE DARK night, we found ourselves back on Peach Blossom Island. As we approached the main hall, *Shifu*'s voice reached us: "Brother Bottom, I never took your Manual. There is nothing to return!"

I had never heard *Shifu* stoop to personal insults!

We peered through a gap in the window. The man *Shifu* was shouting at wore a long beard and seemed some years older. He did not seem at all offended. In fact, he answered with a laugh. "I don't believe you, Old Heretic. Your actions live up to your name."

"I am called a heretic because I refuse to submit to Confucian teachings, because I don't blindly obey the Emperor or my elders. But I live by the four social bonds of propriety, justice, integrity and honour. I said I did not take your Manual, and that is the truth. Even if I did take it, with what I already know, I have no need to stoop to learning from someone else's martial dog farts."

"Well, I can smell something, that's for sure. Come, let's spar a little. Let me see if you took a naughty sniff or not." Chuckling, the man sprang from his seat and waited for *Shifu* to stand up before throwing a punch with his left hand. *Shifu* responded with a move from the Cascading Peach Blossom Palm.

As the blows rained down, the candles flickered. I looked over at Hurricane. He glanced back at me. We had never seen such advanced kung fu before.

The heavens were granting us the chance of a lifetime to take the Manual. This longbeard was holding *Shifu* back for us – we would have free access to his study! If we saw *Shimu*, we would not hurt or frighten her; I would kowtow to her three times to thank her, and then snatch the precious book.

I tugged Hurricane's sleeve, but he would not move an inch. He told me later that he had been convinced one of them would use techniques from the Nine Yin Manual. Seeing the moves in action would be so much more instructive than reading about them. He was too entranced to leave and I was too scared to go alone.

The bearded man's kung fu was like nothing we had seen. But *Shifu* would not attack, he just glided around as if he were on water, evading his opponent. They were now coming towards our window. The man swiped at *Shifu* with his left hand.

Shifu ducked.

The window flew open.

I swerved to the side, but he must have seen my hair flying.

"Cyclone!"

Pang! The man followed up with his right palm and struck *Shifu* on the shoulder.

Shifu's right knee buckled. As he stumbled back, he flicked a finger against his thumb twice. The air whistled and the longbeard's legs gave way. He rolled on the ground and could not stand up again.

"*Shifu* has no need of the Nine Yin Manual, Cyclone. I subdued him with the Divine Flick. What brings you here?"

I leapt up and fell on my knees in front of *Shifu*, tears streaming down my face. "Your disciple has done you and *Shimu* grievous wrong."

"She is no longer with us. Her mourning hall . . . over there."

I ran across the courtyard in the direction he pointed. There it was, her spirit tablet:

Here lies the spirit of my late wife, of the Feng clan.

My head spun. I could hear myself wailing. *Shifu* stood behind me. Then I noticed a small child of no more than two, perched on a chair. She smiled at me. She looked just like *Shimu*. Had she died in childbirth?

"Papa, cuddle."

A smile bloomed like a flower on the little girl's face. She stretched out her arms and threw herself at *Shifu*. He scooped her up protectively just before she toppled from the seat.

I felt Hurricane grabbing my hand and my body hurtling across the island. In no time, I sensed the spray of brine upon my face.

My heart was pounding. I was convinced that it would jump out of my mouth.

Then, *Shifu*'s voice, borne to our boat by the wind: "Make your own way. Meddle no more with the Nine Yin Manual! Preserve yourselves. Stay alive."

Having witnessed *Shifu*'s battle with the longbeard, we were dejected. Eventually, Hurricane spoke: "*Shifu*'s kung fu is at least ten times more powerful than ours. That man is also far more accomplished than us."

"Do you regret what we did?" Then I added, under my breath, "If we had stayed with *Shifu*, we would have learned all that."

"I have no regrets. And neither have you."

After that, he worked even harder to figure out a way to train our internal strength. He kept saying that, though it was not the orthodox way, it would still get us results.

"*Shifu* said we mustn't practise the kung fu from the Manual," I reminded him.

"With his skills, obviously he has no need of it. But can we survive without it?"

So we trained and trained. We managed to master two-thirds of the Golden Bell and Iron Shirt techniques, which toughened our bodies against weapons and blows.

We were now unstoppable. Fear raged wherever Twice Foul Dark Wind blew.

WE WERE practising the Heartbreaker Palm in an abandoned temple when, suddenly, we were surrounded by kung fu masters in every direction. Zephyr Lu, our own martial brother, organised and led the attack. He blamed us for the loss of the use of his legs and he thought that, by capturing us and presenting us to *Shifu*, he would be allowed to return to Peach Blossom Island.

Ha! Twice Foul Dark Wind would not be caught so easily!

My loving bastard dispatched the Flying Divine Dragon, Ke Bixie the Talisman, that day. Or maybe it was I. I cannot remember. It does not matter. We slew half a dozen of Zephyr's martial friends and got away, but I was also badly hurt.

A few months later, even the Taoist monks of the Quanzhen Sect were after us. We had far too many enemies now, we could not beat them all. The only option that remained was to leave the Central Plains. We went far, far away into the west and settled on the Mongolian steppe.

We kept practising the Nine Yin Skeleton Claw and Heartbreaker Palm, and I continued to work on the White Python Whip. Hurricane constantly reminded me that these were legendary techniques we could master in a reasonably short time, it mattered not that we did not have a foundation in *neigong* inner strength.

Then, out of the blue, I was ambushed on a barren hill in Mongolia. "My eyes!"

The pain. The itching. The horrible darkness.

I gathered my *qi* to contain the poison. I crawled away. But I lost my sight. And my burly rogue.

Retribution. We killed Ke Bixie. We killed blind bat Ke Zhen'e's brother. And he had brought his brethren all the way out to Mongolia to seek revenge. The Seven Freaks of the South.

CYCLONE MEI'S jaw clenched at the painful memory, her teeth cracked and her grip tensed.

Guo Jing was convinced that his wrist was about to snap. This is it, he said to himself. She's going to kill me, now, in the most brutal way. But I've still got the herbs Elder Wang needs to cleanse the poison from his injury last night!

"Could you please do one thing for me," Guo Jing began timidly, "after you have had your revenge?"

"You want my help?"

"Yes. I appeal to your kindness. Please take the herbs on my person to Elder Wang. His life depends on them. He is staying at the Peaceful Stay Inn, west of the city."

Cyclone Mei did not answer, but she did not shake her head either.

"You will do it? Thank you – you are so kind!"

"I am not kind and I don't want your thanks."

CYCLONE MEI could not remember all the hardships she had already lived through in her short life. She could not recall how many people she had killed. But she could not forget that night. It was carved into her being.

EVERYTHING WAS cloaked in darkness. The stars had lost their glow.

"Little sister, I can't look after you anymore. You must take care . . ."

These were his last words.

"What's the point of taking care without you?" I asked as he pressed the Manual into my hand. "I've lost my sight. I can never read again."

I put it inside my robe, close to my chest. It was of no use to me, but I would make sure it never fell into enemy hands. One day, I would return it to *Shifu*.

The heavens opened. A torrential downpour. The Freaks slashed and struck. I was hit on the back. A powerful blow. It rocked my bones.

The sky wept. The world had lost its light. Darkness became my cloak.

So I scooped up my storm and ran.

I hurtled through the rain.

My Hurricane was still warm! But, little by little, a chill took over. Like my heart, he turned to ice.

I had never felt so cold.

"Are you really gone? You were supposed to be unassailable. How did it happen? Who was it?"

Shivering, I found the dagger in his navel and pulled it out. I felt his blood gush from his wound. I know how much there must have been. I have killed many times.

"Who will call you 'dearest filthy dog' down there?" I asked out loud. "You won't be alone in the underworld. I won't allow it!"

I slipped the tip of the dagger under my tongue – my most vulnerable point – then I felt it. Words, carved into the hilt. The surname, Yang. The character meaning "vitality". Yang Kang. His murderer. Yang Kang.

How could I die before I had taken my revenge?

My sweet bastard will be avenged!

CAN YOU hear my sigh, burly rogue?

It's all over now.

Have you missed me as much as I've missed you? If you've found yourself some waif as wife down there, I promise you, I will haunt you for eternity . . .

I DUG a hole in the desert and buried him. Without my sight, I could not even find food to feed myself, let alone seek my revenge. Luckily, the Mongolians took pity on a poor blind woman, sharing with me their milk, meat and bread. For several years, their kindness was all that kept me from starvation.

One day, a column of men and horses passed by my cave, speaking in the Jurchen tongue. I asked them for food, and their leader took me in and brought me all the way to their capital, Zhongdu. I only realised later that I had been taken in by the Sixth Prince of the Jin Empire. He let me live in the palace and gave me a job. I became a sweeper in the inner garden, where I made an abandoned underground chamber my den. At night, I practised my martial arts in secret.

Another few years passed, the royal household still looked on me as a poor blind woman. But, one night, the naughty young Prince sneaked into my garden. He was fond of raiding birds' nests for eggs. He saw me practising with the whip and pestered me to teach him. I showed him three moves and he mastered them immediately. He was such a joy to teach, so before long I showed him the Nine Yin Skeleton Claw, and Heartbreaker Palm too. I made him swear to secrecy: he must never speak about it. Not to the Prince, not to the Consort. If he made one squeak, I would put five holes in his skull with my own hand.

The little Prince had already studied some kung fu, so he was not a complete novice.

"*Shifu*, my other teacher is a bad man. I don't like him. I like you!" The boy had a sweet tongue and he knew how to use it to get his way. "I'd never show him the kung fu you teach me. His skills are nothing compared to yours! The things he makes me learn are useless."

But, from what the little Prince could do, I could tell this man was a master. And yet, I was in no place to ask questions, since I had made him promise never to reveal me.

Time stands still for no-one. A few more years had gone by and the young Prince told me his father was going back to Mongolia. I told the boy to ask if I could travel with them to visit my husband's grave. Of course, the Prince agreed – he would never say no to his beloved son.

This was my chance to find the Seven Freaks of the South, to make them pay for what they did to me. Yet, fortune did not smile on me – the Seven Immortals of the Quanzhen Sect were in Mongolia too! One blind woman could not fight seven masters on her own.

Their internal kung fu was as formidable as their reputation. Scarlet Sun Ma Yu sent his voice across great distances with so little effort.

And yet, it was not a wasted trip. I tricked the Taoist into explaining a secret of their *neigong* training. And I worked hard when I got back . . .

But, without guidance, it was impossible to cultivate my internal energy. Two days ago, as I willed my *qi* around my body, my internal life force passed the Long Strong pressure point at the bottom of my spine and got trapped. Nothing I have tried since could make it circulate back, and I have lost all movement in the lower half of my body.

IF THIS boy had not stumbled in, I would have starved to death because I have never allowed the young Prince to visit me. My Hurricane led him here. To rescue me and to avenge him!

Cyclone Mei cackled wildly at the thought, causing her whole person to convulse and release a mighty burst of internal strength through the fingertips still clutching Guo Jing's windpipe.

Guo Jing forced his hands under her wrist and pushed back with every last drop of energy inside him. Having practised orthodox *neigong* for some years under Ma Yu's instruction, his internal strength was not inconsiderable.

Such impressive kung fu!

45

Cyclone Mei had to give the young man credit. Not many could have made her grip slip. She made three quick strikes and he managed to divert her talons each time with the force of his palm.

She drew her arm upwards, shrieked, and slapped it down onto the top of Guo Jing's head. The most lethal move of the Heartbreaker Palm repertoire.

Guo Jing's left hand was still trapped between Mei's claws, so he channelled all his power to his right arm and blocked. He knew it was hopeless, but he had to try. Pain shot down his arm at contact. Then, to his surprise, nothing happened. Had she changed her mind?

Cyclone Mei had remembered at the last moment that Guo Jing was taught by the Taoist Ma Yu, and pulled back.

I am unable to walk now because I have no-one to guide me in my *neigong* training. But he learned it from the source – he can help me. I must avenge my sweet bastard, I must not forget! Luckily, I have not killed him yet.

Annoyed with herself, she grabbed Guo Jing by the throat once more.

"You killed my husband and I'll kill you with this hand. But, if you behave, I'll grant you a quick death. If you play games, I'll make sure you suffer every conceivable pain this world has to offer. I'll start by chewing your fingers off, one by one – and I will do so slowly."

It was not an empty threat. She had not eaten in days.

Guo Jing shuddered at the sight of her gleaming white teeth, too frightened to answer.

"The Quanzhen Sect has a saying: 'Three Splendours Gather at the Crown, Five Forces to the Origin.' What does it mean?"

Guo Jing knew she was after his knowledge of inner strength. I'd rather die than help you improve your kung fu! I know you're planning to go after my *shifus*! he answered silently.

Cyclone Mei squeezed, sending shards of pain into his wrist.

Guo Jing closed his eyes and clenched his teeth, determined not to show his suffering. Then he said, "I'll never share my *neigong* knowledge with you!"

She loosened her grip a little and tried to make her voice sound soft. "I will take the herbs to Wang Chuyi . . . to save his life."

That reminded Guo Jing of the reason he came to the palace in the first place. That was more important than anything, right now! She won't be a bother to my *shifus* anymore if she can't walk.

"Swear you will help Elder Wang first."

"I vow to deliver the herbs to Wang Chuyi after you have shared the secrets of Quanzhen *neigong*. If I break my word, I shall be paralysed for eternity."

5

Guo Jing recognised the voice: Browbeater Hou, the Three-Horned Dragon!

"She can't have got far; there's nowhere for her to go!" A second man.

They were only a few score paces to his left. But it sounded like they were moving away from him.

Lotus is still in the palace? Guo Jing turned to Cyclone Mei. "There's one more thing you must promise me. Or I won't tell you anything."

"What is it?" Mei snapped.

"My good friend is being pursued by the martial masters of this palace. You must give me your word that you will help her escape."

"How do I know where she is?" Mei tensed the hand still wrapped around Guo Jing's throat. "Explain the internal kung fu first!"

"It's down . . . to you . . ."

"I, Cyclone Mei, have never bent to anyone's will. Yet, today, I will let you have your way," she said, with gritted teeth. "Is she your sweetheart? You are devoted to her, aren't you? Let me be clear. I'm only agreeing to help the girl. I'm not saying I'll let you live."

"Lotus, come here! Lotus . . ."

They heard a rustle from a nearby rose shrub, and Lotus emerged. She had been listening in the undergrowth for some time and Guo Jing's words had sent a flood of hot tears down her cheeks. They had only been friends for a matter of days, yet he was thinking of her even when his life was in mortal danger.

Lotus had been dressed as a beggar boy when they met and she had been living the part for some time. She was furious with her father. For the first time in her life, he had reprimanded her.

She knew that, to her father, she was dearer than life itself. Her mother had died in childbirth. As she grew up, she was his only companion. He was an eccentric man. He did not live by assumed etiquette or the prevailing social rules of the time – indeed, he despised and rejected them. He always let her have her way and never said a stern word to her.

All she had done to incur her father's wrath was to go on a wander around the island, find the place he used as a prison and strike up a conversation with a captive therein.

He had been greatly amusing, this captive. He complained the wine her father served was flavourless, so she had the servants bring a flask of their best vintage, together with a few plates of delicacies. They whiled away hours, eating and drinking. The man was thrilled by the feast and she had fun talking to the irreverent uncle.

Why should this have caused such anger from her father? Feeling grievously wronged, she ran away and roamed from town to town, alone and abandoned. She even convinced herself that her father did not love her anymore; she might as well become the most miserable little beggar in the world.

It was in this guise that she met Guo Jing outside an inn, in the fortress town of Kalgan. At first, she abused Guo Jing's hospitality, ordering the most lavish and expensive dishes at her new acquaintance's expense, to vent her anger at her father. But, as they ate and talked, they each felt like they were in the company of an old friend.

When Guo Jing gave her, a mere beggar boy, his sable coat, ingots of gold and his precious Fergana horse at their parting, she recognised the sincerity of his kindness. Now, being called his "sweetheart", she felt a honeyed warmth grow inside her bosom.

"Lotus! She'll help you. Those men won't bother you anymore!"

"Let him go, Flora Mei!" Lotus cried.

"Who are you?" Cyclone Mei's voice trembled. She had not been called by her birth name for decades. No-one in the martial world knew it.

> *"Ghosts of peach blossom cascade as the sword flies,*
> *Tides of the green sea billow as the jade flute sings."*

Lotus recited these words before announcing, "My surname is Huang."

"You – you are . . ." Mei was stunned.

"Fillip Peak, Pure Tone Cave, Verdant Bamboo Grove, Sword Trial Pavilion. Do you remember these places on Peach Blossom Island, in the Eastern Sea?"

The very places Cyclone Mei had learned kung fu! That was a lifetime ago. Yet, how could she forget? She could see the verse inscribed on the pillars of the Sword Trial Pavilion in her mind's eye, even now. They referenced two of her *shifu*'s proudest martial inventions.

"Who . . . ? Who are you to . . . Master Huang?" she stammered at last.

"Good! You haven't forgotten my father. He remembers you too! He's here to see you."

Mei was certain her frightened soul had flown up beyond the highest heavens. She wanted to run away, but her legs would not respond.

Then, a little spark of joy lit up within her. At last, she could see *Shifu* again! She murmured, "*Shifu . . . Shifu . . .*"

"Let him go. Now!"

Suddenly, doubt and distrust gripped Cyclone Mei. *This little girl is trying to trick me. Shifu has not left Peach Blossom Island for* years. He did not even pursue us when we took the Nine Yin Manual. He cannot be here.

Seeing the change in Mei's countenance, Lotus tapped her left foot and jumped high over the blind woman's head.

"Do you remember learning this from my father?"

Cyclone Mei could hear a swooshing in the air. Two rotations mid-air, followed by a downward strike. A move from Cascading Peach Blossom Palm.

Blossoms Fly over River Town.

Mei now knew exactly who this girl was. She removed a hand from Guo Jing to ward off the strike. Lotus took her chance and tugged him free as she landed.

"Little sister, where is *Shifu*?"

Lotus Huang was the young child Cyclone Mei had seen on Peach Blossom Island all those years ago – her *shifu* Apothecary Huang's only daughter.

Though Lotus never knew any of her father's disciples, as they were already banished by the time she was born, she had heard her father speak of them. From Mei's mutterings, she had surmised the woman's identity.

Faced with such a lethal adversary, Lotus felt a small pang of regret at not being more focused on the martial arts in her education. She remembered pestering her father to teach her all his other skills, like yin yang, the Five Elements and other ways of divination derived from the *I'Ching*. Apothecary Huang might have been one of the greatest masters of the age, but Lotus had only just scratched the surface of Peach Blossom Island's vast store of martial knowledge. If only her martial skills were more sophisticated, then she would be able to free Guo Jing with her kung fu. She would not have to pin all her hopes on her wit. Luckily, she had managed to frighten Cyclone Mei with the lie that her father was here too.

By now, Cyclone Mei had flopped to the ground, all her martial training vanished. Her face had turned an earthen hue and she spoke fearfully, as if an enraged Apothecary Huang was standing before her. "Your disciple deserves ten thousand deaths for her crimes. I beseech *Shifu* to take pity on my blind eyes and crippled body, and show mercy with your punishment. I have wronged you grievously, Master. I am a nothing but a beast, even worse than a pig or a dog!" Her voice was trembling.

Then she thought of the kindness *Shifu* had shown her, and the desire to be in his presence overcame her fright. Now, she sounded more certain. "No, *Shifu* must not be merciful. I deserve the most severe punishment you can devise."

Guo Jing was bewildered. Twice he had seen this fearless demon surrounded and outnumbered by martial masters in the treacherous terrain of Mongolia. And now all it took was the mention of Lotus's father to reduce her to a whimpering heap!

Chuckling silently at her effect on Cyclone Mei, Lotus took Guo Jing's hand and pointed towards the palace wall.

Just as they were about to make their escape, they heard a wolf whistle followed by a snigger.

"Little girl! I won't fall for your tricks again!"

Not him again! Lotus recognised Gallant Ouyang's voice. We can't outrun him. His kung fu is too strong. Maybe she could hold him back?

"Sister Mei, my father never says no to me. If you help me, I'll speak for you. He'll definitely forgive you."

"How can I help you?"

"That man is here to make trouble with me. I'll pretend to lose, then you step in and send him packing. My father will be very pleased when he sees you helping me." Lotus pulled Guo Jing behind Cyclone Mei as she spoke.

CHAPTER TWO

ETERNAL SPRING DEFEATED

I

GALLANT OUYANG APPROACHED, FLANKED BY FOUR OF HIS concubines. He glanced in disdain at the shadowy mass of unkempt hair that was Cyclone Mei.

With a casual wave of his fan, he reached over Mei to grab Lotus.

Immediately, he felt a wave of enormous strength rush towards his chest, then saw her flashing claws. He jabbed his fan at her wrist, pivoting himself away from harm.

Cloth tearing, metal snapping, screams of pain.

He looked down and saw that the front of his robe was torn, his metal fan had been broken in two and all four of his women were slumped on the ground in a grey-red pool of blood and brain. Five holes were visible in their skulls, dug by a human hand.

He had never known an attack so fast and so brutal. The crone was still crumpled on the ground, and he concluded with slight relief that she could not walk, then launched into the Snow Mountain Camel Palm, a boxing technique passed down in his family.

Cyclone Mei flashed her talons. Each swipe tore the air with a whistle.

Now, Lotus thought, and tugged at Guo Jing's hand. They must run. But immediately she heard a howl of rage and felt fists flying at her from behind. She swerved to duck. Surprisingly, her attacker pulled back.

Browbeater Hou had remembered, just before his punch landed between Lotus's shoulder blades, that she was wearing the Hedge-hog Chainmail. He most certainly did not want his hands pierced by the spiky steel shirt. He twisted away in time, but he was not able to arrest the momentum of the blow and his fist crashed into the three cysts on his forehead. He collapsed, yelping and bawling in pain.

The commotion brought Hector Sha, Greybeard Liang and Tiger Peng to the scene.

One look at Gallant Ouyang's tattered robe and the woman's claws, and Old Liang recognised the kung fu immediately. The demon in the cave! He lunged at her with a roar.

Sha and Peng watched from the sidelines, stunned by the woman's skill and ruthlessness. They were both thinking the same thing: Where on earth did this hag come from?

"She is Twice Foul Dark Wind!" Tiger Peng gasped.

Meanwhile, Browbeater Hou was on his feet and chasing Lotus, but he was neither fast nor agile enough to catch her. Lotus noticed that he was reaching for her head in an effort to avoid the Hedgehog Chainmail. She dived into a nearby patch of shrubbery and stuck her Emei Needles into her hair.

"I'm here!" She poked her head out through the vegetation.

"I'll get you this time!" He grasped at Lotus's hair.

"Brother, she's got spikes on her head too!"

Too late. Browbeater Hou stared at his bloody palms and started hopping about in pain.

"Shh!" Hector Sha silenced his martial brother and launched himself at Lotus.

Unable to move freely, Cyclone Mei was in danger of being over-whelmed by the joint attack of Greybeard Liang and Gallant Ouyang.

With one arm fending off her opponents, she reached behind her and grabbed Guo Jing.

"Lift me up!"

Guo Jing could not understand the purpose of her instruction. But they were fighting on the same side, for the moment, so he did as she asked, wrapping his arms around her legs.

Mei blocked a palm strike from Gallant Ouyang with her left hand and clawed at Old Liang with her right.

"Make for the Ginseng Codger!"

At last, Guo Jing understood: she could not fight them off sitting down. He hoisted her onto his shoulders, lunging and retreating at her command. Cyclone Mei's slight frame meant that she was an easy load, and did not affect the speed or agility of his lightness kung fu.

Now a good three feet taller than her opponents, Cyclone Mei regained the upper hand. It gave her respite enough to question Guo Jing on the secrets to cultivating internal strength.

"What position should one take to train *neigong*?"

"Sitting cross-legged, with the Five Cores turned skywards."

"What are the Five Cores?"

"The centres of the palms, the soles of the feet, and the crown of the head."

Excited by this knowledge, she attacked with renewed strength. She clawed at Greybeard Liang's shoulder, drawing blood. The older man backed off. But, just as Guo Jing was about to give chase, he noticed that Hector Sha and Browbeater Hou were hounding Lotus.

"We shall get rid of those two first!" He charged at them.

Cyclone Mei thrust her left palm into Browbeater Hou's back. He ducked, certain that he was now beyond her reach. Yet, immediately, he felt himself being lifted up. Can she extend the length of her arm at will?

Petrified, he watched her right hand descend towards his head.

"I surrender!" he squeaked.

Hector Sha leapt up to block Cyclone Mei. Their wrists locked

and their arms quivered in pain. Mei then felt a tremor in the air to her left and tossed Browbeater Hou in that direction.

Aiya! Tiger Peng was hoping to ambush Cyclone Mei using his secret throwing weapons, his Copper Coin Darts, but they hit Browbeater Hou instead, as he sailed through the air.

He'll be seriously hurt if he is dashed to the ground like that, Hector Sha said to himself. He dived forward and thrust his palm into his martial brother's waist.

Browbeater Hou flew up into the air like a paper kite, the momentum of Cyclone Mei's throw broken by his martial brother's intervention, but, as he summoned his *qi* to cushion his landing, he found he was unable to stop his flailing arms from swinging once more into the cysts on his forehead, and he yelped in pain.

It all happened in the blink of an eye – Cyclone Mei's throw and Hector Sha's desperate catch.

All the while, Tiger Peng continued to fling his coins at Cyclone Mei. Gallant Ouyang and Greybeard Liang had repositioned themselves to encircle her.

Cyclone Mei might have been blind, but her ears were as sharp as any eyes. She flicked her fingers in different directions and the clang of metal reverberated through the air. All of Tiger Peng's projectiles were redirected back at him and his three companions. This was the Divine Flick, the technique she had started to learn shortly before her dishonourable departure from Peach Blossom Island. The counterattack bought her enough time to question Guo Jing further on the training of inner strength.

"What is Garnering the Five Elements?"

"Wood of the Eastern Spirit, Gold of the Western Soul, Fire of the Southern Life Force, Water of the Northern Essence, Earth of the Central Mind."

I had it completely wrong, she said quietly to herself. "What about Harmonising the Four Forms?"

"Holding the spirit in the eyes, garnering the tone in the ears, tuning the breath in the nose, binding the energy in the tongue."

"Really? What about the Five Forces to the Origin?"

"Without seeing, gather the spirit in the liver; without hearing, pool the essence in the kidneys; without speaking, form the life force in the heart; without smelling, raise the soul in the lungs; without moving, hone the mind in the spleen."

These were secret formulas of Taoist *neigong* practice that Guo Jing had learned from Ma Yu.

One day, Guo Jing had said, "I feel like there is a warm little mouse running around inside my tummy." It was the first sign of his internal-energy flow being connected. The first step towards acquiring *neigong*.

Ma Yu was not able to tell Guo Jing on the spot, in simple, everyday terms, how he could guide this warm little mouse in his stomach, nor how it could connect and tap into the Conception Vessel and Governing Vessel meridians, the body's main rivers of energy. Nor did he wish to alter the formula of inner kung fu practice that had been passed on to him by his own mentor, aware of the damage a misguided energy flow, however slight, could wreak on the body. So he taught Guo Jing the only way he knew – the Quanzhen Sect's method of channelling internal energy – while holding back from explaining the complexities within. After all, they were not master and disciple.

Guo Jing had memorised the words, as per the kindly Taoist uncle's instruction. He never thought of asking their purpose or meaning. That had always been the way he learned kung fu, by committing to memory tenets given to him and not questioning when he did not understand. When he learned the move Black Tiger Steals the Heart, he knew that it was a right jab to the chest, and that he could never use it on his Seventh *Shifu* Jade Han. He never pondered on *how* the tiger stole the heart. The physical gesture alone was often more than his poor brain could cope with.

Though Guo Jing barely understood the meaning of the phrases he was repeating, he could answer Mei's questions without hesitation. He had no idea that the martial philosophy of Peach Blossom

Island was different in every way from that of the Taoist tradition. He could not have guessed that Cyclone Mei had groped blindly for an interpretation of those phrases in the Nine Yin Manual for more than a decade, nor that her current paralysis had been caused by one of these wild guesses.

"What about Three Splendours Gather at the Crown?" This was the point at which everything began to go wrong.

"Essence into force, force into spirit—"

Cyclone Mei was now paying more attention to Guo Jing's words than to the fight. Her opponents, each of them a martial master with decades of combat experience, saw their opportunity. A palm strike from Gallant Ouyang hit her in the left shoulder, and one from Hector Sha met her ribcage from the right. Even with her body-toughening training, the pain shook her to the core.

Lotus Huang had hoped Cyclone Mei would keep her pursuers busy while she escaped with Guo Jing, but now he was her warhorse and they were stuck.

Under attack from all four sides, Mei was struggling.

"How did you offend so many martial masters? Where is *Shifu*?"

She really hoped he would arrive soon. Not only would he see her risking her life to help his daughter, but he would also dispatch her assailants with ease. But, then again, what punishment would he mete out for her?

"He'll be here any moment. These people can't touch a hair on your head, even if you fight them sitting down."

Lotus hoped that Mei would fall for the flattery and let Guo Jing go, but Mei was running out of tricks and she knew it. A small mistake now could cost her life. Moreover, she was being held aloft by a store of *neigong* knowledge contained within a young boy who also happened to be her husband's murderer. Nothing in the world could tempt her into letting him go.

Another dozen moves were exchanged. Cyclone Mei could feel the air rushing at her from both left and right. She flung her arms out sideways to deflect the blows.

Just then, Greybeard Liang leapt up and grabbed Mei by the hair. Lotus knew she had to step in and she thrust her palm at Liang's back. He twirled his right hand and locked onto Lotus's wrist, his left still gripping Mei's hair. But his attention was now divided and it gave Mei a small window of opportunity to strike. Her palm whipped up a gust into Old Liang's face. He had to let go to avoid it.

"Lying wench!" Tiger Peng shouted. "You *are* Twice Foul Dark Wind's disciple!"

"She's not my *shifu*! Not in a hundred years!" Lotus retorted. "It would be more accurate to say I'm *her* teacher."

The answer took Tiger Peng aback. It was obvious that the girl and Cyclone Mei shared the same martial fingerprint, but no member of the *wulin* would deny their *shifu* outright, to their face. Could she be telling the truth?

"Shoot the horse to take the rider!" Hector Sha called to his companions as he swept his right leg at Guo Jing.

If he gets hurt, I won't survive this fight! Cyclone Mei thought, and she lunged her claws at Hector Sha's foot. But the desperate move exposed her back to Gallant Ouyang. He immediately thrust his palm at her from behind.

Hearing his approach, Mei flicked her wrist and a sliver of glittering white unfurled in the air. White Python Whip. The four men ducked out of the weapon's reach.

We need to kill her quick! It was unlike Tiger Peng to show mercy – not for nothing was he known in the martial world as the Butcher of a Thousand Hands. We'll be in big trouble when her husband Copper Corpse appears.

News of Hurricane Chen's death had not reached the Central Plains, as neither Cyclone Mei nor the Freaks had spoken in the *wulin* about that night.

The unforgiving lash of the White Python Whip could maim anyone within four *zhang*, but Cyclone Mei was not facing common brawlers.

Now at a safe distance, Gallant Ouyang, Greybeard Liang, Hector Sha and Tiger Peng looked for a pattern in her moves.

Suddenly, Peng whistled through his fingers and rolled under the reach of the whip. Mei heard Guo Jing's yelp and extended her left arm with a downward strike. She needed Guo Jing to support her, and it was hard to focus on Tiger Peng while also keeping the other three Masters at bay.

Lotus Huang wanted to help, but she could not get near them. She could see that Mei was struggling to subdue Tiger Peng with one hand. The situation was turning very ugly for Guo Jing. She needed to act fast.

"Stop! Listen!" she shouted. Her words fell on deaf ears.

"Lotus, run! I'll find you!" Guo Jing called back.

"I'm not going anywhere without you!"

2

"STOP!"

This time, the voice came from the top of the palace wall. But mere words can never halt a fight, especially when no-one recognises the speaker. Lotus looked up and saw six disparate figures standing in a line. The diminutive, rotund one leapt down first, with a whip in hand. He was accompanied by a broad-chested man brandishing a shoulder pole.

"You can't run from us, libertine!" the first man cried.

Guo Jing knew the voice very well. "Third *Shifu*! Help me!"

After parting ways with Guo Jing near Kalgan, the Six Freaks of the South had tailed the eight women from White Camel Mount who they had overheard conspiring at the inn. That night, they had discovered that the women were part of Gallant Ouyang's retinue and their master planned to abduct a maiden for his harem. The Freaks could not stand by and do nothing in the face of such moral depravity.

The Freaks had spent more than a decade honing their martial skills in the arid landscape of Mongolia, teaching Guo Jing. Fighting six to one also gave them a distinct advantage against Gallant

Ouyang when they challenged him. The eldest of the Freaks, Ke Zhen'e, the Suppressor of Evil, landed a blow on Gallant Ouyang with his metal staff, and Zhu Cong the Intelligent, the second of this martial brotherhood, fractured the little finger in Gallant Ouyang's left hand with his signature move Split Muscles Lock Bones. Two of Ouyang's female accomplices lost their lives to Woodcutter Nan and Gilden Quan, the fourth and the sixth of the Freaks. The Master of White Camel Mount had fled without his prize.

The Freaks escorted the frightened girl home and they began to track Gallant Ouyang. They knew none among them could beat the rake single-handed, so they stayed together as they searched. Sly though Gallant Ouyang might have been in his decision to take less-trodden paths, the physical appearance of his women – dressed completely in white and travelling on camels – meant they were always noticed. The Freaks were able to follow their trail by questioning innkeepers along the way, until they found themselves at the Prince of Zhao residence, the palace of the Sixth Prince of the Jin Empire, Wanyan Honglie.

Shocked and surprised to find Guo Jing here, Zhu Cong was the first to spot their disciple carrying Cyclone Mei on his shoulders!

Jade Han, the youngest of the Freaks, charged at Mei with her sword raised, and Gilden Quan rolled under Mei's dancing whip to get to Guo Jing.

Tiger Peng could not tell whether these new arrivals were friends or foes, as they were taking on both Gallant Ouyang and Cyclone Mei. He performed several somersaults of the Ground Boxing technique to distance himself from Mei's whip and bellowed, "Stop!"

His voice rang like a mighty bell, crashing and clanging in everyone's ears. Greybeard Liang and Hector Sha took a step back and paused their attack on Cyclone Mei.

"Third Brother, Seventh Sister, stop!" Ke Zhen'e ordered. He knew his martial siblings would not be able to subdue this man whose shout still echoed. Ryder Han, the rotund, bow-legged man Guo Jing called Third *Shifu*, backed away from Gallant Ouyang.

Gasping in pain, Cyclone Mei let her silver whip hang limp. Lotus moved closer and said in her sweetest voice, "You've done brilliantly. Father will be so pleased." At the same time, she gestured wildly at Guo Jing to throw Mei off.

"Essence into force, force into spirit, spirit into emptiness: such is the meaning of Three Splendours Gather at the Crown." Guo Jing summoned his *qi* and hurled Cyclone Mei from his shoulders as she pondered the cryptic explanation. He jumped back to put more distance between himself and the blind woman. But, before his feet could touch the ground, he found the White Python whip hurtling at his face, its hooks glistening under the stars.

Ryder Han let fly his whip with a backhand flick. As it curled over Mei's, a sharp tremor jolted his grip. The weapon flew out of his hand.

Still airborne, Cyclone Mei reached out, tapped the ground lightly with her hand to guide her descent, and landed gracefully.

The Seven Freaks of the South! She recognised Ke Zhen'e's voice as well as Jade Han's moves. Why did they have to come now? On any other day, she would have rejoiced at their arrival. I have been looking for them for so many years, she thought. But I am having trouble enough with these four others . . .

Once again, that fateful night came back to her. She knew what she had to do next. If I am fated to die today, I will take the Freaks down with me. As many of them as I can manage. The other four are of no matter.

She tightened her grip on the whip and listened. How come there are only six? Where's the seventh Freak? She did not know that Laughing Buddha Zhang Asheng, the fifth sibling, was killed by her husband in the same fight that took her sight and the love of her life.

No-one dared stray within the whip's reach. Silence sat heavy in the air until Zhu Cong broke it.

"Why were you helping that witch?" he whispered.

"They were trying to kill me. She saved me." Guo Jing's answer brought more confusion than clarity.

"Who are you?" Tiger Peng demanded. "Why did you break into the Prince's palace?"

"My name is Ke. We siblings seven are known on the *jianghu* as the Seven Freaks of the South."

"The Seven Heroes of the South — we have long admired your reputation." There was not a drop of sincerity in Tiger Peng's voice.

"Excellent! I have always wanted to see with my own eyes what the Freaks are made of." Hector Sha glowered.

The Seven Freaks of the South were a sore point for Sha. His four disciples had suffered a humiliating defeat at the hands of Guo Jing not long ago, in Mongolia, in full view of both the Jin and the Mongolian armies, including his host, Prince Wanyan Honglie.

Hector Sha darted forward with a swerve of his body, swinging his palm at Woodcutter Nan's head with a *whoosh*. Nan thrust his shoulder pole into the ground and lifted his arms to block. Within a few moves, Nan was struggling. Jade Han rushed forward with her sword to aid her Fourth Brother, followed by Gilden Quan with his steelyard.

Howling, Tiger Peng lunged at Gilden Quan and snatched at his weapon. The Sixth Freak jolted backwards, a move that sent the steelyard's hook and counterweight flying at Peng. It was not a weapon Peng had ever seen in his decades roaming the martial world. With a Python Flip, he slipped past the projectiles.

"Is this thing, these weighing scales, your weapon?" Tiger Peng was incredulous.

"It's made for weighing pigs like you!" was Gilden Quan's comeback.

Tiger Peng pounced, thrusting his palms in quick succession. These powerful strikes sliced the air with a roar.

Gilden Quan ducked and dodged. He did not stand a chance against such a skilled fighter. Ryder Han came to his aid, swinging punches and launching kicks. Though competent in hand-to-hand combat, he had lost his Golden Dragon whip, the conduit of his most accomplished kung fu. Even fighting two to one, there were too many close calls for the Freaks.

The two eldest Freaks now stepped in. Brandishing his Exorcist's Staff, Ke Zhen'e joined Woodcutter Nan and Jade Han in resisting Hector Sha. Zhu Cong came to Gilden Quan and Ryder Han's aid, jabbing his oilpaper fan at Tiger Peng's vital pressure points. Their skill far exceeded that of their younger martial siblings. Now fighting three against one, Sha and Peng instantly lost their advantage.

Meanwhile, Lotus Huang was harrying Browbeater Hou once more. He was without a doubt the more skilled fighter, but he was too scared to strike, worried that he would get stung again by the spikes on her body and in her hair. Lotus took advantage of this and launched her armoured body at him.

"Take off your chainmail. Make it a fair fight!" Hou protested as he dodged.

"Well, cut off your cysts then. Otherwise, it's not going to be fair."

"They don't hurt anyone!"

"The sight of them makes me sick. And that's giving you an advantage! Come on, one, two, three, you cut them off and I'll remove my steel shirt."

"No!"

"You said you wanted to fight fair."

"I'm not falling for your tricks again!"

Gallant Ouyang had been watching from the sidelines, calculating his next move. *Cyclone Mei isn't going anywhere in this crippled state; I can deal with her later. I'm going to show these six busybodies some real kung fu and cast them down to the underworld,* he thought.

He leapt up and, suddenly, he was next to Ke Zhen'e. It was a lightness *qinggong* technique known as A Thousand Miles in One Breath.

"I'll show you martial prowess!" Gallant Ouyang slapped down at Ke Zhen'e with his right hand.

The eldest Freak twirled his staff to block, but Gallant Ouyang's attack morphed into a backhand strike from the left.

Ke Zhen'e ducked and swung his staff in a move known as

Protector Adamantine Dharma. But, by now, Gallant Ouyang had moved on to attacking Woodcutter Nan. Darting east and west, he threw a deadly blow at each of the Freaks.

With the Freaks struggling against Gallant Ouyang, Greybeard Liang saw his opportunity. He charged at Guo Jing. Within a couple of moves, he had the young man by the front of his shirt and aimed a sweeping strike at his abdomen. Guo Jing sucked his tummy in and lurched back. His shirt ripped and the herbs he had stolen tumbled out. Recognising the scent, the Ginseng Immortal quickly gathered and stowed the packages, then launched his palms at Guo Jing once more.

Guo Jing managed to swerve away from Old Liang and ran to Cyclone Mei. "Help me!"

"Lift me up. We have nothing to fear from the Ginseng Codger." She still had many questions about Taoist *neigong* training, but she could sense Guo Jing was not going to let her sit on his shoulders again – instead, he ran past her, with Greybeard Liang hard on his heels.

Guo Jing was now within the reach of Cyclone Mei's whip; the time had come to take her revenge. She listened and flicked her wrist. The lash slithered towards its target.

All through her fight with Browbeater Hou, Lotus had kept an eye on Guo Jing. She had been too far away to help when he was grabbed by Greybeard Liang, but he was now racing in her direction and Cyclone Mei's whip was snaking towards him. Lotus launched herself forward and sailed into the path of the lash. The whip's thong coiled around her waist and then cast her high up into the air.

"You'd hurt me, Flora Mei?"

Oh no, *Shifu* will never forgive me now, Cyclone Mei realised with horror. What's done is done. I'll pull her to me and then decide what to do.

With another flick of her wrist, the lash swirled and set its load beside its owner.

Cyclone Mei untangled Lotus from the whip, expecting the hooks to have sunk deep into her flesh, yet only the outermost layer of her clothing was torn and it was curiously dry.

"My clothes! Ruined! You'd better replace them!"

She doesn't sound hurt. Now Cyclone Mei understood. Of course! *Shifu* had given her the Hedgehog Chainmail.

"Forgive me. I shall happily buy you a new dress to replace the one I have damaged."

Lotus beckoned Guo Jing over. They stood several paces from Mei, close enough to keep the Ginseng Codger away, but just out of her reach.

The Six Freaks of the South were now standing back-to-back in a circle, using all their martial knowledge to resist the attentions of Hector Sha, Tiger Peng, Gallant Ouyang and Browbeater Hou. The Freaks had developed this formation when they were in Mongolia, to keep themselves protected from an attack from the rear. Though the arrangement amplified their strength, there were still too many heart-stopping moments.

Ryder Han had suffered an injury to his shoulder, but he pushed through with gritted teeth. If the formation was broken, it would put everyone's life in danger.

Noticing this weak link, Tiger Peng launched a succession of his deadliest moves at Ryder Han.

Guo Jing sprinted over to help his Third *Shifu*, thrusting his palms at Tiger Peng's back in a Dispel the Clouds to Push the Moon. The martial Master sniggered at this feeble effort and had the young man scrambling for his life in just three moves.

Lotus did not have the skills to help Guo Jing, but perhaps she could create a distraction?

"Cyclone Mei —" she raised her voice — "you've stolen my father's Nine Yin Manual. Give it to me and I will bring it back to him."

Gallant Ouyang, Hector Sha, Tiger Peng and Greybeard Liang turned to Cyclone Mei with the same thought: the Manual! It's still in her hands! Once I kill her, it will be mine!

Instantly, their quarrel with the Freaks was entirely insignificant.

Mei realised what was coming. Once more, she created a circle of protection with her silver whip, keeping the four martial masters at bay. For the time being.

Lotus grabbed Guo Jing's hand. "Let's go!"

At that moment, a messenger from the palace arrived in their midst.

"Masters, my father requires your assistance in an important matter." A gold coronet perched on his head, askew. "My mother . . . has been abducted. Please hurry."

It was Wanyan Honglie's son, Wanyan Kang. He had been sent by the Prince, who, after a fruitless search for his Consort, remembered his martial guests and their extraordinary skills. The young man, who was around Guo Jing's age, had come upon the fight in such a distraught state, he did not notice that his father's guests were attacking his clandestine *shifu*.

The four men backed away reluctantly. It would be churlish to refuse the young Prince when his father had showered them with so many lavish gifts, but it was also difficult to let Cyclone Mei go when they were so close to getting their hands on the Nine Yin Manual.

And yet, even if they managed to take the Manual from Cyclone Mei now, they would then have to fight each other for it. Each man was quietly plotting a way to obtain the coveted martial tract, now that he was certain of its whereabouts.

Greybeard Liang glared at Guo Jing as he trudged after Wanyan Kang. The precious snake blood he had cultivated for more than a decade was still inside the boy's body, but he stood no chance against the Freaks and Cyclone Mei on his own.

"Hey, give me back the herbs!" Guo Jing called.

Old Liang flicked his wrist without looking back. A Bone-Piercing Needle whistled through the air, straight at Guo Jing's forehead.

In two quick moves, Zhu Cong knocked the Needle off course with the oilpaper fan in his right hand and caught it with his left. He sniffed its tip. "A Night and Noon Needle. Instantaneous death the moment it draws blood."

The Ginseng Immortal turned, surprised to hear his secret weapon identified so easily.

"Here you go, Master!" Zhu Cong presented the projectile in the middle of his left palm.

Greybeard Liang reached out and took back what was his, paying little attention to the filthy scholar, since he knew he could defeat him with ease. Zhu Cong waved his arm to flick away the dirt on Liang's left sleeve. The older man glowered and walked away.

Guo Jing was dejected. After everything he had been through this night, he had failed to get the herbs needed to purge the poison from Elder Wang's body. He was at a loss what to do.

"Let's go," said the eldest Freak, Ke Zhen'e, as he hopped onto the palace wall. His siblings and Guo Jing followed after him.

Lotus Huang also jumped up, but stayed some distance away from the Freaks. She made no move to greet them.

"Little sister, where's my *shifu*?" Cyclone Mei said.

"On Peach Blossom Island, of course!" Lotus giggled. "Why do you ask? Are you planning to visit him?"

Mei struggled to control her breathing. "You said he was coming," she gasped eventually.

"Oh, he will, once I tell him where you are."

No-one toys with Cyclone Mei! I'll grab this little rascal and drag the truth out of her. She wobbled to her feet and lunged.

In the past days, the more she tried to free her life energy, the more it became stuck. Yet, right now, in her rage, she forgot that she was paralysed from the waist down, and a wave of warmth surged to her heart. Her legs were hers once more.

Shocked by Cyclone Mei's sudden agility, Lotus leapt from the palace wall and disappeared into the streets and alleyways of the Jin capital.

I'm walking! Mei gasped. And yet, just as quickly, the numbness returned to her legs and they buckled. She collapsed on the ground and lost consciousness.

"What about her?" Jade Han, the youngest of the Freaks, asked.

If the Freaks wished to take her life now, it would be as easy as emptying their pockets. But it would be a dishonourable act.

"We promised Elder Ma to spare her life," Ke Zhen'e replied as he landed on the street outside the palace.

3

AS IRONHEART YANG CRADLED CHARITY BAO IN HIS ARMS, A bittersweet rush of emotions overcame him. Reunited at last, after so many years. But he did not have time for reflection. They needed to escape fast. Lifting her tenderly, he scaled the palace wall.

Ironheart's god-daughter, Mercy Mu, was waiting anxiously outside.

"Pa, why is the Consort . . . ?" Mercy asked as she helped them down.

"She is your mother. We need to go."

"My mother?"

"Hush, I will explain later." Ironheart hurried on, with Charity still in his arms.

After they had covered some distance, Charity gradually began to grasp the whirlwind of events that had unfolded over this one night. In the dawn twilight, she could see that the man carrying her was the husband she had yearned for night and day for eighteen years.

She reached out to touch his face. "Am I dead?"

Sobs cracked Ironheart's voice: "We are both alive and well—"

The drumming of hooves cut him short. A company of riders bearing flickering torches was galloping in their direction.

"Get him! Don't let him go! He's taken Her Highness!" The soldiers of the vanguard held their sabres and spears high, ready for combat.

I have her in my arms again; I can die a happy man, Ironheart thought. He turned to Mercy. "Child, take your mother."

Scenes from Ox Village in Lin'an eighteen years ago came rushing back to Charity: Ironheart carrying her as they ran for their lives, the shouts and screams of the soldiers in pursuit. Eighteen years of separation, of heartbreak and disgrace.

It cannot happen again! Charity clung to her husband's neck. I will never let go.

The soldiers were almost upon them. I would rather die defending my love than abandon her again, Ironheart thought. He unwound Charity's arms from his neck and settled her with Mercy before running headlong into the pursuing force. He took out a foot soldier with a punch and snatched up the man's spear.

Now armed, he was ten times the fighter he had been empty-handed.

One thrust and Ironheart managed to unseat the captain of the Sixth Prince's personal guard from his horse.

Having lost their leader, the riders scattered. Relief washed over Ironheart. There were no skilled martial artists among them. But he was also disappointed. He had failed to grab any of their horses.

They pressed on. In the early-morning light, Charity noticed the blood on Ironheart's clothes.

"Are you hurt?"

The mere question sent stabs of pain down the backs of Ironheart's hands.

The ten holes dug by Wanyan Kang's ten fingers.

It had been two days since Yang fought the young Prince. He had refused to acknowledge Mercy as his betrothed, having won her hand in the Duel for a Maiden.

The wounds had started bleeding again. Ironheart had not felt any discomfort while fighting, but now he could barely lift his arms. Just as Charity was about to bandage his hands, soldiers could once more be heard behind them. The dust kicked up by their horses masked their numbers.

"No need." Ironheart sighed. "Run, my child! We will stay here."

"No! I'm staying with you," Mercy said.

"Is she your child?" Charity could not help but ask.

Ironheart was about to answer, but the soldiers were closing in. He turned and saw two Taoist monks heading in their direction. One had a kindly face framed by grey eyebrows and a long, grizzled beard. The other, younger-looking man, with dark hair, carried a sword on his back.

"Elder Qiu! How wonderful to see Your Reverence again!" Ironheart cried.

The Taoists were Scarlet Sun Ma Yu and Eternal Spring Qiu Chuji. They had arranged to meet their martial brother Jade Sun Wang Chuyi here, in Zhongdu, the capital of the Jin Empire, to discuss the contest with the Seven Freaks of the South.

Qiu Chuji's mastery of internal-strength kung fu had kept his features youthful. Even though it had been eighteen years since his encounter with Ironheart Yang, his face had hardly changed at all. The only sign of time's passing was the touch of grey at his temples.

Qiu Chuji studied Ironheart's features. He had never met this man before.

"Eighteen years ago, we drank and fought together in Ox Village in Lin'an. Does Your Reverence remember that day?" Ironheart asked.

"May I ask who . . . ?"

"Your servant, Ironheart Yang." He fell to his knees and touched his forehead to the ground.

Qiu Chuji cupped his hands together to return the honour, but he was hesitant. This man had been scarred by injuries, harsh elements and destitution. He bore little resemblance to the young man Qiu met all those years ago.

The soldiers were almost upon them. There was no time for explanation. Ironheart Yang sprang into a Nodding Phoenix. The spear's red tassel fluttered, its tip flashed inches from Qiu Chuji's chest.

"Elder Qiu, you may have forgotten me, but you cannot have forgotten the Yang Family Spear," he said when the spear was once again at rest.

All at once, that snowy day came back to Qiu Chuji.

"Brother Yang, you're alive! Thank heaven and earth!"

Ironheart bowed in acknowledgement. "Help us, Your Reverence!"

Qiu Chuji glanced at the riders. "Brother Ma, I fear I might not be able to refrain from killing today. Please don't think ill of me."

"Scare them away, but, brother, do not kill," Ma Yu replied.

Qiu Chuji strode forward as the horses thundered towards them. This monk thrived on action. He stretched his arms out and, as the men drew level, he plucked two from their horses and threw them at another two soldiers close behind. The men collided and collapsed in a heap. He seized eight more riders at lightning speed and flung them at another eight, with perfect aim. Terrified, the rest of the company turned their horses and fled for their lives.

A man strode out of the dust. He was tall, stout, and bald as an egg.

"Who is this tawdry monk?"

The man shifted his stance. And then, in the blink of an eye, his feet were planted before Qiu Chuji, his palm striking out. Qiu Chuji raised his arm and blocked.

Their hands met.

Pang!

Both men stumbled back three paces.

Who is he? His strength surprised Qiu Chuji.

The man's arm throbbed. With an angry howl, he launched his fists once more. Qiu thrust out his palms in quick succession.

A dozen blows flew between them.

Five red lines were scored across the man's glossy bald pate. Hot and raw.

I can't take him down barehanded, Dragon King Hector Sha realised. He reached for the iron oar strapped to his back and swung with great force at Qiu Chuji's shoulder, in a move known as Su Qin Carries the Sword.

Qiu Chuji fought back using Bare Hand Seizes Blade technique. But the Dragon King had spent decades fighting with the oar, having killed fearsome tigers on land and giant eels in water. His mastery of this weapon was exceptional and he would not let go so easily.

Impressed, Qiu Chuji was about to ask for the man's name when a voice of rock-shattering hostility boomed out from his left.

"Which Elder of the Quanzhen Sect are you?"

Qiu Chuji leapt to the right, away from the speaker and his three fellows, who had just appeared on the scene. He had never met any of these men before.

"Your humble monk's surname is Qiu. May I ask your names?" He put his hands together in a gesture of respect.

No wonder the Taoist's fame precedes him. He certainly lives up to his reputation, Hector Sha thought. He glanced at his companions and he could tell they were thinking the same.

Tiger Peng might have just arrived, but his mind was already one step ahead: We injured Wang Chuyi the other day, so we are already enemies of the Quanzhen Sect. It matters not if we cross his martial brother Qiu Chuji now. If we defeat him today, then we will be famous across the *wulin* for crushing two of the strongest Quanzhen Masters.

"Attack!"

Hector Sha and his martial brother Browbeater Hou immediately sprang to action at Tiger Peng's battle cry.

Peng charged at Qiu Chuji with a pair of Scribe's Brushes, aiming at the monk's acupressure points – the Cloud Gate, by the collarbone, and the Great Luminance, under the navel. One jab at either spot could be fatal. He meant to kill.

What an unreasonable little man! Qiu Chuji thought as he drew his sword with a *sha!*

In a single move, the Taoist monk repelled all three of his assailants. The sword's point darted towards Tiger Peng's hand and its blade sliced at Hector Sha's waist, while the hilt swept close to Browbeater Hou's ribcage, right at the Camphor Gate.

Sha and Peng twisted their weapons mid-move to block. But Hou was forced to retreat – right into a kick up the backside from the

Taoist. The Three-Horned Dragon fell face down, landing heavily on the cysts on his forehead.

Ignoring their companion's yelps of pain, Hector Sha and Tiger Peng rained down a torrent of blows on the monk. Greybeard Liang, though alarmed by the Taoist's skill, saw the chance to steal in and join the attack.

Watching Qiu Chuji flitting between his three opponents, Gallant Ouyang decided that he would be passing up a golden opportunity if he did not sneak in a death blow from behind. He pulled a feint with his left hand, then thrust the iron-ribbed folding fan in his right at three lethal pressure points on the Taoist monk's back – Kiln Path, Gate of the Soul and Central Pivot.

Qiu Chuji had nowhere to turn to evade the blow.

A movement in the corner of Gallant Ouyang's eye caught his attention. Out of nowhere, three fingers appeared on his fan. A powerful stream of inner strength coursed down the handle. Gallant Ouyang yanked his weapon away.

Ma Yu had intervened.

"Masters, may I ask your names?" His enunciation was soft, but he projected his voice with power. "Though we have never before met, surely we can reason out our misunderstanding, should there be one, without resorting to physical means?"

Each word knocked firm and clear into their eardrums, cutting through the noise of the fight. Hector Sha, Tiger Peng and Greybeard Liang jumped back to appraise the speaker.

"May I ask the Venerable Elder's title?" Gallant Ouyang spoke for the group.

"Your humble monk's surname is Ma."

"Oh, so we are in the presence of Scarlet Sun the Immortal. Pardon us, Elder Ma," Tiger Peng sneered.

"I dare not respond to such an honour, given my meagre knowledge," Ma Yu replied modestly.

Tiger Peng was confident that the five of them could defeat these two Taoists. If they could subdue three of their leading figures in days, they would never have to worry about being troubled by the Quanzhen Sect again. But what if their martial siblings were nearby? He looked around. Her Highness, a wizened peasant and a girl – they would be no bother.

He addressed Ma Yu: "We have long admired the Seven Masters of the Quanzhen Sect. Your fame and reputation reach far and wide in the *wulin*. We hope we will also have the honour of meeting the other five Masters today."

"We reside in different temples and rarely see each other." Ma Yu was a trusting and honest man. The notion that Tiger Peng was trying to find out if he had help nearby did not occur to him. "My brethren ought to be seeking the Way in seclusion, yet they often meddle in worldly affairs, gaining undeserved fame. They are making fools of themselves in the eyes of true heroes like yourself. Qiu Chuji and I are on our way to join our brother, Wang Chuyi, here in Zhongdu. It is serendipitous that we should all meet as we have done. There are many forms of martial arts, but we all strive for the same end. Much like the red lotus and its white roots, they are of the same plant. Why should we not be friends?"

Wonderful! Tiger Peng grinned. The monks aren't travelling with their martial brothers and they haven't seen Wang Chuyi yet. It won't be hard for the five of us to defeat the two of them!

"If Your Reverence doesn't find us too lowly to be troubled by our names, mine is Three – Three Black Cats." He tucked his Scribe's Brushes into his belt and walked towards Ma Yu.

This was unexpected. The Taoists were certain that this man would have a reputation in the *wulin*, but they had never heard such an odd name before.

"Elder Ma, the pleasure's all mine," Tiger Peng offered his right hand, palm facing downwards.

Ma Yu took the man's hand, assured by his smile that it was offered in friendship.

Tiger Peng tightened his grip.

So you're testing my skills, Ma Yu thought. Returning Peng's smile, he summoned his inner kung fu and propelled it into Tiger Peng's palm. A sharp pain ripped into Ma Yu's fingertips and he pulled back quickly.

Tiger Peng hopped away and roared with laughter.

The Taoist looked at his punctured fingertips. Five black holes, cut deep to the bone.

In the world of martial arts, offering a handshake was a common way of testing another's kung fu without exchanging blows. It was particularly useful at first meetings since it would be churlish to start swinging one's fists at a new martial acquaintance. These gestures of apparent goodwill often ended in broken bones, bruised palms and screams of pain, with the weaker party grovelling for mercy.

"What's wrong?" Qiu Chuji was alarmed by Ma Yu's change of countenance.

"The villain has poisoned me."

Tiger Peng had slipped on his secret weapon as he put away his Scribe's Brushes. Its fine steel pins were laced with a poison that could kill within ten hours of contact.

Qiu Chuji had not seen Ma Yu raise his hands against anyone for more than a decade. Yet Ma Yu moved straight into Palm of Treading Frost and Shattering Ice, the most fearsome technique of the Quanzhen Sect. Qiu joined in immediately – *sha, sha, sha!* – slicing his sword at Tiger Peng in three swift strokes.

But Tiger Peng was prepared. Once, twice, his Scribe's Brushes blocked and clashed with Qiu's sword. He even made a quick attack, but he had not reckoned with the monk's thrusting palms. The strikes from Qiu Chuji's left were as sharp as the blade in his right. He twisted his palm and hooked his fingers into a claw, trapping Peng's brush.

"Let go!" Qiu Chuji cried and tugged with his extraordinary internal strength. The sudden force numbed Peng's right arm, and yet he managed to cling on to the brush. Tightening his hold, Qiu plunged his sword forward. Peng had no choice but to let go, tumbling back to avoid being skewered. Qiu flung the brush away and launched into an uninterrupted wave of palm thrusts and sword slashes.

Stunned and sore, Tiger Peng had lost his fighting spirit along with his weapon. Gallant Ouyang and Browbeater Hou came to his rescue, but this fired Qiu Chuji up even more. He was now a storm of razor-edged palm and glittering sword, and showed no sign of fatigue, even though he was outnumbered three to one.

But Ma Yu was struggling. Hector Sha and Greybeard Liang were wearing him down with their relentless onslaught. Liang's weapon was a ginseng hoe. Hack, dig, swipe – he was full of unpredictable moves. Sha swung his iron oar with ferocious force.

The ring of defence Ma Yu was maintaining with his sword was getting smaller and smaller. He was panting now, he felt drained. He had been using his internal *neigong* to suppress the poison, but he also needed to channel energy to the blade in his left hand.

His right palm was swollen and a numbing itch was creeping up the arm. The poison was potent. Ma Yu knew he needed to act fast. The more he used his strength to fight, the faster his blood would pump the venom to his heart.

Steam rose from Ma Yu's head as though it were a pot on the boil. Qiu Chuji wanted to help, but he was unable to shake off his three opponents.

This scholar's moves are peculiar, Qiu Chuji thought. More sinister than Three Black Cat's. They seem familiar . . . Questions raced through his mind. He fights like our foe, Venom of the West. Did he train under him? Is the Venom back in the Central Plains? Is he here in the city, right now?

Qiu Chuji's focus wavered. He nearly took a hit.

Ironheart Yang could not stand by any longer. My kung fu is child's play next to theirs, but I cannot let them hold my enemies back while I run away with my family. He lifted the spear and lunged at Gallant Ouyang's blindside.

"No!" Qiu Chuji gasped. "You'll get—"

Gallant Ouyang leapt into the air. He kicked the spear with his left foot and let his right sink into Ironheart's chest. The spear split in two. Ironheart crashed to the ground.

4

A CLATTER OF HOOVES. ANOTHER COMPANY OF RIDERS WAS racing towards the fight. Leading the troop were the Sixth Prince of the Jin Empire, Wanyan Honglie, and his son, Wanyan Kang.

Wanyan Honglie spotted his Consort from afar and galloped ahead in delight. Yet, as he jumped off his horse, he was welcomed by the chill of steel. He lurched to the side, only narrowly avoiding the blade. A girl in red, standing beside his wife, clutched the sabre – Mercy Mu. His personal guard scrambled forward to restrain the young woman.

Wanyan Kang, meanwhile, had noticed his martial instructor Qiu Chuji.

"Stop! Stop! They're with us!" He had to call out several times before Tiger Peng and his fellow masters heeded his words. The Sixth Prince's personal guard also lowered their weapons.

He was dismayed to find his teacher here in the city, but Wanyan Kang walked up to the Taoist monk and bowed. "*Shifu*, allow me to make an introduction. These gentlemen are *wulin* masters invited here by my father."

With a slight incline of his head, Qiu Chuji went to check on Ma Yu.

His right palm was black. He rolled up Ma Yu's sleeve. The discolouration had reached as far as the elbow. Qiu Chuji was alarmed. How was the poison spreading so fast?

He turned to Tiger Peng. "Give us the antidote."

Tiger Peng did not want to cross the young Prince Wanyan Kang by refusing his mentor, but Ma Yu already had one foot in the grave.

The respite gave Ma Yu a chance to focus on containing the poison. He was able to use his internal strength to push the black blood back down his veins and towards his wrist.

Wanyan Kang now ran towards his mother. "Ma, we've found you!"

"I will never go back," Charity Bao declared.

"What are you talking about?"

"My husband — your father — is still alive. I will never leave his side again."

Shocked and incensed, Wanyan Honglie glanced at Greybeard Liang. Catching the signal, Liang flicked his right hand. Three Night and Noon Needles flew at Ironheart Yang.

Qiu Chuji caught the movement from the corner of his eye. They fly too fast. Ironheart won't have time to duck and I haven't got any secret weapons on me. He seized a nearby soldier and hurled the man into the Needles' path.

The guard screamed as all three projectiles disappeared into his flesh.

That was my ultimate skill, perfected over decades. Old Liang scowled. I've never missed my mark. I'll make him pay! He lunged at Qiu Chuji with a growl.

At this new turn of events, Tiger Peng decided to keep the antidote. The Prince only wants his Consort back, he thought. I'll get her for him. He reached for Charity Bao's arm.

Qiu Chuji twirled his sword, first twisting its sting at Tiger Peng, then slicing its tip at Greybeard Liang, forcing them back.

"Foolish child!" he barked. "You have called a villain 'Father' for eighteen years. The man who sired you stands here before you. Pay your respects!"

When his mother had told him about this man last night, Wanyan Kang had only half believed her. But now his *shifu* was confirming it, he was almost convinced. He looked at the rugged and bedraggled Ironheart Yang. Then he turned to the only father he had ever known, who stood regal and handsome.

Give up my wealth and finery to follow this beggar? No! Never! The young Prince knew where his heart lay.

"*Shifu*, don't listen to his lies. Bring Her Highness to us."

"You animal! You fool!" Qiu Chuji snapped.

The decision had been made for Tiger Peng. He had no obligation to save Ma Yu and could now attack Qiu Chuji without fear of repercussions from the two princes. He let rip his deadliest kung fu.

Wanyan Kang made no move to intervene. In fact, he was secretly hoping that Tiger Peng would kill Qiu Chuji so he would not be bothered by the old man again.

Blood splattered across Qiu Chuji's robe. Greybeard Liang had dug his ginseng hoe into the monk's right arm. A flash of joy lit up Wanyan Kang's face.

"You wolf-hearted beast!" Qiu Chuji shouted, enraged by his disciple's delight at his injury.

Ma Yu pulled a flare from his robe and lit it. A blue flame shot into the sky.

"The old monk's calling for help!" More determined than ever to eliminate the Taoists, Tiger Peng redoubled his onslaught.

Another blue flame answered, flying high above the rooftops.

"Brother Wang's nearby!" The signal energised Qiu Chuji. He switched the sword to his left hand. Bringing his right arm down and lifting his left, he launched a dozen of his deadliest moves in quick succession. His attackers were forced to back away.

Ma Yu pointed north-west. "That way!"

Ironheart Yang and Mercy Mu raised their weapons and rushed ahead with Charity Bao. Ma Yu followed closely behind. Qiu Chuji brought up the rear, brandishing his sword to keep their pursuers at bay.

Hector Sha tried several Shape Changing moves to break through Qiu Chuji's rapid swordplay, but it wove such a tight net of protection that he could not get close to the Consort.

It was not long before the group arrived at the inn where Wang Chuyi was staying. Where's Brother Wang? Why is he not here to help us? The answer appeared before Qiu Chuji's eyes. Wang Chuyi hobbled over, leaning on a wooden staff.

All three of the Quanzhen Sect's most powerful martial artists were injured.

"Give us Her Highness and we shall let you live!" Wanyan Honglie called.

"We don't need mercy from Jin dogs!" Qiu Chuji flashed his sword in defiance.

The Taoist might have been in a tight corner, but he was not going to give up. His blade slashed and stabbed with awesome force and infinite variation. Tiger Peng could not help but admire the man's skill and determination. At the same time, he was thrilled by his stroke of good fortune. He had been handed the chance to eliminate three Quanzhen Sect Masters in one morning.

Ironheart Yang realised death was certain. But, if he took action now, perhaps he could still save Elder Qiu's life. He took Charity Bao's hand and strode forward with his spear.

"Stop! This will end here. Now."

He turned the spear and plunged it into his heart.

With both hands, Charity Bao pulled the spear out and rested the butt against the ground. She turned to Wanyan Kang. "Son, will you not believe that he is your father?"

At which she threw herself down on the spearhead.

"Ma!"

Everyone stopped.

The spear was burrowed deep into Charity's chest. Crying loudly, Wanyan Kang rushed to his mother's limp body.

Qiu Chuji examined their wounds. There was nothing to be done.

"Brother Yang, do you have any unfinished business? Tell me. Whatever it may be, I will fulfil it for you. I . . . I'm sorry that I wasn't able to save you. I . . ." Qiu Chuji broke into sobs.

5

THIS WAS THE SCENE GUO JING AND THE SIX FREAKS OF THE South happened upon when they arrived at the inn in search of Wang Chuyi.

Recognising Hector Sha, Gallant Ouyang and the others from a distance, the Freaks immediately pulled out their weapons, ready to fight. But no-one paid these new arrivals any attention; they were transfixed by the tragedy unfolding before them.

As they approached, the Freaks were surprised to find Ma Yu and Qiu Chuji standing among this group, while Guo Jing broke into a run when he saw that the man lying in a pool of blood was Ironheart Yang.

"Uncle Yang! What happened to you?"

A faint smile appeared on Ironheart's face. "Your father and I made a pledge. If we had one boy and one girl, they would be married . . ." He gasped. "My god-daughter, I consider her as my own blood . . ." He looked towards Qiu Chuji. "Your Reverence, can you see that they are married? Then I . . . I can rest in peace."

"Let it trouble you not. I shall see it done," Qiu Chuji promised.

Lying next to Ironheart Yang, Charity Bao had been drifting in and out of consciousness. She clung to his arm, for fear that they would be separated again. At the mention of the marriage pledge, she summoned her last strength and took something from inside her blouse. "The token . . ."

Qiu Chuji took it from her hands. It was the dagger he had given Ironheart Yang eighteen years before. On the hilt was the name Guo Jing, carved by his own hand.

"I am so happy . . . together again . . . for eternity . . ." Charity exhaled for the last time. The serenity of her face gave no hint of her violent end.

"In the name of your late father . . . look after my daughter . . ." Ironheart choked the words out.

"I . . . I—" Guo Jing stammered.

"I shall take care of everything. Go, go in peace!" Qiu Chuji said softly.

Memories of when he first raised the Duel for a Maiden banner came back to Ironheart Yang. He had not in fact been seeking a suitor for Mercy, but searching for Skyfury Guo's offspring. Now, on this same day, he had been reunited with his beloved wife and had seen with his own eyes his sworn brother's son, all grown up. He had even settled a good future for his god-daughter. He had everything he had ever wanted from life. At that, he closed his eyes forever.

Through the grief, Guo Jing's heart was troubled by Ironheart's last words. How can I marry another? Lotus is devoted to me. Then it dawned on him. The Great Khan's daughter! I've forgotten all about Khojin! Her father has given her hand to me . . . What should I do?

Ever since Guo Jing left the steppe, he had often missed the company of Tolui – his *anda* sworn brother – but he had barely given a thought to Tolui's sister, his betrothed. The Freaks' thoughts turned to her immediately, but, out of respect, they held their tongues.

Wanyan Honglie had dispatched armies and hatched elaborate plots to win Charity Bao for himself, but she had never for one moment forgotten her husband. The Prince catered to her every whim and request. When she wanted the battered old things from her past life as a peasant, he sent soldiers to the south to gather every brick and tile. He had hoped his extravagant gestures would win her affection, but, in the end, he won nothing. As she lay dying, there was such joy, such sweetness. She had never shown such tenderness towards him in eighteen years of marriage. He might have been a prince, but, in her eyes, he was nobody; he could never compare to that simple country fellow. This was no place for a man with a broken heart. He turned back to the palace and his personal guard hastened after him.

Hector Sha and Tiger Peng knew they had lost the advantage now that the Freaks had arrived. They too followed the Prince.

"Not so hasty, Three Black Cats. The antidote!" Qiu Chuji stopped Tiger Peng.

Peng laughed nastily. "My name is Tiger Peng. They call me the Butcher of a Thousand Hands in the *wulin*. Has Elder Qiu mistaken me for someone else?"

That was a name Qiu Chuji had heard before, but the Taoist forced himself to overlook the jibe. Saving his martial brother was paramount.

"I care not if you have three legs or a thousand hands. You're not leaving until you've handed over the antidote."

A glint of metal. The green glow of Qiu Chuji's sword arced towards Tiger Peng. He pulled out his remaining Scribe's Brush to defend himself.

Zhu Cong, the second of the Freaks, had been observing Ma Yu since their arrival. The monk was sitting on the ground, using his internal-strength kung fu to propel his *qi* around his body in an attempt to slow the progress of the poison. His right hand was still completely black.

"Your Reverence, how did it happen?" Zhu Cong asked.

"I shook hands with Tiger Peng. He ambushed me with poisoned pins."

"Oh, did he, now?" Zhu Cong turned to Ke Zhen'e. "Big Brother, may I have a devilnut?"

The leader of the Freaks was unsure why his Second Brother wanted one of his secret weapons, but he trusted that he had a plan. Zhu Cong was named "the Intelligent" and "Quick Hands" precisely because of his quick wits and superb sleight of hand. He reached into his deerskin pouch to fetch a poisoned devilnut.

"I know how to help Elder Ma. Keep Tiger Peng and Qiu Chuji apart for me, please, Big Brother." Zhu Cong took the devilnut with care, then turned to Tiger Peng. "So, it is Butcher of a Thousand Hands, the mighty Tiger Peng! Oh, do stop this silly fight. We are all on the same side. Come, hear me out!"

Zhu Cong tugged at Ke Zhen'e and the two of them placed themselves between Tiger Peng and Qiu Chuji. Zhu Cong raised his oilpaper fan and Ke Zhen'e his metal staff.

Baffled by Zhu Cong's claim, the embattled men stepped back.

"The Seven Freaks of the South and Elder Eternal Spring Qiu Chuji crossed swords eighteen years ago. He injured five of us. But, then again, the fight also left the renowned Eternal Spring more dead than alive. We have yet to settle the score . . ." Zhu Cong turned to Qiu Chuji. "Am I right, Your Reverence?"

"What are you trying to say?" Qiu Chuji roared.

"But we are also guilty of treading on Hector Sha's toes. Our good-for-nothing disciple defeated four of his skilled students single-handedly. We've heard that the Butcher and the Dragon King are such close friends that they would die for each other. So, by that logic, by offending one, we have obviously also offended the other."

Tiger Peng sneered.

"Now, since there is bad blood between us and each of you individually, we are enemies to you both. Doesn't that put the two of you on the same side? So why are you fighting each other? And, Butcher Peng, since we both hold a grudge against Elder Qiu, doesn't that put us on the same side too? Come, let's be friends." Zhu Cong offered his hand.

What is this filthy scholar talking about? Tiger Peng put away his Scribe's Brush and slipped his secret weapon around his fingers. I won't fall for your trap. You can't trick the antidote from me. Wang Chuyi saved your disciple the other day. The Quanzhen Sect is clearly on the same side as the Freaks.

"Brother Zhu, beware!" Qiu Chuji exclaimed. Zhu Cong ignored the warning and kept his hand extended.

"Why not?" Tiger Peng took Zhu Cong's hand with a smirk.

Zhu Cong's little finger pulsed as the two hands joined. They both summoned their inner strength and the grip tightened.

A prick!

Tiger Peng yanked his hand away. Three holes. Much bigger than his pins. Black blood. Numb. Itchy. No pain at all. Lethal poison never hurts.

He had already lost all feeling in his hand. How had this happened? He looked up.

Zhu Cong was hiding behind Qiu Chuji, smirking. Then Tiger Peng noticed his secret weapon dangling from the filthy scholar's left hand, and, in his right, a black object shaped like a water chestnut, its sharp corners glistening.

Blood.

He lunged at Zhu Cong.

"What now?" Qiu Chuji growled, his sword poised for action.

"Butcher Peng, this is our Big Brother's secret weapon. We care not whether you are a tiger, lion, leopard, dog or pig; within four hours all living creatures succumb to the poison." Zhu Cong beamed. "Luckily, you've got a thousand hands. My advice is to cut this one off. You'll still have nine hundred and ninety-nine left. But then you'll have to change your martial title . . ."

Beads of sweat dripped from Tiger Peng's brow. He could not feel his wrist now. Fear shut his ears to the insults.

"You have your poisoned pins and I have my devilnuts. Different poisons, different antidotes. If you want to keep your name, we should really be friends and make an exchange. We're on the same side, after all. How does that sound?"

Hector Sha cut in, "Good! Give us your antidote."

"Big Brother, give it to him."

Ke Zhen'e drew two small packets from an inside pocket in his shirt and Zhu Cong held them out for Hector Sha.

"Brother Zhu, take his antidote first," Qiu Chuji called.

Zhu Cong smiled. "When great men give their word, they keep it. I am sure he won't betray our trust."

Tiger Peng reached into his shirt with his left hand and colour drained from his face. "Where is it?"

"Enough of your tricks!" Qiu Chuji cried. "Brother Zhu, don't give it him!"

"Take it." Zhu Cong offered the packets. "The word of a gentleman is as true as a horseman's whip! We said we would give you the antidote. The Seven Masters of the Quanzhen Sect and the Seven Freaks of the South are men of their word."

Afraid that he would fall prey to Zhu Cong's quick hands, Hector Sha extended his iron oar. "The Seven Freaks of the South are renowned throughout the martial world," he began. "They would not ruin their reputation with fake antidotes, would they?"

"Of course not!"

No-one understood why the Second Freak was so trusting or why he did not press for the antidote.

Zhu Cong handed the devilnut back to Ke Zhen'e, then reached into the pocket inside his shirt. Slowly and deliberately, he drew out a host of objects. A handkerchief. Coin darts. Pieces of silver. A white snuff bottle.

Tiger Peng could not believe his eyes. *Those are my things! How did he get them?* He had no idea that Zhu Cong's left hand had brushed past his shirt and emptied his pockets as they shook hands.

Zhu Cong uncorked the snuff bottle. It had two compartments: one filled with a red powder, the other side with a grey powder. "How does it work?"

"Take the red. Grey's for the wound." His life at stake, Tiger Peng was no longer playing games.

"Fetch two bowls of water. Quickly."

Guo Jing ran into the inn, as ordered. He gave Ma Yu the bowl and helped him take the antidote before dressing his wound. Then he turned to Tiger Peng with the second bowl.

"That's for Elder Wang," Zhu Cong said.

Both Guo Jing and Wang Chuyi were surprised by the instruction, but they raised no objection.

"How do we apply your antidote?" Hector Sha asked.

"Not so hasty. A few more minutes won't kill him." Zhu Cong reached into his shirt once more and pulled out a dozen packets.

"The herbs for Elder Wang!" Guo Jing exclaimed. He unwrapped them and showed them to Wang Chuyi. "Your Reverence, I don't know which ones you need."

Wang Chuyi picked out the five herbs he needed to cleanse his body of the toxic injury he had sustained two nights before. He chewed them thoroughly before washing them down with water.

The packets of herbs reminded Greybeard Liang of his encounter with the Freaks in the palace. *This dirty scholar dusted my sleeves after our fight. He must have stolen them then!* Greybeard Liang raised his ginseng hoe. "Show us your weapon. Let's see who'd win in a proper fight."

"I would most certainly lose," Zhu Cong said with a smile.

"We haven't had the pleasure of your names yet," Qiu Chuji cut in.

Hector Sha introduced his companions one by one.

"All renowned names of the *wulin*! A victor has yet to emerge today, but both sides have already suffered injuries. Let's arrange a date to meet again," Qiu Chuji said.

"We would be sorely disappointed if we didn't get to meet all Seven Masters of the Quanzhen Sect," Tiger Peng replied. "As for the date and location, Elder Qiu, please name it and we will be there."

Qiu Chuji considered their situation. It would take a few months for Brother Ma and Brother Wang to fully recover. It would also take time to gather his martial siblings from different parts of the country.

"Let's meet in six months' time. On the night of Moon Festival," he proposed. "We can gaze at the full moon and discuss kung fu. How does that sound?"

"How poetic! We must find a suitably scenic location." Tiger Peng was turning the proposal over in his head. If all Seven Masters of the Quanzhen Sect turn up with the Seven Freaks of the South, we'll be greatly outnumbered. Yet, six months should give us the time to recruit other masters to our cause. And since we'll be travelling south with the Prince to look for General Yue Fei's final poems, we can hold this fight in that part of the country. Yes, that will work.

"What about the hometown of our Seven Heroes?" Peng said.

"Excellent! Let's meet at the Tower of Mist and Rain, in the South Lake of Jiaxing," Qiu Chuji replied. "You're very welcome to bring friends."

"We shall be there."

"So, we Freaks, being the locals, will have to foot the bill? What a cunning plan you two have cooked up!" Zhu Cong laughed. "Of all the poetic landscapes in China, it has to be Jiaxing."

By now, Tiger Peng could not feel his forearm, and the mere act of conversation took great effort on his part. Zhu Cong's rambling was trying his patience, but with his life in this filthy scholar's hands, he swallowed his pride and waited for further instructions.

"Well, well, it's not every day we get to play hosts to such distinguished masters of the martial world," Zhu Cong continued. "Butcher Peng, take the white one. Yellow's for the wound."

Tiger Peng swallowed the white powder immediately.

"For forty-nine days, you must not drink or copulate," Ke Zhen'e said. "It would be a great disappointment if you weren't there for Moon Festival."

"Thank you for your concern." Tiger Peng glowered as Hector Sha applied the antidote to his wound. They staggered back to the palace with Greybeard Liang and Gallant Ouyang.

WITH EVERYONE else from the palace gone, Wanyan Kang knelt before his mother's body and kowtowed four times. He turned to Qiu Chuji and repeated the action. He then stood up, dusted off his robe and went his own way.

"What was the meaning of that?" Qiu Chuji barked.

Wanyan Kang ignored the question and left without looking back. Qiu Chuji stared after his disciple for a long time, then he bowed deeply at the Freaks. "Without the Heroes' help, we would have died today. That ingrate is infinitely inferior to your Guo Jing. For those of us who practise the martial arts, what matters the most is to live according to the ethics and morals we uphold. Our martial skills are the least of our accomplishments. It is my lifelong shame to have called myself Wanyan Kang's teacher. We need not stage the contest at the Garden of the Eight Drunken Immortals on the twenty-fourth day of the third month, as we agreed eighteen years ago. Today, I admit defeat wholeheartedly. Let it be known in the *jianghu* that Qiu Chuji has been defeated by the Seven Heroes of the South and that he accepts his subjugation with humility. My martial brothers Ma Yu and Wang Chuyi, here, are my witnesses."

Ke Zhen'e replied with a few self-deprecating words of thanks. Qiu Chuji's earnest admission pleased the Freaks enormously. Eighteen years in the Mongolian desert, so far away from the mild weather and comforts of home, had paid off. And yet, it was a bittersweet victory. Oh, how they wished their Fifth Brother Zhang Asheng could have been with them now.

6

THE FREAKS HELPED MA YU AND WANG CHUYI INSIDE AND sent their Sixth Brother Gilden Quan, the Cloaked Master of the Market, to arrange Ironheart Yang and Charity Bao's coffins and burial.

Qiu Chuji did not feel right disturbing the weeping Mercy Mu, but he wanted to find out what had happened to Ironheart Yang since they had parted eighteen years ago.

"Young lady, where did you and your godfather live these last few years?" he asked eventually.

"Papa and I were always travelling. We have never stayed in one place for more than two weeks, ever since I can remember." She wiped her tears. "Papa said he was looking for . . . a young man by the name of Guo . . ." She lowered her head and her voice began to falter. Unmarried young women did not openly discuss men to whom they were not related.

Qiu Chuji glanced at Guo Jing and changed the subject to avoid causing Mercy further discomfort. "How did Ironheart come to be your godfather?"

"I was born in Lotus Pond Village in Lin'an. Papa lived with my family while he recovered from his injury at the hands of the Song soldiers. It was around that time that the plague took my parents and my brother. Papa raised me as his own and taught me kung fu. We travelled everywhere searching for Brother Guo under the banner . . . Duel . . . for a Maiden . . ." It took much courage for

Mercy to overcome her embarrassment and get the last four words out loud.

"Your father's name was Yang, not Mu." Qiu Chuji shifted the topic to spare her. "You should take on his name."

"I am a Mu."

"You don't believe me?"

"Of course I believe you, but I would prefer to stay a Mu," she said, her voice now barely audible.

Qiu Chuji dropped the matter for now, thinking it was her grief that caused her obstinacy and she would soon come round to changing her family name to Yang. He had little idea that it was he who was lacking insight. Mercy had thought things through very carefully. Her hand and heart had been won by the man who had overpowered her in the Duel for a Maiden, and this young man, the young Prince Wanyan Kang, was her papa's true-born son. A Yang. How could she ever hope to marry him if they shared the same name?

Wang Chuyi began to stir, the medicine having revived him somewhat. He had been listening to Qiu Chuji and Mercy's exchange, but his mind kept circling back to the duel, two days before. "Miss Mu, you are much more skilled in the martial arts than your father. Why is that?"

"A master taught me for three days when I was thirteen, but I hardly learned a thing."

"What was his name?"

"I'm afraid I am sworn to secrecy."

Wang Chuyi replayed each of Mercy's moves from the fight with Wanyan Kang, but he could not figure out the origins of her kung fu.

"Brother Qiu, you have been teaching Wanyan Kang for . . . eight or nine years?"

"Nine and a half. I had no idea that in his heart he was such an ingrate!"

Deep in his own thoughts, Wang Chuyi did not seem to hear Qiu's answer.

Ke Zhen'e broke the silence. "Elder Qiu, how did you find Brother Yang's son?"

"It was a stroke of good fortune. After we parted ways eighteen years ago, I travelled far and wide searching for the two families. For years, I searched in vain, but I kept looking. One year, I went back to Ox Village and happened upon a company of soldiers in Brother Yang's home. They were packing and moving everything from the old farmstead. I followed them, listening out for scraps of information. It turned out they were no ordinary soldiers. They were part of the Prince of Zhao's private guard, no less, with orders to collect all personal effects from the house. Broken furniture, rusted spearheads, farm tools. It was all very curious, so I tracked them all the way here."

Now Guo Jing understood why Charity Bao's residence in the palace was so humble.

"I stole into the palace one night. I needed to see for myself why this Prince of Zhao, Wanyan Honglie, wanted these wretched old things so much that he would send his personal guard thousands of miles south across the border to bring them back. That was when I found out that his Consort was Yang's beloved wife, Charity Bao. I was going to put my sword through her for choosing the riches and titles of our country's invaders over the memory of her husband, a patriot. But, seeing her living in that shack amid the grandeur of the palace, cradling Brother Yang's old spearhead, her tears as fresh as the day he died, my heart softened. Her husband still occupied her mind. I also discovered that she had given birth to Ironheart's child and he was the young Prince Wanyan Kang; a few years later, when he was old enough, I went back to teach him kung fu."

"The young man never knew his true parentage?" Ke Zhen'e asked.

"I asked him several times in a roundabout way, but his fondness for wealth and power made me uneasy about his character and I never revealed his heritage. He always feigned obedience with sweet words when I lectured him about the ethics and morals we strive to uphold. If we had not agreed on this contest, I would not have wasted my time on him. I was hoping that, after the fight, regardless of the result, we would make peace. I would tell the boy the truth about his parentage, free Charity from that disgraceful place and find her a quiet home in which to settle down. I never imagined Brother Ironheart could still be alive, or that the pair would lose their lives in such a way as they did today."

Mercy hid her face in her hands and started sobbing again at the mention of her godfather's death.

Guo Jing then told them the story of how he found Ironheart Yang imprisoned in the palace the night before, and of Yang's reunion with Charity Bao. Though Charity had compromised her chastity by marrying Wanyan Honglie, the Freaks and the Taoists understood that she had done so only because she thought her husband was dead. It was not considered immoral for widows to remarry – in fact, it was not an uncommon practice – so no-one could fault her for that. And everyone was moved and humbled by her final act of devotion.

The conversation soon turned to the Moon Festival rendezvous. "There is nothing to worry about," Zhu Cong said. "The Seven Masters of the Quanzhen Sect will be there."

"But if they invite other masters of the *wulin*, we might be outnumbered." Ma Yu was always cautious.

"Who else could they invite? There aren't that many masters in this world!" Qiu Chuji cut in.

"Brother, your martial skills have brought fame and glory to the Sect, but you have yet to rein in the overconfidence of your youth. You know the saying well—"

"Above the sky is a loftier heaven, beyond the man a mightier body." Chuckling, Qiu Chuji supplied the phrase.

"Is that not true? The masters we met today were as skilled as us. We might not win if they bring help."

"You worry too much, brother. How could the Quanzhen Sect lose to such rogues and vagabonds?"

"The calamities of this world cannot always be foreseen. If our friends, the Six Heroes, here, had not stepped forth to help us today, we three would have lost the good name of our Quanzhen Sect, and that took us decades to acquire."

Honoured by Ma Yu's acknowledgement, Ke Zhen'e and Zhu Cong bowed in unison.

"Uncle Zhou was trained personally by our *shifu*," Ma Yu continued. "He was ten times more skilled than us, yet his desire to win and to be proved the strongest was the reason for his disappearance. It has been more than a decade, now. We should learn from this. Be humble and vigilant always."

Ma Yu's speech silenced Qiu Chuji. The Freaks had never heard of this Uncle Zhou. Clearly, this man had done something that was considered a blot on the Sect's name. Although curious, the Freaks maintained a tactful silence. Meanwhile, Wang Chuyi was still lost in thought. He had not spoken a word since his exchange with Mercy Mu.

Qiu Chuji glanced at Guo Jing and Mercy. "Brother Ke, your disciple is honourable and righteous. With him as a son-in-law, Ironheart would for certain find peace in his eternal rest."

Mercy blushed, bowed her head and stood up to leave the room. She was not comfortable with this talk of a marriage to Guo Jing. As she swept past him, Wang Chuyi stood up and thrust his palm at her right shoulder. He waited for Mercy to summon her inner strength to repel him. Just before her strength was fully gathered, he pushed. Mercy teetered and started to fall, face down. Wang Chuyi steadied her with a light touch on the left shoulder. Mercy was once again steady on her feet, standing upright. She stared at Wang Chuyi, wide-eyed.

"Miss Mu, please forgive me. I was testing your kung fu. The master who taught you for those three days, he only has nine fingers and dresses like a beggar, am I right?"

"How did Your Reverence know?"

"The Divine Vagrant Nine Fingers is known for his whimsical

ways. It is the greatest fortune to have received training from the Venerable Master Hong himself. My hearty congratulations."

"It's a pity he was only able to spare three days."

"For anyone else, those three days would amount to decades of hard work."

"If Your Reverence says so . . . Do you know where Master Hong might be found?"

"Well, the last time I saw him was more than twenty years ago, at the summit of Mount Hua."

At this, Mercy left the room in disappointment.

"Elder Wang, can you tell us more about this Venerable Master Hong?" Jade Han asked.

Wang Chuyi sat down with a smile, but it was Qiu Chuji who spoke first. "Perhaps you have heard these names? Heretic of the East, Venom of the West, King of the South, Beggar of the North and Central Divinity."

"Why, they are the greatest martial-arts masters of our age."

"Indeed."

"Master Hong is the Beggar of the North, I believe?" Ke Zhen'e asked.

"Yes. Our *shifu*, Immortal Wang, was Central Divinity," Wang Chuyi replied.

"Your betrothed was a student of the famous Divine Vagrant." Qiu Chuji turned to Guo Jing, laughing. "No-one who knew that would dream of making trouble with you."

Red with embarrassment, Guo Jing wanted to protest that Mercy Mu was not his betrothed, but he only managed to muster a few unintelligible grunts.

"Elder Wang, how did you recognise Mercy's style just by pushing against her shoulder?" Jade Han asked.

"Come here." Qiu Chuji beckoned Guo Jing closer. Instantly, the young man felt a hand pressing down on his own shoulder, weighty with the force of the monk's *neigong*. But, being a better fighter than Mercy Mu and having learned the same internal kung fu from Ma Yu, he was able to hold his ground and stay on his feet.

"Well done!" Qiu Chuji smiled and withdrew his inner strength. There was now nothing for Guo Jing's internal energy to push against. Qiu Chuji then gave him a nudge, tipping him backwards. Guo Jing instinctively extended his arm, pushed against the ground, and jumped right back onto his feet.

"Elder Qiu has just taught you a powerful move. Remember it well!" Zhu Cong teased amid a roomful of laughter.

Guo Jing nodded in earnest, unaware that he was the butt of the joke.

"Anyone trained in the martial arts would fall backwards," Qiu Chuji explained. "However, those trained in the Divine Vagrant's unique kung fu fall forward. His art is rooted in the firmness of his strength. The stronger the opponent, the stronger his moves become. He might have only taught Miss Mu for three days, but that was all the time she needed to learn the essence of his kung fu. She was not able to withstand Wang Chuyi's inner strength, but her training ensured that she did not succumb to it, but rather pushed into it. So, when she fell, she tipped forward, against the direction of the pressure."

Impressed by this martial insight, Zhu Cong asked, "Have you seen the Divine Vagrant in action, Elder Wang?"

"Yes, when our teacher sparred with the other masters at the summit of Mount Hua, more than two decades ago. Master Hong is as much a virtuoso of the martial arts as he is a connoisseur of food, but the summit of a mountain is not a place for gourmet meals, so you can imagine his discomfort. Instead, he treated discussions on martial-arts theory with our *shifu* and Apothecary Huang like banquets and fine wines. It was a real feast of knowledge and ideas. I was very fortunate to be waiting on my Master and was able to listen to the discussions. I'm still reaping the benefits."

"Apothecary Huang is the Heretic of the East?" Ke Zhen'e asked.

"Correct." Qiu Chuji turned to Guo Jing. "Though Brother Ma taught you for a time, it's lucky that he never took you on as a disciple.

Otherwise, you would be a generation beneath your betrothed, in terms of seniority – that's no way to start a marriage!" He laughed heartily at his own joke.

"I'm not marrying her." Guo Jing's face turned bright red.

"What?"

"I'm not marrying her."

"Why?" Qiu Chuji stood up, clearly displeased.

Jade Han came to Guo Jing's rescue. "When we heard that Master Yang had a son, we took it that Guo Jing had gained a sworn brother rather than a bride-to-be. He has since accepted the title granted by Genghis Khan, the Prince of the Golden Blade, as his daughter's betrothed."

Glaring at Guo Jing, Qiu Chuji cried, "A common-born girl is no contest against a princess! You are determined to disregard the future your father settled for you, aren't you? You greedy ingrate! You're no better than Wanyan Kang!"

Guo Jing bowed deeply. "Your student has never met his father. My mother did not mention any last wish. I beg Your Reverence to enlighten me."

"I am always too rash." Qiu Chuji laughed ruefully, and then recounted how he had met Ironheart Yang and Skyfury Guo in Ox Village eighteen years before, and how the two men had made a pact. He also told Guo Jing of his search for the families after hearing that they had been attacked by soldiers, which led to his fight with the Freaks. They were supposed to settle the dispute with a martial contest between their respective disciples, Wanyan Kang and Guo Jing.

The young man sank to his knees. As a son, he should avenge his father; as a disciple, he should repay his *shifus'* kindness. Was one lifetime enough to do both?

"It is common for a man to have three or four wives," Jade Han said, in an effort to comfort him. "When you return to Mongolia, speak with the Great Khan. I am certain he will be understanding and there will be no need for you to break your word. I'll wager the Khan himself has more than a hundred."

"I'm not marrying Princess Khojin," Guo Jing announced.

"What?" It was Jade Han's turn to be surprised.

"I don't want her to be my wife."

"But you are so close, aren't you?"

"She is like a sister, a good friend. I don't want her to be my wife."

This pleased Qiu Chuji. "Good lad! Who cares about the Khan or the Princess? You should follow your father and Uncle Yang's wishes. Marry Miss Mu."

"I am not marrying Miss Mu either," he declared firmly, shaking his head.

"What is going on? Is your heart otherwise occupied?" Jade Han asked quietly, remembering the pretty girl in white she had seen in the palace. She had noticed the way Guo Jing looked at her and how she had come to his aid.

Guo Jing's face flushed bright red once more. After a prickly pause, his chin moved up and down, almost imperceptibly.

"Who?" Qiu Chuji and Ryder Han called out in unison.

Guo Jing opened and closed his mouth. No sound came out. Jade Han knew the boy was too embarrassed to be able to string two words together. "It's the girl in white, isn't it?"

"What girl in white?" Qiu Chuji snapped.

"I remember Cyclone Mei calling her 'little sister' and her father 'Shifu' . . ." Jade Han mumbled.

"Apothecary Huang's daughter?!" Ke Zhen'e exclaimed, jumping from his seat.

Jade Han took Guo Jing's hands. "Is her name Huang?"

"Yes."

She did not know what else to say.

"You want to marry someone associated with Cyclone Mei?" Ke Zhen'e spat the words out.

"Did her father give you her hand?" Zhu Cong asked.

"I have never met him and I don't know who he is."

"You have pledged yourselves to each other?"

Guo Jing gaped at his Second *Shifu*, unsure what the question meant.

Zhu Cong elaborated. "Did you say you would marry her? Did she promise to be your wife?"

"No, we did not say that." Guo Jing paused. "There's no need. We know in our hearts. We cannot be without each other."

"What do you mean?" It sounded ridiculous to Ryder Han, who had never been in love in his life. The words had a very different effect on his cousin Jade, however.

Guo Jing is just like Fifth Brother, she thought, as memories of Zhang Asheng came flooding back. He was in love with me, but he kept it a secret. He thought he wasn't good enough for me. If I had made my feelings known to him, we could have tasted true happiness before he died. But now, he is gone forever.

"Do you know that her father is a cold-blooded killer?" Zhu Cong warned. "Do you think he'll let you live when he finds out? Cyclone Mei has not mastered one-tenth of his repertoire and she is already such a terror. If he wants you dead, none of us can help you."

"Lotus is so nice . . . Her father can't be evil."

"Apothecary Huang is evil incarnate. Swear you will never see that she-demon again. Swear it!" Ryder Han roared.

The Freaks hated everything to do with Twice Foul Dark Wind, for they had killed their Fifth Brother Zhang Asheng; and they hated Apothecary Huang even more, for he was the source of their infernal kung fu. Without this monstrous Heretic of the East, Laughing Buddha Zhang Asheng would still be alive today.

Ryder Han took a step closer. "Say it. Say that you'll never see that she-demon again!"

Guo Jing did not know what to do. He loved and respected his teachers, and he had never gone against their wishes, but he knew what his heart was telling him. He fell on his knees in tears. "*Shifus*, if I'm not allowed to see Lotus, I will not survive three days."

"Have you no shame?" A melodic voice drifted in through the window.

7

LOTUS! GUO JING RUSHED OUT OF THE ROOM. THERE SHE WAS, standing in the courtyard with his horse, Ulaan. The magnificent creature whinnied and reared, excited to see his master.

Guo Jing turned to his mentors as they came out into the courtyard. "Third *Shifu*, this is Lotus. She's a nice girl, not a she-demon."

"Why did you call me a she-demon, tubby man?" Lotus Huang glowered at Ryder Han and Zhu Cong in turn. "And you, you filthy scholar, why did you call my father a cold-blooded killer?"

Zhu Cong had never set eyes on such beauty in all his years. No wonder Guo Jing was so smitten. He smiled foolishly and said nothing.

"Be off with you. Shoo!" Ryder Han's whiskers bristled in agitation.

> "*Squat melon, roll and roll.*
> *One kick to the backside,*
> *And there he goes . . .*"

Lotus Huang sang, beating time with her hands. Ryder Han charged at her. She skipped sideways, evading him with ease.

"They're my teachers!" Guo Jing pleaded.

Lotus pulled a face and stuck her tongue out.

> "*Squat melon, roll and roll.*
> *One kick . . .*"

Lotus took hold of Guo Jing's belt and leapt into the air. They landed together on the horse's saddle. The moment she placed her hands on the reins, Ulaan shot out of the inn like an arrow. However fast Ryder Han's lightness kung fu might be, he could not keep up with a Fergana horse from the Mongolian steppe, whose hooves were so light and quick it was as if they were borne on wind and lightning.

Only moments had passed, but Guo Jing could no longer make out the faces of his mentors and the inn was rapidly reducing to a dot on the horizon. The air parted before him, the wind whistled in his ears. Lotus had taken her left hand off the reins to hold his hand. He felt guilty for running from his *shifus*, abandoning his obligations, but how could he give up Lotus? She was dearer to him than life itself. He would rather lose his head and bleed dry than obey his teachers' wishes and go against his heart.

In a short space of time, Ulaan had taken them dozens of *li* away from Zhongdu. Certain that no-one could catch up with them, Lotus pulled on the reins and stopped by a brook to rest. The magnificent steed rubbed his head affectionately against Guo Jing, delighted to see his master again after a few days of separation.

The young couple had only been apart for a matter of hours, but so much had transpired in that time that they had feared they would never see each other again. There was so much they wanted to say to each other, and neither knew where to start. At the same time, they knew the other person had already understood and there was no need to say anything out loud. Holding hands was enough.

They stood together with their fingers entwined for a long time. Eventually, Lotus took a handkerchief from the saddlebag and moistened it in the stream. She held it out for Guo Jing, but he was lost to the world.

"That's what we'll do," he said suddenly. "We'll go back."

"Together?"

"Yes, I'll tell my *shifus* and the Elders that you're a nice girl, you're not a she-demon, and that I . . . I cannot be without you." Guo Jing took her hand, speaking as if the Freaks were in front of him. "*Shifus*, I could never repay your kindness, but . . . but Lotus . . . Lotus is not a she-demon. She is a very, very nice girl . . . She is very, very . . . nice . . ."

There were so many wonderful things about Lotus, but he had never been good with words. That was the best he could come up with.

Moved by his conviction, Lotus was also amused by how tongue-tied he was. "They hate me. They won't listen to you. Let's run away. We can live in the mountains, or move to an island. We can go to a place where they'll never find us, a place where we can be together."

For a moment, Guo Jing was tempted, then he said, with certainty, "We have to go back."

"They'll split us up. We'll never see each other again."

"I won't part from you, even in death. *Shifus*, I have always obeyed you, but I cannot leave Lotus. You can kill me – I will not run, I will not complain – but I will never part from her."

Lotus had always had a pessimistic streak, despite her outward good humour. She was not hopeful about her future with Guo Jing after overhearing the exchange in the inn, but his resolve restored her faith. After all, their hearts were one. No man or power in this world could separate them.

"I'll always be with you. Death can't part us; not even Papa can split us up."

"See? You're very, very nice . . ."

That made Lotus laugh. "Why don't we let Ulaan rest a little? We should have a snack too." She pulled out a hunk of beef from the saddlebag and coated it in mud, before collecting dried branches for a fire.

IT WAS already afternoon by the time they arrived back at the inn. The innkeeper, remembering Guo Jing's generous tips, welcomed him warmly.

"Sir, your party has already left the capital. Would you like something to eat?"

"Did they leave a message?"

"No, they went south a few hours ago."

"Let's catch up with them."

Guo Jing and Lotus galloped south, but could find no sign of the Freaks or the Taoists. They tried another route, questioning passers-by and shopkeepers along the way, but no-one had seen anyone matching the Freaks' physical descriptions. Ulaan had galloped several dozen *li* with two in the saddle, but he showed no sign of fatigue.

"We'll see your *shifus* in Jiaxing on the evening of Moon Festival," Lotus said, to cheer Guo Jing up. "You can tell them how 'very, very nice' I am then."

"That's six months from now."

"Well, that gives us six months to travel!"

8

THE NEXT MORNING, GUO JING PURCHASED A WHITE HORSE for himself to lighten the load on Ulaan. They travelled southwards at a leisurely pace, enjoying the scenery. Sometimes they slept under the stars, side by side; sometimes they shared a room in a village inn. Close though they were, they were always chaste.

Lotus Huang had been brought up under the influence of her father Apothecary Huang's unorthodox views, rejecting the etiquette and rules of the time. She saw nothing untoward or unusual about Guo Jing's companionship. Guo Jing, with his upbringing in Mongolia, simply followed his heart. He had always done what felt right and natural to him. They also had plenty of gold and silver, so they wanted for nothing on their journey.

By the fourth lunar month, they were approaching the Taining-jun area of Xiqing city in eastern Shandong. Having been in the saddle all morning that warm, sunny day, their faces were sticky with sweat and dirt from the road.

"Let's find a spot of shade," Lotus said.

"The town is just ahead. Why don't we stop there for a pot of tea?" Guo Jing replied.

They soon caught sight of a group plodding ahead of them. A portly man in a purple silk robe sat astride a frail and sickly donkey, fanning himself frantically. The beast buckled under his enormous weight, at least two hundred and fifty *jin*. By his side was a sedan chair. The drapes were tied back, and a plump woman in pink sat within. Her litter was carried by two elderly, stick-thin porters. A maid walked alongside, waving a large fan to cool her mistress.

Intrigued by the spectacle, Lotus said, "I'm going to take a better look at the lady," and urged Ulaan forward.

As she overtook the party, she turned the horse and peered into the sedan chair. She saw a woman in her forties with a face as broad as a washbasin, a pair of small beady eyes, a wide mouth and a flat nose. Her skin was caked in a thick layer of powder, scored through by rivulets of sweat pouring from her forehead. A golden hairpin, a red satin flower and a pair of fleshy ears protruded from her rotund head of hair.

"What are you looking at?" The large lady glared at Lotus.

"I wish to admire your shapely figure and good looks!" Lotus laughed and tightened the reins. Ulaan galloped straight at the sedan chair.

The servants let go and the litter hit the ground, sending the woman tumbling into the middle of the road with a flail, a scream, and then a curse.

Lotus chuckled at such a fine joke. But, before she could ride away, the man on the donkey lashed at her with his riding crop.

"You little rascal!"

Lotus grabbed the end and pulled. The man lost his balance and fell, at which Lotus turned the crop on him.

"Highway robbery! Murder!" the woman screamed.

Lotus pulled out her Emei Needles and sliced the woman's left ear off, making her squeal like a pig at the slaughter.

The man fell to his knees. "Mistress, spare our lives – we will give you gold."

"Who wants your gold? Who is she?"

"She's my wife . . . We're going . . . going to her parents'."

"You're big and strong – can't you walk? Behave, and I'll let you live."

"Whatever Mistress commands!"

Lotus was tickled at being addressed so formally by someone older than her in age. "You three. Into the sedan chair." The porters and the maid straightened the litter and climbed in without a word. There was still room to turn inside.

All eyes were on Lotus. No-one dared guess what she might come up with next.

"You may have a few ingots to your name, but you can't walk over people like that! Do you want to live or die?"

"Live! We want to live!" husband and wife shouted in unison.

"Well, it's your turn. Carry the chair!"

"I . . . don't know how," the woman said, her hand pressed against her bleeding face.

"If you refuse . . ." Lotus swiped her Emei Needle flat against the plump woman's nose.

The woman shrieked and covered her nose. Then she scrabbled to lift the carrying poles onto her shoulders and her husband followed suit. Well fed as they were, the couple were more able to manage the weight than their servants.

Lotus and Guo Jing escorted the group a short distance before galloping away. They turned back to look and saw that the couple were still earnestly carrying the chair.

Lotus giggled. "What a horrible woman. She'd be perfect for Qiu Chuji."

"He doesn't want a wife," Guo Jing said.

"Of course not, but then he'd know how it feels to have one forced upon him. You said you didn't want to marry Miss Mu, but he kept harassing you. One day, when my kung fu is stronger than his, I'll force him to take a nasty wife."

"Lotus, Miss Mu isn't horrible or nasty. But my heart is yours." Guo Jing suddenly realised how much Qiu Chuji's words had troubled Lotus.

"I may be a frightful mistress, but at least I'm pretty. And I'll never be horrible to you!"

∽

ONE DAY, as they ambled along a tree-lined road, the song of a babbling brook caught Lotus's attention. She galloped ahead through the trees and was welcomed by the sight of a deep stream framed by willow branches that reached down to the surface of the water. The water was so clear that she could see pebbles in green, white, red and purple on the riverbed, obscured only by an abundance of fish.

Lotus took off her outer garments and the Hedgehog Chainmail, and jumped into the water. In no time, she emerged with a fish flapping in her hand.

"Catch!"

Guo Jing tried his grappling kung fu on the fish, but it slipped away and lay thrashing about on the ground.

"Come into the water."

Guo Jing did not know how to swim, having spent his whole childhood in the landlocked Mongolia. He took off his shirt and stepped gingerly into the water. Lotus dived and tugged on his leg, upsetting his balance. He panicked and went under, swallowing a lungful of water.

Laughing, Lotus pulled him up and taught him how to breathe and float. The key to swimming lay in controlled breathing, and that happened to be something Guo Jing knew very well from his internal kung fu training. In a few hours' time, he had grasped the basics. They grilled fish for dinner and camped by the brook that night.

Lotus grew up on an island; the sea was her constant companion. Her father Apothecary Huang might have been one of the greatest kung fu masters of the age, but he could not rival his daughter in the water. Guided by such a master and spending at least eight hours in the stream each day, Guo Jing was swimming very well after just one week.

The young couple were swimming upstream when, after a few *li*, a thunderous noise greeted them. They rounded a bend in the stream where the air was filled with vapour. A spectacular sight greeted them: a vast sheet of water crashing down from the cliff edge above, more than a dozen *zhang* high.

"Let's climb to the top!" Lotus was thrilled.

The water beat down hard. They were barely able to hold their ground against the force of the torrent. Whenever they lifted their feet, they were flushed downstream. They struggled for several hours, making very little headway.

"We'll beat it tomorrow!" Guo Jing said.

"Don't take it personally, it's just a waterfall." Lotus laughed.

The next morning, the young couple managed to climb a few *zhang* before falling into the pool below. The depth of the water and their lightness kung fu ensured they were not injured.

They returned to the waterfall every day, learning its topography and the flow of the water. On the eighth day, Guo Jing climbed to the top and pulled Lotus up. Whooping with joy, they jumped down, hand in hand.

After a fortnight of swimming and climbing the waterfall, Guo Jing was now a formidable swimmer, thanks to his considerable internal *neigong*. It would be a long time before he was as comfortable in the water as Lotus, but he was already better than her father. Having exhausted all the sights around the stream, they continued south.

ONE DAY, at dusk, they reached the banks of the Yangtze River. The majestic waters rushed east; white-crested waves splashed and churned. The sight imbued Guo Jing with a great sense of awe, and he felt as if his body and the river were one. The scene captured him for some time.

"Do it!" Lotus cried above the roar of the river. She could tell that he wanted to swim to the other shore. By now, they had developed

such a deep connection that they had little need to give voice to their thoughts.

"Off you go," Guo Jing said as he let the white horse go. He then tied their belongings to Ulaan's saddle. Neighing, the Fergana horse led the way, his masters swimming, side by side, in his wake.

It was a clear night. There was no other sound but the rush of water, as if everything between the heavens and earth belonged to just the two of them.

Clouds began to gather, obscuring the stars. Lightning cracked overhead to the drumming of thunder.

"Are you scared?" Guo Jing asked.

"Not when we're together."

Yet summer storms die down as suddenly as they descend. A bright moon was hanging low by the time they reached the other shore. Guo Jing started a fire and Lotus hung their clothes to dry. They changed into fresh garments and took a nap to the song of the rushing river.

The sky began to glint white. A cock crowed, waking Lotus.

She yawned. "I'm starving!"

Jumping to her feet, she darted towards a nearby farmhouse and soon returned with a large cockerel under her arm.

"Let's go. I don't want his owner to see us," she said.

They walked east for about a *li* before settling down. Lotus gutted the chicken with her Emei Needles and cleaned the cavity. Then, without plucking the feathers, she covered the whole bird with mud and put it on the fire. Soon, a sweet aroma filled the air. She continued to grill the earthen parcel until the mud casing was cracked and dry. When she broke it open, the feathers came off with the baked earth, revealing a perfectly cooked chicken.

CHAPTER THREE

HAUGHTY DRAGON
REPENTS

I

"TEAR IT IN THREE. GIVE ME THE RUMP."

Guo Jing and Lotus Huang turned in surprise. How could they not have heard the footsteps approaching?

A beggar stood grinning at them, his eyes fixed greedily on the chicken.

He looked middle-aged to Lotus; his hair was flecked with grey and a thin beard framed his angular jawline. Strong arms and large feet extended from his patched, but incongruously clean, clothes. He held a bamboo cane, green and polished like jade, and, on his back, he carried a large gourd coated in red lacquer.

He sat down with the young couple without waiting for an invitation and uncorked the canteen. The sweet fragrance of wine drifted into the air. He glugged several large mouthfuls before handing it to Guo Jing. "Go on, lad."

"I'm afraid I don't drink, but thank you, sir." The beggar's behaviour was almost rude, but Guo Jing sensed that there was something exceptional about him.

"What about you, lass?"

She shook her head, and, as she did so, she noticed the stranger was missing an index finger on his right hand. Her father's story about the Contest of Mount Hua came back to her. Could he be the Beggar of the North, the Divine Vagrant Nine Fingers? She decided to sound him out.

The beggar had scarcely taken his eyes off the chicken since he arrived. His Adam's apple bobbed in anticipation. Lotus thought he would take it by force if he had to wait a moment longer. She tore the bird apart and gave him the bottom half.

"Exquisite! Not a single one of my beggar ancestors could conjure up such a delicious beggar's chicken." He wolfed it down as he spoke. With a smile, Lotus handed him the remaining half.

"But you young 'uns haven't eaten yet!" Even as he protested, he grabbed what was left of the chicken and soon it all disappeared down his throat.

A moment later, he spat out a few pieces of chewed bone and patted his belly in contentment. "My dear tum, you haven't tasted such delectable chicken in a long time, eh?"

"What a supreme honour to have my beggar's chicken praised by this dish's namesake." Lotus smiled.

"The lass has a sweet tongue." The beggar chuckled and pulled out a handful of gold darts from his shirt. "I saw a fight the other day. One of the men had his darts gilded with gold. This old beggar couldn't help but filch a few. Here you go, lad. You can probably exchange them for a few *maces* of silver."

Guo Jing declined. "You are our guest, sir; we can't take your gift." According to Mongolian custom, it was a host's duty to feed his guests.

"Now, this is awkward. I'm a beggar and I'm used to scrounging for leftovers, but I took such a wonderful chicken from you kids before you'd even tasted it . . ."

"It's only a chicken!" Guo Jing protested. "And we stole it."

"We filch, you feast — it all works out well," Lotus added.

The beggar chuckled. "I like you two. Is there anything you want? Don't be shy."

Guo Jing shook his head. He had been taught that hospitality should always be freely given without expectation of repayment in any form.

"I'd love to cook you my favourite dish." Lotus, on the other hand, knew what she wanted from this new friend. "We can go to the next town together."

The beggar agreed heartily and the three of them headed south together, to a town called Jiang Temple.

"How should we address you, sir?" Guo Jing asked.

"My last name is Hong and I'm the seventh in the family. Why don't you call me Count Seven?"

So I was right, Lotus thought. He is the Beggar of the North! He doesn't look more than a couple of years older than Qiu Chuji and yet he's ranked as one of the Five Greats, alongside Qiu's Master. Actually, Pa is around the same age, and he's one of the Greats too. What does that say about the so-called Masters of Quanzhen? They're so thick they haven't got a dog's chance of getting anywhere with their kung fu.

Lotus had not forgiven Qiu Chuji for insisting Guo Jing marry Mercy Mu, nor had she forgiven her father.

When they reached the town, they stopped at a local inn and Lotus went to the market to buy ingredients for dinner.

"She's your wife?" Count Seven Hong grinned.

Guo Jing dared not confirm or deny the question, and so answered only with a blush. His awkwardness amused the old beggar no end. Eventually, he stopped laughing and immediately started snoring instead.

When Lotus returned, more than an hour later, she went straight into the kitchen. Guo Jing offered to help, but she pushed him out with a smile.

Another hour passed; the beggar yawned and sniffed noisily. "Curious! What's she cooking? Something's afoot!" He craned to peer into the kitchen, but he could not see much from his seat.

Guo Jing stifled a giggle as the man fidgeted, scratched his face, switched seats and paced the room, growing more and more impatient as the smell of cooking drifted in from the kitchen.

"The mere thought of food makes me lose my wits. You know the saying, 'The index finger pulses when food's about'? It's certainly true for me. This finger –" he held up his right hand – "throbs when I see or smell something delicious. I once botched a very important task because I got so distracted by my aching tummy, so I chopped it off . . ."

Guo Jing gasped.

"But I'm still just as much of a glutton as before," Count Seven said with a sigh.

Lotus finally emerged with a wooden tray: three bowls of white rice, one wine cup and two dishes piled high with her creations. She filled the cup with wine and said, "Count Seven, do let me know what you think of my cooking."

The beggar's chopsticks got straight to work on what Guo Jing thought looked like pan-fried beef strips. But Count Seven knew it was something much more complex than that, as new flavours and sensations unveiled themselves with every bite. One moment smooth, another moment crunchy – it was impossible to predict the next taste or texture. It was as if his tongue was sparring with a martial master. He examined the dish. Each strip was made up of five different layers!

"I can taste shank of lamb, ear of piglet, veal kidney and . . ." The beggar closed his eyes as he savoured each mouthful.

"I'll bow to you if you can identify the others!" Lotus grinned.

"Rabbit saddle . . . and . . . thigh of water deer!"

"Amazing!" She clapped and cheered.

Guo Jing could not believe how much effort she had put into each tiny strip. He was also full of admiration for Count Seven Hong for being able to distinguish the five ingredients.

"Pork and lamb bring out one flavour, water deer and veal another," Hong mused. "I can't work out how many there are in this dish alone."

"Twenty-five, if we ignore the variations you get from layering the meats in different sequences." Lotus smiled. "This dish is called Who Hears the Plum Blossom Fall While the Flute Plays? Five kinds of meat, the same as the number of petals on a plum blossom, and the strip is shaped like the *dizi* flute. It is meant to be a test of your palate, and your tongue affords you the title of Top Scholar."

Count Seven Hong moved on to the other bowl. "This broth is too precious to be devoured." He scooped up a few cherries, tasted them and – *ah!* – gasped with delight.

Refreshing lotus leaf, delicate bamboo shoot, honeyed cherry – their flavours are unmistakeable, Count Seven thought, as he helped himself to a few more cherries. He chewed with his eyes closed. What is the fruit stuffed with? It tastes meaty. Fowl. It has to be . . .

"Partridge?" he said out loud. "No . . . spotted dove!"

He opened his eyes and saw that Lotus had raised her thumb in agreement.

"What outlandish name have you given this lotus leaf, bamboo shoot, cherry and spotted dove soup?" the beggar asked.

"You missed out one ingredient."

"Oh, did I? You mean the petals?"

"Think about the five ingredients. The name is obvious."

"This old beggar doesn't like riddles. Just tell me, lass."

"Well, I'll give you a clue. Think of the *Book of Songs*."

Count Seven waved frantically. "That's no use. This old beggar doesn't know the first thing about books."

"Floral like a visage, cherry-red lips – that's a pretty lady, right?"

"Oh, Beauty Broth?"

Lotus shook her head. "The bamboo is upright and resilient, and, though the lotus grows in mud, its flowers are clean and pure. These are the qualities of a gentleman."

"Gentleman's Soup?"

"We're still missing the dove. Think about the first poem in the *Book of Songs*:

"Coo, coo, the doves sing from the river isle,
The fair maiden is perfect for the lord.

"The dish is called Made for Each Other Broth."

Count Seven bellowed with laughter. "Your creation certainly lives up to its peculiar name. I wonder what sort of eccentric man fathered a funny lass like you. I must say, this is in every way superior to the cherry broth I tried ten years ago, made by the chefs of the imperial household."

"Tell me about their dishes; maybe I can recreate some for you."

Count Seven Hong first satisfied his belly before turning his thoughts to a reply. "There was plenty of wonderful cooking, but nothing as good as this. Well, actually, they did have one outstanding creation, called Contrast of the Five Treasures. I don't know how it's made, though."

"You were treated to dinner by the Emperor?" Guo Jing asked.

"Yes, but he knew nothing about it. I made myself at home on the rafters of the imperial kitchens for three months. I tasted each course prepared for the Emperor. If I liked it, I kept the whole plate. I let him eat what I didn't care for. They thought they were being haunted by the fox demon." Count Seven Hong cackled at the memory.

Amazed by the lengths their new friend would go to for good food, Lotus picked her way through the leftovers while Guo Jing shovelled down four helpings of rice.

Count Seven turned to Guo Jing. "You lucky lad – your little wife is the best cook in the world! Why, by the mother of heavens, did I not meet a girl with her skill when I was young?" He watched as the young man ate, then shook his head. "An ox munching on peonies. What a pity!"

Lotus giggled, but Guo Jing was merely confused. He had looked after many herds, growing up in Mongolia, but he had never seen or heard of a peony. He did not realise that the beggar was lamenting his lack of appreciation for gastronomy.

"I can tell both of you know some martial arts from your physique, and that you have worked out I practise the art too. The lass is clearly trying to entice me, with her cooking, into sharing my kung fu knowledge. It'd be rude of me not to show my appreciation of her culinary kindness. Come, follow me." He patted his tummy happily and headed outside with his gourd and the bamboo cane.

Guo Jing and Lotus followed Count Seven to a pine forest on the edge of the town.

"What do you want to learn?" the beggar asked Guo Jing.

Not the quickest thinker, Guo Jing was stuck for an answer. Besides, there were so many branches and schools of martial arts. How could this man possibly teach him anything he could name?

Lotus answered for him. "He gets annoyed because he can't beat me."

"I've never—"

Lotus cut him off with a withering look.

"How can that be? From the way he moves I can tell he has a sound foundation in internal kung fu," Count Seven laughed. "Show me what you kids can do."

"I'm ready!" Lotus called from several paces away. But Guo Jing was still trying to figure out what to do, so she added, "If you don't show Uncle your skill, how is he going to teach you?"

"I hope the Master will provide guidance," Guo Jing said referentially.

"A little, perhaps. Not much."

"Here it comes!" Lotus cried, as she struck with her palm. He raised his hands to block, but Lotus's move had morphed into a sweeping kick aimed at his legs.

"Good move, lass!"

"Fight properly," Lotus whispered.

Guo Jing thrust and turned his palms in the Southern Mountain style his Fourth *Shifu* Woodcutter Nan had taught him, stirring the air noisily with each move. Lotus fought back earnestly, jinking, ducking and swerving. Her strikes grew faster. A flurry of arms and palms dazzled Guo Jing.

This was a system of attack Lotus's father, Apothecary Huang, had dreamed up while watching peach blossoms swirl in the wind. Cascading Peach Blossom Palm mixed strikes with feints: one sharp blow lurked amid five or eight defensive flourishes. Like flowers fluttering in a breeze, each move was graceful and unforced, yet sharp and sudden at the same time, like petals whipped by a gust.

Lotus had yet to master the sword-like strength that was key to the moves, and she was also holding back for fear of hurting her beloved.

But, to Guo Jing, her fluctuating tempo was enough to confound him. As she performed the flourishes with her arms, her palms struck at him from every conceivable angle. He was dazed by the technique's complexity and speed. He did not know how to defend himself.

Pak, pak, pak, pak! Four loud slaps fell on Guo Jing's shoulders, chest and back. Lotus beamed and leapt away.

"You don't need me to teach you anything, with a father like yours," Count Seven Hong said frostily.

How did he know? Lotus wondered. Papa said he'd never used Cascading Peach Blossom Palm in combat before. "You know my father?"

"He is the Heretic of the East and I'm the Beggar of the North. We've exchanged a few blows in our time."

"How do you know who I am?" Her respect for the beggar was growing. Not many people lived to tell the tale after fighting her father.

"Look in the mirror. Look at your eyes, your nose. He's not as good-looking, or else he would have plunged the world into chaos. I thought you looked familiar, and then your kung fu revealed the rest. I've never seen these moves, but they smack of Peach Blossom Island. Only your father could have come up with something like that, and I bet he named the dishes too."

"You think my father is a martial master?"

"He is certainly formidable, but perhaps not quite the greatest in the world."

"You must be the greatest, then."

"Not necessarily. It was years ago, now, when the five of us sparred at the summit of Mount Hua. We fought for seven days and seven nights, and, in the end, we all had to admit that Central Divinity was foremost among us."

"Who is he?"

"Didn't your father tell you about him?"

"He only told me a little. Whenever I pressed him for more, he'd say that the martial world was full of ill dealings not fit for a girl's ears, and then he'd clam up. He rarely spoke to me about the *wulin*, and then one day he shouted at me to be gone, so I ran away . . ." Lotus trailed off and lowered her head, once again upset by the memory of her last encounter with her father.

"That old monster."

"Hey, he's still my papa!"

Count Seven chuckled. "It's a shame no nice girl wanted to marry me, because I'm a beggar. If I had a good daughter like you, I'd never throw her out."

"That's for sure; otherwise, who'd cook for you?"

"That's true." He sighed, suddenly lamenting that he had no-one in his life to help him satisfy the epicure within. After a pause, he resumed his tale. "Central Divinity was the founder of the Quanzhen Sect. His name was Double Sun Wang Chongyang. It's hard to say who is the greatest, now he's gone."

"I knew three Quanzhen monks: a Qiu, a Wang and a Ma. Useless old cow muzzles! They're utter shams. They all got poisoned after a couple of moves."

"Really? They're Wang Chongyang's disciples. I've heard that Qiu Chuji is the strongest martially, but I doubt any of them could match their martial uncle, Zhou Botong."

"Elder Ma did speak of a martial uncle once, but he never mentioned the Venerable Elder's title," Guo Jing said.

Neither Count Seven nor Guo Jing had noticed Lotus's reaction to the name Zhou Botong. She was about to speak, but then thought better of it.

"He hasn't got a title, because he's not a monk! Heavens, you are a fool, aren't you? I bet your genius of a father-in-law isn't keen on you." Count Seven Hong's jibes reduced Guo Jing to tongue-tied splutters. It had never crossed the young man's mind who his father-in-law might turn out to be, and he knew he had better keep his mouth shut for now.

"Papa hasn't met him yet. But, if you'd give him some guidance, I'm sure Papa will like him," Lotus said, before adding coyly, "As a courtesy to you."

"You can't sweet-talk me into teaching your stupid husband anything! Only you would treat this dullard like some treasure! Trying to lick my boots to get your way!" The beggar was just warming up. "Let me be clear. I don't take on students, and who wants to teach such a dumb lad? You little knave! You haven't picked up one-tenth of your father's kung fu, but you've inherited every drop of his connivance."

Lotus blushed and lowered her head, embarrassed to see her ploy exposed so easily. She had not expected the glutton to be this sharp and she did not like being lectured, so she walked away.

She had never been that interested in kung fu training; she had not even bothered to learn much from her own father, so why would she be interested in the martial tricks of this beggar? She had been thinking of Guo Jing. She was angry his *shifus* had called her a she-demon and it had upset her to see him cowering before the Freaks and those smelly monks, like a mouse among cats. She had thought, perhaps, Count Seven Hong could toughen him up by teaching him some new martial skills.

"He's quite a character," Guo Jing said when he caught up with her.

Lotus heard the rustle of leaves overhead. Count Seven must have skimmed around the woods and hidden himself up a tree to eavesdrop on us, she thought. She answered Guo Jing, projecting her voice more than usual. "He's a good man. His kung fu is much stronger than Papa's."

"How do you know?"

"Papa told me. He said the only person that could overpower him was the Divine Vagrant Nine Fingers, Count Seven Hong. He said that he much desired another chance to spar with Master Hong, but it was impossible to track him down."

Count Seven Hong suspected they had been sent by Apothecary Huang to steal his martial secrets, but he could not help but feel a little pleased with himself at the news that the Heretic regarded his skills so highly. He had no idea Lotus was making it all up.

"I've barely scratched the surface of Papa's kung fu," Lotus continued. "You know me: anything to avoid hard work. I'm sure if Master Hong gave me some pointers, it would be even better than being taught by Papa. I feel so bad that I upset him."

She started to weep. It was all an act, at first, but soon her mind drifted to her mother's early death and the estrangement from her father, and all at once she found that she was really crying. Guo Jing's attempt to comfort her only made the tears flow faster.

"I remember Papa once said that . . ." Lotus choked out the words between sobs. "That Master Hong has gained incomparable kung fu skills . . . on a level unheard of before or since . . . and that even Wang Chongyang of the Quanzhen Sect was wary of him. His speciality is called . . . It's called . . . It's on the tip of my tongue. Anyway, I was going to beg him to teach you it . . ."

Lotus was making everything up. She assumed that Count Seven Hong would have such a particular martial move in his repertoire.

The beggar could not stand it any longer and jumped down. "It's called the Eighteen Dragon-Subduing Palms!"

Startled, the young couple stumbled back a few steps.

Guo Jing was genuinely surprised, while Lotus continued to spin her tale. "Count Seven, how did you end up in that tree? I can't believe I've forgotten the name of your kung fu. Papa always talks about it! It's the martial technique he admires the most."

"I thought your papa considered himself the greatest, now that Wang Chongyang is dead, but I guess even he has to speak the truth from time to time!" Count Seven said gleefully, before turning to Guo

Jing. "Your kung fu foundations are as good as the girl's; you lose out when it comes to technique. Lass, go back to the inn."

Now that everything was going according to plan, Lotus left the two men, with a spring in her step.

2

"KNEEL!" COUNT SEVEN POINTED TO THE GROUND. "SWEAR you'll never teach anyone anything I've taught you, without my permission. And that includes your clever little wife."

Guo Jing knew he could deny Lotus nothing she asked of him, so he said, "Count Seven, I don't think I should learn from you."

"Why?" Such a refusal was a first.

"I would be doing you wrong if I taught her at her request, but I'd be doing her wrong if I refused."

"You may be slow, but your head's screwed on right." The beggar chuckled in approval. "I'll teach you one move: Haughty Dragon Repents. Anyway, I doubt Apothecary Huang would come down from his high horse for long enough to learn from you. The foundations of our kung fu are polar opposites: I could never master his and he could never master my palm strikes."

Count Seven Hong bent slightly from the left knee and raised his right arm, keeping it a little crooked at the elbow. He drew a circle with the right palm, exhaled and thrust it forward. His hand swept in the direction of a nearby pine tree. The trunk snapped with a loud crack.

Guo Jing was amazed by the force contained within this one simple movement of the arm.

"The tree can't move, but people can. The key is to make sure your opponent has nowhere to turn, no way to block. Then, one little push. *Crack!* They will snap like the tree."

The beggar repeated the movement twice before explaining patiently the breathing techniques vital to summoning internal strength, how to convert this strength into the external force of the palm thrust, and how to initiate and conclude the move. He stressed that the key to it, and its most difficult aspect, was not the expulsion of energy, but its retrieval.

Guo Jing was not a quick learner, but the simplicity of the movement suited his character, and his solid foundation in *neigong* inner strength was of great help. After about four hours, he began to grasp the basics.

"Your lass fights mostly with feints. You can never guess whether the next move is real or not. And you can't win if you're running blindly after her. She'll always be faster. The only way is to ignore whatever she's doing. Every move that comes your way – feint or real – you answer with a Haughty Dragon Repents. She'll see its power and she'll have to drop her charade."

"And then?"

"You think she can block it?"

"I don't want to hurt her!"

Count Seven rolled his eyes and shook his head. "Do you know why this kung fu is so special? Because it doesn't just blunder forward, it can be pulled back. It can be a blow or a caress!"

Guo Jing made a mental note not to show Lotus the move until he had mastered how to pull it back.

"If you don't believe me, try it yourself!"

Guo Jing picked the smallest tree and settled into the starting stance. Exhaling, he pushed. The tree began to shake a little.

"Why are you shaking the tree? Are you trying to catch squirrels? Pick pine cones?"

Guo Jing blushed and laughed nervously at Count Seven's frustration.

"I told you already, you need to make sure your opponent has nowhere to turn, no way to block. It's not that your thrust was weak, but it shook the tree and that took the sting out of your attack. Work on how to hit the tree without it shaking, then practise how to snap the trunk."

"So, I have to do it so quickly and suddenly that my opponent has no time to react," Guo Jing said out loud to himself, in a moment of epiphany.

"Obviously! You've been sweating over the move for half a day and you only just realised? You really haven't got much in there, have you?" Count Seven tapped the side of his skull in exasperation. "Remember the name: Haughty Dragon Repents. The essence of the move is not about being 'haughty', it's in the 'repent'. Anyone with a few muscles can muster up fast, brute force. Do you think that's enough to win Apothecary Huang's approval?

"'The haughty dragon repents, what waxes must wane.' Propel and withdraw. For each palm thrust you launch, you must have at least twice the strength reserved in your body. When you understand what 'repent' means in action, then you will have grasped about a third of what this move is about. It's like a vintage wine: smooth on the palette, a powerful kick at the end. This is 'repent'.

"It's the same with everything in this world: once at the peak, the only way forward is down. Dragon-Subduing Palm is rooted in the *I'Ching*: 'From prosperity's peak, adversity grows; from adversity's trough, prosperity climbs.' That's the theory underlying Haughty Dragon Repents. You reserve your strength for the descent, before you even reach the climax. That is why it is a technique that can never be defeated. How often do you hear that? Even if you lose, it's no big deal, because you've got plenty of power left in reserve."

Seeing confusion etched on Guo Jing's face, Count Seven Hong changed tack. "When I first started, I thought, if I put more energy into the thrust, surely it would make it better, so I channelled more and more strength into it. Suddenly, my *shifu* slapped me very hard in the face and said, 'The spirit of this move is the exact opposite of a bull running into a wall. You may be able to summon a force of tens of thousands of *jin* in one move, but you will always reach your limit. A skilled opponent will attack you the moment your strength is drained. Then all it takes is a nudge to overpower you.'

"Haughty Dragon Repents is the cornerstone of the Eighteen

Dragon-Subduing Palms. If you master this, the rest will come naturally. The character 'haughty', here, means fearsome, mighty, spirited. A dragon soaring high in the sky. Fangs and claws glistening. It can't possibly be more frightening, more majestic. And therefore, from this point, it can only dwindle, slow down, fall.

"The character 'repent' is a reminder of the saying, 'After might and hardiness, decline and weakness come.' A ship sailing at full speed, say. It may be fast, but it's also at its most vulnerable should it collide.

"I'm teaching you this because I can see that you are honest and loyal, I can tell you always put others first. This is not a move used to intimidate or subjugate, but rather to get you out of a tight corner, to save yourself."

"I don't want to kill anybody, but I would like to avoid getting killed!" Guo Jing said.

"Good lad." The beggar patted the young man on the shoulder. "You may not be the smartest, but your temperament is perfect for my kung fu. As you have no desire to hurt or kill, you will always hold something back when you channel your strength. This is what 'repent' means, and this is also why, the stronger the enemy, the stronger you will become, to the point where you can even subdue dragons, the strongest opponents of all. This kung fu can also be called Tiger Taming Palm, because the rationale behind it is the same. The hardest part is to find the balance between propelling and reserving. You can't hold back everything. There has to be something behind your strike."

Hong continued his explanation, but he doubted Guo Jing was grasping much of what he was saying. It took him years, after all.

"The theory behind this kung fu extends to how we live our lives. In our actions and our dealings, we should always leave room to turn, to retreat. You probably can't understand it fully, right now. That's fine. Just learn these passages. Their meaning will come to you eventually.

"The first one: 'Perceive before the heavens, and the skies shall not intervene; conceive after the heavens, and the celestial times will decide.'

"The second one: 'Haughty knows only of advance but not retreat, of existence but not demise, of gain but not loss. Is this the basis of a sage? Knowing when to advance, retreat, persist and desist, to be simultaneously upstanding and unerring – is that not the basis of a sage?'"

Count Seven Hong recited the passages slowly. When Guo Jing had memorised them, the older man said, "My clan's martial interpretation is different from Taoist understanding of these phrases. Laozi wrote, 'A master of warcraft once said, "I would rather lead a defence than launch an attack, I would rather retreat a foot than advance an inch."' Taoist martial arts suggest a practitioner should first guard and protect, not attack. They believe in using suppleness to overcome firmness and toughness.

"Whereas, my clan, we adapt, we become firm or supple as the situation requires. It is about noting an opponent's flaws before they are revealed through the moves. Haughty Dragon Repents should be aimed at the cracks that are about to surface. If your opponent has already shown their weaknesses, then you must exploit their vulnerability.

"And when you launch a move, you don't just think about attacking, you must also keep your retreat in mind. You may be alive now, but you could be dead within moments. You must never forget that, though this one move may win you the fight, it can also cost you everything. We all want to come out on top, but losing is not the real catastrophe.

"After all, Haughty Dragon Repents will make sure you never end up screaming 'Mercy!' as someone pins you down and punches you in the face."

Guo Jing committed Count Seven's words to memory, without understanding much. He had always learned kung fu this way, cramming what he had been told into his head without questioning its purpose or meaning. He also knew that what would take an average person one morning to learn would take him ten days.

When he tried the move again, he paid special attention to reserving and retrieving his strength. The pine tree continued to sway after his first dozen palm thrusts, but, as he gained more control of his energy, the trunk only quivered. His palm was now red and swollen, especially along the sides, but he was not one to be deterred by a little pain.

Meanwhile, the tedium had put Count Seven Hong to sleep. The beggar was lying on the forest floor, snoring loudly.

Guo Jing drew a deep breath into the Elixir Field in his lower abdomen, thrust his hand forward then pulled back his strength immediately. He could feel the reserved energy in his body. Nothing happened. The tree did not move. He repeated the movement, keeping the force focused on the edge of his palm.

Crack! The tree fell.

"Wow!" Lotus Huang had appeared with a tiffin on her arm.

"Hmm . . . Delicious!" Count Seven Hong sniffed theatrically before he had even opened his eyes. He leapt up, snatched the food box and ripped off the lid, exclaiming with joy at the contents: smoked frogs' legs, eight-treasures duck and silver-thread rolls. His hands shuttled back and forth between the carrier and his mouth, making grunts of pleasure and praise as he swallowed the delicious meal. By the time he remembered Guo Jing, nothing but a pile of chewed bones remained.

"The rolls are delicious . . . Even better than the duck!" he said sheepishly.

"You haven't tried my best dishes yet," Lotus said.

"Tell me more!"

"There are too many to name. Stir-fried pak choi, steamed tofu, egg stew, slow-cooked white radishes, sliced belly of pork . . ."

Any connoisseur knows that it is only through the simplest dish that a chef's true skill is revealed. The same goes for the martial arts – a true master can perform magic in the most ordinary move. The dishes Lotus named were enough to make the glutton hungry again. "I'll get the ingredients for you right now. I've always said this lass is my favourite person."

Lotus chuckled at Count Seven's eagerness. "It's alright – you don't know what I need, anyway."

"Of course, of course," he said humbly.

Lotus went over to examine the tree Guo Jing had snapped in two. "I saw him break it with just a thrust of his palm. He's much too strong for me now."

"He will need a lot more practice. The trunk should break neatly. Look how it's all bent and splintered. This tree is tiny. Like a chopstick. No. More like a toothpick. He's still got a long way to go."

"But what if he hits me with it? I can't block a move like that!"

"I'd never do that!" Guo Jing protested.

"What do you propose, then?" Count Seven knew that Lotus was tricking him into teaching them more kung fu. And yet his stomach overruled his rational brain.

"Teach me how to beat him. Then I'll cook for you."

"It would be my pleasure! I'll teach you a set of moves I call Wayfaring Fist." Count Seven leapt into the air, darting high and low with grace and ease, his sleeves fluttering in a breeze of his own making.

Lotus watched intently, committing a good half of Wayfaring Fist to memory during Count Seven's initial demonstration alone. A couple of hours later, she had mastered all thirty-six moves. Now she tried the whole set together, with Hong. One started from the left and the other from the right. One light and elegant, like a swallow, the other fierce and quick, like an eagle. At the end of the thirty-sixth move, they landed at the same time, to loud cheers from Guo Jing, and exchanged a smile.

"The lass is a hundred times sharper than you!" Count Seven said.

"How does she memorise so much in a few short hours?" Guo Jing scratched his head. "If I try to learn a new move, the previous one immediately disappears out of my head."

The beggar chuckled. "This kung fu wouldn't suit you, it's true.

You could memorise the moves, I don't doubt, but I imagine, when put together, they would better resemble the Distress Crawl. All bogged down and lumbering."

Guo Jing laughed in agreement.

"I learned the Wayfaring Fist in my youth. I dug it out now, for the lass, because it matched her style, but it doesn't fit with my current martial practice. I haven't used it in more than a decade."

"Poor Guo Jing," Lotus said. "Now I have the tools to beat him again, he must be very upset. Perhaps you could teach him a few more moves?"

"This simpleton hasn't even mastered the move I taught him this morning. Don't make him bite off more than he can chew. But, if you keep cooking for me, your wish may come true." Count Seven Hong laughed and headed back to the inn, leaving Guo Jing to practise in the woods until nightfall.

That evening, Lotus made stir-fried pak choi and steamed tofu. She hand-picked the most tender shoots of pak choi from the core and sizzled them in a hot wok with chicken fat and finely diced, deboned duck feet. She then sliced a whole leg of dry-cured ham in half and carved twenty-four holes into the flesh and filled them with perfectly sculpted balls of beancurd, before placing the tied ham into a steamer. Once it was cooked, the meat was discarded, since its flavours were infused into the tofu. Count Seven was dazzled by the depth of flavour in this simple dish, the name of which, Twenty-Four Bridges on a Full Moon Night, referenced a Tang-dynasty poem.

The Orchid Touch kung fu invented by Apothecary Huang had made Lotus's hands nimble and strong. Without such dexterity, it would be impossible to craft such tender tofu, which was liable to disintegrate upon touch, into perfect balls. Such a skill was comparable to the traditional craft of engraving an essay onto a grain of rice, or carving an olive pit into the shape of a boat. Of course, it would have been easy to simply cube the beancurd, but who ever heard of a square moon? The meal was a demonstration of martial skill as well as gastronomic flair.

3

SINCE GUO JING AND LOTUS HUANG HAD SET OUT ON THEIR wanderings, they had often shared the same room. However, now that they were in Count Seven Hong's company, they took separate chambers. Their sleeping arrangement piqued the beggar's curiosity. "Why aren't you sleeping side by side? Isn't that what couples do?"

"One more silly question and I won't cook for you," a blushing Lotus threatened.

"What? Did I say the wrong thing?" Count Seven laughed. "Oh dear, what an old fool I am. You're still dressed as a maiden. You two arranged your future together without your parents' consent or a matchmaker's promise, am I right? I bet you haven't even bowed to the heavens and earth! Don't worry, this old beggar will be your marriage broker. If your father refuses you, I will fight him for seven days and seven nights, or until he gives you his blessing."

Lotus had been worrying that her father would not like Guo Jing, but with Count Seven as go-between, their future together felt more secure. Thanking the martial master profusely, she resolved to put even more care into crafting the most exquisite dishes for him.

The next day, Guo Jing was back in the pine forest at the break of dawn to practise Haughty Dragon Repents. After twenty or so repetitions, he was drenched in sweat. Just as he was beginning to feel pleased with his progress, a voice broke his concentration.

"*Shifu*, we must have travelled more than thirty *li* by now."

"Indeed, both the strength in your legs and your pace have improved."

Guo Jing thought the second voice sounded familiar.

Four men burst through the trees, and Guo Jing's stomach sank. Striding at the head of the group was a white-haired man with a jarringly youthful face. Greybeard Liang, the Ginseng Immortal.

"Where do you think you're going?" Old Liang spotted Guo Jing trying to get away, and dashed after him. His three disciples spread out to close off Guo Jing's escape.

Guo Jing started to run using his fastest *qinggong*. I'll be fine if I can get to the inn, he told himself.

But Greybeard Liang's lead protégé was faster.

"Kneel, thief!"

He grabbed Guo Jing by the chest in a Power Grapple technique usually only found in China's north-eastern borderlands.

Guo Jing bent his left knee and raised his right arm until not quite straight. He traced a circle with his right hand, exhaled and pushed.

He aimed the Haughty Dragon Repents at his attacker's torso.

The man pulled back to block.

Crack! The bone in his arm snapped. The force of the thrust threw his body back several paces, where he crumpled in a heap.

The result amazed Guo Jing. He had not even used half of his strength.

He turned to run, but Greybeard Liang had already planted himself in his way. Guo Jing bent his knee and raised his arm again. Another Haughty Dragon Repents.

The older man ducked and rolled. The move was too powerful to counter head on.

While Old Liang was finding his footing, Guo Jing grabbed the chance to make one last dash for it. The inn was now in sight.

"Lotus, help! That man is here! The one who wants to drink my blood!"

"Don't worry! We'll teach him a lesson!" Lotus was keen to try out the Wayfaring Fist.

Before Guo Jing could chide Lotus for openly slighting their opponent, Greybeard Liang lunged with fearsome might. Guo Jing scrabbled together another Haughty Dragon Repents, forcing his attacker to twist left.

The Ginseng Immortal managed to dodge Guo Jing, but he still caught a glancing blow to his right arm. The pain halted him.

How can this boy's kung fu have improved so much in just a few weeks? My python's blood! Incensed by the thought, Greybeard Liang dived at Guo Jing again. He could not have known that Guo Jing was receiving guidance from one of the greatest martial masters of their day.

Guo Jing fought back with the same formidable thrust of his palm.

"Is that your only move?" The older man's confidence was returning.

"It's enough to hold you back!" Guo Jing responded, with another Haughty Dragon Repents.

Satisfied that the boy had revealed the extent of his kung fu, Greybeard Liang hopped to one side, then shifted his weight in the opposite direction, whirling around to land securely behind Guo Jing.

Guo Jing spun to face his attacker and settled into his opening stance. He was ready to launch another Haughty Dragon Repents, but his target was gone.

Old Liang was already behind him again. His fists shot towards the young man's back. Guo Jing turned. Within just three moves, the old man had Guo Jing spinning in circles.

The young man flapped his arms this way and that in a feeble attempt to protect his exposed back, then torso. There was no chance for him to launch another Haughty Dragon Repents.

"Let me deal with him!" Lotus flew up and landed between them, simultaneously thrusting with her left palm and kicking with her right foot. Guo Jing took two steps back to catch his breath.

Old Liang pulled in his chest and retaliated with a double punch. Lotus fought back with the Wayfaring Fist. Her interpretation was full of unexpected feints and twists, and yet she was unfamiliar with its power and unable to tap into the technique's full potential. Soon, she began to struggle. After all, Greybeard Liang had decades of combat experience. By this point, her Hedgehog Chainmail was her only real protection. Without it, she would have taken many punches and already be out of the fight.

Greybeard Liang's two remaining disciples, who had been help-ing their injured martial brother, cheered as their *shifu* steadily gained the upper hand.

Guo Jing was about to come to Lotus's aid when Count Seven Hong called from inside the inn, "His next move will be Rabid Dog Blocks the Way!"

Greybeard Liang had lowered himself into the horse-riding stance, with his feet apart and his fists raised. Count Seven Hong was right, he was about to launch a move known in the *wulin* as Fearsome Tiger Blocks the Way.

Count Seven knows the move before he even makes it! How does he do it? Lotus asked herself.

"His next one is Rancid Snake Fetches Water!" Hong's voice again.

Lotus knew he meant Blue Dragon Fetches Water, a forward punch that left the upper back unprotected. Armed with this knowl-edge, she darted in behind Old Liang and aimed a fist at his spine.

Already more than a foot off the ground, the older man threw himself forward at the last moment. If he had been a less experienced fighter, he would not have been able to dodge the blow.

The Ginseng Immortal tapped the ground with the tip of his foot and flipped upright. "Who presumes to predict my kung fu? Show your face!"

No answer.

Now that Count Seven Hong was watching over her, Lotus attacked with renewed confidence. Greybeard Liang fought back with his deadliest moves. Lotus quickly found herself in a tight cor-ner once more.

"No need to fear!" the beggar called from his room. "The Bare-Arsed Monkey is Mounting the Tree!"

Chuckling, Lotus raised both fists over her head and smacked down hard. Greybeard Liang was about to vault high and strike in mid-air. But, if he followed through on his move, Gibbon Climbs the Tree, he would be jumping head first into her punch, so he wrenched sideways awkwardly.

When an opponent can predict one's kung fu in a fight, mortal danger awaits within a handful of moves. Luckily for Greybeard Liang, he was fighting a novice.

"Show your face, sir! Or I won't show mercy!" Greybeard Liang rained down a torrent of overlapping attacks, each move launched before the last one had connected, too fast for Count Seven to call them out. Even if he were able to, there would be no time for Lotus to react.

Hard pressed, Lotus's responses became jumbled as she scurried and scrambled out of harm's way. Guo Jing stepped up and launched a Haughty Dragon Repents.

Old Liang tapped his right foot and hopped away from Guo's thrust.

"Give him three more like that!" Lotus shouted as she ran back to the inn.

Guo Jing lowered into the opening stance once more and waited. The Haughty Dragon Repents was only set loose midway through one of Greybeard Liang's attacks.

Has he only got one move? The Ginseng Immortal was infuriated by the absurdity of the situation. And yet, it was enough to keep him at bay. There was no obvious way to overpower the young man.

Frustrated by this impasse, Greybeard Liang had an idea. He sprang with a roar of defiance, knowing Guo Jing would answer with his only move. Yet, this time, the older man spun mid-flight and flicked with his right wrist.

Three Bone-Piercing Needles. Coming straight at Guo Jing's chest, abdomen and hip.

The young man managed to scuttle out of the way, but his panicked retreat gave Liang the chance to charge. With lightning speed, he pinched the back of Guo Jing's neck.

Guo Jing elbowed back at him. But, somehow, Old Liang's chest was as soft as a bale of cotton.

Greybeard Liang had at last caught the boy who killed his precious python. He could take back what was his. He raised his arm, ready to discharge the death blow.

"Ginseng Codger, look what I've got!" Lotus cried from the inn.

Knowing that the young woman was full of tricks, he immobilised Guo Jing by jabbing his Shoulder Well pressure point, then looked up.

She had raised in one hand a bamboo cane as green and glossy as jadeite.

"Let him go!" Lotus demanded as she ambled over.

"Chief Hong . . ."

The old man was visibly dismayed. His arms dropped to his sides. Guo Jing was free!

It had badly shaken Greybeard Liang to have his moves called out before he even initiated them. Now, the bamboo cane confirmed that the voice belonged to the one man he feared the most.

"The Divine Vagrant Nine Fingers Count Seven Hong wishes to know why you insist on behaving in such an abominable manner." Lotus held up the bamboo cane with both hands. "Explain yourself!"

The Ginseng Immortal sank to his knees. "Your humble servant had not realised that Chief Hong had graced this region with his presence. Your servant would never dream of attempting anything that might displease the chieftain."

Why is he so frightened? And why does he call him Chief Hong? Lotus tried to hide her surprise.

"What should be your punishment?"

"I entreat my lady to speak a few kind words on my behalf. Greybeard Liang regrets his trespasses and begs Chief Hong for mercy."

"I will say one kind word and no more. You must never trouble the two of us again."

"Your humble servant has offended my lady and lord out of ignorance. Rest assured that I shall never be so reckless again."

Satisfied, Lotus took Guo Jing's hand and disappeared inside the inn. Count Seven Hong was seated at the table, wine cup and chopsticks in hand, busying himself with four plates piled generously with the finest food.

"His knees are nailed to the ground," Lotus reported gleefully.

"Do what you want with him. He won't fight back now."

Guo Jing looked out of the window. Greybeard Liang was kneeling stiffly; his three disciples had joined him in this show of repentance. Guo Jing was starting to feel sorry for them. "We should let him go."

"Heavens, what's the matter with you? You were defeated and I rescued you. And now you want to let him go?" Count Seven Hong fell into a thoughtful silence. "Actually, forgiveness is the higher virtue. It is the underlying idea of Haughty Dragon Repents."

"I'll send him away." Lotus picked up the bamboo cane and headed outside once more.

Greybeard Liang was still on his knees, his deferential stance barely hiding the whiff of panic.

"Count Seven Hong would have taken your life today for your misdeeds, but Guo Jing is merciful and he entreated on your behalf." At this, she smacked his backside with the cane. "Shoo!"

"Chief Hong, please grant me an audience. Please allow me to thank you personally for your magnanimity," Greybeard Liang called out in the direction of the inn.

Silence.

Eventually, Guo Jing stepped outside, waving for him to be quiet. "Count Seven Hong is sleeping. He should not be disturbed."

Greybeard Liang glared at the young couple, climbed back onto his feet and left with his disciples.

Count Seven Hong was snoring, face down on the table, by the time Guo Jing and Lotus returned inside. Lotus shook him lightly by the shoulder. The beggar yawned and stretched.

"Your little bamboo cane is very powerful. Can I have it? You don't use it, anyway."

He grinned. "A beggar can't do without his cane. Or else how do I chase the dogs away? Not for nothing does it have the name Dog-Beating Cane."

Lotus would not be brushed off so easily. "Your kung fu is so strong, and your voice alone instills fear. What do you need the cane for?"

"Make something nice for me and I'll tell you the whole story."

Lotus disappeared into the kitchen and soon re-emerged with three more delicious plates.

"You've heard the saying, 'Things gather by kind and people band together by groups', haven't you?" Hong began, waving his wine cup while chewing a mouthful of dry-cured pork knuckle. "Landlords belong to one class. Highwaymen another. Beggars—"

"You're the Chief of the Beggar Clan!"

"Indeed! Beggars are abused and looked down upon, even by dogs. If we don't work together, we can't survive. There are very few of us who don't need to belong, deep down. Grand figures, like your father. He can get by on his own and no-one dares cross him. Our northern folk are ruled by the Jin, for now, and those in the south by the Song Emperor, but beggars of both realms are—"

"Ruled by you!" Lotus completed the sentence for him.

Count Seven nodded, with a smile. "This cane is the emblem, the sign that I am Chief of the Beggar Clan, like the Emperor's jade seal or an official's golden stamp. It's several hundred years old, passed down through generations of chieftains since the end of the Tang dynasty."

"Thank the heavens you didn't give it to me, then." Lotus stuck her tongue out. "It would be horrible if the world's beggars came after me, pestering me with all their troubles."

"You have the right of it. I love food and I hate dealing with all their petty complaints. It's a burden, being the chieftain, but I can't find anyone to take my place."

"That's why Greybeard Liang was so afraid of you. If every beggar put a flea into the old Codger's hair, he'd scratch himself half to death!"

The room erupted in laughter.

"But that isn't the reason he fears me," Count Seven Hong said, after some time.

"What is it, then?" Lotus asked.

"About twenty years ago, I happened upon him while he was up to no good . . ."

"Tell us!" Lotus loved a good story.

"Well . . . the Codger fell for some evil notion . . . of gathering yin to replenish yang. He captured a lot of maidens and . . . deflowered them in the hope of gaining immortality."

"What do you mean?"

The beggar struggled for words. He could not have known that Lotus's mother died in childbirth, nor that she had grown up around male and female servants who had been forbidden to speak by her father. She knew nothing of the physical matters that connected a man and a woman. She thought that a husband and a wife would always stay together, like she and Guo Jing would. She knew the sweetness she felt around Guo Jing, and the pain when they were forced apart. But what happened between the sheets . . . ?

"Did he kill them?" she pressed on.

"No . . . For a woman, it's a fate worse than death. You've heard the saying, 'Grave is the loss of chastity, trifling is the loss of life', right?"

"Did he cut off their ears and noses?"

"Fie! Stop pestering me! Ask your mother!"

"I don't have one."

"Oh . . . Then you'll find out on your wedding night."

She finally understood – that act of shame – but her curiosity was not bound by modesty. "What happened next?"

Count Seven sighed, relieved that she did not press him further for the details of Liang's misdeeds. "I caught him and gave him a good beating, before pulling out his whole head of hair. I made him send the girls home and swear never to do it again. He knew, if I caught him at it one more time, I'd make him beg for death. I heard that he has stayed away from it since, so perhaps I was right to let him go. Has he got hair now?"

"A head full!" Lotus chuckled. "It must have hurt."

With a laugh, Count Seven Hong turned back to the more important business of eating. When they had finished the meal, Lotus said, "I won't take your cane, even if you give it to me. But we won't be travelling together long, anyway. What if we bump into him again? 'I backed down to please Chief Hong,' he'll say, 'but, now you're alone, I'll avenge myself and pull out all your hair!' What should we do then? Haughty Dragon Repents is powerful, but Guo Jing only learned this one move from you. I bet you the Codger will tell people, 'Chief Hong's kung fu is powerful, but he hasn't got much to teach others.'"

"I know what you're trying to do. You won't be short-changed if you keep the tasty food coming."

Lotus took Count Seven by the hand and led him and Guo Jing back to the forest. The beggar taught Guo Jing the second move of the Dragon-Subduing Palm – Dragon Soars in the Sky. It was three days before Guo Jing grasped the essential technique of springing up and using his own momentum to strike down, while Count Seven was treated to a dozen new delicacies by Lotus, who no longer pestered him to teach her kung fu.

4

A MONTH PASSED. BY NOW, GUO JING HAD LEARNED FIFTEEN out of the Dragon-Subduing Palm's eighteen moves, from Haughty Dragon Repents all the way to Dragon in the Field.

Dragon-Subduing Palm had long been regarded as the ultimate external kung fu, invincible and indomitable. During the Northern Song period, at the turn of the first millennium, Xiao Feng, then Chief of the Beggar Clan, staged a contest with the heroes of the martial world. Few could withstand more than three moves of his Dragon-Subduing Palm, and no-one had ever found a way to overcome its might. At the time, there were twenty-eight moves, but Xiao Feng and his sworn brother, Hollow Bamboo, later distilled it down to eighteen, making this already matchless kung fu even more impregnable. Decades later, Count Hong used the repertoire to win the respect of the martial Greats at the summit of Mount Hua.

Count Seven Hong only intended to teach Guo Jing two or three moves, more than enough to keep the young man alive against any opponents. Yet the culinary magic conjured by Lotus Huang had ensnared the gourmet in Count Seven Hong. He could not find the will to tear himself away. The young man might be slow on the uptake, but he compensated with persistence, practising night and day. He had already grasped the essence of the moves; the rest would come as his internal strength and control grew. In this short space of time, Guo Jing had become a formidable martial artist.

One day, as the three of them were eating breakfast, Count Seven Hong said, "It's time to go our separate ways."

"But I've still got lots of dishes I want to cook for you," Lotus replied.

"As the saying goes, 'There's no such thing as a never-ending banquet', but there are more delicacies than one can eat in a lifetime. I've never taken on any disciples or taught any one fighter for more than three days. Yet we've spent more than thirty together. If I stay any longer, I'll be in big trouble."

"Why's that?"

"You'll have learned all my tricks."

"Wouldn't it be nice to teach him all eighteen moves?"

"Fie! Nice for you, perhaps, but not for me!" Count Seven Hong picked up his gourd and left without another word.

Guo Jing hastened after Count Seven, but the beggar's lightness kung fu was extraordinary. In the blink of an eye, he had vanished out of sight.

"Master Hong! Master Hong!" Guo Jing ran into the pine forest. Lotus followed, calling his name too.

Count Seven stopped and came back to meet them. "Why are you following me? I'll never teach you again!"

"Sir, your student is deeply grateful and has no wish to test your patience. Please allow me to thank you for your generosity." Guo Jing kneeled and kowtowed, knocking his head audibly on the ground before standing up.

"Stop! I taught you in order to satisfy my belly. You've paid me fair and square. I'm not your *shifu* and you're not my disciple." Hong dropped to his knees and began to kowtow.

Flabbergasted by such an unorthodox response, Guo Jing kneeled once more. Count Seven caught him mid-motion and jabbed at the pressure point in his armpit. Guo Jing was frozen. The beggar then kowtowed at Guo Jing four times before he let him move again.

"Never speak of your kowtows. You are not my protégé."

Guo Jing understood that Count Seven meant what he said, and kept quiet.

"You've been so kind to us. I was hoping to cook for you again, when we next meet, but . . . I fear . . . it won't be possible." Lotus was starting to sound teary.

"What do you mean?"

"There's a host of dangerous men out there who wish to do us harm. The Ginseng Codger is just one of them. They mean to kill us!"

"We all die sooner or later."

"That's not what I'm afraid of," Lotus said with a shake of her head. "They're going to find out that I cooked for you and, in exchange, you taught me kung fu. They'll force me to make Floating Moon in the Fragrance of Twilight or When Will the Moonlit River Shine on Her? – delicacies you haven't tried yet. What an insult to your name!"

Count Seven Hong knew she was bluffing – provoking him, in fact – but the thought that someone else might taste dishes he had yet to try upset him all the same.

"Who are these men?" Hong asked.

"The Dragon King Hector Sha, for one. The way he eats is most disgusting. Spitting everywhere. Onto my beautiful dishes!"

"Hector Sha is a nobody," Count Seven snorted. "Your silly lad will beat him easily, in a year or two."

Lotus then named Lama Supreme Wisdom Lobsang Choden Rinpoche and Tiger Peng, the Butcher of a Thousand Hands, who were both dismissed by Count Seven Hong as nobodies too.

The last name Lotus mentioned piqued the beggar's interest. Listening closely to Lotus's explanation of his moves and stance, Count Seven nodded and said, "It's him, then."

"Is he scary?" Lotus was surprised by how grave his expression turned upon hearing the name of Gallant Ouyang, Master of White Camel Mount.

"Another nobody. But his uncle, the old Venom—"

"Surely he can't beat you?"

Count Seven fell silent.

"We were about equal, but that was two decades ago . . ." he said at last. "He works hard on his kung fu, whereas I just like to eat. But, then again, it's not easy beating this old beggar."

"I'm sure he couldn't."

"It's hard to say . . . We'll see. If the Viper's spawn wants to make trouble for you, then we must be careful. I'll stay with you for another fortnight, on the condition that you won't cook me the same dish twice, or else I'll slap my arse and go. And you must serve me your very, very best. So, if you are caught one day, they won't get better food than me."

Delighted, Lotus put her heart into preparing every meal – even the side dishes and staples were unique. Pot stickers, siu mai, steamed dumplings, boiled dumplings, wontons, pak choi rice, fried rice, rice soup, rice cake, flower rolls, rice noodles, shredded tofu, bean noodles, scallion pancake, garlic chive buns . . . Count Seven Hong also honoured his part of the bargain, honing their reactions and giving them guidance on self-defence during combat. And yet, he did not quite get round to teaching Guo Jing the last three moves of Dragon-Subduing Palm. He did continue to help the young man consolidate his understanding of the first fifteen moves, which only increased the potency of the kung fu he had learned from the Six Freaks of the South.

Count Seven Hong was a vast repository of martial arts techniques in every style known to the *wulin*. He selected the more quirky ones for Lotus, to keep her amused. They were full of dizzying flourishes, to be sure, but none of them could overpower opponents as effectively as the straightforward Dragon-Subduing Palm.

One evening, at dusk, Guo Jing was finishing up his daily practice in the woods as Count Seven Hong lounged on the forest floor, half watching and half dozing, and Lotus Huang foraged for pine nuts nearby. She had already begun naming the dish she was going to prepare for dinner: Three Friends of Winter, if she matched the pine nuts with bamboo shoots and salted plums; or Longevity Pine and Crane, if she added chicken broth to the three ingredients. Her deliberations were making Count Seven Hong's mouth water.

Hmm! The beggar huffed and hopped onto his feet. He stooped and swept his arms through the undergrowth. When he straightened up, he had a snake pinched between the thumb and index finger of his right hand. Two-foot long and bright green. He pushed Lotus lightly with his other hand, sending her stumbling back.

"Snakes!" Lotus yelped.

The shrub rustled. More serpents reared their heads. Count Seven Hong brandished his bamboo cane. Each flick of his wrist felled an unsuspecting snake instantly, as he struck it seven inches from the head.

Lotus cheered. But, even as she did so, Count Seven noticed two vipers slithering up her dress. At that moment, they lodged their fangs into her back. He was familiar with the venom of the green tree viper. There was no time to lose if he was going to neutralise their lethal poison.

A crescendo of hisses. From all directions. The grass had come alive. Flickering and slithering.

Count Seven Hong grabbed Lotus's belt and took Guo Jing's hand. Using his fastest *qinggong*, he flew out of the woods until they reached the inn.

"How are you feeling?" He was surprised by how unaffected Lotus seemed to be by the snake bites.

"I'm fine." She smiled.

Guo Jing now noticed the snakes dangling from her back and

tugged at one of them. Count Seven shouted – "Stop!" – but he had already pulled it off.

"Of course, your father gave you his Hedgehog Chainmail." The beggar looked at the snake that was still stuck to Lotus's back.

Just as Guo Jing was about to remove it, a mass of the creatures emerged from the forest. Count Seven took a yellowish cake of herbal medicine from his shirt and chewed it vigorously. Hundreds of luminous green snakes were slithering towards them. Countless more were spilling out between the trees.

Guo Jing grabbed Count Seven Hong's hand. "Let's go inside!"

Ignoring Guo Jing, Count Seven pulled the gourd from his back, unplugged it and took a big gulp of wine. He gurgled loudly, mixing the wine with the chewed herbs. Then he pursed his lips and a jet of wine shot out from between them like an arrow. Turning from left to right, he sprayed a perfect arc of wine across the ground before him.

The scent instantly put the nearest snakes into a stupor and they were paralysed on the spot. Those further back hesitated, then turned on their tails, tangling with the thousands more swarming in the opposite direction.

Shrill calls emanated from the trees and three men in bright white robes emerged. They each waved and jabbed a wooden staff, more than two *zhang* in height, through the sea of snakes, herding them like cattle. Lotus found it amusing at first, but soon she began to feel as if hair had sprouted from her throat and she was overcome by nausea.

Count Seven Hong flicked a snake up with his cane and caught it between the index and middle fingers of his left hand. He then sliced open its belly with the extra sharp nail of his little finger and pulled out a green blob.

"Swallow this whole. Don't chew. It's very bitter."

Lotus gulped it down and felt better at once.

"Do you feel sick?" she asked Guo Jing.

He shook his head. He had not noticed that the snakes were avoiding him as he fled from the forest. He did not realise that the blood of Greybeard Liang's python, which he had sucked in a desperate attempt to free himself from its stranglehold in the Jin Prince's palace, had imbued him with a scent repellent to serpents. Not only that, but it made him immune to most venoms.

"They keep the snakes!" Lotus squealed in alarm.

Count Seven nodded, his eyes fixed on the three men.

The snake herders were incensed by the beggar's audacity. How dare he kill their snake and give its gall bladder to the girl! They whistled a command to settle their flock and started marching, side by side, towards them.

"Are you trying to get yourself killed?" one of them bellowed.

"Are you?" Lotus retorted.

Count Seven patted her on the shoulder in approval.

The snake herder nearest Lotus swung his staff at her. He looked jaundiced and past the prime of his youth, yet he wielded the weapon with strength.

Count Seven Hong tapped his cane lightly against the man's staff, halting it in mid-air. He then turned his wrist and cried, "Shoo!"

The man sailed backwards and landed flat on his back, crushing at least a dozen snakes. He too must have taken a herb mixture, as the snakes refrained from attacking him.

Frightened by the unexpected turn of events, his companions stumbled back several paces. "What's going on?" one of them managed to stutter.

Meanwhile, the first man tried to scrabble to his feet, but he was still winded from his fall. He crashed to the ground once more, killing even more snakes. Grabbing the tip of the staff offered by his fellow herder, he hauled himself upright. Together, they retreated to stand among the snakes.

"Who are you?" the jaundiced man cried.

Count Seven Hong laughed, ignoring the question. Once again, it was Lotus who spoke. "Why are you herding these snakes?"

The snake herders exchanged a look and one of them made as if to respond. Just then, a fourth man emerged from the woods. Dressed in a snowy white scholar's robe, the man walked among the serpents as if they were not there, lazily wafting his gentleman's folding fan. The creatures parted as he approached. Guo Jing and Lotus watched in astonishment.

The snake herders approached the newcomer deferentially and whispered a few words, stealing glances at Count Seven Hong. A flash of surprise crossed the scholar's face. He collected himself immediately and nodded at his men.

He put his hands together in greeting and addressed Count Seven Hong. "Pardon my servants; their ignorance has caused offence and I am grateful for your forbearance." He then turned to Lotus. "What good fortune that my lady is here. I have been searching far and wide for you."

"Count Seven, he is a nasty man; you must teach him a lesson." Lotus ignored him completely.

The beggar nodded. "There are specific rules and standards governing the herding of snakes. And none of them permits it in broad daylight."

"These snakes have travelled a long way and they are famished. It is not possible to abide by the rules always." The scholar spoke politely, but his demeanour was defiant.

"How many people have fallen prey to your creatures?" Count Seven asked.

"Hardly any; we only herd them through the wilderness."

"Your name's Ouyang, isn't it?"

"My lady must have told you. May I ask the Elder's name?"

"His name alone will leave you cowering in fear," Lotus interjected.

The man was not bothered by the insult. Instead, he cocked his head and leered at her.

"You're Viper Ouyang's son, aren't you?"

"How dare you use our Master's name, beggar!" one of the herders cried.

Count Seven Hong tapped his cane, flew up and swooped down like a bird of prey.

Smack, smack, smack!

Another tap of the cane and the beggar glided back to the inn. His feet never touched the ground.

"Teach me, please!" Lotus was amazed.

The men groaned in pain and cradled their chins. Count Seven had dislocated their jaws using a Split Muscles Lock Bones move.

"Sir, you know my uncle?" The scholar was shocked by the display.

"I haven't seen the Venom for more than twenty years. I trust he still lives?"

Furious as he may have been, Gallant Ouyang knew his kung fu was no match for the beggar's; he must tread carefully. "Uncle often jokes that he intends to cling to life long enough to see all his friends meet their end."

"Think you're smart enough to insult me?" Count Seven laughed, then pointed at the snakes. "What are you doing with these precious little creatures?"

"This is my first trip to the Central Plains; I picked them up along the way to keep me entertained—"

"Enough of your lies," Lotus cut in. "Surely the women you brought provide entertainment enough."

Gallant Ouyang unfolded his fan and tapped it against his chest.

> *"My heart quivers for you alone,*
> *You are the reason for these heavy sighs."*

Unimpressed by his quoting from the *Book of Songs*, Lotus pulled a face. "I'd rather you didn't think of me at all."

Gallant Ouyang was pleased just to have elicited a reaction. For a moment, his soul faltered and his voice disappeared.

"You and your uncle may tyrannise the Western Regions, but if you think your philanderings will be tolerated on the Central Plains, you are wrong! But, as a courtesy to your uncle, I shall let you pass in peace today. Be off with you!" Count Seven said.

Gallant Ouyang knew he should bite his tongue and walk away, but he was not in the habit of letting slights pass. "Allow me to take my leave of the Master. Should you not fall prey to ill health or calamity in the next few years, it would be my honour to receive you at White Camel Mount."

"A stripling like you dares to challenge me?" Count Seven chuckled. "This old beggar never makes dates with anyone. There is no enmity between your uncle and I, nor do we fear each other – we had a good fight twenty years ago. He couldn't overpower me, but neither could I defeat him. We don't need to meet again." Suddenly, the good humour disappeared from the beggar's face. "Get out of my sight!"

Gallant Ouyang was taken aback. *I haven't mastered a third of Uncle's kung fu. If this man's claim is true, then I'd better keep my distance. A wise man does not walk knowingly into a swamp.*

So, with gritted teeth, he reset the jaws of his men and stole one last look at Lotus Huang before retreating into the woods.

Shrill whistles were once more heard echoing between the trees, but now they were muffled with many a *Yi!* and *Ah!* as the three men in white cradled their bruised faces. The snakes heeded the call, and the wave of green ebbed into the forest.

"Can he really keep so many snakes?" Lotus could hardly believe her eyes.

Count Seven Hong took a large swig from his canteen and wiped his forehead with his sleeve. "We had a lucky escape . . . They could have swarmed over us like a tide, and there is nothing I could have done. It was fortunate that they weren't experienced enough to see through my tricks. If the Venom had been here . . ."

"We could have run," Guo Jing suggested.

"You think you young 'uns can outrun the Venom of the West?" Count Seven laughed.

"Is he really that dangerous?" Lotus asked.

"There are Five Greats, as you know. Your own father, the Eastern Heretic. And me, the Northern Beggar. Then we have the Southern

King and the Western Venom – that's the boy's uncle. Now that the greatest amongst us, Immortal Wang, has passed, we four that remain are of roughly equal prowess. Think about my kung fu, or your papa's. Then you'll have an idea of what Viper Ouyang can do."

With a harrumph, Lotus fell silent. Eventually, she said, "I don't like people calling Papa the Heretic."

"Your father likes the name very much. He's an eccentric, unorthodox. He cares not for conventions. He disagrees with Confucianism, the court, the state, and all the traditions they uphold. What does that make him, if not a heretic? He stands firm and acts alone, he doesn't fawn over wealth or power, and I have always respected him for that. But, when it comes to the martial arts, the Quanzhen Sect is the orthodox school, and I admire them unreservedly." Count Seven turned to Guo Jing. "You've trained with them, haven't you?"

"Elder Ma Yu taught me for two years."

"That's why you can attain this level of prowess with the Dragon-Subduing Palm in just a month."

"Who is the Southern King?" Lotus asked.

"His Majesty, of course."

"The Song Emperor in Lin'an?"

"Him?" Count Seven laughed. "He barely has enough strength to lift a golden rice bowl. Southern Fire overcomes Western Gold – the Venom's nemesis."

Count Seven looked at the sky. He seemed troubled. His face bore no trace of his usual joviality. Guo Jing and Lotus wanted to hear more about the Southern King, but they did not feel they should press him further.

Eventually, the beggar made to move inside. As he passed through the doorway, his sleeve caught on a nail, but he was so lost in his thoughts that he did not notice the material rip.

"Let me mend it." Lotus approached him with a needle and thread she had borrowed from the innkeeper's wife.

Count Seven snatched the needle and rushed outside. With a flick of his right hand, he sent a silver thread through the air.

The needle skewered a grasshopper and pinned it to the ground. Lotus clapped in delight at the display.

"Yes, this could work," Count Seven muttered, more to himself than anyone else. "Viper Ouyang has always loved to keep snakes and poisonous insects. It is most impressive how he controls so many with such ease. He must use some powerful drugs . . . That nephew of his is no doubt as crafty as the old man. He will speak ill of me, for sure. I need a plan to hold back the Venom's creatures the next time we meet."

"Pin them down with needles!" Lotus had reached the same conclusion.

Count Seven rolled his eyes. "You little imp! You always know what I'm thinking."

"And you've got the herbs, too. They stopped when you sprayed them with it."

"That will only hold them back for a moment." Count Seven was still mostly talking to himself. "I could try the Skyful of Petals technique with needles, but if there are as many snakes as today, it would take a week or two to skewer the lot, and by then I'd have died of hunger . . ."

"You could cook the snakes in chicken broth, then scatter some chrysanthemum petals and finely-shredded lemon leaves over it. Delicious!"

Count Seven's left index finger pulsed at the thought of snake soup, a welcome – if momentary – distraction from the prospect of an encounter with Viper Ouyang.

"Right, I'll find you your needles!" Lotus dashed out of the inn.

Count Seven sighed. "You really should get her to give you a little of her wit."

"I'm not sure that's possible." Guo Jing grinned sheepishly.

In no time at all, Lotus returned with two large packets. "I've bought every single needle in the town. The local men will know all about it tomorrow when they don't manage to buy any for their wives!" Lotus giggled.

Count Seven bellowed with laughter. "Thank the heavens this old beggar was smart enough to avoid the trap of marriage! Come, come, let's start. I know you kids are desperate to learn this little trick."

Lotus jumped to her feet immediately, but Guo Jing stayed seated. "I don't think I'll join you."

That was not the response Count Seven was expecting. "Why?"

"I've learned more than I can remember already today."

Count Seven Hong was impressed by Guo Jing's sense of honour. Though the beggar had insisted that he would not teach the young man again, he was prepared to go back on his word to ready him for their next encounter with Gallant Ouyang's snakes. Yet Guo Jing had no interest in taking advantage of his great idea.

So, while Count Seven taught Lotus the basics of the Skyful of Petals technique, Guo Jing practised the first fifteen moves of Dragon-Subduing Palm. He now felt as if he had glimpses of its subtle intricacies, but still suspected he would never be able to master the true depth and breadth of the moves.

A fortnight later, Lotus had grown quite competent at the Skyful of Petals needle throw. She could send more than a dozen sewing needles flying at a target's fatal points with a flick of her hand. However, she had yet to master the art of hitting several attackers at once with just one handful of needles.

When not practising, Lotus also made use of the snakes, preparing them in a myriad different ways — stir-fried, stewed, boiled into soups . . . She braised one coiled up, tucking its head under its tail.

"I name this Haughty Dragon Repents, for this snake is as flexible and adaptable as a true hero!" Lotus declared, making Count Seven Hong and Guo Jing howl with laughter.

That morning, Count Seven Hong had succeeded in casting several dozens of needles over an area of two *zhang* in one throw. He laughed heartily, but his delight was short-lived. "What is the Venom planning with those snakes?" he asked himself for the hundredth time.

"If there are only three masters of the *wulin* who can match Viper Ouyang's kung fu, why does he need to use the snakes at all?" Lotus said.

"You're right, he must be planning to use them on us – the other three Greats. The Beggar Clan and the Quanzhen Sect have many followers and allies. The Southern King obviously has his guards and soldiers. Your father is most skilled in divination and strategy – he can defeat an entire army on his own. If the three of us take on the Venom together, he won't stand a chance . . ."

"That's why he needs his creatures!"

"Catching and keeping snakes is a trick of the beggar's trade. A handy way to swindle a few coins out of rich young ladies. It's a feat to capture even a dozen snakes, but the Venom is herding thousands at a time. He must have spent a lot of time and energy on honing this skill. This is not a game to him."

"He must be planning something nasty, but we're lucky that his nephew exposed their scheme. He couldn't help showing off!"

"I'm not so sure. Those snakes couldn't have travelled thousands of miles from the west. He must have collected them in the mountains around here. He's flippant, to be sure, a most slippery young man, but I doubt he would have done it just to show off. There's something else at play here."

The Beggar Chief began to pace up and down. "What if the Venom keeps me so busy that I can't spare a hand? What if his minions herd all the snakes towards me, all at once? What should I do?" he wondered aloud.

Lotus laughed. "Well . . . there's one strategy that never fails – run!"

"Fie! What kind of a man would do that?"

"I've got an excellent idea," Lotus said, after a moment.

"What is it?"

"You can keep us with you. You fight the Venom, Guo Jing keeps his nephew busy, while I throw needles to skewer the snakes. The only problem is, Guo Jing hasn't even learned the whole of

Dragon-Subduing Palm. He'd probably struggle to beat that smarmy rogue."

Count Seven glared at Lotus. "You're the rogue, here! All you ever think about is how to trick those last three moves out of me. Guo Jing is a good soul. I wouldn't mind teaching him the rest of the moves. But that would make him my disciple and I'd be a laughing stock for taking on such a doltish protégé. And that won't do."

Lotus knew nothing she could say or do would change Count Seven Hong's mind, so she headed to the market to provision a spectacular meal to thank him. As she sauntered back to the inn with a basket full of fresh produce, she made little flourishes with her right hand, practising Skyful of Petals kung fu.

5

A PINTO HORSE CANTERED PAST LOTUS HUANG IN A TINGLE OF bells and stopped at the inn. She recognised the dismounting rider immediately. A resentment she had not felt for weeks resurfaced.

Why do they want Guo Jing to marry her? What's so special about her? Lotus decided to make her feelings known. She set down her basket and followed Mercy Mu inside.

Lotus watched Ironheart Yang's god-daughter sit at a square table, and noted how her whole being seemed weighed down by melancholy.

When the waiter came for Mercy's order, she responded without lifting her eyes from the table. "A bowl of noodles and four *taels* of boiled beef."

"Boiled beef! How boring."

Mercy looked up and was surprised to see the girl who had ridden away with Guo Jing standing by her table.

"Please join me, sister," she said as she got out of her seat.

"Are you travelling with the short, fat man and the filthy scholar? What about those meddling Taoists?"

"I am alone."

Her answer brought a grin to Lotus's face. She did not have to worry about Qiu Chuji or Guo Jing's *shifus*, then.

Mercy seemed scrawnier than when Lotus had last seen her, a couple of months ago, yet her despondent air somehow enhanced her beauty. Her travelling boots stood out from her white mourning clothes, as did the mourning flower in her hair.

Lotus noticed the dagger tucked into Mercy's belt – the marriage token – and asked sweetly, "Sister, would you let me look at your dagger?"

Mercy glanced at the outstretched hand, unsure what to do. She found the glint in the young woman's eyes unsettling, but common courtesy compelled her to oblige. She removed it from her belt and handed it over.

Lotus examined the carving on the hilt. Two characters: the surname Guo, and Jing, meaning "serenity".

I can't let her carry a dagger with Guo Jing's name, Lotus told herself. She drew the blade. The chill of the metal instantly cooled the air. What a weapon!

"I'll return it to Guo Jing." Lotus resheathed the knife and put it inside her shirt.

"What are you doing?"

"His name is carved on the hilt. It clearly belongs to him."

"This is the only memento I have of my parents." Mercy sprang to her feet. "Give it back!"

"Catch me if you can!" Lotus darted out of the inn and turned left, heading away from the pine forest where Count Seven Hong was napping and the clearing where Guo Jing was practising the Dragon-Subduing Palm.

Mercy followed as fast as she could, calling out after Lotus. I'll never be able to catch her if she gets on her red horse, she thought.

Lotus took a few sharp turns before stopping near a row of scholar trees. "If you can beat me, I'll give it back to you. Duel for a Sword, this time, instead of Duel for a Maiden."

"Sister, please don't make fun of me," Mercy begged, her face flushed with embarrassment. "It's the only connection I have left to my godfather."

"Who are you calling 'sister'?" Quick as the wind, Lotus swerved close to Mercy and struck out with her palm.

Mercy twirled aside. But Lotus's Cascading Peach Blossom Palm was much faster.

Smack, smack!

Pain rattled Mercy's ribcage. She skittered to the left and turned to face Lotus. Her palms flew hard and fast.

"Wayfaring Fist – how awfully common!"

How does she know? It's Count Seven Hong's unique kung fu! Mercy was taken aback.

Lotus cut a backhanded slice with her left palm and thrust her right fist forwards.

She knows it too! Mercy scuttled back, surprised. "Who taught you Wayfaring Fist?"

"I invented it." Lotus fired off two moves from that very same repertoire: Alms at the Gates and Hands Extended for Charity.

Mercy blocked with a Roam the Four Seas. "You know Count Seven Hong?"

"He's an old friend," Lotus said with a dazzling smile. "You fight with the kung fu he taught you and I'll use mine. Let's see who wins!"

Mercy could not recognise a single move of Lotus's rapid-fire onslaught and she did not stand a chance against a girl who had been taught by two of the greatest martial artists of the age.

Lotus's left palm shot up and hewed to the side, like a longsword. Mercy swerved away from the sharp edge of the strike. All at once, she felt the back of her neck growing numb. Lotus had flicked her Great Hammer pressure point with the Orchid Touch.

This was an important intersection of the Governing Vessel Meridian along the spine and the Triple Heater Channel that extended down the arm. A touch on this spot drained all energy from the limbs.

Mercy watched helplessly as Lotus took a step closer and jabbed at the Will Chamber point on her right flank. She felt herself tipping backwards.

She had lost all control of her body.

She looked on as Lotus unsheathed the dagger and brought it sweeping down towards her face.

This is it, she thought, squeezing her eyes shut.

The swish of the sword, the chill of the blade . . . a dozen times over, but she felt no pain. She opened her eyes to the flash of the dagger. Its point glided past her cheek and ear. No more than an inch away.

"Just kill me. Don't play games!" Anger swelled through Mercy's veins.

"Why would I want to kill you? I have no quarrel with you." Lotus paused, then added, "I'll let you go if you do as I say. If you make this promise."

"No! Kill me, if you dare. I never beg!" Mercy closed her eyes and prepared to die.

"It would be a shame to perish at such a tender age." Lotus fell silent. When she spoke again, her tone had softened. "We are true to each other. Even if you marry him, he won't like you."

"What do you mean?" Mercy's eyes flew open and she stared at Lotus.

"It's fine if you don't want to promise. I know he won't marry you."

"Who are you talking about?"

"Guo Jing."

"Guo Jing? What do you want me to promise?"

"Swear you'll never marry him. Swear on your life."

Mercy smiled. "I would not marry him, even if you forced me at knifepoint."

"Really? Why?"

"It might have been my godfather's dying wish, but . . . he wasn't in his right mind then . . . He had forgotten . . . he betrothed me to another . . ." Mercy's voice had suddenly gone very quiet.

"I'm so sorry. I got it all wrong . . ." Lotus quickly released the lock on Mercy's pressure points and massaged her limbs to ease the discomfort. "Sister, who is your betrothed?"

A blush spread across Mercy's cheeks. "You've met him," was all she was able to whisper.

"Have I?" Lotus tried to recall all the men she had encountered in the past few months, but no suitable candidate came to mind. "I can't think of anyone good enough for my peerless sister, here."

"Your Guo Jing isn't the only good man in this world."

"But why wouldn't you want to marry Guo Jing? Is it because he's too thick?"

"Not at all! I admire him very much. So pure-hearted, so righteous. He was kind to Papa and me. He stood up for us, with no regard for his own safety. I am forever indebted to him. He is a rare breed."

"Then why?"

Mercy took Lotus by the hand. "Brother Guo is in your heart and you will never look at another man. Isn't that so, sister? Even if they are more wonderful than him in every way."

"Of course, but there can't be anyone better than him."

"So you understand . . . The Duel . . . I lost . . ."

"The Jin Prince Wanyan Kang!"

"It doesn't matter if he's a prince or a beggar, kind or cruel, my heart and my being will always be his." Mercy's voice was still barely audible, but she spoke with absolute certainty.

Lotus took Mercy's hand and they sat, side by side, under one of the trees. She felt a profound connection to Mercy. Somehow, this young woman was able to put into words what she had been feeling all these weeks.

"This is yours." Lotus offered Mercy the dagger.

"You should keep it. It has his name on it. It is . . . inappropriate for me to carry it on my person."

"Thank you, sister," Lotus said, putting the dagger back inside her shirt. She wondered how she could return this gesture of kindness.

"What brought you to the south? Is there something I can help you with?"

"Nothing in particular." The blush returned to her cheeks.

"I will take you to Count Seven."

"He is here?"

Lotus heard a creak overhead, then saw a faint shape hopping from branch to branch, retreating through the treetops. She stood up, just as a piece of bark fell from above. On it was carved a short message, inscribed with a needle: *Should Lotus misbehave again, she will be boxed on her ears*. There was no signature, just the outline of a gourd.

Count Seven heard everything! It was Lotus's turn to blush. She showed Mercy the note.

The young women could not find any sign of Count Seven Hong nearby. They headed back to the inn, arm in arm, but found only Guo Jing.

"Sister Mu, when did you last see my *shifus*?" he asked.

"We travelled south together, but parted ways in Shandong. I haven't seen them since."

"Did they seem well?"

"Don't worry, they coped after your departure."

The answer did not set Guo Jing's mind at ease at all. All he could think about was how angry his martial teachers must be.

Noticing the effect of her words on Guo Jing, Mercy chose to change the subject. "Sister, you are so blessed to have spent all this time with Master Hong. I've longed to see him again, but he hasn't even let me catch so much as a glimpse of him!"

"He was watching over you, though," Lotus said. "If I'd tried to hurt you, he would have intervened."

"Lotus, you tried to hurt Sister Mu?"

"Of course not!"

"She was afraid that I . . ." Mercy paused, feeling slightly awkward.

A flustered Lotus resorted to tickling Mercy's armpits. "Are you sure you want to continue?"

"No, of course not! Would you like me to swear?" Mercy stuck out her tongue.

Lotus turned a deeper shade of red as she recalled how she had threatened Mercy earlier.

Never one to read into any exchange, Guo Jing was just happy to see how close the young women seemed.

After dinner, the three took a stroll in the woods. Mercy told her friends about her encounter with Count Seven Hong.

"I was very young then. Papa and I were in Bianliang. I was playing by the entrance of the inn where we were staying. I saw two beggars collapse, all bloodied and covered in stab wounds. No-one helped them because they were so filthy. I felt sorry for them, so I helped them into the room I shared with Papa. I didn't really have any medical knowledge. I could only help them clean and bind their wounds. When Papa returned, he was pleased with what I had done. He said I was kind-hearted, just like his wife. He gave them a few *taels* of silver and they left full of thanks. A few months later, we came across those same beggars in Xinyangzhou. They had made a full recovery. They brought me to an abandoned temple to meet Master Hong. He was pleased with my actions and taught me moves from the Wayfaring Fist, for three days. When I returned on the fourth day, he was gone, and I never saw him again."

"Count Seven forbade us to share his kung fu," Lotus said. "But, if you are interested, we can spend a fortnight or so together and I can teach you some of the moves I learned from Papa." Relieved that Mercy had so resolutely refused to marry Guo Jing, and grateful for her generous gift of the dagger, Lotus wanted to do something to repay the kindness of her new bosom friend.

"Thank you, sister. That's very sweet of you, but I'm afraid I can't stay. There's something I have to attend to first. Once that's done with, I'll come back begging to learn!"

Lotus was curious. What did Mercy have to do that was so urgent? But she could tell from Mercy's expression that she did not wish to speak about it. Over the past few hours, Lotus had come to realise that, although Mercy looked meek and bashful, she was headstrong and firm. Once she had made up her mind, she would not waver. Since Lotus would not be able to prise anything out of Mercy that she did not wish to divulge, she would have to find out her friend's secret another way.

6

MERCY MU RUSHED OUT AFTER LUNCH AND DID NOT COME back until dusk. Lotus wondered what could occupy her friend for a whole afternoon in this small town, and she was even more intrigued when Mercy returned, visibly excited. Lotus was determined to uncover the mysterious business that had caused their paths to cross.

That night, the young women shared a room. Lotus took the *kang* bed-stove that was situated so as to allow her to observe her friend from behind. Mercy seemed more distant than ever, since retiring to their room, resting her head in her hands, staring at the lamp in a daze.

Lotus tucked herself into bed and kept very still to feign sleep. Before long, Mercy pulled a piece of material out of her bag. Tenderly, she brought it to her lips, a soft kiss. She gazed at it, lost in her own world.

Without moving, Lotus craned to get a better look. What was it? Silk? An embroidered handkerchief, perhaps? She couldn't quite make out the pattern.

At that very moment, Mercy turned to face Lotus. She held the cloth high and performed a graceful flourish. Lotus squeezed her eyes shut, her heart thumping. She had come very close to being discovered.

Lotus felt a gentle rush in the air and let her eyelids part a little. The silhouette of Mercy weaved in and out of her vision, acting out what seemed to be different martial moves. The fabric was now draped around her arm.

Now Lotus remembered: Mercy had torn the sleeve of the Jin Prince when they duelled.

A smile hovered on Mercy's lips. A light kick here, a soft punch there. She lifted her eyebrows and flicked her sleeve. Haughty and nonchalant.

A perfect impersonation of Wanyan Kang, Lotus thought.

Mercy indulged herself in this way for quite some time before turning to Lotus once more. Lotus shut her eyes quickly, but she could feel Mercy's eyes on her, gazing intently through the half-light.

A sigh, then a whisper. "You really are beautiful."

After that, Lotus heard the door being opened and closed, followed by a moment of silence. The last thing she could pick up from outside was the sound of nimble feet landing lightly on the ground.

Did she just jump over the inn's wall? Lotus leapt out of bed and ran after Mercy, her curiosity reaching boiling point.

As she vaulted the inn wall, she caught a glimpse of Mercy sprinting westwards and followed silently with lightness kung fu. Catching up with Mercy took only a matter of moments, though she was careful to keep a safe distance of a dozen paces.

When Mercy reached the town centre, she leapt onto a roof and looked around. Once she saw a tall structure in the south side of the town, she began to run towards it, bounding from roof to roof.

The Dai Mansion? Why is she going there? Lotus knew every house in the town, from her daily trips to the market. Has she run out of silver? Is that why she is heading for the wealthiest family, this late at night?

The gates of the mansion were brilliantly lit. Two large red silk lanterns hung high on either side of the doorway, the characters *Imperial Envoy of the Great Jin Empire* emblazoned in gold on the fabric, in an elegant flattened script. Four Jin soldiers stood guard under the lanterns, with their sabres raised. Lotus had walked past the household many times, but she had never seen it so heavily protected.

Maybe she's here to steal from the Jin envoy? I'll tag along and see what trinkets I can find for myself.

Shadowing Mercy, Lotus circled to the back of the estate and saw her friend pausing at the perimeter wall, before scaling it. Lotus followed suit and found herself in the Dai Mansion's walled garden. She trailed after Mercy, scurrying between scholar's rocks and miniature artificial mountains, winding between flowers and trees, until they reached a courtyard.

Flickering candlelight illuminated a chamber on the eastern side, and Lotus could make out, cast on the window paper, the ever-shifting silhouette of a man pacing back and forth.

Lotus watched Mercy approach the room slowly, her eyes fixed on the moving shadow.

And then she stopped.

Lotus was confounded by Mercy's curious inertia. What's she doing? She could easily barge in now and immobilise him through his vital points!

I know what I'll do. I'll surprise her and lock his pressure points. With that thought, Lotus repositioned herself on the other side of the building and found a window that was unlatched.

She was about to climb through the window when she heard the sound of the chamber door creaking open, followed by a man speaking in a most deferential tone.

"Your Excellency, a messenger has just arrived from the relay station. The Song escort for our Imperial Envoy, Commander Duan, shall arrive in the next two days."

The message was received with a grunt. His Excellency, left to his devices, resumed his pacing of the room.

He must be the Jin envoy, Lotus said to herself. But maybe Mercy isn't here to steal from him, after all. I'd better stay put, for now. I don't want to ruin her plan.

She licked a finger. With the moistened nail, she cut a slit in the lowest pane of paper. She pressed her eye to the gap and saw a man draped in a silk robe that was fastened with an embroidered belt. She knew this man!

Wanyan Kang, the son of the Sixth Prince of the Jin Empire.

He was holding something, stroking it as he paced about. But she could not make out what it was. His eyes were fixed on a point beyond the rafters, his mind clearly preoccupied. When he came close to the candle, Lotus finally got a glimpse of the object in his hand: a rusty spearhead, still attached to about a foot of the shaft.

Lotus did not know that the spear had once belonged to Ironheart Yang, the young man's father by birth and Mercy's godfather, nor that it had been his late mother Charity Bao's most treasured possession, but something in the way he caressed it reminded her of Mercy and the torn sleeve. She guessed his odd behaviour had to be in some way connected to her friend, and the thought made her giggle out loud.

"Who's there?" Wanyan Kang snarled, extinguishing the candle with a wave of his hand.

Lotus darted behind Mercy. With the lightest of touches, she pressed both hands onto Mercy's torso in a Reverse Lock, one of the seventy-two techniques of Grapple and Lock kung fu. By the time Mercy felt anything was amiss, her movement was already disabled.

"Don't be scared, sister." Lotus chuckled. "I'm sending you to your beloved."

Wanyan Kang pulled the door open and was greeted with a girlish titter. "Your sweetheart's here. Catch!"

A warm, fragrant body fell into his arms.

"How will you thank me?" A peal of giggles rang out from a nearby roof.

Wanyan Kang retreated further into his room, a little fearful.

"Who are you?" he growled.

"Don't you remember me?" Mercy murmured.

She sounded familiar. Could it be . . . ? Wanyan Kang had not expected to encounter her again. "Is it . . . Miss Mu?"

"It is I."

"Who else came with you?" There was still suspicion in his tone.

"My mischievous friend. I had no idea she was following me."

Wanyan Kang took a moment to collect himself, then relit the candle he had extinguished.

"Please take a seat."

Mercy Mu perched on a nearby chair, her head bowed. She could hear her heart pounding.

Wanyan Kang observed the young woman in the candlelight. A hint of pink was blossoming on her pallid cheeks, accentuating her maidenly demeanour. He could feel something stirring inside – a heady mixture of surprise and excitement.

"What brings you here at this late hour?" His tone was softer now, almost gentle. His mind returned to what he had been dwelling on before the intrusion: his mother, his birth father – her godfather – and their untimely death. He felt tenderness take root in his heart.

"Your father has sadly passed away, but I will look after you like my own sister. You should come and live with us."

"I wasn't born to him . . ." Mercy stared into the floor as she spoke. "I am his god-daughter only."

Wanyan Kang was struck by the significance of her answer. She is telling me we are not related by blood.

He smiled and took her right hand. She blushed a shade darker. She waved his advances away, half-heartedly, but his grip remained firm. She relented. Her head sank even lower.

Emboldened, he put his arm around her shoulders.

"This is the third time I've held you," he said softly into her ear. "The first was at our duel. The second at the door just now. And, this time, we are alone. There is no-one else." He was intoxicated – by her proximity, her fragrance and the slight tremble of her body.

Mercy had never felt like this before. A sweet tingle rushed through her, taking over her senses.

They stayed like this for some time without speaking. Eventually, Wanyan Kang asked, "How did you find me?"

"I followed you from the capital. I keep watch every night. But I never . . ."

He brushed his lips against her cheek at this confirmation of her

feelings for him. Her skin seared like fire, swelling his passion further. He pulled her closer and kissed her. It was a long time before he allowed his arms to slacken.

"I have no father, no mother. Please don't . . . cast me aside."

Pulling her against his chest, Wanyan Kang caressed her hair. "Don't you worry. I'll always be yours. And you'll always be mine. Yes?"

For the first time, Mercy raised her head, looked straight into Wanyan Kang's eyes and nodded. She feared her heart might burst from this onslaught of emotions.

Her cheeks flushed. Her eyes glittered with expectation. Wanyan Kang could no longer contain himself. He blew the candle out and carried her to his bed. He held her close with one arm while the other hand worked at the knots that held her clothes together.

Feeling his hand on her skin, Mercy was jolted back to reality. "No! We can't." She struggled out of his embrace and rolled further into the bed.

But Wanyan Kang caught her in his arms again. "Should I ever be unfaithful, let me be cut into pieces."

She put a finger to his lips to silence him. "I believe you."

"Then let me . . ." He pressed his weight on her and tugged harder at the ties on her shirt.

"No . . . Please . . ."

He was deaf to her objections. His hands kept tugging at her clothes.

Mercy squirmed. Summoning her strength, she shoved him with both arms, driving him away with ease. He had not expected her to resist him with her kung fu. She jumped off the bed and grabbed the iron spearhead on the table.

"If you force me, I will kill myself, right here." She pointed it at her heart as tears rolled down her cheeks.

"Let's talk. There is no need for that." Wanyan Kang could feel his passion turn to ice.

"I may be poor, I may be wandering the rivers and lakes alone. But I am not base. I am not a loose woman. If you truly love me, you must respect me, respect my honour. You already know my future is tied to yours, no matter what. One day . . . if . . . on our nuptials . . . we shall . . ." she faltered. When she spoke again, her soft voice had gained an edge that could cut through steel. "If you dishonour me today, then death is my only way out."

"I see that the fault is mine." He was beginning to feel a quiet respect for this young woman. He got out of bed and lit the candle.

"I will wait for you at my godfather's home in Ox Village, in Lin'an. It doesn't matter when you come . . . with the matchmaker . . ." His apologetic response had softened her resolve. "Even if you don't come, I will still be waiting."

"Please be assured that, when I have finished my duty here, I shall personally lead the entourage to welcome my lady. Always faithful, always constant — this I vow, for life."

Mercy smiled at his promise and left.

"Please stay," Wanyan Kang implored. "So we can talk."

She turned and waved, but her feet did not stop.

Wanyan Kang watched her disappear over the roof and stared at the void she left behind. When he realised the dark sky, the night breeze, the rustling trees and the twinkling stars were his only companions, he went inside.

The encounter had been as unreal as a dream, but her scent lingered in his room, the spearhead still glistened with her tears and a few stray strands of her hair clung to his bedding. He picked up the precious threads and put them in a pouch for safekeeping.

When Wanyan Kang had taken part in the Duel for a Maiden, he had done it for fun, without any intention of marrying Mercy Mu. But now, having held her in his arms again, heard her speak about her silent nightly visits and watched her protect her virtue, something seeded in his heart. He turned the encounter over and over in his mind as smiles alternated with sighs.

He was smitten.

CHAPTER FOUR

THE CRIPPLE
OF THE FIVE LAKES

I

LOTUS HUANG SLEPT SOUNDLY THAT NIGHT, CONVINCED THAT she had done good by bringing Mercy Mu and Wanyan Kang together. When she told Guo Jing the next morning, he too was pleased that Mercy's feelings were reciprocated. He had taken on the Jin Prince, he recalled, to make him honour his prize: he had defeated Mercy in the Duel for a Maiden and thereby won her hand. This latest development was also a relief for him, because it meant Qiu Chuji and his *shifus* could not force him to marry Mercy. As for his betrothal to Khojin, he had not given it much thought since he left Mongolia. There was no need to tell Lotus, since he had decided to refuse the honour from Genghis Khan.

There was still no sign of Mercy after lunch. "I don't think she's coming back," Lotus said as she disappeared into her room. She re-emerged dressed in men's clothes, ready for the road.

They went into town to find a horse for the journey and passed by the Dai Mansion. The livery of the Jin Imperial Envoy had disappeared. Mercy must have left with them.

Guo Jing and Lotus travelled south along the Grand Canal, taking in the many sights along the way. Before long, they arrived at Yixing, the world capital of pottery. Mounds of purple stoneware were stacked in every corner of the city.

They continued eastwards and soon arrived at Lake Tai. This enormous body of water was the culmination of many streams that ran through eastern and southern China, and its shores embraced three major cities – Pingjiang, Changzhou and Huzhou. Known in ancient times as the Five Lakes, its shoreline ran to some five hundred *li*.

Guo Jing stood, hand in hand, with Lotus, marvelling at the rippling expanse. Growing up in landlocked Mongolia, he had never set eyes on such natural beauty. A lush jade green filled his vision. Verdant peaks stood proud against a sea of rolling waves, which stretched as far as the eye could see. Overcome with awe, he howled with delight into the sky.

"Let's explore the lake," Lotus said.

They rode to a nearby fishing village to settle the horses and hire a boat. As they rowed from the shore, they could no longer tell the sky from the water, as if all the layers of heaven and earth were contained within the grand sweep of this lake.

"Official Fan was smart. He chose to roam the Five Lakes with Xi Shi instead of grinding away at court," Lotus mused, her hair and her robe fluttering in the breeze. "Dying of old age out here would be so much better."

"Tell me about this Official Fan. I've never heard of him," Guo Jing said.

Fan Li was a courtier of the Yue state, from around one thousand five hundred years ago, Lotus explained. He helped his king, Goujian, avenge the humiliation suffered at the hands of the Wu king and return the Yue kingdom to prosperity. When Goujian eventually annexed the Wu state, Fan retired from the court with his beloved Xi Shi and lived as a recluse on Lake Tai.

Lotus went on to tell the stories of Fan's contemporaries: Wu Zixu, a general of the Wu state, and Wen Zhong, an official who stayed in King Goujian's court after the conquest of Wu. Unlike Fan, they were both forced by their kings to commit suicide, in spite of their contributions to their kingdoms.

It was some time before Guo Jing could grasp the significance of the story. "Fan Li showed foresight in choosing the smart way out, but Wu Zixu and Wen Zhong were honourable for putting the needs of the state ahead of their own. They served their country loyally to their very last breath."

"'When good prevails in the country, strong are those steadfast to the morals of a less abundant age. When dissolution is rife in a state, strong are those who hold firm to their principles unto death'," Lotus quoted Confucius.

"Can you explain?"

"A real man of honour is one who maintains his integrity, even as he grows wealthy and powerful in an age of peace. A man of honour is also one who gives his life to uphold his ethics in corrupt times."

"You are so wise to have thought of that!"

"Oh, that was Confucius, not me! Papa taught me, when I was little."

"There's so much I don't understand about this world. I wish I knew more about these great thinkers, then perhaps I could comprehend things a little more."

"Papa always says that most of what these philosophers come up with is empty rhetoric! He always mutters – 'Nonsense!' 'Hogwash!' – when he reads. People ridicule him as the Heretic because he sneers at the sages and mocks the Emperor for not standing up to the Jin. But they should praise him as a strong man. Great scholars and Emperors aren't always right, don't you agree?"

"I suppose we should always think and judge for ourselves."

"I really regret spending time studying the sages. I used to harass Papa to teach me everything – painting, divination, anything you can think of. If I had simply focused on martial arts, we wouldn't have to fear Cyclone Mei or Greybeard Liang. But, now you have learned the Eighteen Minus Three Dragon-Subduing Palms, at least that makes the Ginseng Codger less of a threat."

"I'm not so sure." Guo Jing shook his head.

"It's a pity that Count Seven left us so suddenly. I was going to hide his Dog-Beating Cane until he agreed to teach you the last three moves."

"You can't do that! He's your senior! I'm more than happy with the fifteen moves."

They let the waves take them forward. Soon, they were more than a dozen *li* from the shore. A shallow skiff floated some distance away. On the bow of this leaf-like vessel sat a man fishing with a rod. At the stern, a serving boy stood.

"This is like an ink-wash landscape. A lone fisherman amid the misty expanse."

"What do you mean?" Guo Jing knew nothing about literati culture.

"It's a style of painting using only black ink."

Guo Jing looked around him. The hills were green, the water blue, the setting sun – yellow and orange – was painting the white clouds in shifting shades of pink and red. The one colour missing was black. He shook his head, unable to see what she meant.

Lotus looked over at the fisherman again. "What a patient man!"

He had not moved at all, as still as a figure in a painting.

A light wind stirred. Ripples lapped gently against their boat. Lotus broke into song as she picked up the oar.

> "*Cast into waves stretching thousands of* li,
> *Verdant hills of the south roll by unseen.*
> *Clouds gather over the star of rain,*
> *The river runs with the goddess,*
> *Eastwards, into the sea.*
> *This northern traveller drifts,*
> *His heart shaken, his vision misplaced,*
> *Headlong into twilight years.*
> *My mountain hermitage,*
> *My friends from home,*
> *A dream, an illusion, gone!*"

She was drawn into the lyrics as she sang; her voice was tinged with grief and tears glistened in her eyes. "That was the first half of 'Water Dragon Chant' by Zhu Xizhen. Papa sings it all the time."

Just as Guo Jing was about to ask the meaning of the song, mournful singing swelled from the lake. Even he could tell it was the same tune. The stranger's voice conveyed much anguish.

> "*Looking behind, evil remains unvanquished.*
> *Where are the heroes of our time?*
> *Strategies to save the state*
> *Lie disregarded and unused,*
> *Only dust and defeat.*
> *The iron gates stood across the river,*
> *Yet the fleet rode down the waves,*
> *And left the monarch mourning.*
> *I can but beat tempo with my oar,*
> *As I chant with grief*
> *In a torrent of tears.*"

"I can't believe the fisherman knows the song too." Lotus rowed towards the skiff. "It's about an old man sailing down a river and grieving for his country, which has lost half of its land."

By now, the fisherman had put away his fishing rod and was making his way towards Guo Jing and Lotus. When he was a short distance away, he called out over the water, "What a happy encounter! May I invite you for a cup of wine?"

"We should not impose ourselves on you, sir." Lotus had not expected the fisherman to be so well spoken.

"It would be my pleasure to make your acquaintance." He dipped his oar and brought the two boats together.

Guo Jing and Lotus tied their rowing boat onto the skiff's stern and hopped across. Once aboard, they put their hands together respectfully in greeting.

The fisherman returned the salute. "Please forgive me for not standing up to welcome you. My legs are not as strong as they once were." He invited his guests to sit down.

The fisherman appeared no more than forty, but his sallow complexion and hollowed-out cheeks gave him the look of someone long haunted by illness. Despite the problem with his legs, he was curiously well built – half a head taller than Guo Jing sitting down.

"His name is Guo, and mine is Huang. Our impromptu singing must have disturbed sir's enjoyment," Lotus said.

"Your aria washed away my worldly worries. Is it your first time on Lake Tai? My name is Lu."

"Yes, sir," Guo Jing answered.

At the fisherman's signal, the serving boy left his place at the stern, where he had been fanning the stove to heat wine, to set up the banquet.

The host personally poured the wine, demonstrating that he held his guests in great esteem. The four dishes served were not as delicate as Lotus's creations, but the elegance of the presentation and crockery indicated to the young couple that they were in the company of a wealthy and important man.

"My young friend, you sang the 'Water Dragon Chant' with such melancholy and gusto," the fisherman said after the second toast. "It is exceptional to have grasped the sentiment contained in the lyrics at your tender age."

"Every literati has lamented the fate of our country since the Song court retreated south. Zhang Yuhu expressed similar emotions in 'Prelude to Six Provinces'." Lotus started to sing:

> *"I heard our countrymen left in the north,*
> *Oft looked towards the south*
> *For the Emperor's procession.*
> *To see them fills travellers with anger and pity,*
> *To see them fills eyes with tears."*

Smacking the table in agreement, the fisherman sang the last two lines again and poured yet more wine for his guests, and they toasted three more times.

The fisherman talked about poetry with passion and Lotus responded with the same animation, adapting her father's commentaries. But, deep down, she knew she was too young to grasp the concern for king and country expressed by the verses.

Greatly moved by Lotus's insight and her elegant phrasing, the fisherman struck the table again and again in impassioned approval. Guo Jing understood little of their discussion, but was pleased to see the fisherman's reaction.

Soon, twilight fell, shrouding the lake in mist.

"My humble abode is on the lakeshore; might I be so bold as to invite you to break your journey for a few days?" Before they answered, the fisherman added, "I am fortunate that my home is surrounded by abundant natural beauty, and since my young friends are here on Lake Tai to enjoy the scenery, please do not imagine that you would be imposing."

"Well, we shall trouble you then, Master Lu," Guo Jing answered, moved by Lu's earnest invitation.

Happy that his new friends had agreed to stay, the fisherman ordered the serving boy to steer them ashore so Guo Jing and Lotus could return their boat.

"We will be back once we have made arrangements for our horses," Guo Jing said, when he and Lotus were on land.

"I am familiar with the inhabitants of this area; please allow him to attend to your needs," the fisherman said, pointing at the serving boy, who now stood next to them on the shore.

"My ride is of rough temperament; it is best if I settle him personally."

"In that case, I shall await your arrival." With these words, the fisherman and his skiff disappeared among a thicket of weeping willows.

2

AFTER THEY HAD RETURNED THE ROWING BOAT AND retrieved the horses, the serving boy led Guo Jing and Lotus Huang to a household one *li* along the shore, to board a larger vessel. Six stout rowers ferried them across the lake for several *li* to a stone pier on an islet populated by a series of buildings and pavilions interlinked by covered corridors.

The young couple exchanged a look of surprise. What a grand manor for a fisherman!

Across an imposing stone bridge leading to the gate of the manor, a youth of eighteen stood before a formal line of half a dozen servants.

He stepped forward. "Father sent me to welcome you to Roaming Cloud Manor."

Wrapping an open palm over a fist in a gesture of thanks, Guo Jing and Lotus marvelled at the resemblance. Here was a strapping, youthful version of the fisherman. He wore a robe of fine silk over his broad shoulders and muscular torso.

"Please call me by my first name, Laurel," the young man said deferentially as he led the way.

This manor was worlds away from the simple grandeur Guo Jing had found in the architecture of the north. Here, every beam and pillar was carved and painted according to an elaborate decorative scheme. But it was the layout and arrangement of the paths and walkways that caught Lotus's attention as they were guided through the estate. After meandering through three courtyards, they at last reached their destination.

"Please come in!" they heard the fisherman call.

"Due to his indisposition, my father will receive you in the east study." Laurel Lu led them around the screen wall to an open doorway.

Seated on a couch, with a white goose-feather fan in his hand, the fisherman was now dressed in a scholar's robe. He cupped his hands together in greeting and invited his guests to sit. Laurel Lu stood to attention in a corner of the study.

Lotus looked around the room. It was full of artefacts and ancient books, with antique bronzes and jades displayed on every surface. Her eyes fell on an ink-wash scroll of a middle-aged scholar, which was hanging on the wall. The forlorn figure stood with his hand resting on the hilt of his sword, seemingly sighing into an empty courtyard, under a moonlit sky. A lyric poem was inscribed on the top left of the picture plane:

> The autumn cricket chirped incessantly yesternight.
> Startled from the land of dreams a thousand li away,
> Midnight had already passed.
> Out of the bed, alone in the courtyard pacing,
> Solitary was I.
> Beyond the blinds, the moon was shrouded in haze.
>
> Striving for honour and rank has turned my hair grey.
> The ancient pines and bamboos of the old mountain
> Stand in the way of return.
> I wish to confide by the music of my zither,
> But who will listen?
> Who will hear when my string snaps?

Lotus remembered her father teaching her this verse, then she read the signature: *Scribbled by the Cripple of the Five Lakes, in an infirm state*. Their host must have painted this, though she had doubts how ill he could have been at the time. The powerful brushwork slashed like a sword and quivered with pent-up force, as if each stroke could pierce through the paper and take flight.

Noticing Lotus's interest in the painting, Squire Lu said, "Brother, please honour us with your thoughts."

"I hope I am not being impertinent," Lotus replied. "The painting portrays some of the frustration expressed in Yue Fei's 'Layered Hills'. However, General Yue wanted military action against the Jurchen after they annexed the northern part of our realm. He believed he owed it to the people to repel the invaders, but the Imperial Court was more interested in negotiating peace treaties – no-one heard Yue Fei's plea. Though he wholeheartedly opposed talks with the Jin, he did not wish to openly defy the court.

"It's as though indignation, a sense of being wronged, fuelled sir's creation of the work. The brushstrokes are imbued with might, but they are also sharp and spiky, as if the brush was fighting its nemesis to the death. In that sense, perhaps it does not quite match the helplessness and concern Yue Fei felt for the country and the people.

"I once heard that, if one is to attain mastery in the art of the brush, one should never simply pursue force at the expense of the more subtle nuances of control."

Squire Lu sighed and said nothing.

"Forgive my unchecked tongue, Squire Lu." Lotus had parroted her father's interpretation of the poem and his views on artistry. She had not thought it would upset her host so.

Her words jolted Squire Lu out of his gloom and now he seemed pleased. "Brother Huang, please, there is no need to apologise. You are the first person to perceive the state I was in when I created this painting. You can't imagine what joy this understanding brings me. The sharpness of my brushwork is something I've never managed to rectify and I am grateful of this reminder." Squire Lu then turned to his son. "Send word for the banquet to be prepared." The young man left the study quietly, with a bow.

"Brother, you are a true connoisseur," he continued. "I am sure you come from a cultured family. Might I ask your father's name?"

"I don't deserve such praise, sir. My father runs an academy in the country. His name is not known at all."

"The world sighs for talent so neglected."

AFTER A sumptuous feast, they returned to the study. "The caves of Celestial Master Zhang and Hermit Shan Juan the Virtuous are some of the most exceptional sights under the heavens and they are only a short distance away," Squire Lu said. "Please stay for a few days and explore at your leisure. Would you like to retire for the evening?"

Guo Jing and Lotus stood up to take their leave. On the way out, Lotus noticed eight pieces of iron nailed into the lintel over the study door. The metal strips had the outline of the Eight Trigrams, yet they were arranged in slanted, asymmetric disarray. Keeping the discovery to herself, she followed Guo Jing and the servant out of the east study.

The guest room was elegantly furnished with two beds covered in tasteful linen. The servant brought tea. "Should my lords require anything, please pull the bell by the bed. We shall be at your service instantly. Might I bid my lords to stay in the room during the night?" Softly, he shut the doors.

"There's something queer about this place. Why did he say we should stay inside?" Lotus spoke quietly.

"Maybe they don't want us to get lost? The manor is huge and the paths are confusing."

"It is built in an odd way," she said, pondering the estate's layout. "What do you think our host does?"

"A retired official?"

She shook her head. "He's trained in the martial arts. A master, probably. Did you notice the iron Eight Trigrams over the study door?"

"Huh?"

"They are set up for the practice of Splitting Sky Palm. Papa tried to teach me, but it was boring; I gave up after a month. I never imagined I'd see it here."

"Squire Lu has no ill intent towards us. Just pretend you didn't see it."

Nodding with a smile, Lotus swung her palm in the direction of the candlestick and the light went out with a hiss.

"Impressive! Was that Splitting Sky Palm?"

"That's all I know. Good for showing off, no use in a fight."

3

THE LOW BLAST OF A FARAWAY CONCH JOLTED GUO JING AND Lotus awake, some time after midnight. A moment later, a similar groan sounded from another direction. A call and response, messages passed over distance.

"Let's take a look," Lotus whispered.

"We were told—"

"Come on, just a peek."

They nudged a window open and peered into the courtyard. Men rushed to and fro, lanterns in hand. A few dark shapes squatted on the roof. Metal glinted in the movement of the lights. Soon, the men in the courtyard marched off in formation. Lotus took Guo Jing's hand and went to the window on the other side of the room. Not a soul in sight. She leapt out and beckoned Guo Jing to do the same. Instead of following the group, Lotus headed in the opposite direction. The armed men on the roof did not register that the guests had left their room.

There was not a single path that followed a straight line. They meandered left and snaked right. At every corner of the grounds, the banisters, buildings and vegetation were identical. Guo Jing was hopelessly lost, yet Lotus hurried along without hesitation, as if she was at home. Time and again, Guo Jing was certain that they were at a dead end, but Lotus would burrow into a hidden passage through an artificial mountain, or hop around some shrubbery, and suddenly the walkway reappeared. Every time Guo Jing thought they must have reached the outer perimeter of the estate, Lotus found the entrance to another courtyard or garden lurking behind a screen or a tree. Often, she ignored the open entry of a moon gate and pushed at the wall to reveal a hidden door.

"How do you know your way around?"

Lotus put a finger to her lips to silence him. She navigated another half a dozen turns before stopping at the wall of the rear garden. She looked around, counting with her fingers as she paced.

"Thunder in the First, Reluctance in the Third, Nourishment in the Fifth, Returning in the Seventh, Earth . . ." Lotus's mumbled calculations made no sense to Guo Jing.

Eventually, she stopped. "This is it. We can get out from here. The rest of the wall is fitted with traps."

When they were safely on the outside, Lotus explained. "The manor was built according to the directions of the sixty-four hexagrams of Fuxi the Sovereign, which stems from the knowledge of the Mysterious Gates and Eight Trigrams. Papa is a master of the subject. This place may confuse most people, but not me."

Lotus marched to the summit of the small hill behind the manor for a better vantage point. To the east, a procession of lanterns and torches was making its way towards Lake Tai. She tugged on Guo Jing's sleeve and they sprinted to the shore together using their lightness kung fu. When they were near the water, they hid behind a large rock.

Streams of men boarded a fleet of fishing boats anchored along the bank. The moment each man stepped aboard, he snuffed out his light. Now that the last of them had embarked, the lake was plunged into darkness once more, giving the young couple the cover they had been waiting for. They hopped silently onto the stern of the largest barge as it set sail and climbed onto the cabin's canopy. Peering through the gaps of the woven bamboo awning, they were surprised to find their host's son, Laurel Lu, seated below.

The fleet cruised for several *li* across Lake Tai. Then the seashell horn was heard once more. A man emerged from the cabin to sound a reply from the bow. The barge covered another few *li*, reaching a stretch of the lake that was dotted with skiffs as far as the eye could see, as if countless ink droplets were splattered across a large piece of green paper.

Three blasts of the conch and the barge dropped its anchor. A dozen small boats hastened towards it from all directions. Could this be an attack? The idea occurred to the young couple, but Laurel Lu's demeanour showed no concern.

The launches closed in and men began to board Laurel Lu's barge in twos and threes. They bowed deferentially at the young man, then headed to their seats. There was a clear hierarchy: some early arrivals sat down at the back, while others had a place close to the front. In the time it takes to drink a pot of tea, everyone had settled. The men were all dressed as fishermen, but each of them was of a martial bearing, tough and strong. They could not possibly make a living simply from fishing.

Laurel Lu raised his hand, then spoke. "Brother Zhang, what news?"

A compact, wiry man stood up. "The Jin envoy will cross tonight. Commander Duan will be here in about two hours. His arrival is delayed because he has been extorting and plundering along the way on the pretext that he was leading the welcome party to receive the Jurchen forces."

"How much did he take?"

"Every town and province offered their respects. His soldiers pillaged every village they passed. I saw his men carrying more than twenty chests, and they appeared very heavy."

"What about the troops?"

"Two thousand cavalry, and as many infantry again. But there aren't enough boats. Only one thousand infantrymen will make the crossing."

"What do you say, my brothers?"

"We will follow our leader's order!" everyone cried in unison.

"They took our people's livelihood. They seized what belongs to Lake Tai." Laurel Lu folded his hands on his chest. "It is not against the Way of the Heavens to reclaim what is ours. And we will reclaim it all!"

The men exploded in cheers.

"We will distribute half of our booty to the poor living around the lake," he continued. "The rest will be split among the crews."

Now Guo Jing and Lotus understood. These men were pirates, and Laurel Lu was their leader.

"What are we waiting for?" Laurel Lu roared, before turning back to Brother Zhang. "Take five skiffs as scouts." The man disembarked with a curt nod.

He then gave orders to his band of outlaws, assigning the vanguard, the reserve, the water ghosts who would scuttle the Jin envoy's fleet, squads to seize valuables and to guard the prisoners . . . This softly spoken, scholarly young man was turning out to be a confident commander of ruffians.

"Surely we've already made enough from wealthy merchants?" a pirate said, just as everyone was leaving to take their posts. "Is there really a need to wage war on government officials? What will become of us? The Great Jin Imperial Envoy isn't the sort of enemy we want."

Guo Jing and Lotus recognised the speaker immediately – Ma Qingxiong the Valiant, an apprentice of Dragon King Hector Sha and one of the Four Daemons of the Yellow River. How had he got involved with this band of robbers?

"Brother Ma, you are new to our crew – and perhaps unfamiliar with our rules." Laurel Lu's face darkened and his voice boomed above the jeers of the pirates. "Every one of us here is committed to our mission, wholly and with one heart. Our force might be wiped out tonight, but we will give our lives without regret."

"Do what you will! I want nothing to do with this cesspool!" The Soul Snatcher Whip, Ma Qingxiong, spun away, looking for a way out of the cabin.

Two men blocked his exit. "You beheaded a chicken and pledged to share our every fortune and misfortune!" one of them cried.

"Out of my way!" Ma Qingxiong's fists shot forward and both men fell to the side. He darted towards the open deck as a rush of air closed in from behind, then he swivelled to dodge, pulling a dagger from his boot and, as he did so, jabbing the blade in a backhand thrust at his pursuer.

Laurel Lu pushed the knife aside and launched his other palm. Ma Qingxiong twisted and shoved. He raised the knife again.

At first, Guo Jing was concerned for Laurel Lu. Yet, within a handful of moves, his host's son was firmly on the offensive and Ma Qingxiong could only shift and swerve in the narrow cabin.

Why was the Soul Snatcher Whip's kung fu so weak now? Guo Jing was surprised, but then quickly realised: I was attacked by the Four Daemons all at once, in Mongolia. This time, he's alone in enemy territory.

Little did Guo Jing know that it was the tremendous improvement in his own martial skills that made Ma seem less threatening. In the past two months alone, he had learned one of the most powerful forms of kung fu known to the *wulin*, Dragon-Subduing Palm. Each tip and suggestion he had received from Count Seven Hong as they sparred was a nugget of supreme martial wisdom from one of the greatest masters of the age. Hong's knowledge was on a level far beyond the collective expertise of his *shifus*, the Seven Freaks of the South. Though Guo Jing barely understood a tenth of what Count Seven had said, he held each word firmly in his mind. That alone was enough to propel his martial prowess onto an equal footing with his teachers. Ma Qingxiong now seemed trivial by comparison.

Laurel Lu lunged and threw a left punch – *pang!* – square in Ma Qingxiong's chest.

Ma stumbled and tipped backwards. Two men hacked down with their sabres, killing the Soul Snatcher Whip instantly. Then they tossed his bloodied, lifeless body into the lake.

"Brothers, let courage be our watchword!" Laurel Lu cried. The pirates returned to their vessels with a rousing roar of agreement.

Thousands of oars propelled this fleet eastwards. Laurel Lu's boat held up the rear as they glided across the dark lake.

The pirates soon spotted a squadron of several dozen brilliantly lit ships sailing west.

That must be the government convoy! With that thought, Guo Jing and Lotus scaled the mast for a better view. They sat on the yard, shielded from view by the sail.

The pirate fleet was fast approaching the government ships. A conch blasted from one of the scouting skiffs. Moments later, shouts, clangs and splashes swelled from the lake, drifting faintly towards Guo Jing and Lotus.

Now, a burst of fire engulfed the Jin flotilla, lapping at the night sky and painting the dark water crimson.

A group of launches skimmed across the water and approached Laurel Lu's barge. "We have captured the commander of the warden's office. His entire fleet is lost, and the Jin infantry with it!"

Visibly elated, the pirate commander stood on the bow and bellowed, "Keep up the great work! Let's take the Jin ambassador!"

"Aye!" The messengers sped away to deliver the order.

That's Wanyan Kang! What will he do? Guo Jing and Lotus reached for one another's hand at the thought of Mercy Mu's sweetheart.

Beckoned by a chorus of seashell horns, the marauders raised their sails and sped westwards on the midsummer easterly wind. Laurel Lu's barge, equipped with the largest sail, pulled ahead, in hot pursuit of the Jin envoy. Guo Jing and Lotus, too, were caught up in the excitement of the chase. Roused by the rushing wind at their backs, the glittering sky and the misty expanse ahead, they felt an overwhelming urge to sing at the top of their voices.

The sky began to grow light in the east. By now, the pirates had been stalking the Jin fleet for two hours. Two launches glided close to the barge. A pirate on the first waved a green flag, signalling to the larger ship. "The Jin fleet is in sight! Captain Ke is leading the assault," he cried.

"Excellent!" Laurel Lu responded from the barge.

Before long, another small boat slipped close. "The Jin dog has sharp claws! Captain Ke is injured. Captain Peng and Captain Dong are fighting him together."

Shortly after, two pirates carried the unconscious Captain Ke onto the barge. Laurel Lu hurried over to check his wounds. Just then, another two launches arrived with Captain Peng and Captain Dong. Both were injured, and they brought the news of the death of Quartermaster Guo of West Dongting. He had taken a spear from the Jin ambassador and fallen into the water.

"I'll kill that rabid Jin dog myself!" Laurel Lu roared.

Guo Jing and Lotus were angry at the brutal way Wanyan Kang dealt with his own countrymen. Yet they were also concerned for his safety, since Mercy's heart was tied to him.

"Should we help him?" Lotus asked quietly.

Guo Jing paused before answering. "We'll save him, but he must change his ways."

Lotus nodded, pointing at Laurel Lu as he boarded a launch. "Let's follow him."

They were ready to leap down onto another skiff when a great roar rose from the lake, spreading from pirate to pirate. The Jin envoy's fleet was slowly sinking, ship by ship. The pirates, the scourge of the water, had succeeded in their efforts to scuttle the enemy craft.

The green flag was raised again. A boatswain called from one of the two approaching launches. "The Jin dog is in the water!"

"We've got him!" another reported.

At that news, Laurel Lu climbed back aboard his own vessel.

Soon, conch shells were sounding from every direction. The Jin ambassador and his personal guard and staff were brought onto Laurel Lu's barge by a series of skiffs.

His hands and feet bound, Wanyan Kang's eyes were tightly shut, but his chest was heaving. It seemed the young man had swallowed a lungful of water.

By now, the rising sun had chased away the last traces of the night. Rays of light danced on the waves as if thousands of golden snakes were gliding across the surface of the lake.

"All captains, return to Roaming Cloud Manor! Quartermasters, lead your crews back to camp. Await instruction for the division of the bounty," Laurel Lu announced, to thunderous cheers.

The pirate fleet dispersed in four directions, accompanied by wisps of mist clinging forlornly to the morning breeze.

Lake Tai returned to its usual peaceful self. Flocks of gulls soared and swooped as the green hills watched on from a distance.

Guo Jing and Lotus Huang waited until the last pirate had disembarked before jumping ashore. They re-entered the manor the same way they had left, through the rear garden perimeter wall.

The servants had checked their room several times that morning, assuming they were sleeping in after a long day's journey. The very moment Guo Jing opened the door, two serving men rushed forward with a breakfast tray of noodles and soup dumplings.

"Squire Lu would be honoured if you would grace him with your presence after breakfast."

Guo Jing and Lotus ate quickly and followed the servants to the study.

"The wind was high last night. I hope it didn't disturb your sleep," Squire Lu said, with an apologetic smile.

"We slept very well, thank you," Lotus answered immediately, knowing Guo Jing would not be able to come up with a lie quick enough and might reveal their whereabouts last night. "Was there a ritual to appease hungry ghosts? We thought we heard a conch sounding in the middle of the night."

Squire Lu smiled and changed the subject. "I would love your opinion on my small collection of calligraphy and paintings." He ordered the servants to bring the art works. Lotus admired the scrolls one by one; Guo Jing looked on, unsure of what to think.

Suddenly, the peace in the study was broken by shouts and cries and pounding feet. It sounded like someone was running from a group of pursuers.

"You'll never find your way out of Roaming Cloud Manor!"

Pang! The study's doors flew open. A man barged in, dripping wet. Guo Jing and Lotus recognised him immediately – Wanyan Kang!

"Look at the painting, not at him," she whispered, tugging Guo

Jing's sleeve. They lowered their heads and pretended to study the scrolls.

Wanyan Kang had fallen into the water when his boat sank. He was unable to swim, and his martial knowledge counted for nothing once in the lake. He had gulped a bellyful of water and passed out. Coming to, he found his hands and feet bound. He had been delivered to Laurel Lu at knifepoint for questioning. The moment the blade was removed from his neck, he had summoned his inner strength and ripped his binds using Heartbreaker Palm. With an effortless swing of his arms, he had dispatched the two guards who tried to restrain him. He sprinted onto the first path that crossed his way.

Laurel Lu had not been too concerned about his prisoner escaping when he broke his restraints. As Lotus had surmised, Roaming Cloud Manor was built according to the rules of the Mysterious Gates and the Eight Trigrams. Without a guide familiar with the layout or knowledgeable in the underlying concepts behind its construction, Wanyan Kang would never find his way out. However, as they neared his father's study, Laurel Lu rushed into the room after Wanyan Kang, ran forward and placed himself protectively in front of his father. The pirate captains spread out in a line across the doorway, blocking the study's only exit.

Realising he was trapped, Wanyan Kang jabbed his finger at Laurel Lu. "You sank my fleet with your dirty tricks. You'll be laughed out of the *jianghu*."

"What does a Jin Prince know about the *jianghu*?" Laurel Lu sneered.

"I heard that the heroes of the south were honourable men. Well . . . having seen you in action first hand, I can see that this reputation is ill deserved!" The pirates snarled, but Wanyan Kang continued unfazed. "A swarm of cowards and rogues who got lucky through sheer weight of numbers, that's what you are!"

"Will you submit to your fate if we defeat you in one-to-one combat?"

Wanyan Kang smiled to himself. He's fallen for my taunt! "I shall yield to your ropes without another word. Who would like to display their martial knowledge first?" He folded his arms behind his back and cast his eyes around the room, regarding each of the pirates with disdain.

"This old man will rip the feathers off this foreign peacock!"

Captain Shi, known as the Golden Turtle, charged at Wanyan Kang. His fists flew at the Prince's Great Sun vital points, at each of his temples, in a move known as Bell and Drum.

Standing tall, with his hands still behind his back, Wanyan Kang turned a fraction and evaded the punches with ease. With a twist of his right hand, he grabbed Captain Shi from behind and propelled the pirate's fleshy bulk back towards the doorway.

"It would be my pleasure to sample your excellent kung fu in the courtyard." Laurel Lu gestured outside. He knew none of his men could beat Wanyan Kang – he was too fast and too brutal – and he could not let this fight unfold near his father and the guests. They were not trained in the martial arts and might get hurt.

"Why not here?" Wanyan Kang was confident that he could tackle his captor within moments. "Please honour me with your first move."

"You are our guest; the first is yours."

Wanyan Kang thrust his left palm in a feint. It masked the deadly Nine Yin Skeleton Claw that tore at Laurel Lu's chest.

The young master of Roaming Cloud Manor held his ground. Hunching his shoulders so that his torso was just beyond reach, Laurel Lu threw a right punch at the Prince's elbow. At the same time, he jabbed two forked fingers at his opponent's eyes.

The speed of the attack took Wanyan Kang by surprise, forcing him to step sideways. He flipped a clawed hand into a Grapple and Lock and seized his captor by the arm. Laurel Lu twisted away, then drew his arms in a circle with his thumbs outstretched, in an Embrace the Moon. Recognising the move's potency, Wanyan Kang launched into the Quanzhen Sect's defensive fist technique.

A student of Abbot Withered Wood of Cloudy Perch Temple in

Lin'an, Laurel Lu was well versed in the boxing techniques of the Immortal Cloud Sect. A branch of the Shaolin Temple on Mount Song in Henan, their kung fu, together with that of the Quanzhen Sect, was considered a fundamental part of the orthodox martial lineage.

But this was the first time Laurel Lu had fought such a powerful opponent. Treading with care, he kept his arms close to his body to fend off Wanyan Kang's savage talons. His feet were ready to kick out the moment he saw a gap in the Jin Prince's defence.

Fists and feet flew faster and faster. The two young men were now nothing but blurred outlines flitting around the room.

For fear that Wanyan Kang might recognise them, Lotus and Guo Jing had retreated behind the bookshelves to watch the fight.

Wanyan Kang had expected to beat Laurel Lu quickly, and he would have done so had he not been so shaken by his ordeal during the night.

If I let this fight go on much longer, I won't have any strength left to take on another challenger. With that thought, he redoubled his efforts, employing some of his most brutal moves.

Thwack! Laurel Lu took a punch to the shoulder. He staggered back several steps.

Revelling in the hit, the Jin Prince lunged. A crushing pain rocked his chest. How had his opponent hit back while in retreat?

Laurel Lu's kung fu was grounded in muscular strength and agility. It stressed the collaboration between hands and feet, a repertoire of kicks forming his most potent offensive technique. "One-third punches, two-thirds kicks" and "Hands are doors, kick to win" were well-known mantras of this style.

Laurel Lu stumbled, and yet struck his left leg at Wanyan Kang, quick as lightning, in a kick called Arrow to the Heart. He had toiled over this move since childhood, pulling, stretching and hoisting his ankle high using a rope thrown over a roof beam. The speed, the force and the extreme overhead angle made the kick all but impossible to dodge.

Wanyan Kang felt the wind knocked out of him, but still he managed to twist his left hand and impale Laurel Lu's calf with all five fingers before the young man could pull back.

"Down!" He smacked his other palm into Laurel Lu's hip.

Laurel Lu lost his footing. After all, he was only supported by one leg. The young man flew across the room, straight into his father.

Confounding all expectations, Squire Lu placed his hand on his son's back and set him down with ease. A scarlet line on the floor marked the young man's trajectory.

"Who are you to Twice Foul Dark Wind?" Squire Lu hissed.

Needless to say, the room was stunned by Squire Lu's reaction, except for Lotus and Guo Jing. Even Laurel Lu had assumed his father's disability and his interest in music and literature precluded any real knowledge of the martial arts. But the hand that guided him down was certain and steady. The touch of a master.

"I've never heard of this Twice Foul Dark Wind!" Wanyan Kang said with disdain. He had learned kung fu from Cyclone Mei for years, but he did not even know her name, let alone her past.

"Then who taught you the Nine Yin Skeleton Claw?"

"I haven't got time for this!" Wanyan Kang turned to leave. The pirates immediately raised their weapons.

"Are you not honourable men of your word?" the Jin Prince drawled.

"The heroes of Lake Tai never go back on their word." A pallid Laurel Lu signalled his men to stand down, and, grudgingly, they obeyed. "Captain Zhang will see you out."

"Follow me." The pirate glowered at Wanyan Kang.

"And my entourage?"

"They too will be freed," Laurel Lu conceded.

"The word of a gentleman is as true as a horseman's whip!" Wanyan Kang raised his thumb in approval. "Captains, fare you well." Smug in his triumph, the Jin Prince put his hands together and gave each pirate a mocking salute.

"Do indulge this old man and show me once more the Nine Yin Skeleton Claw." Squire Lu spoke softly.

"Happy to oblige."

"Pa . . ."

"He hasn't mastered it yet; there is no need to worry." Squire Lu turned to Wanyan Kang. "I can't walk, so you have to come to me."

Sneering, Wanyan Kang stayed put.

"I'd like to sample your kung fu on behalf of my papa." Despite his injury and almost certain defeat, Laurel Lu could not let his father put himself at risk.

"It would be my pleasure," the Jin Prince said.

"Out of my way, son!"

Squire Lu gently tapped his seat and instantly propelled himself across the study, his left palm held high, ready to strike down at the Jin Prince's head.

Wanyan Kang lifted his arm to block, but, instead of pain, he felt a tightness around his wrist. Then, outlines of hands and palms weaved back and forth before his eyes. A right hand struck at his shoulder. The Jin Prince had never seen such fast and unusual grappling kung fu. Defending himself with one hand, he struggled to free himself from Squire Lu's clutches.

Meanwhile, Squire Lu's feet had not touched the ground. The weight of his whole person pivoted on Wanyan Kang's wrist. His palm cracked over Wanyan Kang like lightning, five or six savage blows in the space of a single breath.

Wanyan Kang writhed and turned, his legs kicked and flew, but he could neither free himself nor hit back at Squire Lu.

Gasps of surprise overtook the room, as all stood transfixed by Squire Lu's extraordinary skill.

The master of Roaming Cloud Manor brought his palm in attack once more at Wanyan Kang. This time, the Jin Prince scratched his talon-like fingers at the offending hand.

Squire Lu dipped his elbow and knocked the bony joint into the young man's Shoulder Well pressure point, just above the collarbone. Instantly, numbness spread over half of Wanyan Kang's body. His other wrist fell to Squire Lu's grip.

Crack! His joints popped simultaneously.

By the time Wanyan Kang registered the gentle push to his waist and his shoulder through the pain in his wrists, Squire Lu had settled back on his couch. The young man's legs gave out.

The pirates gaped in stunned silence. Then cheers lifted the roof.

"Pa, you're not hurt, are you?" Laurel Lu hobbled over.

Squire Lu reassured his son with a smile, then a look of concern darkened his face. "You must question him thoroughly about the lineage of his kung fu."

Seeing his fellows approach Wanyan Kang with ropes to bind him, Captain Zhang said, "We took some steel manacles last night. They'd be perfect."

A pirate dashed off to fetch the fetters. When he returned, the metal shackles were clamped around Wanyan Kang's wrists and ankles.

"Bring him here," Squire Lu requested.

Two pirates dragged Wanyan Kang over by his arms. Intense pain ripped through his broken wrists. Beads of sweat the size of soybeans formed on his forehead. He fought hard to swallow his groans of pain.

Pop, pop! Squire Lu snapped the dislocated joints back into place with expert precision. He then tapped the pressure points at the bottom of Wanyan Kang's spine and on the left side of his torso.

The Jin Prince could feel the pain fading away as anger and shock took its place. Before he could get another word out, he was escorted back to the prison at Laurel Lu's order.

Once the study was empty, Guo Jing and Lotus Huang emerged from behind the bookshelves. They were confident that Wanyan Kang had not noticed them.

"Please forgive my ungentlemanly conduct," Squire Lu said.

"Who was that man?" Lotus feigned ignorance, quietly noting the similarity between Lu's kung fu and hers. "Did he steal something from you?"

"He has taken rather a lot from us." Squire Lu laughed. "Come, we mustn't let this little rascal spoil your stay."

Squire Lu and Lotus returned to the paintings, discussing each work's composition and admiring the brushwork. Guo Jing listened to this talk of trees and rocks, insects and flowers, but he could comprehend little.

After lunch, Squire Lu sent two servants to show them the caves of Celestial Master Zhang and Hermit Shan Juan the Virtuous. They explored the subterranean wonder until dusk.

That night, as they were getting ready for bed, Guo Jing asked Lotus, "What should we do? Should we help him?"

"Let's wait a few days. I can't quite figure out Squire Lu yet."

"His kung fu is very similar to yours."

"I know!" Then she lowered her voice. "Could he have known Cyclone Mei?"

The line of conversation ended there, for fear that someone might be eavesdropping.

4

NOT LONG AFTER MIDNIGHT, LOTUS HUANG AND GUO JING woke up to the quiet rattle of roof tiles overhead. Then they heard a light scraping on the ground outside. They tiptoed to the window and saw a dark shape duck behind a rosebush. The figure looked around, then ran eastwards. Only an intruder would move with such stealth.

Having witnessed Squire Lu's martial skills, Lotus decided Roaming Cloud Manor must be more than just the base for Lake Tai's pirates. Perhaps this trespasser would lead them to their host's secrets. She jumped out of the window and beckoned Guo Jing to follow.

After trailing the intruder for several dozen paces, Lotus realised she was following a woman and that her kung fu was no better than mediocre. Quickening her steps to take a better look, Lotus caught the interloper's starlit profile as she glanced around, trying to work out her route.

Mercy Mu!

She must be here to rescue her sweetheart! Lotus smiled to herself.

Mercy darted hither and thither around the garden and was soon completely lost. But Lotus knew where they could find Wanyan Kang. The holding cell must be located at the Gnawing Bite, she figured, based on what she had learned from her father. The *I'Ching* stated that this hexagram – with the trigram for Flame placed above the trigram for Thunder – was a suitable location to exercise the law, mete out punishments and build gaols.

Roaming Cloud Manor might be a maze to those unfamiliar with the principles of its construction, but, to Lotus, its layout was straightforward.

Lotus watched with amusement as Mercy hesitated at a fork in the road. The way you bumble around, you won't find him in a hundred years!

She grabbed some earth and flicked a speck to the left.

"That way," Lotus croaked, deepening her voice.

Mercy spun, with her sabre raised. But her reactions were not quick enough. The young couple had long sprinted out of sight using lightness *qinggong*.

Do they mean well? Mercy wondered. She was hopelessly lost. She might as well place her faith in her unseen guide and head down the path as indicated. A flying grain of earth pointed the way whenever the path split. She meandered through courtyards and gardens for some time. Suddenly, something swished past and there was the quiet sound of earth hitting the window frame of a nearby hut. Two blurry shadows flitted past her, heading towards the unassuming structure, then disappeared.

Mercy rushed towards it. As she neared the bungalow, she could make out two stout men lying on the ground by the entrance, clutching their blades. She could feel their eyes following her every move, but they were paralysed by means of their pressure points.

Relieved that a master was watching over her, she nudged the door open, stepped inside and listened.

Yes. She could hear breathing.

"Kang, is that you?" she whispered.

"Yes!" Wanyan Kang replied at once. He had been woken by the thump of the guards hitting the ground.

"Thank the heavens and earth!" Mercy moved closer, guided by his voice. "Let's go."

"Have you got a blade on you?"

"What do you mean?"

Wanyan Kang shifted on the straw mat and his shackles clanked.

Mercy tugged at the fetters. "I shouldn't have given Lotus the dagger. It would cut through this as if it were soft clay."

Of course, she had no idea that Lotus and Guo Jing were listening outside. And no notion of the thought that was going through Lotus's mind: I'd be happy to give you the dagger, but only when you're desperate.

"I'll find the keys."

"No, don't. You can't beat them. You'll put yourself in danger and it won't make any difference."

"Then I'll carry you out of here."

"They've chained me to a pillar."

"What should we do?" She sounded tearful.

"Kiss me."

"This is not the time for jests!" Mercy stamped her foot in exasperation.

"I've never been more serious."

Mercy ignored him. Freeing him was the only thing on her mind.

"How did you know I was here?"

"You know I've been following your entourage."

"Come into my arms. Let me speak to you."

She obeyed without protest, falling into his embrace.

"I'm the Imperial Envoy of the Great Jin Empire. They won't harm me. But, as long as I'm stuck here, I will be thwarted in an important matter Father has entrusted to me." He paused, then added sweetly, "You will help me, won't you, my dear?"

"What is it?"

"Take the gold seal from around my neck."

Mercy felt under his collar and untied a silk cord.

"This is the seal of the Imperial Envoy. Take it to Lin'an and ask for an audience with the Song Chancellor Shi Miyuan."

"The Chancellor? He'd never receive a commoner like me."

"He'll welcome you quickly enough when he sees the seal."

Darkness hid a smug smile from Mercy.

"Tell him I can't be there personally because I'm being held by the pirates of Lake Tai, but that I have one simple message for him. He must not grant the Mongol emissary an audience. The moment they arrive in Lin'an, he must order their arrest and beheading immediately. This is a secret decree, direct from the Great Jin Emperor. It must be followed to the word."

"Why?" She stiffened.

"It's a military matter of the greatest import. You won't understand, even if I explain it. Just repeat what I said to the Song Chancellor and you will have done me a great favour. If the Mongolians get to Lin'an before me, it will be very bad for our Great Jin Empire."

"Our Great Jin Empire? I am Chinese, an honest subject of the Song. I will not do this for you until you have explained everything."

"Aren't you a future royal consort to the Great Jin Empire?"

Mercy shot to her feet. "You are the true-born son of my godfather. You are no Jurchen. You are Han Chinese. Do you really intend to stay a Jin prince? I thought . . . I thought you . . ."

"What?"

"I thought you were a brave and wise man. I thought you were just pretending to be a Jin prince, biding your time so you could do something great for our fatherland. Our Song Empire. Yet, you . . . you actually see that Jin invader as your father!"

Wanyan Kang was alarmed by this change in her. He could sense the words and emotions choking in her throat, and maintained a tactful silence.

"Half of our country is occupied by the Jin." Mercy had found her voice once more. "Our people are murdered, tortured, robbed, suppressed by the Jurchen. Do you really not feel a thing? You . . . You . . ."

She tossed the seal to the floor and made for the door, her face buried in her hands.

"Mercy! I was wrong. Come back."

She stopped.

"When I'm free, I won't play this silly envoy game anymore. I won't go back to Zhongdu. I'll travel south with you. We'll live together, as recluses. We'll be farmers! It would be so much better than feeling wretched like this all the time."

Mercy sighed. When she had lost the Duel for a Maiden to Wanyan Kang, she thought she had given her heart to a hero, an outstanding man. She had convinced herself that he had refused to recognise his birth father, Ironheart Yang, for some noble reason she was yet to understand. When he travelled as the Jin Imperial Envoy, she decided he must be using his position of influence to do something spectacular, something that would aid the restoration of the Song Empire. All along, she had been nothing more than deluded, blinded by her feelings.

He was no great man. He would not hesitate to betray his ancestors for personal gain.

He was a scoundrel.

This was a rude awakening.

"Mercy? My dear . . ."

No answer.

"Ma told me I was sired by your godfather. But, as you know, before I could ask her more about him, they both departed from this world. You don't know how heavy it weighs on my heart. One's birth and bloodline is an important matter. I can't let it lie in doubt like that."

I'm too harsh on him. He doesn't understand his lineage yet. Mercy's heart was softening. "Don't ever mention going to the Song Chancellor again. I will find Lotus and come back with the dagger."

But Lotus had changed her mind: He can stay locked up, for all I care! Papa hates the Jin.

"How did you find your way? This place is a maze," Wanyan Kang asked, after a pause.

"I was guided by two masters, but they stayed in the shadows."

Lotus chuckled silently at being called a master.

Wanyan Kang pondered Mercy's answer. "I worry you might be discovered by the martial masters of this manor when you return with the dagger. If you really want to help me, there's someone I need you to find."

"I'm not going to any Chancellor."

"I know. You've made that very clear. I'm talking about my *shifu* ... Take my belt. Carve this message in the gold hoop: 'Wanyan Kang in trouble at Roaming Cloud Manor on Lake Tai's western shore.' Thirty *li* north of Pingjiang, you will find a desolate hill. Look for a stack of nine human skulls. One on top, three in the middle, five at the bottom. Put the belt under the top one."

"Eh?"

"*Shifu* is blind. Carve it deep. It has to be legible by touch alone."

"I thought your teacher was the Immortal of Eternal Spring. When did Elder Qiu lose his sight?"

"This is my other *shifu*. She will come when she finds the message. Don't tarry in the area once you've set down the belt. *Shifu* can be ... unpredictable. I don't want you to get hurt. Her kung fu is superb; she'll set me free. Wait for me at the Temple of the Impenetrable Sublime, in Pingjiang."

"You must give me your word. Swear to me, you will never betray your country. Promise me you will never again call Wanyan Honglie Father."

"I will act according to my conscience when I understand everything." A distinct note of displeasure had crept into Wanyan Kang's voice. "What's the point of making me swear now? If you don't want to help me, that's fine. It's your decision."

"Fine! I'll deliver your message." Mercy untied Wanyan Kang's belt.

"You're leaving already, my dear? Let me kiss you farewell."

"No!" She was already at the door.

"I fear they'll kill me before *Shifu* arrives. I may never see you again."

Mercy sighed and turned back. It was impossible to steel her heart against him. She leaned into his embrace and let him kiss her on the cheeks.

Wanyan Kang had hoped to use physical contact and sweet whisperings to weaken her resolve, so she would agree to see the Song Chancellor. He could feel her body responding to his tactics. The tingling tremors, the shallow breathing. Mercy's desire was being rekindled.

"If you prove to be dishonourable, there is only one fate left to me. To kill myself before your eyes."

Wanyan Kang had not expected her to speak with such detachment and conviction in this heightened state. By the time he had come to terms with her words, Mercy had left.

Lotus and Guo Jing guided Mercy out of the manor in the same way as they had led her to Wanyan Kang's cell.

After scaling the perimeter wall, the young woman fell to her knees. "Masters, please accept this gesture of gratitude." She kowtowed three times.

A girlish giggle rang in the air. "Oh dear, we don't deserve that."

Mercy looked around. The stars were shimmering, the flowers fluttering in the breeze, but there was not so much as half a shadow in sight.

The voice sounded so like Lotus. But why would Lotus be here? Even if it was her, how would she know the way?

Mercy turned the night's events over and over in her head as she walked away from the manor. Before long, she had traversed more than a dozen *li*. Tired, she rested under a tree until the morning, when she would find passage across Lake Tai to Pingjiang.

5

PINGJIANG WAS A FLOURISHING CITY OF SILKS AND GARDENS, almost as wealthy and bustling as the capital, Lin'an. There was a well-known saying, comparing the glory of the two cities with the celestial realm: "Above are the heavens, on earth Pingjiang and Lin'an." Now, with the Song Imperial Court's relocation to the south, all the riches south of the Huai River were gathered in these two cities. Nowhere else in the world could compare with their opulent architecture or the affluence of the inhabitants. The Song Emperor and officials, indulging in the peace and prosperity that yet reigned in the south, had forgotten the groans and sufferings of their people in the north, who were being trampled daily under the iron hooves of their Jurchen overlords.

Yet, Pingjiang's urbane sights were of no interest to Mercy Mu. She found a quiet corner in which to carve the message into Wanyan Kang's belt hoop. Holding the belt, her mind wandered back to yesternight, when it was still fastened around its owner's waist. She prayed it would encircle his body once more, and that one day she would have the pleasure of clasping it shut. That would mean he had understood his parentage and sworn allegiance to a just cause. There would be hope for their union.

She tied the belt under her outer garments and felt her heart pounding. It was as if she was wrapped in his embrace. She blushed at the thought.

The sun had started to sink below the horizon in the west and she turned her mind to the task at hand. She had a quick snack at a noodle shop and went north, as instructed.

As she left the city, her surroundings grew desolate. The sun disappeared behind the hills to the cries of unseen birds in the distance. Though unnerved, she pushed on, veering off the road into a valley.

By now, only the last hint of twilight remained. There was no sign of the skulls Wanyan Kang had described. She would have to spend the night here in the wilderness and resume her search when it was light again. She climbed up a hill to look for shelter. Eventually, she spotted some structures by a hillock in the west.

Relieved that she had found a roof for the night, she ran towards them. She was greeted by a dispiriting sight. A broken sign hung above the entrance: *Temple of the Earth God*. Gingerly, she gave the doors a nudge. They tipped back and crashed to the ground, throwing up a great cloud of dirt and soot as they did so. She waited a moment before tiptoeing into the main hall. The Earth God and the Earth Goddess were cloaked in dust and wrapped in spider webs. A large altar table sat before the deities. She pressed her weight on it. The wood felt strong and the structure solid. It would work as a bed. She busied herself making the place habitable for the night. She collected some straw and wiped the dust off her makeshift bed, then propped the doors back up to block the entrance — two flimsy guards against the outside world. When all was ready, she ate some dried bread and rested her head on her knapsack.

But Mercy could find no rest. Wanyan Kang filled her thoughts. Tears fell down her cheeks as she thought about his continued allegiance to the Jin, a dark cloud over their future together, but she smiled all the same at the memory of his sweet words and even sweeter touch. Conflicting feelings kept sleep at bay until late into the night.

Waves of whirring and hissing washed over the abandoned temple, waking Mercy from her uneasy sleep. She sat up and listened. The noise was coming closer. She peered through the gap between the doors. What she saw made her tremble in fear.

Hundreds, perhaps thousands of snakes were slithering eastwards past the temple. Their scales glistened under the moon. A peculiar stench filled the air. It was a long time before the serpents began to thin out. Then she heard footsteps. Three men, dressed head to toe in white, brought up the rear, each prodding the ground with a long staff.

Mercy huddled behind one of the doors, hoping that the men had not noticed her. Once out of earshot, she peeped her head out again. Her surroundings were once again returned to their night-time hush, giving no hint of the scene Mercy had just witnessed. She opened the doors wider and stuck her head out completely. Tentatively, she stepped into the open and ventured in the direction the snakes had taken, but the three men had disappeared into the night. There was no point in looking. As she headed back to the temple with relief, she caught sight of a splash of white shimmering against a nearby rock. She slowly approached, and then barely suppressed a yelp.

Skulls, stacked neatly.

One on top, three in the middle and five at the bottom.

Exactly nine skulls.

The very thing she had been looking for all evening. Nonetheless, this unexpected encounter set her heart racing. She edged near the grotesque objects and, trembling, reached for the skull at the top. Her fingers slipped into the five holes in the crown. The cranium opened up and swallowed her hand! Jolting back, she screamed. She stumbled back a few steps, before managing to gather her wits. She paused, then laughed a little at herself.

What a strange *shifu*! Is she as frightening as these skulls? Mercy wondered, as she walked back to the pile of bones and placed the belt under the top skull.

Master, I hope you will find the belt and free him, she prayed silently. I hope you will guide him to change his ways, so he can become the honourable man he was born to be.

Just then, a tap on her shoulder.

The shock chased Wanyan Kang's handsome face from Mercy's mind. She leapt over the pile of skulls. Holding her arms over her chest for protection, she turned.

Another tap on the shoulder. She turned again. No-one.

Tap. Turn. Nothing.

Nothing behind her, not even a shadow.

Tap.

Mercy was now too spooked to move. Is this a ghost? A demon? A monster? A cold sweat broke out across her skin as her mind raced through a list of all the kinds of supernatural beings that haunt the night.

"Who are you?" A feeble squeak.

"Hmm . . . Such a sweet scent!"

Someone was sniffing the back of her neck.

"Guess who?!"

She spun round.

A white scholar's robe. A gentleman's folding fan. He's one of the men who drove Papa to his death!

Mercy fled.

But he was much faster. Suddenly she found that she was throwing herself headlong into his open arms. She veered to the left. With a couple of strides, the man overtook her. Waiting, arms wide to receive her. He leered. She dashed in another direction. But there he was again.

It was all a game to Gallant Ouyang. He only needed a fraction of his kung fu and the girl would be firmly in his clutches. But why spoil the fun?

Sha, sha! Mercy hacked her willow sabre at his head.

"My, my! Like it rough, eh?"

Gallant Ouyang reclined a little as he lifted his right hand to guide her arms away. He grabbed the chance to snake his arm around her waist.

Mercy squirmed and struggled against his inappropriate embrace. She felt a numbness between her thumb and forefinger. The sabre was snatched from her grasp and clattered to the ground. For a moment, she thought she had repelled his offensive hands. But they returned, twining tighter around her body. His fingers closed around her wrists, squeezing her pulse and cutting off her strength.

"Call me *Shifu* and I'll let you go this instant." Gallant Ouyang flashed an amorous grin and shifted her arms into the grip of one hand so he could caress her face. "I'll also teach you how to break free. But I suspect, by then, you'd want my arms around you all day."

Paralysed by the fear that he might rob her of her chastity, Mercy blacked out. When she came to, she felt limp and unable to summon any energy in her body.

For a moment, she thought the strong arms encircling her were Wanyan Kang's. She opened her eyes. Gallant Ouyang's face filled her vision. She tried to kick and scream. But her body would not respond and her cries were muffled, gagged by a handkerchief that had been tied over her mouth.

Her captor ignored her. His entire focus was taken up by something ahead. Why did he look anxious, suddenly?

Though Mercy had lost control of her body, she could still move her eyes and turn her head. She could feel through her back that she was lying across Gallant Ouyang's lap and he was sitting cross-legged on the ground. She glimpsed four women flanking them on either side, dressed in matching white outfits. Their weapons unsheathed, they were staring at the same fixed point in nervous anticipation.

She followed their gaze.

The skulls.

They're waiting for his *shifu*, she thought, as she looked in the other direction.

A waking nightmare confronted her. The dark landscape had come alive in a moving sea of red ripples, as far as her eyes could see. Tens of thousands of snakes, wiggling their forked tongues. The three men she had seen earlier stood among the serpents, their staffs raised in expectation.

Mercy looked across at the skulls and focused her eyes on the golden hoop of Wanyan Kang's belt, watching as it glimmered in the moonlight. She came to a sudden realisation: they must have planned this attack on Wanyan Kang's *shifu*. How could she take on so many enemies and snakes on her own?

Terror seized Mercy. Part of her prayed that Wanyan Kang's *shifu* would not appear, as she would not want anybody important to her beloved to be in danger. Yet, this mysterious mentor was also her only hope. Who else could defeat her villainous captor and deliver her from this horrible fate?

By now, the men and the snakes had been waiting for more than an hour. Gallant Ouyang was checking the position of the moon with increasing frequency.

Maybe his *shifu* will arrive when the moon reaches its highest point, Mercy thought, as she watched moonbeams caress the tips of the nearby pine trees and colour the cloudless night with a wash of indigo.

There was no sound but the screeching of owls over the ever-present humming of insects. Gallant Ouyang looked at the sky once more and passed Mercy Mu into the arms of one of the women next to him. He stared at the hills beyond, his folding fan poised in his right hand.

Wanyan Kang's *shifu* must be about to arrive, any moment now.

A distant shriek punctured the air.

At the foot of the hill, a whirlwind of a shadow morphed into a woman with long unkempt hair.

Iron Corpse Cyclone Mei had managed to unblock the trapped energy in her Long Strong pressure point within a month of learning the secrets of *neigong* from Guo Jing. Not only had she regained the use of her legs, her internal strength had also grown significantly. But with her hideout in the Prince of Zhao's residence exposed, she had travelled south with Wanyan Kang's entourage. She had no desire to sail across Lake Tai with them, however, as being confined to a small cabin would force her to abandon her midnight kung fu practice. So she travelled on foot around the lake instead, having arranged to rejoin the young Prince at Pingjiang.

Of course, she did not know that Wanyan Kang had been taken prisoner by the pirates of Lake Tai. Nor that Gallant Ouyang had been following her, plotting to avenge the insult he suffered, for she had killed four of his concubines and torn his robe. Moreover, he was determined to get his hands on the Nine Yin Manual and had been waiting for an opportunity to ambush her.

The moment Cyclone Mei emerged from between the hills, she slowed.

Breathing. More than one person. And what was that faint hissing noise?

She halted.

The blind hag has sensed us! Gallant Ouyang cursed silently, but they still had the element of surprise to their advantage.

Flicking his fan, he stood up, ready to lunge. Just as the energy coursed to his toes, the appearance of a second figure forced him to pull back.

Hovering on cloud and riding on fog, this newcomer drifted in like a phantom, his feet barely touching the ground. He stood behind Cyclone Mei and cast his eyes over Gallant Ouyang and his creatures.

Tall and thin, he wore a green robe and a square scarf over his hair – the trappings of an educated man. Yet, one look at his face would make anyone's skin crawl. Cold to the core. Wooden to the extreme. Lifeless and expressionless, his was the look of the undead, frozen except for the eyes.

However, it was the stranger's kung fu that really gave Gallant Ouyang the chills.

Even Cyclone Mei walks with a scratching noise, Gallant thought. Somehow, this man moves in almost complete silence. I must act fast.

With that thought, the Master of White Camel Mount made a signal with his left hand. The snake herders whistled and the serpents surged, slithering around Mercy Mu and the eight women in white.

Cyclone Mei gathered her *qi* and leapt back several paces. She had, by now, worked out that the unusual noise was the sound of thousands of writhing snakes. With a twist of her body, she unwound a long whip from her waist and whisked up a silvery circle of protection.

Mercy could see the fear in the woman's face. Was this his *shifu*?

The snake herders brandished their staffs and the serpents

scattered. In no time at all, the snakes had surrounded Cyclone Mei. Those in the front line sprang to attack at the whistles' urging, but Mei's lash sent them flying back.

"Give me the Nine Yin Manual and I'll let you go, hag!" Gallant Ouyang called.

He had been planning the attack since he learned the Manual was in Cyclone Mei's possession, in Wanyan Honglie's palace. His uncle, Viper Ouyang, had spent decades searching for the coveted martial-arts tract. If he managed to seize it from her, it would elevate his standing, not only in his uncle's eyes, but in the eyes of the whole martial world. It would make his trip to the Central Plains worthwhile.

Receiving no reply, the Master of White Camel Mount said, "I don't mind waiting. Go on. Wave your whip. You can do it for hours. Until daybreak, if you like. Let's see who gives up first."

The moonlight danced with the silver coil. A thousand rays flashed.

Cyclone Mei kept her tongue in check and her whip airborne. Time was not on her side. Her strength, as he had predicted, would soon be spent. Was there a way out? Deadly serpents in every direction. She might be bitten if she moved her foot by a mere inch. And once the venom had entered her bloodstream, no kung fu would be able to help her.

Relishing his control of the situation, Gallant Ouyang sat down again and addressed Mei with mock familiarity. "Sister Mei, you've had the Manual for twenty years. Surely you know it by heart, by now? Why hang on to a tatty old book? Lend it to me and we can be friends."

"Call off your snakes first."

"I'll happily oblige, as soon as I hold the Manual in my hands."

I'll tear it to pieces first, Cyclone Mei thought to herself. The Manual was the only memento she had left of her husband, Hurricane Chen. It was dearer to her than life itself. And she had vowed never to let it fall into enemy hands.

Mercy Mu wanted to shout, *Jump into the trees!* but the gag swallowed her words. Without her sight, Cyclone Mei did not realise she could find refuge in the silent pine trees standing just beside her.

Mei reached inside the pocket in her shirt. "Fine! I admit defeat. Come and get it."

"Throw it to me."

"Catch!"

She flicked her right hand. The air murmured.

Two women in white were hit by something and slumped sideways. Gallant Ouyang threw himself to the ground and rolled away.

"You'll regret this, crone!" he yelled in anger. "You'll be begging me for death when I've finished with you!" He regained his footing and retreated to a safe distance as a cold sweat broke out across his back.

Cyclone Mei had not expected to miss her target. Few could detect her Vanishing Needles, lightning fast and silent as they were. Even fewer could evade them. She felt a grudging respect for her opponent's kung fu.

Gallant Ouyang watched her hands carefully, now that he was out of her range. She continued to lash her whip, but, having done so for more than an hour, her defences were beginning to weaken. Gallant urged the snakes forward.

Mei could sense the hundreds of snakes at her feet, and could still hear thousands more approaching. She could last only so long. How am I going to get out of this? she asked herself as she tightened the circle of protection to conserve energy.

Noticing how she was growing short of breath, Gallant Ouyang knew the moment was close and signalled the herders to keep the pressure up. Yet, a part of him feared closing in on her too quickly, in case she realised death was upon her and she destroyed the Manual. His whole focus was now on her free hand, ready to intercept the second he sighted the Manual.

Mei clutched onto the Manual in her shirt pocket as the snakes edged closer. She was angry at the thought of being bested by these legless, scaly creatures, and frustrated because her husband's death would go forever unavenged.

Just then, music resounded in the hills, clear as the twang of a zither string or the clang of jade. The night quivered to the airy bright tones of the *xiao* flute.

The tune came from the green-robed man, now sitting atop a pine tree.

When did he get up there? Gallant Ouyang prided himself on his powers of observation. It was inconceivable that he could have missed the man climbing the tree on such a clear, moonlit night. He was even more alarmed by the way the stranger was perched on the tip of a branch, swaying to and fro with the wind. Effortlessly steady. Even if he spent years devoting himself to the practice of lightness kung fu under his uncle's guidance, Gallant Ouyang would never be able to attain such ease. Could he be a ghost?

The man had only been playing for a short time, yet Gallant Ouyang began to feel the corners of his lips tugged upwards by the melody. As each note wove tightly into the next, an indescribable feeling rose and spread like wildfire inside him. How he yearned to feed the rapture with dancing!

As he lifted his arm and kicked his foot to the rhythm, he noticed his women and snake herders careering towards the tree from which the music was emanating. Spinning and raving, they tore at their clothes, pulled at their hair and scratched their cheeks. Manic grins split their grazed, bloodied faces. Intoxicated by the flute song, they did not seem to feel pain.

A feeble voice of clarity warned Gallant Ouyang to control his heart and mind. Tapping some hidden resource of strength, he dug out six poisoned silver shuttles and flung them at the musician's head, chest and abdomen. The man flicked each of them away with the end of his *xiao*. All the while, the flute's mouthpiece never left his lips. The music did not pause for a second.

The melody turned and soared. Gallant Ouyang could no longer steel himself against its call. He unfurled his fan, ready to dance.

Right then, the last remaining kernel of self-control acquired over decades of kung fu training spoke to him: *Tear a piece of cloth from your sleeves. Seal your ears against his music. Or you'll dance to your death if he keeps on playing.*

Cyclone Mei was also struggling. She sat cross-legged, her head bowed, in an attempt to gather her inner strength to resist the lure of the music. Meanwhile, Mercy Mu had had a lucky escape. Though the melody played havoc inside her, she lay in perfect stillness, her movements locked through her acupressure points.

Gallant Ouyang managed to wrench his arms from the music long enough to tear a piece of fabric from the front of his shirt. But his hands hovered just beyond his ears, unwilling to shut out the bewitching song. Three of his women with lesser kung fu were now completely ensnared, rolling on the ground as they ripped and shredded their clothes.

The mental battle against the music had drenched Gallant Ouyang in sweat. His cheeks were flushed, his heart raced, his throat was parched and his tongue dry. If he let the frenzy within boil over, he would not survive till morning.

Mustering all the strength and willpower left in him, Gallant Ouyang crushed his teeth down on his tongue. The pain pierced through the music's hold for a brief moment, giving him the chance to flee. And flee he did, until the ghost of the flute song could no longer haunt him. When he finally stopped, several *li* away, he was drained, as if his body were fighting against a grave illness.

Only one thought remained in his tortured mind: Who was that?

6

BACK AT ROAMING CLOUD MANOR, GUO JING AND LOTUS Huang spent their days sightseeing around Lake Tai and their evenings discussing painting and literature with Squire Lu.

"We should tell Squire Lu about Cyclone Mei." Guo Jing knew her arrival would bring carnage to the manor. "We can persuade him to let Wanyan Kang go, to save everyone on the estate."

Lotus shook her head. "There's something rotten about Wanyan Kang. He won't change if he's let off the hook so easily."

In truth, Lotus cared little about Wanyan Kang's rotten nature. As the disciple of two great evils – Qiu Chuji and Cyclone Mei – he could never be any good. Yet she was counting on him as Mercy Mu's betrothed, so no busybody could make Guo Jing marry that poor orphan. And, to fulfil that role, Wanyan Kang would have to mend his ways.

"What do we do when Cyclone Mei arrives?" Guo Jing had his mind on more pressing matters.

"We can try out Count Seven's moves!"

Knowing Lotus's temperament, Guo Jing knew nothing he could say would persuade her to warn Squire Lu. He promised himself he would do anything in his power to help their host.

Three days after Mercy's midnight break-in, while Lotus and Guo Jing were having their morning conversation with Squire Lu, Laurel rushed into the study with a strange look on his face. A servant hurried after him, carrying a wooden tray covered in a green cloth.

"Pa, this was delivered to the manor just now," Laurel Lu said, unveiling the object on the tray.

A skull. Five holes in the crown. The emblem of Cyclone Mei.

"Who . . . ? Who brought it?" The blood had drained from Squire Lu's face.

"We don't know. I have already sent men to find the messenger, but we've had no luck yet," Laurel Lu replied, shaken by his father's reaction. "It was dropped off like an ordinary delivery. There was nothing unusual about the box or the bearer. The servants thought it was a gift, so they tipped the man and sent it to the bookkeeper's office to be logged. Do you know what it means, Pa?"

Squire Lu pushed himself up from his seat to examine the skull. His fingers slotted smoothly into the holes.

"Are they made by a human hand?" Laurel Lu could not imagine anyone with such strength.

Squire Lu nodded, but did not speak for a long time. "Pack up the valuables at once and escort your mother to our northern mansion in Wuxi. Order the captains and their men to stay in their camps for the next three days. No matter what happens at Roaming Cloud Manor, they must not interfere. Hurry!"

"Why, Pa?"

Squire Lu ignored the question and turned to his guests with a wry smile. "Alas, your stay here is cut short. I had hoped that we might have longer together. However, I have, over time, made two fearsome enemies and they will soon be here to take their revenge . . . A disaster is about to befall Roaming Cloud Manor. If I survive, we shall meet again, but the likelihood is very slim . . ." He trailed off and addressed the pageboy instead. "Fetch fifty *taels* of gold."

Laurel Lu knew better than to ask questions, and slipped away to carry out his father's orders, followed by the pageboy.

When the servant returned with a tray of gold *sycee* ingots, Squire Lu said to Guo Jing, "Brother Guo and the young lady are a match made in the heavens. Please accept this humble gift for the day you become man and wife."

Lotus blushed, dying to ask Squire Lu when he had first seen through her disguise and how he had worked out that the two of them were yet to marry. However, she knew it would be rude to interrupt her host at this moment, and kept quiet.

Not versed in the etiquette of ritual refusal, Guo Jing thanked his host and accepted the generous gift.

Squire Lu picked up a porcelain bottle from his desk and carefully tipped dozens of small crimson pills onto a piece of soft parchment paper. "I acquired a little medical knowledge from my gracious teacher. These pills took some effort to make. They can improve your health and extend your years. A small token to celebrate our friendship."

They had a delicate fragrance that Lotus knew well. She had

helped her father make them, collecting the morning dew from petals of nine different flowers and pairing it with the rarest and most precious medicinal herbs. She remembered how each step in the process could only be performed during a particular season and at a specific time of day. This was a truly lavish gift.

"The Dew of Nine Flowers is very hard to come by. This is too great an honour," Lotus said.

"My lady knows about them?" Surprise flashed across Squire Lu's face.

"I was a sickly child and was once given three such pills. Their effect was exceptional."

Squire Lu put the pills back in the bottle and sealed it tight. Then, taking great care, he wrapped it twice in tin paper. They were clearly very precious to him. "I have little use for them. Please accept this gift."

It was obvious Squire Lu was not expecting to survive his encounter with Cyclone Mei. Lotus accepted the pills with gratitude.

"A boat will be ready to take you across the lake at once. No matter what you encounter along the way, you must not turn back."

Guo Jing was about to offer his help, but, after one look at Lotus, he swallowed his words and nodded.

"Might I ask sir an impertinent question?" Lotus said.

"Please."

"I surmise that you are not confident that you can subdue your enemies, and yet you also have no intention of taking refuge. I am not sure I understand."

"They are the source of my misery." Squire Lu sighed and pointed at his legs. "This is their bequest. But my suffering is insignificant compared to the wrong they have done my mentor. And this is the offence I must avenge. I shall defy them unto death. I doubt I will overcome them, but I hope my demise will also be theirs. And that is the only way I can repay the immense kindness *Shifu* has shown me."

Why does he keep saying "them"? Does he not know Copper Corpse Hurricane Chen is dead? How did he get tangled up with

Twice Foul Dark Wind? Though curious, Lotus kept these questions to herself.

Laurel Lu re-entered the study and made his report quietly. "Captain Zhang, Captain Gu, Captain Wang and Captain Tan refuse to leave the manor. They said they would sooner lose their heads for insubordination than desert Roaming Cloud Manor in its hour of need."

Squire Lu smiled at the pirates' devotion. "Son, see our guests out safely, and quickly."

Guo Jing and Lotus bid their host farewell and followed Laurel Lu out of the manor. Ulaan and their other horse were already waiting on the boat.

"Shall we go aboard?" Guo Jing whispered.

"Yes, and then we will turn back."

Just as they were about to step aboard, Lotus saw a man striding towards them along the waterfront, balancing a large vat on his head. She pointed at him.

Grizzled and bearded, the man wore a summer shirt woven from arrowroot and held a palm-leaf fan in his hand. The vessel on his head was wrought iron, and must have weighed hundreds of *jin*. However, his steps were light and nimble, and he hurried past them without as much as a glance in their direction.

Once he was several paces past their boat, the man swayed casually and water sloshed over his head. An iron tub full of water! Laurel Lu was astonished. That surely doubled its weight. He must be a martial master. Otherwise, how could he walk with such an enormous weight, as if it were nothing?

Could he be Papa's enemy? Ignoring the danger, Laurel Lu went after the stranger.

Guo Jing caught Lotus's eye and followed Laurel Lu. He remembered his *shifus* telling him about the fight with Qiu Chuji at the Garden of the Eight Drunken Immortals, and the wine-filled bronze censer they had hurled around to test each other's strength.

This tub is bigger than the one my *shifus* told me about. Could this man be more skilled than Elder Eternal Spring? Guo Jing was impressed.

The man carried the load for another *li*, to where a stream fed the lake, its banks scattered with untended graves. Laurel Lu knew there was no bridge in the vicinity and wondered which way he would turn.

An incredible sight stopped all three in their tracks. The man walked straight into the water and crossed the stream. Only his feet were submerged. His body was as steady as if he were walking on land. He set down the vat on the far bank and returned in the same way – treading on water!

Lotus had heard of many martial sects and kung fu moves, but nothing of what she was witnessing now. Walking on water was a mythical skill in the *wulin*. It was impossible. But she had just seen it with her own eyes. This man must be an extraordinary master.

The man addressed Laurel Lu. "You must be Young Squire Lu, leader of the Lake Tai pirates."

"Might I ask the Elder's name?" Laurel Lu bowed.

He stroked his beard and laughed. "And our young friends over there. Do come over here!"

Laurel Lu turned and, to his surprise, found Guo Jing and Lotus Huang kowtowing to the stranger, not three paces from where he himself stood. He had never imagined that his father's guests were skilled in lightness kung fu and could move so fast in near total silence.

"You're too polite." The older man waved the homage away, but was clearly pleased. He addressed the pirate leader once more. "Is there somewhere we can sit and talk?"

"Does the Elder know my father?" Laurel Lu asked warily.

"I haven't had the pleasure of making his acquaintance yet."

"My father received an unusual gift today. Does the Elder know anything about it?" The young man wanted to gauge whether this stranger had anything to do with his father's enemies.

"What was it?"

"A skull with five holes in the crown."

"How peculiar! Could someone be playing a trick on your esteemed father?"

If he was Papa's enemy, he wouldn't need to lie. With kung fu of that level, he could have easily come straight to our main gate, Laurel Lu reasoned. With a master like him on our side, we won't have to fear whoever sent the skull.

He relaxed visibly and said with warmth, "It would be my honour to serve the Elder tea at our humble estate."

The stranger considered the invitation before nodding. "Our young friends are from the manor too?"

"They are my father's friends," Laurel Lu replied deferentially. He invited his guest to lead the way.

The man took no further notice of Guo Jing and Lotus. When they arrived at Roaming Cloud Manor, Laurel Lu settled everyone in the front hall before hurrying inside to inform his father.

A few moments later, Squire Lu was carried by two servants into the room on a bamboo chair. He cupped his hands in respect. "We are honoured that the Elder has deigned to grace our humble manor with his presence."

"There is no need for ceremony, Squire Lu." The man inclined his head fractionally in acknowledgement.

"Might I ask the Elder's name?"

"My family name is Qiu, the given name is Qianren."

"The Master is honoured as Iron Palm Water Glider in the *jianghu*." Squire Lu sounded surprised.

The man smiled. "I thought my name had long been forgotten."

Squire Lu knew that Qiu Qianren led the Iron Palm Gang and wielded great influence over Hunan and Sichuan, in the south and south-west of China. Many years ago, this Master of the martial world had put up his sword and become a recluse. Young people of the *wulin* today would not have heard of this great man.

"Might I ask what important business brings Master Qiu to this part of the country?" Squire Lu had many more questions, but he did not want to appear impertinent, so he added, "If I could be of service, I would most certainly oblige."

"My business here is too trivial to trouble you with." Qiu Qianren smiled and stroked his beard. "Suffice to say that I am not finished with the martial world just yet ... Indeed, with your leave, I would find a quiet spot to practise in now. We shall speak at length this evening."

Although Qiu Qianren had signalled the conversation was over, Squire Lu persisted with one last question. "Did Master Qiu come across Twice Foul Dark Wind on his way here?"

"Oh, are that infernal pair still alive?"

Smiling with relief, Squire Lu said, "Son, please show Master Qiu to my study." The martial Master nodded in farewell and followed Laurel Lu out of the hall.

"I am happy you are back. Master Qiu's martial training is far beyond the reach of us mere mortals. With him among us, I do not fear my enemies. You will be safe if you stay in your room," Squire Lu said to Guo Jing and Lotus.

He recalled that Qiu Qianren was invited to the Contest at Mount Hua to fight the Five Greats – Heretic of the East, Venom of the West, King of the South, Beggar of the North and Central Divinity. Though Iron Palm Water Glider did not take part, he must have been a martial master of the very highest level just to receive an invitation. The idea that such a man was here as his guest was a great comfort to Squire Lu.

"Oh, but we'd love to watch the fight!" Lotus said.

"I worry my enemies might bring help and I'd be too preoccupied to look after you. I would not wish any harm to befall you." After a pause, Squire Lu continued, though perhaps speaking more to reassure himself, "However, with Master Qiu here, we shall have nothing to fear. Please make sure you stay by my side at all times."

"I love kung fu fights." Lotus clapped her hands together. "Your exchange with the little Jin Prince was thrilling!"

"My enemies taught that young man, but they are far stronger. That is why I was so concerned."

"Really?"

"Miss Huang, perhaps you do not quite understand martial matters. Remember how he hurt my son? That very same kung fu dug the holes in the skull you saw this morning."

"So the martial arts are just like painting and calligraphy? Where one can tell at a glance which school and style a work belongs to?" Lotus was playing the innocent, as ever. "Like how we can tell from Wang Xianzhi's calligraphy that he studied under his father, Wang Xizhi, who was taught by Madam Wei, who in turn learned from Zhong Yao?"

"Indeed, my lady is most perceptive. However, these enemies of mine are ruthless and brutal. The comparison may offend our great calligraphers."

Lotus smiled and took Guo Jing's hand. "Shall we pay the whitebeard a visit and see what he's doing?"

"We mustn't disturb the Master." Squire Lu tried to stop her politely.

"We'll be as quiet as a mouse!" Giggling, she headed for the study, hand in hand with Guo Jing.

Confined to his chair, Squire Lu called after Lotus, "The Master might get upset if you watch him train, without an invitation."

The servants scrambled to lift their master's chair and hurried after the mischievous couple. By the time Squire Lu had caught up with Lotus and Guo Jing, their faces were already pressed up close to one of the study windows, peering through the holes they had made in the window paper.

Hearing the servants' approach, Lotus signalled them to stay quiet and beckoned Squire Lu to come over.

If she continues in her wilful ways, Qiu Qianren will know we're spying on him. I'd better indulge her, Squire Lu thought, and so he gestured at his servants. They lifted him off the chair and steadied him as he walked over to the window on tiptoes. Lotus stepped back to let him look in on the remarkable scene that had so transfixed her and Guo Jing.

The martial Master sat cross-legged, with his eyes half closed. A stream of smoke billowed from his mouth.

Squire Lu remembered his *shifu* telling him about the most advanced kung fu from different martial branches and styles, but he had never heard of this technique. But he should not be snooping on his guest, and he tugged at Guo Jing's sleeve. The young man understood at once. Straightening up, he took Lotus's hand and returned to the hall with his host.

Lotus giggled. "The whitebeard is great fun! He has a fire burning in his belly!"

"It seems he was practising an extremely potent inner-strength technique."

"Can he breathe fire?" Lotus found Qiu Qianren's kung fu truly mystifying.

"What Master Qiu was doing is no conjurer's trick."

Lotus's antics gave Squire Lu an idea. He sent his son to the pirate captains with a new command: Waylay any martial heroes sailing on the lake or travelling on nearby roads and invite them to the manor. He also ordered his household to throw open the main gate and stand by to welcome guests.

That evening, the main hall of Roaming Cloud Manor was bright as day. Dozens of enormous candles illuminated the round banqueting table in the middle of the room. Laurel Lu personally led Qiu Qianren to the best seat at the table. Guo Jing and Lotus Huang were each shown to a secondary place of honour, while Squire Lu and his son took their seats last.

After a few rounds of wine and a gentle discussion about the area surrounding the manor, Qiu Qianren cleared his throat and said, "Squire Lu, you must be an exceptional martial artist to lead the pirates of Lake Tai. Could I persuade you to show us a few moves?"

"I have long been indisposed and what little I learned is long out of practice."

"Who is your *shifu*? Perhaps I know him."

Squire Lu heaved a sigh and did not speak for a long time. "I was young, and through my ignorance I was brought down by another. Master, pardon my silence, I do not wish to tarnish my teacher's reputation."

That's why he hides his martial knowledge from us. Papa was thrown out by his *shifu*! Laurel Lu now understood. Whatever happened back then, it must be a most painful memory. If the Jin dog hadn't injured me, Papa would have never revealed that he knew any martial arts at all.

"My friend, you are in your prime and a leader of a formidable company of men, no less. You should seize life in your hand and do something worthy of your standing," Qiu Qianren said, paying no attention to Squire Lu's reticence and resignation. "It will ease the grievances you have suffered. Your martial elders must certainly regret their behaviour towards you."

"I am crippled, Master. I appreciate your kind advice. I might have the will, but my body will not stretch to great deeds."

"You are too modest. I see a bright path ahead of you."

"Please point the way, Master."

With a cryptic smile, Qiu Qianren turned his attention to the feast. Squire Lu knew his probings must relate to the matter that had enticed the martial Master back to the *jianghu* after more than a decade. Only etiquette held his curiosity in check. It would be unmannerly to question his guest and social senior outright.

"I am certain the man who built Roaming Cloud Manor's great reputation was a disciple of the most esteemed martial master of the *wulin*," Qiu Qianren said, breaking a long silence.

"My son manages the affairs of the manor. He studied under Abbot Withered Wood of Cloudy Perch Temple in Lin'an."

"Ah, Withered Wood of the Immortal Cloud Sect. This Shaolin branch has passable kung fu. Perhaps the Young Squire would care to show this old man a few moves?"

Laurel Lu stood up and bowed. "I humbly seek your guidance, Master." He knew a few words of advice from this martial great would bring a lifetime of benefits.

The young man positioned himself in the centre of the hall and settled into the opening stance of the Tiger Taming Arhat Fist, a kung fu he was most proud of. His punches roared with force, his kicks flew like shadows. The power and precision of the moves were testament not just to his talent, but also to the skill of his teacher.

Suddenly, he howled like a tiger and the candles flickered. The elaborate sequence of punches had whipped up a draught in the hall. The servants glanced at each other, trembling in fear.

Leaping, turning, rolling, pouncing, he prowled and growled like a tiger on the hunt. Then he held his left palm upright over his chest in the Tathagata Buddha's Mudra, his thumb curled and the rest of the fingers straight and pointing upwards. The predator sprang. The monk struck. The animal's snarls weakened as the arhat's blows quickened.

He hurled his fist down. *Thwack!* A floor tile fractured at the impact. He then flattened his palm to the ground and thrust, extending himself to his full height with mighty force. His left palm pushed skywards and his right foot kicked high, steady as a sculpture of he who attained nirvana.

Laurel Lu held the pose for some time before drawing his strength back into his core, to thunderous cheers from Guo Jing and Lotus Huang. He cupped his hands over his chest and bowed deeply at Qiu Qianren. The old man smiled but said nothing.

"I hope my son did not embarrass himself." It was Squire Lu who broke the silence.

"The young man has shown us an excellent exercise for strengthening the body, but it is useless in combat."

The bluntness of Qiu Qianren's words took everyone by surprise. Squire Lu replied humbly, "We should be most grateful if Master would illuminate the Way."

The martial Master left the table and wandered into the courtyard, without another word.

Guo Jing, meanwhile, was scratching his head. How could it be useless? Laurel Lu may not be a master, but he has a strong grasp of his branch of kung fu.

When Qiu Qianren returned, he held a brick in each hand. He closed his fingers around them. With very little effort on his part, they crumbled into small pieces. Then he clenched his fists. What was left of the bricks disintegrated into powder. Two handfuls of dust poured down onto the table.

Yet another type of kung fu no-one had ever seen before.

After demonstrating this incredible move, Qiu Qianren pulled open the front of his shirt, swept the dust inside, then went out again to empty it in the courtyard.

"It is impressive, shattering a tile with a punch," the martial Master said when he had finished cleaning up. "But your opponents aren't going to stand still and wait for your attack. If they have more developed inner strength, then all the power in your strike will rebound onto you and cause you grave injury. So, for your skill to be of any use, you need to be able to crush stone into dust."

Laurel Lu nodded at the profundity of the words.

"There are many who attempt to learn the martial arts," Qiu Qianren continued, "but only a small handful manage to master true kung fu."

"Who are these masters?" Lotus Huang asked.

"The Heretic of the East, the Venom of the West, the King of the South, the Beggar of the North and Central Divinity are regarded as the greatest martial masters of our time. Central Divinity Wang Chongyang possessed superior internal energy, whereas the other four have their unique strengths and weaknesses. If one comes to understand their individual shortcomings, it would not be so difficult to overpower them."

The only person in the hall not astonished by this claim was Laurel Lu, as he had never heard of the Five Greats. Lotus, though impressed by the older man's display, would not let a slight on her father slip by so easily. "Master, you should confront these Five Greats to make your name!"

"Central Divinity has passed away now. I had affairs of my own to tend to that year when they held the Contest of Mount Hua," Qiu Qianren said. "That is why the Taoist monk was named the Greatest Martial Master Under the Heavens.

"At that time, the five of them were fighting over some martial tract called the Nine Yin Manual. Whoever had the strongest kung fu would take custody of the book. After seven days and seven nights, Eastern Heretic, Western Venom, Southern King and Northern Beggar all admitted defeat.

"Apparently, before Wang Chongyang died, he passed the Manual to his martial brother Zhou Botong. But the Heretic of the East, Apothecary Huang, defeated this Zhou Botong and took the Manual for himself. I am not certain what happened after that."

Lotus and Guo Jing looked at each other. This was the first time they had heard the Manual's complex history. Their minds turned to the next thieves to steal the Manual, Twice Foul Dark Wind.

"Since the Elder's kung fu is the greatest, the Manual should belong to you!" Lotus said, with a provocative giggle.

"I am not interested in taking up arms over a book," Qiu Qianren replied. "Now that Wang Chongyang is gone, we are left with four masters who are just about equal. I know they have all been working hard to gain the supreme title for themselves in the intervening years. The second contest will be quite an event."

"When will it be held?"

"The contest takes place every twenty-five years, so the next one is in a couple of years' time. It looks like it will be us old hands again. There's no-one new to take on the mantle. Our art is dying. Each generation is less capable than the last." Qiu Qianren sighed and shook his head.

"Can you take us with you to the next contest, please? I love sparring matches."

"There's much more to it than that. Titles have little meaning when you have one foot in the grave. But we live in a time of great change. I would be neglecting my duty as a martial man and putting tens of thousands of lives at risk if I hid my knowledge to preserve the peaceful anonymity I have been enjoying." He paused and turned to Squire Lu, gesturing at Guo Jing and Lotus. "Our young friends, here, have no dealing in the *jianghu*. It is for the best if they know nothing of this."

"Squire Lu would not keep such things from a good friend." Lotus smiled sweetly.

The Master of Roaming Cloud Manor silently cursed Lotus's sharp wit and quick tongue. For she was right. It would be an affront to the rules of hospitality to deny one's guests.

"Please do not speak of this matter to anyone." Qiu Qianren was ready to explain the reason of his visit.

"Allow us to bid you good night," Guo Jing stood up and took Lotus's hand. He did not feel comfortable being party to the conversation against Qiu's wishes.

"You are a friend of Squire Lu, so you are no stranger to me." Qiu Qianren placed his hand on Guo Jing's shoulder. "Please sit."

Guo Jing was surprised by how light the push was. He held back his inner strength and sat down obediently.

The martial Master got to his feet and raised his cup before he spoke. "Are you aware that the Great Song will face its sorest trials within half a year?"

Laurel Lu gestured at the household staff to step out of the hall, while the servers retreated out of earshot, though they remained on hand to assist the diners.

"I have confirmed intelligence that within six months the full force of the Jin army will march south. The Great Song will certainly lose the remnants of its realm. This is its fate," Qiu Qianren declared.

"Master Qiu, we must inform the Song court immediately," Guo Jing exclaimed.

"What do you know of such matters, young man?" He shot a look of disdain at Guo Jing. "Informing the Song court would only intensify the misery of the coming battle."

No-one could quite grasp the logic behind his words.

"I have thought long and hard," Qiu Qianren continued. "There is only one way to keep our beautiful land from being razed and plundered. It is the only path open to us if we are to protect our people so they can live in peace and prosperity.

"This is the cause of my journey to Jiangnan, to the heartlands of the south. I have heard that my esteemed hosts have taken the young Prince of the Great Jin Empire, as well as Commander Duan of the warden's office, captive. Why don't we invite them to join us?"

Squire Lu sent for his prisoners, though he could not help but wonder how Qiu Qianren knew about them and what he wanted with a traitor and an enemy prince.

Once the captives were brought to the hall, Squire Lu ordered their shackles to be removed and assigned them the least prominent seats at the table, though he did not send for cups or cutlery.

"Your Highness," Qiu Qianren said in greeting to a sallow-looking Wanyan Kang. He merely glanced at the terrified Commander Duan, a bearded man in his fifties.

The Jin Prince nodded in acknowledgement, but he was more concerned by Guo Jing's presence. What is he doing here? He did not know Guo Jing had seen his fight with Laurel Lu, and he did not recognise Lotus Huang in her disguise. He kept his expression neutral, and Guo Jing, in turn, made no move to greet him.

"This manor houses riches and honour beyond imagination," Qiu Qianren said cryptically.

"You hold me in too high esteem, Master. I am but a ruffian living a simple life," Squire Lu said, with guarded courtesy. His guest's familiarity with the Jin ambassador was making him feel uneasy.

"Death and destruction are inevitable as the Jin army moves south," Qiu Qianren continued. "I have travelled here to bring the heroes of the south together, so we can rise up in unison to find a way to forestall the horrors of war."

"We martial men are trained to serve our country and to deliver our people from their plight. My loyalty to our land never found an avenue of expression, thanks to our muddled and corrupt court.

But now, the chance to fulfil our duty to our country is worth more than earthly wealth or rank." Squire Lu spoke with barely contained fervour. "I implore the Master to point the way."

Stroking his beard, Qiu Qianren smiled at Squire Lu's impassioned words, but a servant rushed in before he could reply.

"Captain Zhang is outside with six extraordinary heroes he met on the lake."

"Invite them in."

Have Twice Foul Dark Wind brought help? Squire Lu's face darkened at the thought.

CHAPTER FIVE

LORD OF
PEACH BLOSSOM ISLAND

I

"FIRST *SHIFU*, SECOND *SHIFU*, THIRD *SHIFU*, FOURTH *SHIFU*, Sixth *Shifu*, Seventh *Shifu*!" Guo Jing cried in one breath, as a woman and five men were led into the banqueting hall.

Armed and of exceptional appearance, the Six Freaks of the South had not disclosed their names when their vessel was hailed by Captain Zhang's men on Lake Tai, but exchanged a few words in the dialect of the rivers and lakes and accepted the invitation. The loyal pirate followed Laurel Lu's order to the letter, personally escorting the Freaks back to Roaming Cloud Manor, fearing the whole way that he was leading Squire Lu's enemies inside the estate.

Guo Jing's reaction had somewhat reassured Squire Lu, but before he could find out more about these newcomers, a voice boomed, "Is the she-demon here with you?"

"Not now!" Pulling him back, Jade Han hushed her cousin, Ryder Han. She'd recognised the boy sitting next to Guo Jing the moment she stepped inside – Lotus, in male disguise.

The Cyclone Mei I remember doesn't look or sound like her,

Squire Lu observed with relief. He put his hands together in a gesture of respect as Guo Jing introduced his teachers.

"I have long admired the Heroes' unparalleled reputation. Pardon my rudeness for staying seated — I do not have full use of my legs."

He then ordered the servants to set a second table for the new guests.

Qiu Qianren, meanwhile, had paid no attention to the Six Freaks, other than flashing a half-smile when they appeared at the doorway. He was entirely focused on the feast.

"Who is that?" Once again, it was Ryder Han who spoke.

"One of the supreme martial masters of our age. His reputation is paramount in the *wulin.*"

"Apothecary Huang of Peach Blossom Island?" Jade Han said.

"The Divine Vagrant Nine Fingers?" Ryder Han guessed.

Squire Lu shook his head. "This is Master Qiu, Iron Palm Water Glider."

"Master Qiu Qianren?" Ke Zhen'e, the most senior of the Freaks, was impressed.

Qiu Qianren was visibly pleased by the reaction to his name. He stopped eating for a moment and threw his head back in laughter.

Once the table was set, the Six Freaks seated themselves according to their seniority. Guo Jing turned to Lotus. Smiling, she shook her head and he moved over alone.

After Guo Jing had settled at his *shifus'* table, Squire Lu said with a smile, "I didn't think Brother Guo knew any martial arts. It turns out he is a disciple of the most esteemed masters."

"I hope sir will forgive me for concealing my martial knowledge." Guo Jing jumped to his feet reverentially. "I am not naturally gifted and I have barely scratched the surface of my mentors' kung fu." The Freaks were pleased by this humble response.

"It is said that the Six Heroes have won fame across the south." For the first time, Qiu Qianren addressed the new arrivals. "If the Heroes would join us, it would be of immense benefit to our enterprise."

"Master Qiu was about to explain the business that brought him here, just as you arrived," Squire Lu added.

"We are all men of the martial world. Our code of heroic right-eousness requires us to prevent suffering from befalling our fellow men," Qiu Qianren said proudly. "The Great Jin Empire's army is poised to head south at any moment. War is inevitable. As the two armies clash, how many lives will be lost? How many ruined?

"We all know the saying, 'Fortune smiles on those who oblige the heavens, death descends on those in opposition.' I am here to make contact with the martial masters of the south, so we can work together to make sure the Song court will not ignore the escalating situation and will at last understand the precarious position it is in.

"With pressure mounting from within and without, it has become clear that the best option would be to surrender before we are forced to endure the humiliation and the strife that would follow a defeat on the battlefield.

"When we accomplish this task, the people's gratitude alone shall justify our efforts. Needless to say, wealth and rank would also be bestowed on us."

The Sixth Freak, Gilden Quan, shot a warning glance at his breth-ren – *Let our host respond first* – while giving the most hot-headed among them, Ryder Han and Jade Han, a sharp tug on the sleeve.

"I may keep the company of pirates and thieves, but I know where my allegiance lies." Squire Lu chose his words carefully. He was aghast to hear a master he so respected make such a treacherous sug-gestion. "If the Jin army comes to take our realm, I shall fight to the death alongside the martial masters of the south." He paused and then decided to make a jest of it. "I think Master is testing our loyalty."

"My dear brother, don't be so short-sighted!" Qiu Qianren exclaimed. "What good can come of helping the Song against the Jin? The only fate that awaits is that of Yue Fei – a lonely death in the Storm Pavilion."

"My enemies will be here at any moment. I was hoping to ask Master for his assistance. But, since our principles are irreconcilable, I would rather see my throat slit and my blood pouring out onto the floor than seek your help . . . Please!" Squire Lu cupped his hands in a perfunctory gesture of farewell, then pointed towards the way out.

The Freaks, Guo Jing and Lotus Huang were impressed by Squire Lu's bold response.

Smiling, Qiu Qianren pinched the lip of his wine cup between his thumb and his index finger. He turned the cup around before releasing his hold and striking its rim with the base of his palm. A ringlet of porcelain half an inch deep clattered to the table with a *pop*. He placed the drinking vessel next to its severed rim, showing off the clean edge.

Smashing ceramics required no skill, but to crack it so neatly with only his palm? That demonstrated exceptional mastery of internal *neigong*!

"Traitor! Enough of your tricks!" the fiery Ryder Han exploded, before his host could think of a rejoinder to the threat. He hopped out of his seat and planted himself before Qiu Qianren. The Freaks would never let a traitor slip away without a challenge.

"Nothing pleases me more than the chance to put a great martial reputation to the test. All of you together, please," the martial Master said.

"Indeed, the Six Heroes of the South are a united front, against one man or a thousand," Squire Lu added.

The Second Freak, Zhu Cong, understood the warning – none among them could beat Qiu Qianren in single combat. "We six martial siblings would be honoured to learn from a renowned master of the *wulin*," he said, with a wave of his hand. The rest of the Freaks leapt to their feet.

Qiu Qianren stood up and carried his chair to the centre of the hall, away from the tables.

"Come, we'll play sitting down."

He settled on the chair and rested his ankle on the opposite knee. The other foot tapped at the ground.

The Freaks inhaled sharply at this arrogant response. Only the most supreme martial master would slight his opponents so.

"Master, allow me to fight on behalf on my *shifus*." Guo Jing planted himself in front of his teachers. He had seen Qiu Qianren's strange skills and knew none of his teachers could match him. Even though he would likely die at the hand of this Master, as a disciple, it was his duty to keep his mentors from harm.

"Raising you was no mean feat. Why throw your life away so young, boy?" Qiu Qianren cackled.

"Move!" the Freaks ordered in unison.

Afraid that he would be restrained, Guo Jing bent his left knee and drew a circle with his right palm, without another word.

Haughty Dragon Repents.

He had been working hard on this move and his control over its power had grown exponentially since the day he learned it from Count Seven Hong. He thrust his palm, channelling only two-fifths of his inner strength, with ample back-up in reserve.

Qiu Qianren had noted how mediocre Ryder Han's kung fu was when he leapt out of his seat, so he had assumed the apprentice's skill would be negligible. Little did he imagine that a boy barely out of his teens could produce such a mighty force. He threw his feet down and sprang into the air.

Crack! The red sandalwood chair splintered.

"Insolent boy!" The first crack in Qiu Qianren's composure.

"I hope the Master will deign to instruct me," Guo Jing said referentially, well aware that it was very rude to strike one's senior, especially a master with such exquisite kung fu.

While Guo Jing hesitated over his next move, Lotus cried out, "No need to be civil to this awful old fossil." A ploy to distract the Master. Never before had insult been thrown with such audacity into his face.

Outraged, Qiu Qianren lunged at Guo Jing, his palms thrusting furiously. Then he remembered he was fighting a novice; he must maintain his composure. At the last moment, he turned a blow with his right hand into a feint, and with a disdainful sneer let his left hand fly in a Brow Brush Palm. Guo Jing swivelled away.

The martial Master changed the failed attack into a probe, pulling back in a Grappling Hook. Now, he struck once more in a Brow Brush Palm, before spinning into a low stance, his hand sinking into a Crushing Collapse.

"That's a dreadfully common move!" Lotus cried. "Wild Goose Leaves the Flock, from the Palm of Connected Arms and Six Unions."

Qiu Qianren had spent decades perfecting this very kung fu. Evolved from the Palm of Connected Arms and Five Elements, the moves themselves were not surprising, but the way in which the two arms interacted was unusual. As one palm thrust, the other would twirl, channelling its force into the attacking hand. The arms were connected in a cycle of energy, boosting each other with every blow.

Guo Jing had never seen such seamless coordination between the two sides of the body. His confidence wavered. At a loss whether to block or to attack, he just ducked and shied away. All he could think of was Count Seven Hong's explanation of "repent" and "retreat".

The boy's kung fu is most average. No finesse, just brute force. With that observation, Qiu Qianren fired three successive moves – Palm Piercing Strike, Yin Stirring Push and Mount the Tiger, Scale the Mountain – each one quicker than the last.

Lotus edged closer to the fight, ready to help.

Guo Jing veered from a sideways kick, then hesitated as he noticed the concern in Lotus's eyes.

Qiu Qianren saw his chance. He smacked the young man square in the chest, in a White Snake Spits Tongue.

Gasps filled the hall. No-one could survive such a heavy blow!

The blood drained from Guo Jing's face. Fear rushed through him, and yet he felt no pain. He flexed his arms and shoulders. Nothing.

How was that possible?

Lotus ran to steady Guo Jing. He looked dazed, his eyes had glazed over. "That stinking whitebeard must have knocked him out," she cursed under her breath. "How do you feel?" Tears were rolling down her cheeks.

"I'm fine." He smiled. "Let me try again."

He puffed up his chest and strode over to Qiu Qianren. "Hero of the Iron Palm, please strike me once more."

Seething, the older man summoned his strength and – *pang!* – hit Guo Jing again. Directly at his heart.

"*Shifus*, Lotus, this old man's kung fu is very common!" Guo Jing chuckled. "His moves look powerful, but, by striking me, he showed his hand." Then he took a step forward – "Now it's my turn!" – and swung his left arm horizontally.

Circling his arms over his chest, Qiu Qianren thought Guo Jing's swipe would turn into a punch. He had no idea that he was about to face the most intricate move from the Dragon-Subduing Palm: Dragons Tussle in the Wild.

Left arm sweeping, right palm thrusting, each could be a feint or an attack. It was impossible to predict which hand would land the blow.

The moment Qiu Qianren made to block, Guo Jing slapped his other palm into the old man's right shoulder.

Pang!

Like a kite with a snapped string, the martial Master careered through the doorway.

2

A WOMAN OUTSIDE THE HALL CAUGHT THE HURTLING QIU Qianren. She hoisted the martial Master back inside by his collar and dumped him on the floor.

Iron Corpse Cyclone Mei.

She planted herself in the middle of the room, her face, partially obscured by her unkempt hair, turned up to the rafters.

But the horror that followed eclipsed her dramatic entrance.

A tall, lanky figure, clad in a light green robe. Waxen complexion, mouth, nose, facial muscles stiff and dead as wood or stone. Only the eyes were capable of movement. The head of a corpse on a living human body. One look at his face and a chill descended down the beholder's back. Everyone in the banqueting hall averted their eyes as their hearts raced and spines shivered.

Any amusement Squire Lu had felt at Qiu Qianren's humbling by Guo Jing was snuffed out when he caught sight of the new arrivals. She had changed almost beyond recognition, but there was no mistaking her identity. Fear, and grief, took root in his heart.

"*Shifu!*" To everyone's surprise, Wanyan Kang rose to greet Cyclone Mei.

"Cyclone, my martial sister, it has been more than ten years. Finally, we meet again." Squire Lu cupped his hands in respect. "How is our brother, Hurricane?"

Guo Jing and his *shifus* looked at each other, startled by this revelation. Had they walked into a trap? Cyclone Mei alone was hard enough to defeat, now they had to deal with her martial brother, too?

Meanwhile, Lotus Huang was pleased that her intuition had been vindicated: I knew he was Papa's disciple! Everything about him reminded me of Papa.

"Zephyr Lu? My little martial brother?" Cyclone Mei's voice was cold as ice.

"Yes, it is I," the Master of Roaming Cloud Manor answered. "I trust you have been well?"

"Well? Can't you tell I'm blind? Hurricane was murdered years ago. Isn't that what you always wanted?"

"Who killed our brother? Was his death avenged?"

Zephyr Lu was surprised to hear that someone had got the better of Twice Foul Dark Wind, but also relieved that this was one enemy he no longer need worry about. He sighed, thinking of those days, another lifetime ago, when they were martial siblings on Peach Blossom Island.

"I'm still looking for them."

"Before we settle the grievances between us, I shall help you find this killer of our kin."

Cyclone Mei snorted in contempt.

"Seek your vengeance here!" Ryder Han bellowed as he smacked the table. He would have leapt out of his seat if Gilden Quan had not restrained him.

"No more empty talk of petty revenge!" Qiu Qianren had finally recovered from the heart-shattering, lung-piercing blow he had suffered at Guo Jing's hands. "You strut around, calling yourself heroes and great men, yet you know nothing of your own *shifu*'s death. Spare me your posturing!"

Cyclone Mei flipped her hand and locked on to Qiu Qianren's wrist. "What did you say?"

The pain bore deep into his bone. He shrieked. "Let go!"

"What did you say?" Mei asked again.

"Apothecary Huang. Lord of Peach Blossom Island. Murdered!" He spat the words out. Cyclone Mei's grip went slack.

"Is it true?" Zephyr Lu did not care about the etiquette of hospitality anymore.

"Why would I lie? He was hunted down by the Seven Immortals of the Quanzhen Sect – Wang Chongyang's disciples – and killed."

Cyclone Mei and Zephyr Lu sank to their knees, sobbing. Lotus Huang fainted, crashing to the floor along with the chair she had been sitting on.

No man, without help, could inflict mortal harm on the Lord of Peach Blossom Island. But, outnumbered and surrounded by Ma Yu, Qiu Chuji, Wang Chuyi and their martial siblings . . .

"Lotus! Wake up!" Guo Jing cradled her. Her pale cheeks and shallow breathing frightened him. "Help her, please, *Shifu*."

Zhu Cong held his hand under her nose.

"Don't worry; she will be fine. She's passed out from grief." He massaged the Palace of Toil pressure point in the centre of her palm.

She began to come to.

"I want Papa! Papa! Where are you?"

Realisation dawned on Zephyr Lu, despite the double onslaught of shock and grief. Of course! She's *Shifu*'s daughter! That's why she recognised the Dew of Nine Flowers.

"Little sister, we'll kill the Quanzhen monks!" he spluttered through tears. "Cyclone, are you coming with me? If not, then I'll have to kill you first!"

"Papa, we must plan this properly." Laurel Lu had never seen his father so overcome with emotion.

"It's . . . It's your fault, Cyclone Mei. You brought this onto *Shifu*! You brought this onto me!" There was no stopping Zephyr Lu now. "It was bad enough you did that shameful thing with Hurricane. Why did you have to steal the Nine Yin Manual too? Did you know *Shifu* broke our legs because of it? All three of us. Your martial brothers! And banished us! I've longed for *Shifu* to change his mind, to take me back, so I can wait upon him once more, so I can repay his kindness in teaching me. But now he is no more. All my dreams, my hopes – dashed! Gone! Because of you!"

"Stop! I've cursed you for your lack of backbone in the past, and I curse you again now! It was you who wouldn't stop hunting us. It was you who pushed us out to Mongolia. Without you, Hurricane would not have met his death out there! Why are you still wailing about settling our old scores? You should be focused on how we are to avenge our *shifu*! We must find those Taoist bastards. If you can't walk, I'll carry you myself." Her tears were falling as fast as her words.

"Papa! I want my papa!" Lotus had been repeating those few words for quite some time now.

"We should question him properly," Zhu Cong whispered to Lotus. He went over to Qiu Qianren, flicking his sleeve over the dust and dirt on the martial Master's shirt.

"Our disciple's ignorance has offended the Master. Please forgive him."

"My eyes aren't as sharp as they once were. It didn't count. Let's do it again."

"It was obvious that the Master's kung fu is far superior. There is no need to fight again." Zhu Cong patted Qiu Qianren on the shoulder and shook his left hand.

The Second Freak returned to his seat and picked up his wine cup with a smile. He pinched the edge of the vessel with his thumb and index finger, as Qiu Qianren had done. After turning it a full circle, he touched his palm against the rim. A porcelain ring, half an inch deep, fell to the table. It was exactly the same kung fu.

"The Master's kung fu is most superb. Pardon me for stealing the move. And thank you!" Zhu Cong grinned. "Come, Guo Jing, I'll teach you. Now you'll be able to trick people and give them a good fright."

The colour drained from Qiu Qianren's face. How did he discover my secret? I had it on my person just a moment ago!

No-one could work out how Zhu Cong had managed to replicate the trick.

The Second Freak removed a ring and held it up. "Put it on. Pinch the rim. Make sure the ring is touching it. Now turn." Guo Jing did as he was told. Another ceramic ring fell onto the table. "Many thanks to Master Qiu for lending us the ring. See, this is an adamant – the hardest material in this world."

So it wasn't thanks to his extraordinary control of inner strength! Lotus joined in the laughter before succumbing to tears once more.

"Don't cry, my lady," Zhu Cong said. "Our Master Qiu lives to deceive and play tricks. Your esteemed father's martial skills are incomparable. The Seven Immortals of the Quanzhen Sect are principled. Why would they kill your father for no reason?"

"Qiu Chuji and his cow muzzles must have heard about their martial uncle, Zhou Botong," Lotus blurted out.

"What do you mean?"

"Nothing. Nothing that concerns you . . ." She started to cry again. Under normal circumstances, she would not have fallen for Qiu Qianren's trick. But, for the first time in her life, it had been months since she had last seen her father, and, furthermore, if the Seven Immortals had found out what had happened between her father and Zhou Botong, then they would have had just cause for a fight.

To distract Lotus from her thoughts, Zhu Cong pulled out two bricks, one bundle of tightly rolled reeds, as well as tinder, a flint and a flint cutter. "Master Qiu keeps all kinds of funny things up his sleeves. Shall we guess their purpose?"

Lotus picked up a brick and tightened her grip. It disintegrated at the slightest pressure. She rubbed a fragment of the remnants between her fingers and it crumbled into dust. A smile spread over her face. "This brick is made of flour! He showed us how he could crush it with his inner strength!"

Qiu Qianren's face flitted between sickly green and pallid white. He had been hoping the lie about Apothecary Huang would create an opportunity to escape. But all his illusions were being exposed by the filthy scholar. He turned and tried to slip away.

Cyclone Mei grabbed the martial Master and hurled him to the ground with a backhanded throw.

"What you said about my teacher just now. Was it a lie?"

Qiu Qianren whimpered in pain.

Lotus noticed that one end of the reed was scorched. "Second *Shifu*, can you smoke this and conceal it in your sleeve?"

The Freaks were wary of Lotus Huang because of her father, but, for the moment at least, they were united against Qiu Qianren. Zhu Cong was quietly pleased she called him *Shifu*, as he had always felt a connection with her irreverent quick wit. He did as she requested, and, with a serious expression, he inhaled.

Laughing and clapping, Lotus turned to Guo Jing and Zephyr Lu. "That's what the awful old fossil was doing when he was practising his internal kung fu!"

She approached Qiu Qianren and smiled sweetly. "Allow me."

As she helped the martial Master back onto his feet, she tapped his Spirit Path pressure point, positioned under his fifth vertebra, with her Orchid Touch.

"So, what happened to my papa?" she barked. "I'll kill you if you say he's dead!" Her hand flourished. The steel point of her Emei Needle was now pressed into his chest.

Everyone suppressed their laughter at her interrogation methods.

Qiu Qianren succumbed to waves of aches and itches. "Perhaps he is not dead. It is impossible to be sure."

"That's more like it!" Beaming, Lotus rubbed the Empty Basin point on his right shoulder blade to ease the discomfort.

"You said the Seven Immortals of the Quanzhen Sect killed our teacher. Did you see the fight with your own eyes? Or did you simply hear about it?" Zephyr Lu asked, hoping to get more information out of the martial Master than Lotus had.

"I heard about it."

"From whom?"

Qiu Qianren said, after a pause, "Count Seven Hong."

"When was this?" Lotus cut in.

"A month ago."

"Where?"

"At the summit of Mount Tai. We were duelling. He lost and he mentioned it in passing."

Laughing, Lotus grabbed him by the shirt and plucked a handful of his beard. "Another lie! We were with Count Seven a month ago!" She turned to Guo Jing. "Show him another one of your palm thrusts."

"Of course!" Guo Jing leapt over.

Qiu Qianren spun and scampered away from the young man. Seeing Cyclone Mei in the doorway, he scurried back into the hall.

Laurel Lu stepped forward to restrain Qiu Qianren, but the older man pushed back and Laurel stumbled backwards. The so-called martial master was not entirely without skill, or he would not have challenged the Freaks.

"Tell me how you walk on water with the iron tub on your head." Lotus put a restraining hand on Qiu Qianren's shoulder.

"That was my unique lightness kung fu. It is why I'm known as Iron Palm Water Glider."

"Really? Are you still trying to fool us?"

"At my old age, my martial skills aren't what they used to be. But I never lost my *qinggong*."

"In that case, show us your Water Gliding kung fu. There's a big fish pond in the courtyard. Through the doors, under the osmanthus tree on the left."

"A pond? I can't possibly—" A flash, and something tightened around his ankles. The White Python whip. Before he knew it, he was hanging upside down.

"You've talked enough!" Cyclone Mei dragged Qiu Qianren through the banqueting hall's doorway and, with a flick of her wrist, tossed him into the fish pond in the courtyard.

Lotus followed him outside and held her Emei Needles over the edge of the stone pond.

"Show us how you glide on water! Or my needles will make you sink to the bottom!"

Qiu Qianren pushed off with his feet, hoping to jump out. But he launched himself straight at Lotus's steel spikes. Pricked on the shoulders, he fell back with a splash.

"I put logs on the riverbed. Five or six inches from the surface," the old man confessed, shamefaced and dripping wet. "The vat is made of a very thin sheet of iron. Its opening is sealed and it only holds three inches of water."

Her curiosity satisfied, Lotus went inside with a chuckle. Qiu Qianren hopped out of the pond and disappeared into the night, his head hung low.

3

CYCLONE MEI HAD COME TO ROAMING CLOUD MANOR BENT ON unleashing carnage, but, after the tears and the laughter, her bloodlust had been chased away. Now, her thoughts had turned to her *shifu*. As she listened to Lotus Huang's giggly, animated re-enactment of Qiu Qianren's tricks, Cyclone Mei knew she could no longer steel her heart against her martial brother.

"Zephyr Lu, set my disciple free. In honour of our *shifu*, I shall let our past enmity go." She sighed. "You drove my husband and I into Mongolia . . . It's all been the work of fate."

"He is yours."

Zephyr Lu had also realised how futile it had all been: Cyclone Mei has lost her husband and her sight. She has nothing and no-one left in this world. I might be crippled, but I have my wife and my son, I have a home and I have my business. My life is a hundred times better than hers. What sense is there in raking up the past?

"I shall set off for Peach Blossom Island tomorrow," he said, after a pause. "Would you care to join me?"

"Really?" This one word crystallised years of fear and yearning.

"Yes. I know to step foot on the island without invitation is a grievous offence, but Qiu Qianren's lies have made me miss our gracious teacher even more."

"We'll go to see Papa together," Lotus said. "I'll entreat him on your behalf."

Cyclone Mei stood rooted to the spot, lost to the present. Tears began to roll down her cheeks. "No, I can't. I'm too ashamed. Our teacher took pity on me and granted me a new life. Raised me, taught me. And I, this feral heart, spawn of wolves, betrayed him. I'm worse than a beast . . .

"Every day, I think of him. I pray for his good health and that he might set me free with a strike to my cheek!" She struck herself twice across the face.

"*Shifu*, I . . . I've wronged you." She struck herself once more. Her cheeks burned fiery red. "I shall take my life, once I have avenged my husband. The Seven Freaks of the South, fight me if you dare!"

Ke Zhen'e stepped forward and banged his iron staff on the floor. "Cyclone Mei, you can't see me, nor can I see you," he said, his voice rising above the ringing of metal on stone. "Your husband lost his life that night, but he also took our Fifth Brother Zhang Asheng with him."

"That's why there are only six Freaks now," she said aloud to herself.

"We promised Elder Ma Yu we would never seek you out for revenge, but today you have found us. The heavens and earth might be infinite, yet our paths always converge. Perhaps the Lord of the Heavens does not wish us to exist together in this world. Please make your first move."

"After you." Cyclone Mei sniggered. "All of you."

The rest of the Freaks had long taken up position behind Ke Zhen'e. Now, they brandished their weapons as one.

"Your disciple shall make the first move against Cyclone Mei." Guo Jing bowed at his mentors.

"Please hear me out!" Zephyr Lu wished he had the authority or the kung fu to diffuse the situation. "There might be past discord between Sister Mei and the Six Heroes, but both sides have already suffered bereavements as a result. Might I propose that, today, we only fight to win, without causing injury? The Six Heroes are united in all their deeds, but fighting six to one might appear unfair. Dare I ask my sister to teach our young friend a few moves?"

"How could I fight with a nameless youth?"

"It was I who killed your husband," Guo Jing said. "My *shifus* have nothing to do with it."

Cyclone Mei had already determined Guo Jing's location from his voice. She howled, sprang and plunged her claws at the crown of his head.

Guo Jing swerved aside. "Master Mei, I was only six years old. I was a child. It was by accident that I hurt Master Chen. But I take full responsibility. You need only come for me. I will not run. Kill me, skin me alive, deal with me as you wish. But you must promise never to trouble my six *shifus* again."

"You won't run?"

"I won't."

"Very well! The Freaks and I both have lost someone dear to us. It's my wretched fate, and theirs too. What can we do? All the hatred and animosity between us belongs to the past. Now, boy, come with me."

"Sister Mei," Lotus interrupted. She had an idea. "Guo Jing has shown he has courage and yet the *jianghu* heroes will laugh at you until their jaws ache!"

"What do you mean?" Cyclone Mei snarled.

"He is the only disciple of the Six Heroes of the South. The Heroes' martial skills have improved phenomenally in the past few years; they could take your life with a wave of a hand. But they chose to let you go, to let you save face. Yet, here you are, boasting with your big words."

"Pah! I don't want their mercy. Freaks, let's see if your kung fu has really improved!"

"They have no need to fight you. You probably can't even beat their disciple!"

"If I can't kill that boy within three moves, I will smack my head into a pillar and die right here!" Cyclone Mei remembered Guo Jing's kung fu from the Prince of Zhao's residence. She had no idea of the vast improvements he had made under the guidance of the Divine Vagrant Nine Fingers.

"Three moves? That's too few. Let's do ten. We all stand here as witness."

"I would be honoured to receive fifteen moves from Master Mei." Guo Jing had caught on to Lotus's ploy. He was confident his Dragon-Subduing Palm could withstand Mei's attack.

"We shall ask Brother Lu and the gentleman accompanying you to keep count," Lotus said.

"Who? I came here alone. I have no need of company!"

"Then who is standing behind you?"

Cyclone Mei swung a backhand, swift as lightning. But the man in green was faster. He evaded her, silent as a ghost.

Since Cyclone Mei had come to the south, she had had this queer feeling, as if she were being followed. She had called, lashed out around her, but had found nothing. She had even begun to think her mind was playing tricks on her. Yet, that night, when she was ambushed by Gallant Ouyang's snakes, someone had sent her attackers away with flute song. She had kowtowed in gratitude, kneeling for hours, but received no reply. Nothing. Not a sound. No departing footsteps. Lotus's words at last confirmed her suspicions.

"Who are you?" Mei asked. "Why are you following me?"

The man ignored her questions. Cyclone Mei lunged. The man did not lift his feet or shift his body, but she only managed to grab at air. The room was shocked by the stranger's skill. It was far beyond anything they had known.

"Master, I have been tardy with my welcome," Zephyr Lu said. "Would you care to sit down and join us for a drink?"

The man turned and drifted out of the hall.

"Was the Master the flute player?" Mei asked. "Cyclone Mei is most grateful."

"He's gone," Lotus said.

"Gone? I . . . I heard nothing."

"Go after him!"

Cyclone Mei seemed far, far away. She did not hear Lotus. Then the malice, the thirst for vengeance returned. "Here comes the first move, boy!"

She flashed her talons. They glowed a ghostly green, poised to strike.

Guo Jing shouted, "I am ready—"

Mei's right palm swirled before he could finish the sentence. Her left hand darted. The sharp claws scratched at Guo Jing's face. He tilted out of the way, flipped his left palm and thrust.

Cyclone Mei heard the approach, but there was no time to dodge.

Pang! Her shoulder.

The force pushed her back three steps. Yet, in an instant, she was on the offensive again. Moments later, she had Guo Jing's left wrist in her grip, her claws digging into three vital points – the Inner Pass, the Outer Pass and the Gathering Convergence.

Numbing pain radiated from his arm. Guo Jing had heard about Cyclone Mei's explosive speed and unpredictable moves from his *shifus*. He knew he would not have the skill to dodge or block, but he did not expect her to turn on him so quickly after taking a blow.

And yet, true to the spirit of the Dragon-Subduing Palm, Guo Jing had strength in reserve. Now, he unleashed it. Curling the index and middle fingers of his right hand, he struck her in the chest.

This was half of Shun the Concealed Dragon. His other hand was supposed to reach in with a Grappling Hook, but Mei had it in her grasp.

A punch? A palm thrust? Cyclone Mei twisted to the right.

Once more, the same shoulder was hit.

Though she avoided the full brunt of the blow, an enormous force drove her back. She flicked her wrist and flung Guo Jing away.

Thwack! They each slammed into a pillar. Roof tiles, bricks and dust rained down. The waiting staff fled into the courtyard, yelping in fear.

The Freaks looked at each other. When had Guo Jing learned such superior kung fu?

Ryder Han glanced at Lotus Huang. She must have taught him the move! He was grudgingly impressed by the martial arts of Peach Blossom Island.

Cyclone Mei darted back and forth. Ruthless claws scratched at Guo Jing from every direction. Lightning quick and never the same stroke twice. A strong gust trailed every move.

But Guo Jing stood his ground, each counter-thrust fierce and powerful. He knew he was not quick enough to respond creatively to each individual attack, so he stuck to Count Seven Hong's advice. Whatever came his way, he answered with the Dragon-Subduing Palm.

Starting from the Haughty Dragon Repents, he launched the moves one by one, until the fifteenth and final in his repertoire. Then he began again.

The tactic worked. Forty moves on, Cyclone Mei had not advanced half a step.

A triumphant smile spread over Lotus's face. The Freaks stared at their disciple in wonder.

Zephyr Lu was dazzled by the improvement in Cyclone Mei's kung fu. If he were fighting her, he would have been dead within ten moves.

And how extraordinary is our Brother Guo, he thought with admiration. To attain such deep martial knowledge at his tender age! I overlooked his talent. How fortunate that I treated him with the utmost courtesy.

Zephyr Lu turned his eyes back to his martial sister. In the flickering candlelight, her face glowed with a luminescent pallor acquired over years of hiding from daylight. She had also dabbed some petal sap on her cheeks, as if it were rouge.

Memories from Peach Blossom Island invaded Zephyr Lu's mind. He was too young to have had romantic thoughts then, but he remembered how much he had adored his beautiful, kindly big sister. She looked after him like he was her own brother. Her beauty had not waned, but an air of malice clung to her. Zephyr Lu knew it did not stem from her time on Peach Blossom Island. He thought of his crippled legs and the hatred he had felt towards Twice Foul Dark Wind after his banishment. He prayed the fight would end amicably.

Wanyan Kang watched in envy and frustration. It was only a couple of months since he had almost defeated this young man. Now, he stood no chance.

"Sister Mei, admit that you have lost! You have already exchanged more than eighty moves!"

Cyclone Mei knew Lotus was exaggerating. The true count was closer to sixty, but it was already sixty too many. She had sacrificed so much to hone her kung fu. And yet she could not defeat a teenaged boy!

She clawed and slashed, desperate to deal the death blow, so intent on revenge and so surprised by Guo Jing's improvement that she had forgotten a frenzied mind in combat can lead to the downfall of even the most seasoned martial master. She had driven herself into a state that – compounded by her blindness – curtailed the power of her far superior martial skills.

So far, thanks to his strength and stubbornness, Guo Jing had managed to keep Cyclone Mei at arm's length. However, he had already repeated Count Seven Hong's formidable palm thrusts in the same sequence half a dozen times.

Soon, he had reached a hundred moves.

Cyclone Mei was confident she had the measure of his limited repertoire and changed tactics. No more fighting at close quarters. She stepped back ten paces. Flitting back and forth, she drew out his palm thrusts to drain his strength.

As she had predicted, great focus and much energy was required to launch the Dragon-Subduing Palm. Soon, the might of Guo Jing's blows began to diminish.

Cyclone Mei lunged, sweeping her arms up and down. A deadly fusion of the Nine Yin Skeleton Claw and Heartbreaker Palm.

Fearing for Guo Jing, Lotus Huang shouted, "Sister Mei, why won't you admit you've lost? It's almost two hundred moves now!"

Mei was by now a whirlwind of palm thrusts and sharp claws, impervious to any distraction.

"Psst! Over here!" Lotus beckoned Guo Jing.

He threw a Traverse Great Rivers, followed by a Wild Goose Approaches Land, pushing Mei away. Then he looked up.

Why is she pointing and running around the pillar? He could not understand.

"Fight her from here!" Lotus cried.

Ah! Now he got it.

Guo Jing leapt to the closest column. Cyclone Mei lunged, following the sound of his feet. He ducked. Her talons sunk into the wood.

Whoosh! A palm thrust.

No time to dodge. Mei pushed back with her left hand. The fierce force sent her stumbling back, freeing her claws from the wooden support.

Immediately, she pounced. Her talons flashed with the fury of lightning.

Guo Jing was still finding his footing after the last clash. A strip ripped from his sleeve. His arm was scored, but no blood was drawn. He threw another palm thrust and ducked.

Once more, Mei's left claw dug into the column. She shrieked in frustration.

"Master Mei, my kung fu is no match for yours. Please have mercy!" Guo Jing lowered his guard.

It was obvious Guo Jing could not lose, fighting in this new way, but his words gave Cyclone Mei the chance to claim victory and save face. Zephyr Lu hoped this would signal the end of the duel.

"If this was a simple martial contest, I would have admitted defeat after three moves. But this is revenge. I may have lost, but I shall kill you all the same!" Cyclone Mei replied.

Three thrusts from her right hand, then three from her left. All striking the same spot on the pillar. With a roar, she launched both palms.

Crack! The support snapped.

There was barely time to react. A thunderous crash pursued Laurel Lu into the courtyard as he ran with his father in his arms. Half of the hall had collapsed.

The only one who failed to escape was Commander Duan of the warden's office. Without the benefit of martial-arts training, he could not foresee the consequences of the blind woman's actions. He screeched for help, his legs pinned under the main lintel. Wanyan Kang dived into the rubble, shoved away the wooden beam and yanked the man back to his feet. He did so only because he thought the chaos would give them a chance to escape. Just as he turned to make a run for it, the Jin Prince felt a spot of numbness spreading from the small of his back. He did not see the person hitting his acupressure point.

Cyclone Mei had ears only for Guo Jing. She picked out his footsteps, despite the commotion, and lunged.

They were once again consumed by their duel. Their faint silhouettes blurred into one shadowy storm. Hands sliced the moonless night with shrill cries. Kicks whipped up a dusty wind. Cyclone Mei's joints cracked and popped.

The night robbed Guo Jing of his sight; defeat was surely imminent. He dodged and ducked blindly. A murky shadow of Mei's sweeping left foot. A hasty right kick at her shin.

"It's a feint!" Laurel Lu cried. That was how Wanyan Kang had defeated him the other day.

If Guo Jing's kick found its target, it would fracture the leg at contact. But Cyclone Mei had already twisted away. He was now swinging straight into her talons. He shot his left hand at her wrist with the inner strength he held in reserve.

A quick move, but of limited power.

Mei twirled her claws, deflecting the shove with ease. She dug three nails into his hand and dragged. Guo Jing thrust his right palm in a last-ditch defensive block. She swerved away and, laughing, jumped back, out of range.

Guo Jing looked at the back of his hand.

Three red lines. Each with a hint of something darker than blood. Scorching hot and a little numbing. Like he had been burned.

Mongolia, the cliff. A long night, like tonight. Fragments came to Guo Jing. Skulls, in a stack of nine. His *shifu* talking. The Nine Yin Skeleton Claw. Deadly venom. Her talons.

She scratched my arm earlier tonight, but did not draw blood, and now . . .

"Lotus, I've been poisoned."

Guo Jing lunged, throwing two palm strikes at once. In desperation, he stamped and swatted in one movement. He wanted to subdue her quickly so he could force her to give him the antidote.

Mei felt the air stirring long before the blows could find their mark.

Ke Zhen'e charged, with his iron staff raised. His martial siblings and Lotus Huang followed, hot on his heels, forming a ring around Cyclone Mei.

"Sister Mei, why are you still fighting?" Lotus demanded. "You have lost! Give him the antidote!"

No answer.

Mei had to keep her focus on the gusts of air that hinted at Guo Jing's palm thrusts. She could not afford to be careless against such powerful moves.

Picking up on his exertions, she thought with satisfaction, The poison will only spread faster. I don't care if I die here today – I have at last avenged my Hurricane.

Guo Jing was now blundering about with a lazy half-smile on his lips. His head felt light. His sight was becoming blurry. He was not sure why he was fighting. A rising tide of tranquillity washed over his body. The numbing ache had deadened his left arm.

The poison was taking root.

"Guo Jing, step back!" Lotus charged at Cyclone Mei with her Emei Needles.

Her voice dispelled the fogginess in his head for a moment. He pushed his left palm in a Sudden Advance, the eleventh move of the Dragon-Subduing Palm. Sluggishly, his palm drifted towards Cyclone Mei.

She stood firm and let it hit her on the shoulder.

The blow pushed her over.

Ryder Han, Woodcutter Nan and Gilden Quan rushed to restrain Mei. She flexed her arms and flung Han and Quan away. Then she swiped at Nan with her claws. He ducked and rolled out of her reach.

Mei had just got to her feet when Guo Jing's palm arced into her back. She fell forwards and landed, sprawled, face down on the floor.

Had she not heard him coming? No-one had the mental energy to comprehend how Guo Jing could have sent Cyclone Mei flying, not once, but twice.

The world had become a swaying blur. Guo Jing fell to his knees, not far from his opponent.

Lotus dashed over to steady him. Cyclone Mei's talons flashed once more at the sound of footsteps, and she climbed to her feet.

An incredible pain ripped through her fingertips. Hedgehog

Chainmail! She flipped into a Jumping Carp to put some distance between her and Lotus.

"Hey, catch!"

Cyclone Mei did not recognise the voice, but she could sense something sizeable hurtling towards her. What kind of weapon is this? she wondered, as she swung her right arm to block. *Crack!* The object was smashed into pieces.

An even stranger noise followed. She could feel the shift in the air. Something even larger was hurtling towards her. She shot out her left hand to bat it away.

Everywhere she struck was flat, smooth and hard.

Unable to find anything to grip on to, Cyclone Mei sent it flying with a kick. Just then, she felt something wriggling inside her shirt. Cold and slimy.

What kind of sorcery is this? She reached in and closed her fingers around . . .

Cyclone Mei froze, still as a statue, her hand held awkwardly in her shirt pocket. The only signs of life were the beads of sweat rapidly forming along her hairline.

Where are my things?

She could hear a bottle being uncorked.

"Is this it?" The same voice that shouted at her just now.

Sniffing.

"Ingest it and put it on the wound." An older, gruffer voice.

Cyclone Mei understood. Distractions, they were, so the thief could empty her pocket.

Zhu Cong had known that the antidote must be on Cyclone Mei's person. But what could he do to circumvent her sharp senses and quick reflexes? He noticed a few goldfish flapping in a puddle, their tank shattered by a falling pillar from the hall. They would do, he thought, scooping them up. He hurled the chair at Mei and charged at her with the table, buying enough time to plant three goldfish inside her collar. That final shock had allowed him to put his sleight of hand to use, lifting the contents of her pockets. Not for nothing was Zhu Cong known as both "the Intelligent" and "Quick Hands".

Cyclone Mei turned on the last person to speak, and clashed with a metal staff.

So, it was Ke Zhen'e who figured out my antidote!

As she began to understand what had just happened, three weapons struck at her simultaneously: Ryder Han's Golden Dragon whip, Gilden Quan's steelyard and Woodcutter Nan's shoulder pole.

Holding them off with one hand, she reached for the White Python whip, coiled around her waist. A chill blade sliced at her wrist: Jade Han's sword.

Zhu Cong handed Lotus Huang the antidote and said to Guo Jing, "Yours, I believe." He put the dagger he had taken from Cyclone Mei inside his disciple's shirt, then lunged at Mei, brandishing his folding fan.

This was the fight Cyclone Mei and the Freaks had trained hard for, over the past decade.

"Please stop! Please – listen to me!" Much as Zephyr Lu admired the extraordinary skills on display, he wanted to stop it before things got even more out of hand. But no-one heard him.

The stupor clouding Guo Jing's mind began to clear. The wound on his arm still hurt, but the venom in his veins was neutralised.

Once more, Greybeard Liang's python blood had saved Guo Jing, though the young man had yet to realise it. This time, instead of repelling serpents, it had slowed the spread of Cyclone Mei's poison. Without it, not even the remedy Zhu Cong stole would have been able to revive him.

Back on his feet, Guo Jing joined his *shifus*, biding his time. He let his palm float forward, slow and deliberate. He held his strength back until his hand had almost reached their blind opponent.

The sudden impact of his Thunder Rocks a Hundred Miles knocked Cyclone Mei off her feet.

"*Shifus*, please let her live!" Guo Jing stooped to hold back Ryder Han and Gilden Quan's weapons.

Cyclone Mei vaulted back up and lashed the White Python whip into a circle of protection once more. She had been defenceless against Guo Jing's silent approach.

"We won't trouble you again, Master Mei," Guo Jing said. "Please go in peace."

"Give me back the Manual and all our grievances will be forgotten." She stopped whipping. "Words on paper are no use to a blind woman, but I would like to take it back to its rightful owner."

Zhu Cong had witnessed the evil deeds she had committed with the infernal kung fu from the Manual. How could he let her have the book again? Yet, what she said was true. She had no eyes to read. Seeing her standing on her own, lost and crestfallen, he reached inside his shirt.

"Is it this one?"

4

A WHIRL OF GREEN MATERIALISED BEHIND CYCLONE MEI AS she snatched the Manual from Zhu Cong. No-one could tell how the man had crept up on her, nor could they understand how he had seized her. Somehow, he managed to grab the back of the fearsome martial Master's shirt and carry her off. She did not have the chance to lift a finger against him. In the blink of an eye, they disappeared into the woods beyond the manor, leaving in their wake a shocked silence, broken only by the faint gurgle of waves lapping at the shore.

The man kept his fingers locked onto the major pressure points on Cyclone Mei's back, rendering her immobile. Once deep in the forest, he threw her down.

"You wailed and grieved at the craven's lie." He pointed at her heart. "Does that mean *Shifu* is still in there, somewhere?"

"*Shifu*!" Cyclone Mei cried. She crawled over to hug his legs tightly. "Thank the heavens and earth! You are well!"

"Aren't you ashamed to call me thus?"

"Strike me dead. Please. *Shifu*!" she sobbed. "If I could hear you say yes, I'd die with a smile on my lips. I have wronged you and I have wronged *Shimu*. *Shifu* . . ."

She reached up and took his hand, swinging it gently, as she had done whenever she'd had something to ask of him. He had never once refused her.

Apothecary Huang grunted in half-hearted agreement. He felt a flush of warmth swell through him, accompanied by a wave of memories.

Cyclone Mei bowed joyfully, knocking her head against the ground. She lifted the Nine Yin Manual high with both hands.

"*Shifu*, I have been carrying this book on my person. I am blind, I will never see again, but I am determined to return it to you."

Apothecary Huang took the Manual and put it inside his shirt. "Far too much damage has been done by this book. The martial arts you learned are included in this second volume for one reason alone – to be unpicked and countered with the skills discussed in the first volume. You would have known, if you had read it. You and Hurricane must have suffered so much trying to master these techniques, but you do realise that it has all been in vain, don't you? If the Nine Yin Skeleton Claw, Heartbreaker Palm or White Python Whip had any power, do you think Hurricane would have been killed by a child?"

She kowtowed fervently, agreeing with his every word.

"Once you defeat that boy who wields the Old Beggar's Dragon-Subduing Palm, make yourself a quiet life with Zephyr. You wouldn't want people in the *jianghu* making trouble with you because you can't see."

Realising he still cared for her, Cyclone Mei let her emotions get the better of her. "*Shifu*! *Shifu*!" she cried loudly, tugging the hem of his robe.

"Come, let's go." Apothecary Huang did not want his heart to soften further, for fear it would complicate their already troubled relationship. He offered a few more words of advice and led her back.

At Roaming Cloud Manor, everyone was struggling to comprehend the latest turn of events. How had the stranger in green managed to spirit Cyclone Mei away so effortlessly?

Eventually, Ke Zhen'e spoke. "Our heartfelt apologies for the damage our disciple has caused to your beautiful manor."

"Master Ke, please," Zephyr Lu replied. "It would be remiss of me not to thank you for averting disaster with your presence."

"Shall we retire to the inner hall?" Laurel Lu said, then turned to Guo Jing. "Brother Guo, does your wound still hurt?"

"It's much better—"

Before Guo Jing could say any more, the green swirl reappeared with Cyclone Mei.

Crossing her arms over her chest, Cyclone Mei said to Guo Jing, "Boy, you struck me with the Dragon-Subduing Palm you learned from Count Seven Hong. I was not able to counter it because I am blind. I haven't got long in this world and I don't care about winning or losing, but if word gets out that Cyclone Mei failed to defeat the Old Beggar's teenage disciple, I will have brought shame to Peach Blossom Island. So, we will fight again."

"I was never your match," Guo Jing replied. "The only reason I escaped with my life was because I took advantage of your impediment. I admitted defeat long ago."

"There are eighteen moves to the Dragon-Subduing Palm. Why didn't you use them all?"

"Because I am slow and stupid . . ." He saw Lotus signalling at him to hide the truth, but he decided to answer honestly. "Master Hong only taught me fifteen moves. He also said I am not his disciple."

"So . . . You only learned fifteen moves and you still got the better of me. Can that Old Beggar be so powerful? No, we must fight again."

Cyclone Mei had moved on from the urge for vengeance. This was now a matter of protecting Apothecary Huang's martial reputation.

"I can't even beat young Miss Huang. How could I hope to defeat you? I have always held the martial arts of Peach Blossom Island in the highest regard."

"Sister Mei, why are you going on about this? We all know no-one can beat Papa!" Lotus tried to lighten the atmosphere.

"No! We must fight again!"

Cyclone Mei decided to let actions speak. She swiped her claws at Guo Jing, forcing him into a hurried response.

"In that case, I hope to learn from Master Mei," Guo Jing said humbly.

"Use your silent palms," Cyclone Mei demanded, turning her wrists to flash her talons. "You can't beat me with these noisy moves!"

Guo Jing hopped back several paces. "No. I cannot oblige. If someone took advantage of my First *Shifu*'s indisposition with such tricks, I would hate them with every fibre of my being. How could I do to you something I would despise in others? Just now, I fell for your poison and it slowed my movement, so you weren't able to hear the approach of my attacks. Faced with a life-and-death situation, the silent strikes saved my life. But, in a contest, it would be immoral and unfair. I fear I cannot follow your command."

"I told you to use them because I have my ways to overcome it. I have no need of your moralising!" She was quietly impressed by his principled stance.

Guo Jing glanced at the stranger. Did he teach her a countermove while they were away?

"It would be my honour to receive another fifteen moves from Master Mei," he said, knowing he had no choice in the matter. He hoped the Dragon-Subduing Palm would be enough to keep him alive.

Guo Jing stepped back before tiptoeing towards Cyclone Mei. His palm floated forward. Then he heard a very faint hissing sound approach.

The next thing he knew, Cyclone Mei had twirled her wrist in a backhanded Grapple and Lock, straight at his attacking arm. Her aim was so precise, he swore she had regained her sight.

He recoiled in shock and sidled to her left, settling into a Traverse Great Rivers at an even more ponderous pace. He had barely gained an inch when another hiss ripped through the air.

Somehow, Cyclone Mei had figured out exactly where he was and rained down a torrent of attacks. Her talons almost caught him.

How does she know where I am? he thought as he scurried away. He took extra care with his third, and most confident, attempt. Haughty Dragon Repents.

Hiss!

Mei's claws, hard as steel, lashed out at his wrist.

Guo Jing was now certain that her new prescience was related to the noise. He glanced at the stranger as he held off Cyclone Mei with his fourth move. The man flicked his finger surreptitiously and a speck of earth tore through the air.

That's how he warns her! How can he predict my moves? Guo Jing decided to admit defeat immediately after the fifteenth exchange.

Cyclone Mei could now draw on the insights she had gained into the young man's unchanging kung fu to devise ways to counter his attack.

The stranger sent three crumbs of masonry flying one after another. Suddenly, she switched to the offensive. She ripped the air with three lethal moves. Guo Jing buckled under the weight of the onslaught, and only managed to send two palm thrusts in response.

The air fizzed with whooshing clumps of earth. Lotus was flinging handfuls of rubble into the air, some aimed at the stranger's pebbles, others just to create a distraction. But, as his projectiles flew into the cloud of dust, the hisses became shrill whistles. They knocked any debris out of the way without slowing or veering from the trajectory the man had set.

The Freaks and Zephyr Lu lamented the failure of Lotus's intervention, but, at the same time, they were awestruck by the stranger's power. At mere flick of his finger, a speck of earth could pierce through flesh and bone.

Lotus stared at the man in disbelief. Cyclone Mei had gained control of the fight and Guo Jing was struggling to defend himself.

Whoosh! Another bit of masonry zoomed past. Then one more. They crashed together in an explosion of sparks and shrapnel.

Cyclone Mei swooped on Guo Jing with all her strength.

Guo Jing was outmatched and overwhelmed. Woodcutter Nan's advice flashed across the young man's mind: *If all else fails, run!*

5

"PAPA!" LOTUS CRIED, THROWING HERSELF AT THE STRANGER in the green robe. "Pa! Your face . . . What happened?"

Cyclone Mei paused mid-move, tilting her head to listen.

This is my chance! Guo Jing pushed his right palm forward slowly, so there was no sound or movement of air to alert Cyclone Mei of its approach. The moment his hand connected with her shoulder, he unleashed all his inner strength, holding nothing in reserve. He then struck her other shoulder with his left hand in the same manner. The combined force sent Mei tumbling in a somersault. She lay on the ground, unable to stand up.

At Lotus's words, Zephyr Lu rose to his feet, forgetting his disability. But, the moment he lifted his foot, he was toppled by his decades-old injury.

Holding Lotus close, the man peeled a layer of skin from his face to reveal handsome, chiselled features. Lotus snatched the mask and, with a smile, put it over her tear-stained cheeks.

"What brings you here, Papa?" She coiled her arms around his neck, bobbing with joy. "Why didn't you teach that awful old fossil a lesson when he cursed you?"

"What brings me here? You, of course!" Apothecary Huang replied, with a touch of sternness.

"So you've done it, at last, Pa? What great news!" Lotus clapped, taking no notice of his tone.

"No. I have broken my word in order to come looking for you."

That dampened Lotus's mood somewhat. She knew how much the theft of the Nine Yin Manual by Hurricane Chen and Cyclone Mei had weighed on her father. He had vowed to use his wit and knowledge to recreate the kung fu in the stolen second volume, using only the contents of the volume that was still in his possession. He would often say, "The Nine Yin Manual was written by a mortal man. If it can be done, then Apothecary Huang can do it too! If I cannot recall the martial skills set down in the second volume, I will not take one step beyond Peach Blossom Island!"

Realising she had caused her father to break a promise he had kept for as long as she had been alive, Lotus said solemnly, "I'll be good, Pa. I'll always listen to you, until the day I die!"

"Help your Sister Mei."

In truth, Apothecary Huang was delighted to find Lotus unharmed. Her words melted away the last traces of anger he had felt when she ran away.

As Lotus lifted Cyclone Mei back to her feet, Zephyr Lu came forward, supported by his son. Together, the two disciples of Peach Blossom Island bowed at their teacher's feet, sobbing with joy.

Apothecary Huang sighed. "Good Zephyr, stand up. I was too quick to blame you."

"I trust *Shifu* has kept well?" Lu asked referentially.

"I have yet to succumb to rage."

"You aren't talking about me, Pa, are you?" Lotus giggled.

"You have played your part," Apothecary Huang replied, with a snort.

Lotus stuck her tongue out, then changed the subject. "Pa, can I introduce you to my friends? They are Guo Jing's *shifus*, the renowned Six Heroes of the South."

Apothecary Huang looked to the heavens. "I am not here to make the acquaintance of strangers."

The snub riled the Freaks, but they knew it would be better to swallow their pride for now, having witnessed his extraordinary martial skill.

"Do you need to pack? We shall head home at once," Apothecary Huang said to Lotus, ignoring everyone else.

"I have no luggage, but there is something I should like to return to its owner." Lotus took the bottle of the Dew of Nine Flowers from inside her shirt. "Brother Zephyr, these pills are not easy to make. I should give them back."

Zephyr Lu declined Lotus's offer with a polite wave. "It is the most joyous surprise to set eyes on *Shifu* again. If you would stay for a while, it would be—"

Taking no notice of the invitation, Apothecary Huang pointed at Laurel Lu. "Is he your son?"

The young man immediately kowtowed. "Grandmaster!"

Apothecary Huang grunted an acknowledgement at the fourth bow. Instead of helping the young man to stand, he grabbed Laurel Lu's collar with his left hand and thrust his right palm into his shoulder.

"He is my only son . . ."

It was not a weak strike. Laurel Lu stumbled and fell backwards. When he found his feet again, he seemed unhurt.

"Well done for not teaching him your kung fu," Apothecary Huang said to Zephyr Lu. "The child was trained by the Immortal Cloud Sect?"

Zephyr Lu was relieved that Huang was only testing his son's martial skills. "As your disciple, how could I forget *Shifu's* rule? I would never dream of sharing my knowledge without permission. His mentor is Master Withered Wood, Abbot of Cloudy Perch Temple in Lin'an."

"Master? That man isn't worthy of that title. His offshoot of Shaolin Temple kung fu is so feeble, they aren't even worthy of being our servants. You are a hundred times his superior. From tomorrow, you may teach your son yourself."

Overjoyed, Zephyr Lu said to his son, "Quickly, thank the Grandmaster for his benevolence!"

Laurel Lu prostrated in gratitude, knocking his head on the ground four more times. Apothecary Huang held his head high and showed no acknowledgement of the honour.

For years, Zephyr Lu had watched his son's kung fu training from afar, frustrated that his hard work brought little advancement. All Laurel needed was a nudge in the right direction, he often thought.

Although he had lost the full use of his legs, Zephyr Lu never neglected the training of his arms. He was also learned in martial theory. But he had hidden it all from his family, fearing his son might ask him for lessons if he found out. Zephyr Lu could not betray the bond of trust bestowed upon him by his mentor.

And now, in one day, not only had he been welcomed back to Peach Blossom Island, he had also been granted the permission to share his hidden knowledge with his only son. At last, the young man's kung fu would improve! Zephyr Lu wanted to thank his *Shifu*, but his words were caught by the lump in his throat.

Apothecary Huang shot a look of disdain at Zephyr Lu's emotional display and said, "This is for you."

He waved his right hand and two pieces of paper drifted towards Zephyr Lu, one after the other. He was standing more than ten feet from his disciple, yet the two leaves fluttered in the air as if borne on a breeze. Only a consummate master could channel his inner strength into something so soft and light, and manipulate it as if it were weighty and substantial. To hurl a rock hundreds of *jin* would have been much easier. Everyone watched in awe.

"What do you think of Papa's kung fu?" Lotus asked proudly.

"It's magical." Guo Jing was gobsmacked. "You must learn properly when you get home."

"You're coming too, aren't you?"

"I'll travel with *Shifus* first – but I'll visit!"

"No! We have to stay together!" Lotus grabbed his hand, but Guo Jing had accepted with a heavy heart that, after tonight, they would have to part.

Zephyr Lu caught the flying pages and saw that they were covered in script. By the light of a torch, he recognised Apothecary Huang's handwriting. Both pages were filled with a martial training formula.

Shifu's calligraphy is so much more powerful and alert these days, he observed as he skimmed the pages.

On the top right of the first leaf was the title *Swirling Leaf Kick*. He knew this and the Cascading Peach Blossom Palm were his teacher's most cherished inventions, but neither Lu nor his five martial siblings had been taught this kung fu.

I haven't got the legs to learn this now, Zephyr Lu thought, regarding the pages wistfully. But Laurel does, and I will help him master it. He carefully stowed the instructions in his shirt and bowed in gratitude.

"This is all very different from what you may remember. The moves might be the same, but this starts from a foundation in *neigong*," Apothecary Huang explained. "If you meditate and cultivate your energy according to my formula, your inner strength will build up, and if your progress is quick, you will walk without crutches in five or six years." The martial Master sighed. "Your legs will never regain their full strength, they will never be fit for martial arts – but, if you follow my instructions, you will walk again."

For years, Apothecary Huang had regretted his rash punishment, so he had set his mind to creating a way to help his four blameless, exiled disciples regain the use of their legs. When he succeeded, his pride led him to name the new technique after an existing, unrelated martial skill – Apothecary Huang would never admit he was wrong.

"Find Tempest and your two little brothers. Share it with them," Apothecary Huang said, after a pause.

"Alas, Brother Wu passed away some years ago. I have yet to find news of Big Brother Qu and Brother Feng, but search for them I shall," Zephyr Lu promised, struggling to keep his emotions in check. *Shifu* has been thinking about us, all these years!

Apothecary Huang had not known of Brother Wu's passing. He turned his hawk-like gaze onto Cyclone Mei, his heart aching at the loss of yet another disciple. She could not see his glare, but its sharpness made everyone else uneasy.

"Cyclone, you have committed great evil, but you have also endured great suffering. Though your sight is gone, if you stay on the righteous path, I doubt anyone would wish to trouble a disciple of Old Heretic Huang."

Mei knew that was a public acknowledgement of her readmission to Peach Blossom Island. Tears burst forth once more at this unexpected good news.

Paying no attention to Mei's emotional outburst, he continued, "Stay at Roaming Cloud Manor. Zephyr will look after you."

Cyclone Mei and Zephyr Lu thanked their *shifu* as one.

Laurel Lu stepped forward and took Cyclone Mei by the arm. "Allow me to show you to your room. My mother will wait upon you with refreshments." Gently, he led her to the private quarters at the heart of the manor.

"Might I invite *Shifu* to step inside to rest his feet?" Zephyr Lu asked.

Ignoring the invitation, Apothecary Huang glared at everyone gathered, before focusing on Guo Jing. "You are Guo Jing?"

"Yes, Master Huang." The young man kowtowed.

"You killed my disciple Hurricane Chen? You must have some skill!"

"I was a child." Guo Jing was alarmed by Huang's tone. "I was captured by Master Chen and I panicked. I hurt him by mistake."

Apothecary Huang snorted at the response, then he said frostily, "Treacherous though Hurricane Chen was, it was a matter for us to deal with. Not an outsider!"

"He was six years old, Papa!"

Unsettled by his daughter's decision to stand on the boy's side, Huang continued, "Old Beggar Hong has never taken a disciple, yet he taught you fifteen moves of his most celebrated kung fu. You must have something about you. Or perhaps you tricked him into indulging you? You defeated my disciple with the Old Beggar's moves. The next time we meet, I'll never hear the end of it!"

"Pa, look at him! Does he look like he knows how to flatter? It was me! I coaxed Count Seven into teaching him. Don't be so mean – you're scaring him!"

"I know the Beggar only taught you so he could make fun of me," he said, furious that Lotus should choose to defend Guo Jing once again.

He had expected to find his beloved daughter ill at ease in the *jianghu*, having run away in a fit of petulance. After all, she had never set foot beyond the comforts of Peach Blossom Island until a few short months ago. Yet, here she was, blossoming with confidence and speaking up for the boy against her own father. A kernel of jealousy took root, nourished by the anger he felt towards Guo Jing for killing his disciple, and the slight estrangement he could discern in Lotus's attitude towards him.

"I know he taught you so you could defeat Cyclone Mei, so he can rub in my face the fact that I have no disciples and those I once had are useless—"

"Pa, who said Peach Blossom Island has no disciples?" Lotus cut her father off. "Guo Jing took advantage of Sister Mei's indisposition. He just got lucky! When we were in Yanjing a few months ago, Sister Mei had him completely in her power, riding on his shoulders like he was a horse. I wish you had seen that. He looked so downtrodden! And the Old Beggar couldn't do anything about it!" Lotus was happy to bend the truth to sway her father. "Tell him to blindfold himself and fight Sister Mei. No, better still, let me show him the might of Peach Blossom Island."

Since her kung fu was at about the same level as Guo Jing's, if she made a good show of fighting him, perhaps she could appease her father by coming to a draw after a few dozen moves.

"I'll fight with my father's most simple kung fu," she announced. "You'll see it's more than a match for Count Seven Hong's most vaunted moves."

"You always beat me," Guo Jing said, picking up on her ploy.

"Take this!" Lotus swung her arm in a horizontal swipe known as Torrent and Tempest, from the Cascading Peach Blossom Palm repertoire. The air parted with a *whoosh*.

Guo Jing responded with the Dragon-Subduing Palm, but how

could he put genuine power into his moves? In no time at all, he was overcome by Lotus's complex and ever-changing martial choreography, taking several painful hits to the body.

"You've lost!" Lotus made a point of not holding back, or else her father would not be appeased. She knew Guo Jing was stout enough to stomach it.

"Enough of your games!"

Apothecary Huang's face had turned the hue of cast iron. No-one had caught how he had repositioned himself to enter the fight. His movements were as hard to see as the words he uttered. In a trice, he had lifted each of them up by their collars. He set Lotus gently down with one hand and hurled Guo Jing away with the other.

Guo Jing careered through the air, unable to summon his strength. Nonetheless, the moment his feet reconnected with the earth, he found his footing, standing upright and tall, as steady as if his feet were nailed to the ground.

If Guo Jing had crashed face down, purple and swollen and sore, perhaps Apothecary Huang might have been satisfied. Though grudgingly impressed by the young man's footwork, such an act of defiance could not be left unchallenged.

"Since I have no disciples, I shall test your kung fu personally." Apothecary Huang could barely contain his fury.

The young man bowed deeply. "A lowly novice like myself would never dream of fighting the Master."

"Fight me? A boy like you?" Apothecary Huang sneered. "I shall stand here, perfectly still. You will launch your Eighteen Dragon-Subduing Palms. If I so much as flinch or lift a finger in my defence, then I have lost. Understood?"

"I—"

"You have no say in this."

Guo Jing assumed that Apothecary Huang would deflect his strength and send him flying. If that's all it takes to fix everything, then it's worth falling over a few times, he told himself.

"Come, make your move, or I'll come after you!" the martial

Master taunted. He could detect a hint of eagerness in the young man's show of reluctance. After all, it was a rare and valuable opportunity to try out one's martial learning on a master.

"It would not be my place to defy the Master's orders."

Guo Jing lowered into his opening stance, his elbow slightly crooked. Then he traced a circle with his palm to gather his inner strength before launching the hand at Apothecary Huang. Haughty Dragon Repents. His most confident move. He channelled less than half of his strength, as he was wary of hurting Lotus's father – and was even more afraid that the force of the thrust would rebound back onto him.

The moment he pressed his hand on Huang's chest, it skidded away. The martial Master's torso was slippery, as if slick with oil.

"Why are you holding back? You think I can't withstand your precious Dragon-Subduing Palm?"

Guo Jing mumbled an apology and launched the second move, Leap from the Abyss. Inhaling deeply, he drove his left hand forward as his right palm darted low to strike at Apothecary Huang's abdomen.

"That's more like it."

Guo Jing held back his strength until his fingertips touched Apothecary Huang's clothes, just as Count Seven Hong had taught him.

Yet, in that split second between unleashing the energy and feeling it reaching its target, Guo Jing's connection with his opponent vanished – the martial Master had tugged in his stomach.

It was too late to retrieve his force now.

He heard the crunch of bone snapping out of joint.

Guo Jing jumped a few steps back. A shattering pain shot down his wrist. He could not lift his hand.

Never put all your strength into the attack – he remembered Count Seven Hong's warning too late.

The Freaks were outraged, but they could not fault Apothecary Huang. He had kept his word. He had not dodged or struck back.

"Now it's my turn."

The air stirred with Apothecary Huang's words. A flying palm. Though in great pain, Guo leapt back and ducked sideways. He dodged the palm thrust, but threw himself straight into the kick that followed, which morphed into a sweep and then a hook. Guo Jing was sent sprawling to the ground.

"Papa, no!" Lotus threw herself over him.

Apothecary Huang's strike eased into a claw, and he grabbed at Lotus. The moment he had lifted her out of the way, he sliced down with his left hand.

Not a hint of mercy. He meant to kill.

The Freaks charged in unison. Gilden Quan was the closest and he swung his steelyard into the wrist of Apothecary Huang's attacking hand.

Apothecary Huang took no notice of the attack until he had set Lotus down. Then, for the first time that night, he turned his attention to the Freaks. In an instant, he had snatched up Quan's steelyard and Jade Han's sword, striking them together. They clattered to the ground in four useless pieces.

"Shifu . . ." But what could Zephyr Lu say to dissuade his teacher?

"Pa, if you hurt him, you'll never see me again!" Lotus sprinted towards Lake Tai.

Stunned by her words, it was some time before Apothecary Huang reacted. By then, all that remained of Lotus Huang was a straight line cutting into the surface of the water.

He followed her to the shore and gazed at the swell she left in her wake. He knew she was an excellent swimmer, having grown up with the tides of the East Sea. As a child, she often spent whole days in the water. And this was only a lake. But it is in the nature of parents to worry.

Zhu Cong took advantage of the respite to set Guo Jing's wrist, and this stoked Apothecary Huang's anger further. "Kill yourselves. All seven of you. Now. You will suffer much more if you don't."

Ke Zhen'e held his iron staff sideways across his chest. "A true man has no fear of death. What is there to fear in suffering?"

"The Six Freaks of the South are finally home. If we should meet our fate by Lake Tai, we'll have no regrets," Zhu Cong added. They were now in combat formation; whether they had their weapons or not, they were poised.

I can't let my *shifus* throw their lives away because of me! Guo Jing scrambled forward and stood in front of his teachers.

"It was I alone who caused Hurricane Chen's death. My *shifus* have nothing to do with it." He took a step towards Apothecary Huang. "I will pay with my life."

Then it occurred to Guo Jing that, if Apothecary Huang struck him down, here and now, given his mentors' fiery temperament – especially First *Shifu*, Third *Shifu* and Seventh *Shifu* – they would immediately take up arms to avenge him. It would still end the same way, with all of them dead because of him.

So Guo Jing straightened up and said, "However, I have yet to avenge my father's death. Would the Master kindly grant me thirty days to fulfil my duty as a son? Then I shall go, willingly and promptly, to Peach Blossom Island to meet my fate."

By now, Apothecary Huang's rage had subsided somewhat and he was more occupied with thoughts of Lotus. In no mood to wrangle with Guo Jing, he gave a dismissive wave of his consent and disappeared into the night.

Everyone was left rooted to the spot, dazed by all that had transpired in just one evening. No-one believed Apothecary Huang would let Guo Jing off so easily. One thing was certain: darker plans were at work.

It was Zephyr Lu who broke the silence. "Please come to the rear hall to rest."

CHAPTER SIX

DRAGON WHIPS TAIL

I

"I PROMISED YOUR *SHIFU* I'D LET YOU GO," ZEPHYR LU SAID to Wanyan Kang, as Laurel Lu lifted the Jin Prince to his feet.

The young man could only glare back. Of course, Zephyr Lu was aware that Wanyan Kang's limbs were locked through his acupressure points — he even noticed it had been done in a way different from that taught on Peach Blossom Island. Though he could free the young man, it might be deemed impolite by the person who had put Wanyan Kang into that state. He was certain he would be released when the moment was right.

Zhu Cong stepped forward and pinched Wanyan Kang in the waist a few times, then patted him on the back. The young man regained the command of his body immediately.

Having seen Wanyan Kang fight, Zephyr Lu was impressed how Zhu Cong had immobilised the Jin Prince without exchanging a blow. Under normal circumstances, the Second Freak would not have been able to subdue the young man so easily. Yet, in the chaos after the roof's collapse, Wanyan Kang was busy freeing the Song official that had been travelling with him. That had given Zhu Cong the chance to steal close and restrain them both.

"Take him with you," Zhu Cong said, as he massaged the captured official's vital points.

The man bowed deeply when he could move again, overcome with euphoria; he had been delivered from the jaws of death. "Your humble servant Justice Duan thanks the magnanimous hero for sparing my life. Should my lord—"

"You are . . . Justice Duan?" The name rang and rang in Guo Jing's ears.

"Yes, young hero."

"You were a martial officer in Lin'an, eighteen years ago."

"Indeed, young hero." He then turned to Laurel Lu. "Abbot Withered Wood is, in fact, my uncle. In a way, we are related!" He laughed awkwardly.

Guo Jing looked Justice Duan up and down, silently taking in everything about this desperate man as he ingratiated himself with smiles and small talk.

"Squire Lu, may I use the rear hall for a moment?" Guo Jing said at last.

"Of course."

Guo Jing grabbed Justice Duan by the arm and marched off. The Freaks followed, thanking the heavens for this stroke of luck. If this vile traitor had not revealed his own name, they would not have realised that he was the very person they had tracked for tens of thousands of *li*, all those years ago.

Zephyr Lu, Laurel Lu and Wanyan Kang, mystified by Guo Jing's reaction, trailed after them.

As they entered the rear hall, Guo Jing turned to one of the servants lighting the candles and asked for a brush and some paper. When the writing instruments were brought to him, the young man said, "Second *Shifu*, please write a spirit tablet for my father."

HERE LIES THE SPIRIT OF PATRIOT SKYFURY GUO. Zhu Cong wrote the characters large and clear, and placed the paper reverentially in the centre of the table.

Justice Duan shrivelled at the sight of the name. He had hoped the nice young man was taking him for a late-night meal to calm his nerves. He so desperately wanted to flee, but the rotund figure of Ryder Han filled his vision before he could lift so much as a toe.

Duan immediately felt his trousers clinging to his legs, warm and sodden. He had seen this frightening form before. At an inn in Yangzhou, he had caught a glimpse of him between the door and the jamb. This man and six others, they had followed him as he dragged Skyfury Guo's widow north.

Duan looked from face to face, silently counting, before crumpling into a trembling heap on the floor. Though he had seen the Freaks earlier, at the banquet, he had been too preoccupied by his predicament and had not put two and two together.

"What would you prefer, a quick death or a bit of pain first?" Guo Jing barked.

Justice Duan realised his only hope of survival was to own up and shift the guilt onto someone else. "Though this lowly man played a small part in Patriot Guo's misfortune, I was simply following ord—"

"Who gave the order? Who sent you to kill my father? Speak now!"

"Wanyan Honglie! The Sixth Prince of the Great Jin Empire."

"How dare you!" Wanyan Kang cried.

Justice Duan reasoned that he might mitigate his guilt if he dragged another into the mire, if he could argue he was simply a pawn in someone else's game. So he relayed in great detail how Wanyan Honglie had met and fallen for Ironheart Yang's wife, Charity Bao, how the Jin Prince had used his influence to bribe the Song officials with gold and silver to send soldiers to get rid of Ironheart Yang and Skyfury Guo, and how Wanyan Honglie had pretended to happen across the raid and mount a heroic rescue of Charity Bao. He also told Guo Jing how he had escaped to Zhongdu with the boy's mother as hostage, how they were captured by the Jin army and pressed into service as porters on their march to Mongolia, and how they had been separated in battle. He even explained how he had found his way back to Lin'an and found his path to preferment, to his current high position in the government. He fell to his knees as he concluded his tale.

"Hero Guo, Lord Guo, this is the truth. I am nobody. I remember your honourable father. A real man – righteous, handsome, such a commanding presence – I didn't want to hurt him. It would have been an honour to befriend him. But . . . but I was just a soldier, a lowly official. I received a command – it wasn't up to me. I truly admired your father, I would have spared his life if . . . Justice is my name and I have aspired, ever since I was a child, to live up to it, it's just . . ."

The man glanced up from his grovelling. Guo Jing glared back, dark like iron and hard as steel. The official prostrated himself before Skyfury Guo's memorial, knocking his head loudly and fearfully against the ground in a sign of the utmost respect and submission.

"Grandmaster Guo, I submit myself to your spirit in the heavens. You must understand it was Wanyan Honglie, the Sixth Prince of the Jin Empire, who was your nemesis. Yes, that beast! Not me, not this nobody. Why, I'm no more significant than an ant. Your spirit above must rejoice to see your son so upstanding and heroic. Please, my lord, be merciful. Please ask him to spare this wretched life of mine . . ."

Duan continued to ramble and kowtow to the spirit of Skyfury Guo, but his appeals were soon cut short. Wanyan Kang leapt up, then came swooping down, crushing his fellow captive's skull with both hands.

Guo Jing collapsed by the table in a torrent of tears. Zephyr Lu, Laurel Lu and the Six Freaks took turns to pay their respects to Skyfury Guo.

Wanyan Kang followed, sinking to his knees and touching his head to the ground. He stood up and turned to Guo Jing. "Brother Guo, I had no idea until just now that . . . that Wanyan Honglie is our enemy. I have behaved most unnaturally through ignorance; I truly deserve ten thousand deaths." He thought of the suffering his mother had been through and started to cry.

"What will you do?" Guo Jing asked.

"I now know the name Wanyan has no meaning for me," he said. "From now on, my name will be Yang. I am called Yang Kang."

"These are the words of a man who remembers his roots," Guo Jing said. "I'm leaving for Yanjing tomorrow. To kill Wanyan Honglie. Will you come with me?"

Yang Kang was not sure how to answer. After all, Wanyan Honglie had raised him and treated him as his own blood. However, noticing Guo Jing's face darkening, he immediately said, "Of course! I shall follow my brother's lead."

"Excellent! Your late papa and my mother both told me that our fathers once pledged that we should be sworn brothers. How does that sound?"

"There is nothing I want more."

Yang Kang asked Guo Jing his birthday to determine who would be the elder brother. It turned out he was one month younger than Guo Jing.

Kneeling side by side, they bowed eight times at Skyfury Guo's memorial and became brothers.

2

THE NEXT MORNING, ZEPHYR LU PRESENTED THE FREAKS AND Yang Kang with generous parting gifts as they said their farewells. Guo Jing, however, refused to take anything more from his host. Meanwhile, Cyclone Mei was beginning to settle in at Roaming Cloud Manor. She was given her own quarters as well as dedicated servants and ladies in waiting.

"Brother Yang and I will head north to find Wanyan Honglie," Guo Jing said to his *shifus* as they strolled away from the manor with their horses.

"We will come with you," Ke Zhen'e said, and there was a chorus of agreement from his martial siblings. "We have no engagements until our contest with Tiger Peng on Moon Festival."

"*Shifu*, it would not be right for me to take you north again. You haven't been back to the south for two decades because of me – and your home is just a few days' ride from here. Wanyan Honglie knows no kung fu. With Brother Yang's help, I am sure it won't be difficult to kill him."

Though the Freaks were keen to accompany Guo Jing on his quest, the call of home was strong too. They also had little cause to fear for his safety, given the vast improvement in his kung fu. So, they took turns to bid the young man farewell and offer advice.

Jade Han was the last to speak. "You don't have to go Peach Blossom Island." She knew Guo Jing would never break his promise, but she had at least to try to stop him from walking knowingly into danger. Apothecary Huang's cruel ways were legendary.

"I cannot go back on my word."

"What's the point of keeping faith with such a vile, evil man? Brother, you are too inflexible," Yang Kang interjected.

Ke Zhen'e snorted and turned to his disciple. "We martial men must always honour our word. You need not travel with your sworn brother. Mount Ulaan and gallop to Zhongdu for your revenge. If you succeed, excellent; if you fail this time, remember that it may take years for a man of principle to be avenged. There will always be another chance to plunge a blade into that villain, Wanyan Honglie.

"Today is the fifth day of the sixth month. Meet us at the Garden of the Eight Drunken Immortals in Jiaxing on the first of the seventh month, and we will go to Peach Blossom Island with you."

Guo Jing fell to his knees and bowed in gratitude.

Yang Kang had sped up to distance himself from the group as he heard Ke Zhen'e's pointed remark. Gilden Quan now took the chance to whisper a word of warning: "He's born to wealth and rank. He doesn't seem like an upright man of honour to me. Beware."

Guo Jing nodded solemnly.

"That daughter of Apothecary Huang is nothing like her old man, eh?" Zhu Cong said with a chuckle, in an attempt to diffuse the tension. "We aren't upset about her anymore, are we, Third Brother?"

"She called me a squat melon!" Ryder Han tugged at his beard. "But I'll admit she's a bit better looking than me." He giggled at his own joke.

Guo Jing laughed along with the rest of the Freaks, pleased that his *shifus* had come around to Lotus. However, their current separation and the uncertainty of their reunion weighed heavy on his heart.

"Swift be your ride! We'll await your good news in Jiaxing."

With these parting words from Gilden Quan, the Freaks mounted their horses and rode south.

3

GUO JING WATCHED HIS *SHIFUS* DISAPPEAR BEYOND THE horizon before mounting Ulaan to catch up with Yang Kang.

The two young men rode slowly northwards. It was Guo Jing who broke the silence. "My horse is very fast. It will only take me a fortnight to ride there and back. But let's travel together for a few days at first."

Yang Kang did not reply, trying to hide the upheaval churning inside. Just a month ago, he had come south as Imperial Ambassador of the Great Jin Empire, escorted by a large envoy of guards and attendants. Now, he rode north all alone. His retinue, his wealth, his status – all had vanished like a spring dream. Though he was relieved that Guo Jing had stopped pressing him to come along to Zhongdu for the assassination, he was torn as he tried to resolve one burning question: should he find a way to warn Wanyan Honglie?

Guo Jing noticed Yang Kang's unease, but the simple-minded fellow assumed his sworn brother was thinking about his late parents, and left him to grieve.

At around midday, they arrived in Liyang. Just as they started to look for a place to rest, a man waved at them to stop.

"Sirs, are you Master Guo and Master Yang? We have food and drink ready for you; please come with me."

Guo Jing and Yang Kang exchanged a look of surprise.

"How do you know our names?" Yang Kang asked.

"A gentleman gave us your description this morning and bade us to prepare lunch for your arrival." The man smiled and took the reins of the horses. "Allow me to show you to your table."

The waiter first brought a flagon of Floral Carving yellow wine of good vintage, then returned with bowls of fine noodles accompanied by a variety of elegantly prepared dishes, one of which was Guo Jing's favourite – braised chicken with mushrooms. It was an unexpectedly good meal.

When they asked for the bill, the waiter told them it was already settled.

"Such generosity from Roaming Cloud Manor," Yang Kang sneered as he handed the waiter one *tael* of silver as a tip. The man bowed repeatedly as he saw his patrons all the way to the door, unable to believe his luck.

When they were on the road again, Guo Jing recounted how hospitable Squire Lu had been when he and Lotus had stayed at the manor.

"That man is a fraud. He clearly bought his place among the heroes of the *jianghu* with gold," Yang Kang said sourly, still insulted by the treatment he had received at Zephyr Lu's hands. "What he just did for us – I'm sure that's how he became the leader of the pirates of Lake Tai."

"He's your martial uncle, isn't he?" Yang Kang's attitude took Guo Jing by surprise.

"Cyclone Mei did teach me some martial arts, but I can't really say she's my *shifu*." The flippant answer was followed by a wistful muttered aside. "If only I'd known, I would have stayed away from such unorthodox kung fu. I wouldn't be in such a sticky situation today."

"What do you mean?"

Realising he had let his tongue run away with him, Yang Kang blushed and forced a smile. "Oh, I've always felt there was something not quite right about the Nine Yin Skeleton Claw and all that."

Guo Jing nodded and said, "You're right. Your *shifu* Elder Eternal Spring is a true master of the most orthodox school of martial arts. If you explain everything and promise to practise earnestly, I'm sure he'll forgive you."

Yang Kang made a point of ignoring his sworn brother's words.

At sunset, the young men arrived at Jintan. Once again, the local inn had been informed of their arrival. The same thing happened in every town they stopped at for the next three days. On the fourth day, they crossed the Yangtze River and arrived at Gaoyou. The moment they rode into town, an innkeeper welcomed them.

"How far is Roaming Cloud Manor going to see us off?" Yang Kang scoffed.

But Guo Jing had long suspected it was someone else. There was always one or two of his favourite dishes at each meal. How would Laurel Lu know his tastes so well?

Once they finished eating, Guo Jing said, "I'll go ahead to see who's behind this."

Guo Jing sped through the next three towns without stopping. When he reached Baoying, there was no innkeeper watching out for his arrival. He found the largest inn in town, asked for the room closest to the reception and waited.

At nightfall, he heard a peal of bells and a horse whinnying outside. Then footsteps approached the reception and he heard a voice asking for a room, and for a Master Guo and a Master Yang to be received the next day.

Guo Jing's heart fluttered with joy to hear Lotus's voice again, but he decided not to show himself yet: Lotus loves to play tricks; I'll surprise her tonight!

He got out of bed quietly after the second watch was sounded and tiptoed to Lotus's room. On his way, he caught a glimpse of a shadow hurtling across the rooftops.

Where's she going, this late at night? He gave chase, using his lightness kung fu.

Lotus did not stop until she reached a stream, out in the countryside. She sat down under a willow tree and took a few things from the pocket inside her shirt.

"Now, sit nicely," she muttered. "Face each other. Yes, that's it."

Nocturnal insects chirped over the sound of the babbling brook. The low-hanging moon cast its beams sideways through the night sky. A breeze wafted through the willow branches, ruffling Lotus's sleeves.

Guo Jing stole closer and found shelter a short distance behind Lotus. On the ground before her were two clay dolls, a boy and a girl, chubby and full of life. He remembered her telling him about the earthen figures she'd had growing up on Peach Blossom Island. They came from a city called Wuxi, on the shore of Lake Tai. Even though they were children's playthings, they were skilfully crafted and most lifelike.

Intrigued, Guo Jing crept forward a few steps to get a better look. Placed between the figurines were tiny clay bowls and plates, filled with flowers, grass and leaves.

"This one's for Guo Jing and this one's for Lotus. I made them just for you. Do you like how it tastes?"

"Very much so!" Guo Jing replied, running up behind her.

A glorious smile lit up Lotus's face as she turned and threw her arms around Guo Jing. They held each other tight, refusing to let go. Eventually, they sat under a willow tree, shoulder to shoulder, telling each other all that had happened since they had parted. Though it was only a few days, it felt like months, nay, years.

Guo Jing listened intently, intoxicated by her laughter, her words, her presence. He remembered how Lotus had defied her father to protect him, jumping into Lake Tai to prove her point. But he did not realise that she had swum back after two hours to make sure he was out of danger, and had spent the night in the woods outside Roaming Cloud Manor to keep an eye on him; nor that she had lurked in the undergrowth by the manor's entrance and watched him heading north with Yang Kang, before overtaking them to arrange their meals. He felt blessed that Lotus cared so much, but also a

little uncomfortable with the rift he had caused between father and daughter. He could tell Lotus regretted her harsh words.

By now, the moon was high and the refreshing night breeze lulled Lotus into a languid contentment. Her eyes started to grow heavy and she began to slur her words. Soon, she fell asleep in Guo Jing's arms, her breathing soft and light, her skin cool and smooth. Fearing he might wake her, he slowly leaned his weight against the tree, and he too dozed off.

When Guo Jing woke up, the morning sun was peeking over the horizon. The willow branches rustled to the oriole's song and there was a sweet scent of Lotus in the air. He watched her sleep.

Her eyebrows, perfect crescents. Her cheeks, rosy and immaculate. Her lips, curved upwards in a smile. He decided not to interrupt this perfect image of sleep and turned his attention to counting her eyelashes.

"I scouted out Miss Cheng's chamber. It's behind the Tong Ren Pawnbroker, in the rear garden." The speaker was only a dozen or so paces to the left of Guo Jing.

"Excellent. Let's do it tonight," came the hoarse, whispered reply.

Guo Jing was certain these two men could not be up to any good. Perhaps they were the lecherous flower thieves his *shifus* had told him about? He must thwart their plans.

Right at that moment, Lotus jumped up and ran away from him, calling, "Catch me if you can!"

Guo Jing was confused. What's she doing? Why's she waving at me from behind the tree? After a moment, he understood. She's pretending to be playing in the woods! Chuckling, he ran towards her, making sure his footsteps were heavy and loud enough to disguise his martial training.

The two men were alarmed to find they had company so early in the morning. They relaxed a little when they saw it was a young couple frolicking in the forest, and slunk away in silence.

When the men were out of earshot, Lotus said, "What business do you think they have with Miss Cheng tonight?"

"They're up to no good. We should help her!" Guo Jing replied.

"Do you think they're Count Seven's people? Their clothes were dirty and patched."

"I doubt it, although Count Seven did say he's the chieftain of all beggars. Maybe they're rogues dressed as beggars?"

"No, they're real beggars. You can't fake boils like those on their legs, and their feet were bare and callused." Lotus fell silent for a moment. "Count Seven may have amazing kung fu, but there's only one of him. And there are tens of thousands of beggars under the blue sky. They can't all be good; there must be some rotten ones. He can't possibly keep every single one in line. We should discipline these two for him. I'm sure it'll please him, and it's the perfect way to thank him for being so kind to us, too."

Guo Jing nodded, happy for a chance to repay Count Seven's generosity, and impressed by Lotus's sharp eyes. He certainly had not noticed their legs.

4

GUO JING AND LOTUS HUANG RETURNED TO THE INN FOR breakfast and spent the morning strolling around Baoying, searching for the pawnbrokers mentioned by the beggars. They eventually found it on the western side of the town.

The Historical Tong Ren Pawnbroker was a grand structure. Its name was proudly painted on its white wall, each character taller than an adult man. Beyond this imposing façade was a garden, just as the beggars had described. Among the buildings in the grounds was one particularly ornate tower, its windows shielded by jade-green bamboo blinds. Pleased to have located Miss Cheng's chamber, the young couple continued to explore the rest of the city, hand in hand.

That evening, they went straight to bed after dinner, napping until the first watch was sounded. Then they returned to the pawnbrokers and hopped over the garden wall. A faint light was visible from the tower. They climbed up to the roof, hooked their feet on the eaves and hung upside down to peer inside.

It was a warm night and the windows were all open. Through the slats of the bamboo blind, they could make out seven women in the room. One of them was reading. She looked no more than eighteen or nineteen. She must be Miss Cheng. Around her were six maidservants. Yet, instead of waiting upon their mistress with the usual trappings of a maiden's chamber, they each clutched a weapon, ready for combat. Even their flowing garments were tied back to ensure ease of movement. From their demeanour, it was clear these young women had some kind of martial training.

Guo Jing and Lotus had thought they were here to deliver a young woman from trouble, but, since she was so well prepared, something else must be afoot. Sharing a smile, they swung back up to the roof and waited for the excitement to begin.

Half an hour later, a quiet *pop* sounded from beyond the garden wall. Lotus tugged Guo Jing's sleeve and they ducked down, out of sight, behind an upturned corner of the roof.

Two dark shapes scaled the wall and one of them gave a short, low whistle as they hurried across the garden to Miss Cheng's building. Their outlines very much resembled the beggars from that morning.

A maid lifted a corner of the blind. "Are you the heroes of the Beggar Clan? Please come up."

Guo Jing and Lotus glanced at each other. They had been expecting a fight. Who would have thought the beggars would turn out to be friends with Miss Cheng?

When the two men entered her chamber, the young woman stood up and made a gesture of welcome. "Might I ask your names?"

"My family name is Li. This is my martial nephew, Prosper Yu." Guo Jing and Lotus recognised his voice immediately – the second speaker that morning, the man with the hoarse voice.

"Master Li, Brother Yu, it is my honour to be acquainted with such revered names. The heroes of the Beggar Clan are admired throughout the *wulin* for their righteous sense of justice. Please take a seat."

Miss Cheng's words were a standard welcome in the dialect of the rivers and lakes. Yet she spoke in such a bashful, halting manner that it was clear to all that these martial courtesies fell outside her usual manner of speaking, and nor were her guests her usual conversational companions.

The young woman's face was flushed crimson. Eventually, she mustered enough courage to lift her eyes for the first time since the men's arrival. The mere sight of them sent her head sinking even lower in maidenly discomfort. "The Elder is the Serpent Lord of the Eastern Shores, Vigour Li?"

"The lady is most perceptive." Li smiled. "I once had the pleasure of meeting your honourable teacher, the Sage of Tranquillity. I have always held her in the utmost respect and admiration."

The Sage of Tranquillity? Could he mean Sun Bu'er the Faithful, one of the Seven Immortals of the Quanzhen Sect? Guo Jing wondered. If so, I'm martially related to both Miss Cheng and the beggars.

"I am immensely grateful for the heroes' assistance," Miss Cheng said. "I shall obey your instructions."

"The lady is of such sanctity that it would be a disgrace if that despicable rake were to clap eyes on you even momentarily." Vigour Li's words caused the maiden to blush again. "Might I ask the lady to retreat to your mother's room with the esteemed ladies here? I know just the way to deal with such a miscreant."

"My martial skill is rudimentary, but I do not fear the ruffian. It would be improper of me to let the heroes take all the responsibility."

"Our Chief Hong and Immortal Wang were great friends. We are one family – your troubles are our troubles too."

A little part of Miss Cheng wanted to stay and take part in the action, but she was brought up to obey her seniors' instruction. Accepting the decision, she bowed. "I shall entrust the matter to Master Li and Brother Yu." With that, she hurried downstairs with her ladies-in-waiting.

Vigour Li lifted the embroidered quilt and planted himself –

grubby clothes, dirty feet, unwashed body – onto Miss Cheng's scented silk bedding.

"Go downstairs and keep watch with our men," he ordered Prosper Yu. "No-one strikes before my signal."

When his companion had left the room, Vigour Li blew out the candle, let down the gauze around the bed and pulled the quilt over himself, before turning to hide his face against the pillow.

Lotus chuckled silently. *Miss Cheng will never want to use those bedclothes again. Looks like the chieftain's mischievousness has rubbed off on his beggar followers. Who are they waiting for? This is going to be a fun night!*

Lotus retreated further up the roof with Guo Jing. She could hear the men from the Beggar Clan positioning themselves around the garden.

Dik dok, dik dok, dong dong dong. The third watch.

A clattering stone broke the stillness of the night. Shadowy figures leapt over the garden wall in quick succession. Eight in total. They disappeared into the tower. The spark of flint and tinder flickered briefly in Miss Cheng's room. Guo Jing and Lotus caught a glimpse of the intruders – they were dressed from head to toe in white – Gallant Ouyang's disciples!

The women approached the bed. Stealth was their watchword. Two of them took up defensive positions as four more lifted the gauze, pulled the quilt over the sleeper's head and pressed the covers down. Their bounty was then deftly bundled up into a large sack, held open by the last two accomplices, who yanked the drawstring tight the moment the silk-cocooned captive was rolled inside.

The abduction only took a few moments. They had clearly done it many times.

As the kidnappers made their way downstairs, Lotus restrained Guo Jing from intercepting them. "Let the beggars go first."

Watching from their high vantage point, they made out four women darting across the garden, each holding a corner of the sack. The others guarded their flanks. A group of ten or so beggars set off after them with wooden staffs and bamboo canes in hand.

Once the two groups were some distance ahead, Guo Jing and Lotus jumped down from the tower and followed them all the way to a large house on the outskirts of the town. The women disappeared inside and the beggars scattered, surrounding the building.

Lotus led Guo Jing by the hand to the back of the house, where they scaled the perimeter wall. They tiptoed to the candlelit main hall and found a window to peer through.

This residence was not built for the living. Rows and rows of spirit tablets lined the walls. Horizontal wooden plaques, inscribed with the titles and ranks of illustrious forebears, covered the tie beams. This was a family temple, built to honour the dead.

A lone figure sat in the middle, illuminated by a handful of red candles. The flames flickered as he wafted his fan.

Gallant Ouyang. Just as Lotus and Guo Jing had expected.

They ducked and kept very still, lest he discover them.

The kidnappers entered and spoke in perfect unison as they set down their load: "My lord, Miss Cheng."

Gallant Ouyang's reply was addressed to those waiting beyond the confines of the room. "Why don't you come inside, friends?" he said with a sneer.

The beggars stayed silent, waiting for their leader's signal.

Tilting his head, the Master of White Camel Mount studied the sack. "I didn't expect such a great beauty to come with so little effort." He edged closer as he spoke, folding his fan slowly into an iron brush.

Judging from his actions and his expression, it was clear that Gallant Ouyang knew the bag did not contain Miss Cheng. He was prepared to use force on the imposter. Guo Jing and Lotus both knew that he was not a man given to mercy. Lotus held three steel needles between her fingers, ready to help the beggar the moment Gallant Ouyang lashed out.

But before anyone made a move – *whoosh, whoosh!* – two sleeve arrows hurtled at Gallant Ouyang's back. One of the beggars outside had deemed the situation too dangerous to wait for Vigour Li's sign.

The libertine reached casually behind him with his left hand and caught the first arrow between his index and middle fingers. With a slight twirl of his wrist, he trapped the other arrow between the fourth and little fingers of the same hand. Moments later, the arrows clattered to the floor in four broken pieces.

"Come out, Uncle Li!" Prosper Yu cried.

The sack containing Vigour Li ripped open and out flew two glinting daggers. The beggar rolled out and leapt to his feet, whipping the bag around him to create a soft shield.

Vigour Li knew it was unlikely he could subdue Gallant Ouyang through force alone. He had hoped the element of surprise would play to his advantage, but the Master of White Camel Mount had seen through his ploy.

"What an excellent transformation trick!" Gallant Ouyang jeered. "A young beauty turned into an old beggar!"

"In the last three days, four maidens have gone missing in this town. These were your fair deeds, were they not?"

"Surely the constables of a town as wealthy as Baoying aren't forced to beg on the side?"

"This town isn't my patch, but a little beggar told me about the abductions yesterday. I must say, it rather piqued this busybody's curiosity."

"Well, those girls weren't anything special. Since we're both martial men, if you want them, you can have them. I hear beggars find dead crabs delicious, so I'm sure you'll treasure them."

At Gallant Ouyang's signal, several of his women slipped out of sight and returned dragging four young women with them. The girls were visibly distressed, their clothes in disarray, their eyes bloodshot and swollen from crying.

The sight made Vigour Li's blood boil. "What is your name? Which martial school do you belong to?"

"My name is Ouyang," came the nonchalant reply. "So? Do you like them?"

"Prepare to defend yourself, scoundrel!"

"Happy to oblige." Gallant Ouyang stood back and let the beggar make the first move.

Vigour Li raised his right arm. Before he could launch his attack, a blur of white flew behind him and a gust of air fluttered at the back of his neck. If he had dived forward a fraction slower, Gallant Ouyang would have caught him by his vital points. He would have lost before the fight had even started. Embarrassed by his near defeat, the beggar swung his palm in a backhand slice without turning to face his opponent.

"Dragon-Subduing Palm," Lotus muttered.

Guo Jing nodded in agreement, watching closely.

Gallant Ouyang realised he could not counter this blow directly and swerved sideways, beyond its reach.

This gave a window for Vigour Li to turn and take a step closer for his next attack. Lifting his hands over his chest, the beggar drew a circle in the air before punching forward.

"Wayfaring Fist?" Guo Jing whispered.

Lotus nodded. The beggar's movements were heavy and leaden, lacking the necessary ease and fluidity. They would not have known that Vigour Li was a senior and respected figure of the Beggar Clan, in charge of the eastern and western routes of Huainan, which covered a large stretch of the Jiangsu and Anhui regions, nor that he was considered a formidable fighter of his rank, Disciple of Eight Pouches.

Taken aback by the beggar's steady stance and intricate moves, Gallant Ouyang started to take the fight seriously. Tucking his fan into his belt, he veered away from the beggar's attack and let his fist fly in retaliation – a bolt of lightning – at his opponent's right shoulder. Vigour Li blocked with a Beg for Alms, another move from the Wayfaring Fist.

Now, Gallant Ouyang threw a left hook. He waited until his opponent had raised his arms to block, then he darted round. He stood behind Vigour Li, his hands shaped like beaks, then pecked at the major acupressure points on the beggar's back.

Guo Jing and Lotus gasped. There was nothing Vigour Li could do to save himself.

The beggars outside had rushed into the hall when the fight started. Now, they all scrambled forward, desperate to help their Elder.

Vigour Li heard the air part behind him and felt the pressure bearing down on his back. He swung his arm sideways again in a backhand slice.

The same move from the Dragon-Subduing Palm he had used before.

This move was inspired by the way a tiger swings, jaws snapping, when its tail is pinned. It was also rooted in the Treading hexagram from the *I'Ching*. When the Dragon-Subduing Palm was distilled from twenty-eight to eighteen moves, the strike was sharpened and its name changed from Trapping the Tiger's Tail to Dragon Whips Tail.

Gallant Ouyang tilted backwards quickly to avoid its sting.

That was close! Vigour Li thought, as he turned to face his opponent once more.

The beggar managed to withstand another thirty or so moves by the skin of his teeth. He turned to Dragon Whips Tail another five or six times to get out of danger.

"Count Seven only taught him one move," Lotus observed quietly. Nodding, Guo Jing remembered how he had fought Greybeard Liang with just Haughty Dragon Repents. He felt even more honoured that he had learned fifteen moves, when this man from the Beggar Clan only knew one.

Gallant Ouyang was taking a step forward with each attack. He wanted to trap the beggar in a corner, to deny him of the space he needed to launch his one powerful strike.

But Vigour Li saw through the tactic. He stepped sideways to bring the fight back to the middle of the hall. Then he heard Gallant Ouyang laugh in derision.

Pang! A fist connected with his jaw.

Blinded by pain, it took a moment for Vigour Li to collect himself. By the time he had raised his arms to block, a second punch had connected with his body. Five or six blows landed in quick succession on his face and chest. His head started to spin and he could not summon any strength to his limbs. He swivelled and collapsed to the floor.

Several beggars rushed forward to catch Vigour Li. Gallant Ouyang grabbed the two closest to him and flung them aside. The men hit the wall with a sickening thud, slumping to the floor in an unconscious heap. Everyone else froze, rooted on the spot.

"Did you really think I'd fall for a beggar's trick?" Gallant Ouyang's voice was dripping with disdain. He clapped once and two women ushered another young woman into the hall.

The tearful girl's hands were bound behind her. Her unblemished cheeks were devoid of colour, like a piece of white jade.

Miss Cheng.

Her capture shocked the beggars. They looked at each other, appalled by their failure. Even Lotus and Guo Jing could not fathom how she had been abducted.

Gallant Ouyang gave the signal and his women dragged Miss Cheng away.

"While our beggar friend was playing hide and seek upstairs, yours truly had the pleasure of meeting Miss Cheng downstairs and invited her back here to await your arrival."

He unfurled his fan and began to wave it leisurely. "The reputation of the Beggar Clan travels far and wide. Now, having crossed paths with the renowned Clan, I can only say that my jaw aches from laughing. Your fists may come in handy when stealing chickens and swiping dogs. Your palms may be helpful when begging for food and catching snakes. But to interfere with my business? I'll do your Chief Hong the honour of sparing this old beggar's life, but I'll gouge out his eyes so that no one will forget this day!" His hand was raised like a claw, ready to jab into Vigour Li's eyes.

5

"STOP!"

Before Gallant Ouyang could register who it was who stepped between himself and Vigour Li, he felt an enormous force closing in on his chest. He twisted out of its path. Though the palm strike never connected with his body, the fringes of its power rocked him off balance, forcing him to stumble two steps back.

Who has such mighty strength? Gallant Ouyang was shocked to find the youth he had first encountered at the Prince of Zhao's residence. He remembered the boy's kung fu being average, at best. How had he improved so much in just a few months?

"You feel no remorse for the evil you have done and you would hurt a good man. Chief Hong's followers will not be intimidated by the likes of you!"

"You're from the Beggar Clan too?" Gallant Ouyang cast Guo Jing a condescending look. The young man must have got lucky just now.

"I am not worthy to stand among the valiant men of the Beggar Clan. But may I offer a suggestion? Free Miss Cheng and go back west."

"What if I don't take your advice, child?"

"He'll beat you up!" Lotus answered for Guo Jing.

"My dear lady, I shall free Miss Cheng this instant if you wish it." Gallant Ouyang's heart leapt at the sight of the girl. "I would only ask for one thing in return. You. And I promise, not only will I free Miss Cheng, I will free all my women. And I will never seek another. What do you say?"

Lotus smiled back. "I'd love to see the west." She turned to Guo Jing. "What do you say?"

"No, no, no. Just you. Not that meddling fool."

Lotus swung a backhand – "How dare you insult him!" – catching Gallant Ouyang square in the face.

Under normal circumstances, Gallant Ouyang would never have let his guard down like that. But the sight of Lotus Huang sauntering over to him – her smile, her voice, her charm, her innocence – dazzled him. The last thing he had expected was for her to attack him, least of all with one of the most intricate and unpredictable moves from the Cascading Peach Blossom Palm. Even though her inner strength was limited, his left cheek now stung, as much with shame as anything else.

"Fie!" Gallant Ouyang lashed out with a strike aimed at her chest.

Standing her ground, Lotus flung both fists at the crown of his head.

A punch is a small price to pay to feel her bosom, Gallant Ouyang said to himself. His angry reaction was the perfect cover for a lecherous grope. But the moment his hands grazed her clothes, a fierce pain skewered his fingertips. Hedgehog Chainmail, he recalled with a grimace, flinging his arms up hurriedly to block her.

Lotus chuckled. "It's a bad idea to fight me. Only I get to do the hitting; you can't touch me!"

Her taunt fanned the flames of Gallant Ouyang's desire. It was like an itch he could not scratch. Surely, if he killed the boy, she would have no reason to resist his advances. Keeping his eyes trained on her, he kicked back, fast and merciless, in one of his uncle Viper Ouyang's deadliest moves. Once his foot connected with Guo Jing's chest, the young man's ribs would shatter, puncturing his lungs.

The attack was so sudden, there was no time for Guo Jing to duck. But no-one, least of all Gallant Ouyang, foresaw that Guo Jing would fight back head on, swinging his arm horizontally in a backhand slice.

Pang!

Guo Jing took the kick on his hip, but he struck Gallant Ouyang on his leg. The force of each impact sent a bolt of excruciating pain through their bones. They kept their eyes locked as they spun round to face each other. Then they lunged simultaneously.

The beggars could not believe their eyes. How could this boy know Elder Li's life-saving move? His was faster and more powerful too!

In fact, Guo Jing had not studied the move, but since it was rooted in Dragon-Subduing Palm, he could imitate its form well enough to protect himself. If he had known how to channel his full strength into it, Gallant Ouyang would have suffered a crippling injury to his thigh.

By now, Vigour Li had been dragged out of harm's way and he was marvelling at Guo Jing's seeming mastery of Dragon Whips Tail. He watched the young man battle Gallant Ouyang – each palm strike appeared to be in the same vein.

Where had he learned so many moves of Dragon-Subduing Palm? the Beggar Clan Elder wondered. It's Chief Hong's most coveted repertoire. I was only taught one as a reward for risking my life for the Clan! Who is this young man?

Gallant Ouyang was also amazed by Guo Jing's improvement.

In no time, Guo Jing had taken more than forty moves from Gallant Ouyang and responded with the fifteen palm strikes several times over. His knowledge of the Dragon-Subduing Palm was sufficient to keep him from harm, but it was not enough to turn the fight to his advantage. Gallant Ouyang's kung fu was not only far superior, he also had years of combat experience and training over Guo Jing.

After a dozen or so more moves, the Master of White Camel Mount changed his tactics. Darting back and forth with dazzling speed, he bombarded Guo Jing with feints and punches from all directions.

Guo Jing was quickly overwhelmed. He suffered a kick to his hip and, for a moment, lost his footing. He had become predictable. Starting from the fifteenth move, he launched the full repertoire in reverse.

The new sequence forced Gallant Ouyang back onto the defensive. He had to work out the new pattern and watch for gaps again before he could swoop in with a deadly attack.

Guo Jing had now performed the Dragon-Subduing Palm two

more times, first in reverse and then in sequence. For a moment, he wavered.

What should come next? Haughty Dragon Repents? Dragon in the Field?

His hesitation gave Gallant Ouyang the chance he had been waiting for.

Gallant Ouyang pounced, grabbing at his shoulder.

Nothing Guo Jing had learned could counter this blow. He stopped mid-move, flipped his palm and slapped downwards.

Smack! A blow to the wrist.

Gallant Ouyang leapt back in surprise, turning his sore arm to check for injury. Luckily, there was no fracture.

The Master of White Camel Mount had been certain that the boy had a limited repertoire of palm thrusts. Where had this new move come from?

Guo Jing was equally shocked by the efficacy of his improvisation.

My shoulder, left hip and the right side of my waist are exposed; perhaps I could come up— Before Guo Jing could finish this thought, Gallant Ouyang rained down another torrent of thrusts and punches.

Quick wits had always eluded Guo Jing. He would not be able to create a new move even if he had a fortnight of peace and quiet. It would take a miracle to do so in the heat of battle, when his mind could barely react fast enough to fend off his opponent's attacks. Nonetheless, he tried.

Where had these three new moves come from? Gallant Ouyang was infuriated. He had thought he had the measure of Guo Jing's repetitive kung fu and could soon defeat him. Now, he had to bide his time once more while he worked out these new patterns. He had yet to realise that Guo Jing's new moves contained no substance. He would slow down, wear out Guo Jing through a battle of attrition instead.

Then he noticed one of the moves had changed.

He hasn't mastered this one yet! Gallant Ouyang congratulated himself.

He leapt up. His left hand struck down at Guo Jing's cranium. His right foot flew towards Guo Jing's left hip.

Guo Jing froze. What should he do to deflect this brutal attack on his weakest, undefended parts? He abandoned his move and swerved sideways.

But Gallant Ouyang had put all his strength into the kick. There was no chance Guo Jing could react fast enough to evade the blow.

Lotus flicked her right hand, hurling eight steel needles at the cad.

Still in mid-movement, Gallant Ouyang reached for the folding fan tucked into the back of his collar, flicked it open and knocked the needles off course with a gentle flourish.

Lotus's intervention had not made the slightest difference to the power of his kick. It was going to force Guo Jing to the ground and keep him there – too injured to fight back.

But, before his foot could make contact, Gallant Ouyang felt a light tap on his ankle. Then a mild numbing sensation spread, as if he had been struck on a vital point. He managed to land the kick on Guo Jing's side, but all the strength had drained from his leg.

Gallant Ouyang backed away, shocked.

"Who dares to interfere with the Master of White Camel Mount? Show yourself!"

He felt the air stir above his head and he ducked. But, whatever it was, it was travelling at great speed . . . He could feel something in his mouth. He spat it out in a panic.

A chicken bone?

Gallant Ouyang looked up.

A cloud of dust was drifting down from the tie beams.

He jumped sideways.

Pop!

He had barely found his footing when it struck him. Something landed in his mouth. His teeth rattled, his gums felt sore.

A chicken thigh bone.

Gallant Ouyang was consumed with rage. He had never been

toyed with like this before. He sprang up and struck at the shadow scurrying across the beams. While he was still airborne, he felt a hand glide across his face and then something was stuffed into his hand. He landed and unfurled his fingers.

The half-chewed remains of two chicken feet.

Laughter rang out from above.

"So, what do you think about us beggars now? Did our chicken-stealing, dog-swiping kung fu impress you?"

6

"COUNT SEVEN!" LOTUS HUANG AND GUO JING EXCLAIMED, AS the beggars bowed and hailed their leader with a cry of "Chief!"

Perching aloft on a tie beam, his legs swinging in the air, Count Seven Hong paid little attention to the commotion at ground level; the remnants of a chicken in his hand held his full interest.

Not him again! Gallant Ouyang groaned inwardly as a chill spread through him. He could have killed me thrice over just now. If he had used darts or needles instead of chicken bones . . . A smart man would make an exit while he still could.

He made a show of faux deference, proclaiming in his most sonorous voice, "Uncle Hong, what a pleasure to see you again! Your nephew kowtows to you." Yet he remained resolutely upright.

"Why are you still dallying in the Central Plains?" Count Seven said, his mouth full of chicken. "Your wicked ways will get you killed here. Is that what you want?"

"I was told that Master Hong is the only truly invincible martial master of the Central Plains," Gallant Ouyang said. "I would survive if my elder could refrain from harassing me. My uncle the Viper bade me to always be reverential in your presence. He said that a master such as yourself would not lower himself to enter into an altercation with a junior, for such behaviour would make him a laughing stock among the heroes of the *jianghu*."

"I know you're trying to outmanoeuvre me with your clever words – make it seem unmannerly for me to strike you," Count Seven said with a hollow laugh. "But there are many in the Central Plains who would gladly take your life. This old beggar needn't raise a hand. However, there is one thing we do need to settle. I heard you were disdainful of my chicken-stealing, dog-swiping fists and my food-begging, snake-catching palms. Did my ears deceive me?"

"I did not realise this old hero was your disciple. Those were rash words spoken in the heat of battle. I am certain Uncle Hong and the old hero will overlook any inadvertent offence."

"You call him a hero, but he can't beat you." Count Seven leapt down from his perch. "So, are you saying you're the greater hero? Have you no shame?"

Gallant Ouyang bit his tongue and swallowed his retort, knowing he had no chance against this rambling old codger.

"Think you can make the Central Plains cower with what the Venom taught you?" Count Seven snorted. "Alas, there's no place for you here, so long as this old beggar is still around."

"You and my uncle are both regarded to be among the Five Greats. As a junior, I have no choice but always to obey my seniors."

"Oh, so now you're insinuating that I'm using my seniority to bully you!"

Gallant Ouyang's silence was a clear affirmative.

"I have a large family of beggars – big ones, small ones, middling ones – yet not one of them is my disciple. Li over there learned one simple move from me. I didn't teach him Wayfaring Fist. And he's still got a long way to go with that. You may look down on my chicken-stealing moves, but if I did pass my knowledge on to one person, I'm certain that they'd be just as good as you."

"Of course, your disciple would most certainly prevail. But we all know how advanced your kung fu is. I fear it would be difficult for any disciple of yours to acquire even one-tenth of your skills."

"Is that another of your veiled insults?"

"Definitely, Count Seven," Lotus Huang cut Gallant Ouyang off before he could deny it. "He's cursing you. I know what he's thinking. He thinks that, although you're a great martial artist, you're an awful teacher. You've never managed to pass on your knowledge. You just share a piece here, a morsel there. There isn't a single student who's successfully learned all you know."

Glaring at Lotus, Count Seven said, "Lass, I know what you're trying to do, and I know what the lad is saying." His hand shot out like a flash of lightning and snatched Gallant Ouyang's fan from his grasp.

With a flick of his wrist, Count Seven unfolded it and studied its decorations. Several peonies, with the signature *Xu Xi*. He was unfamiliar with the famous artist of the Northern Song period, but even he could tell it was masterfully painted.

"Awful!" he spat.

The calligraphy on the flip side was signed *Master of White Camel Mount*. He pointed this out to Lotus. "What do you think?"

"Vulgar." Lotus lifted her eyebrows in disdain. "I'm certain a scribe at the Tong Ren Pawnbroker wrote it for him. He doesn't look to me like someone who knows how to use a brush."

Gallant Ouyang glowered at Lotus. He was incredibly proud of being both a consummate martial artist and a first-rate calligrapher. Yet, it only took one look from her coy, half-smiling eyes for all his annoyance to dissipate.

Count Seven wiped his lips with the fan, smudging the painting and the calligraphy with the chicken grease. He then crushed the fan and tossed it away like a piece of waste paper. No-one else gave much thought to Count Seven's actions, but they struck fear into Gallant Ouyang – the fan's monture was made of the strongest steel.

Then the Beggar Clan Chief spoke. "If I were to fight you, you'd never admit defeat, even with your last breath. But I can take a disciple now and you two can fight."

"I had the pleasure of exchanging a few dozen moves with our brother, here," Gallant Ouyang said, pointing at Guo Jing, "and I was fortunate enough to gain the upper hand before Master Hong's interference. Were you close to winning the fight, Brother Guo?"

Guo Jing shook his head. "I cannot beat you."

Gallant Ouyang beamed.

Count Seven threw his head back and laughed. "Are you my disciple, Guo Jing?"

"No, sir, I cannot claim such an honour," Guo Jing replied, remembering how Count Seven had responded to his kowtows in the pine forest.

The exchange perplexed the Master of White Camel Mount. *I don't think the old man would lie about such a thing. But then who taught the boy those intricate palm thrusts?*

"See?" Count Seven glared at Gallant Ouyang, then turned to Guo Jing. "If I refuse to take you as my disciple, the lass will haunt me with all her infernal tricks until I change my mind. This old beggar hasn't got the patience to tussle with little girls. I'll admit defeat and take you as my protégé."

"How are you going to thank me?" Lotus asked with a smirk. "I've found you a good disciple. Now you've got someone to pass on your knowledge to. I deserve some credit, don't I?" She had got her way at last.

Guo Jing fell to his knees, knocked his head on the floor and cried, "*Shifu!*" He had told the Six Freaks of the South at Roaming Cloud Manor about his encounter with Count Seven and how he had learned Dragon-Subduing Palm. They were thrilled by Guo Jing's good fortune and gave their blessing should the legendary Master wish to take him as a disciple.

"Come, silly lad, let's get started!" Count Seven began to demonstrate the remaining three moves from the Dragon-Subduing Palm – in front of everyone.

The Beggar's so eager to win, he's forgotten I'm right here! He's clearly soft in the head, Gallant Ouyang said to himself as he watched Count Seven Hong intently.

The moves seemed rather uninspiring to Gallant's eyes, but the intricacy probably lay in the explanations whispered in Guo Jing's ear. The theory behind them must be quite complex, since Guo Jing kept shaking his head in confusion.

Count Seven Hong repeated the instructions again and again. Eventually, his patience was rewarded by a few hesitant nods from his new disciple. It was clear, however, that the young man had comprehended little.

He must be incredibly thick, Gallant Ouyang concluded. I won't complain, though – he's given me more time to observe!

Guo Jing was at last ready to try out the moves. After going through them half a dozen times, Count Seven said, "Well done, lad. You've mastered half their power. Now, the time has come to beat this wicked lecher."

Guo Jing took two steps forward – *whoosh!* – his palm forced Gallant Ouyang to shift sideways. But Gallant Ouyang latched onto his own momentum, swinging his fist back.

Gallant Ouyang expected to defeat Guo Jing easily. Not only could he anticipate the boy's moves – old and new – he was also confident that Guo Jing had barely grasped one-tenth of the intricacy of these new techniques. But Gallant Ouyang had not understood that the power of the Dragon-Subduing Palm lay in the channelling of strength, not the complexity of the movements. That was why he – or martial masters like Greybeard Liang and Cyclone Mei – could not unravel its secrets, even when Guo Jing repeatedly launched the same few sequences on them. Nor did he realise the three moves Guo Jing had just learned completed the set of the Eighteen Dragon-Subduing Palms, and that this knowledge amplified the force of every other thrust Guo Jing made.

Gallant Ouyang was now struggling. He had tried four different boxing techniques in succession. None of them could stand up to Guo Jing's steady and repetitive onslaught.

Another score of moves were exchanged. Gallant Ouyang was growing anxious.

My uncle has trained me personally since childhood and this boy has studied with the Old Beggar only a few minutes. I might not be able to win this without resorting to our secret kung fu. I cannot allow the Beggar to appear stronger than my uncle!

Steeled by fresh resolve, he threw a straight punch at Guo Jing.

Guo Jing raised his arm to block, but immediately felt a thump on his neck. Somehow, Gallant Ouyang had managed to snake around his guard by bending his arm at a distinctly unnatural angle. Had the bone in his forearm just melted away?

Guo Jing ducked in shock and pulled himself away. Then he twisted round, palm thrusting in near panic.

Gallant Ouyang stepped sideways and threw another punch.

Guo Jing swerved, avoiding contact. But the fist pursued him whichever way he dodged, as if Gallant Ouyang's arm could bend like a whip.

Guo Jing moved to block a jab to his right. Yet, somehow, the fist slipped and slithered away, connecting with his left shoulder. He had no idea how to counter these wandering punches and took three heavy blows, one after another. He was flummoxed.

"Guo Jing, stop. Let him have this round."

Guo Jing backed away to lick his wounds, putting several paces between them.

"I am full of admiration for your exceptional kung fu," Guo Jing said to Gallant Ouyang. "It is amazing how you bend your arms."

Gallant Ouyang turned to Lotus, puffed up in triumph.

"This Flaccid Snake Fist must have been inspired by the Venom's serpentine companions," Count Seven Hong said, still mulling over Gallant Ouyang's last phase of attack. "It is indeed exceptional and I will admit that I can think of no way to overcome your kung fu right now. It's your lucky day . . . Now, get out of my sight!"

Gallant Ouyang was horrified that the Beggar had recognised the source of his martial secret instantly. His uncle's warning came back to him: *Use the Sacred Snake Fist only in matters of life and death.*

If Uncle knew what had just happened, he would mete out the worst form of punishment . . . The thought wiped out all the joy of victory. He grudgingly put his hands together in a gesture of respect and turned to leave.

7

"NOT SO HASTY," LOTUS HUANG CALLED.

Gallant Ouyang spun around, his heart thumping in anticipation. But she took no notice of him and spoke only to Count Seven Hong.

"Why not consider taking on two disciples today?" She fell to her knees. "Good things always come in pairs."

Count Seven shook his head and laughed. "I've gone against every principle I hold dear by accepting him. Your father ranks with me as one of the Greats. Why would he let you call me *Shifu*?"

"Oh, you're afraid of Papa!" As usual, Lotus knew exactly how to get her way.

"What? No! I'll take you as my disciple. What can the Heretic do? Eat me alive?"

"It's settled, then! You can't go back on your word. Papa will be thrilled! He's told me many times that there are only two truly great martial masters left in the world, now that Double Sun Wang Chong-yang has passed. You and him. He thought the Southern King was very good too. But, as for the rest –" she glanced at Gallant Ouyang – "for them, he has only disdain. Now, *Shifu*, how do beggars catch snakes? Will you teach me?"

The Beggar was not entirely sure why she wanted to learn that. But, since she had many tricks up her sleeves, he played along and instructed her with mock gravitas: "Fork two fingers, like this. Pinch the snake seven inches from its head, and it will be instantly immobilised."

"What if it's particularly big and strong?"

"Wiggle your fingers as bait, to draw its attention. Then strike with your other hand."

"I'll need to be very agile."

"Of course." Count Seven Hong paused. "There's also an ointment you should spread on your hands. That way, even if you get bitten, you'll be fine."

"*Shifu*, would you put the ointment on my hands?" Her earnest tone belied a wink.

Snake tricks were the work of the most junior beggars of the Clan, and, as their leader, Count Seven Hong did not carry the ointment on his person. So he improvised. He uncorked his red gourd and rubbed some wine into Lotus's hands.

Lotus sniffed and pulled a face. At last, she turned to Gallant Ouyang. "I'm the latest and last disciple of Hero Hong, chieftain of all the beggars. I'd like to take on this Flaccid Snake Fist of yours. The ointment on my hands is poison to your kind. Don't say I didn't warn you!"

"It would be my pleasure to die in your hands," he replied, flashing her a lecherous grin. He knew he only had to reach out and he would win. Nonetheless, he silently promised to avoid her hands.

"Your other moves are too common, hardly worth my while. I'm only interested in your Flaccid Snake Fist. If you use anything else, then you lose."

"Your wish is my command."

Lotus smiled sweetly. "You may be a villain, but you're always rather civil to me. Here comes the first move!"

A punch flew at Gallant Ouyang – *whoosh!* – Count Seven Hong's Wayfaring Fist.

Gallant Ouyang leaned to the side and out of its path. She immediately followed up with a horizontal left kick and a grappling right hook. This was her father's invention, Cascading Peach Blossom Palm. It did not matter who had taught her the attacking move, as long as it helped her defeat him.

The speed and the complexity of her attack forced Gallant Ouyang to take her challenge seriously. His arm shot forward with explosive speed, then bent suddenly, his fist hurtling towards her shoulder. Then he remembered – Hedgehog Chainmail! He wrenched it back at the last moment to avoid a bloody fist.

Lotus saw her chance and raised her palms to box his ears.

Gallant Ouyang twirled his sleeves upward with a flick of his wrists to guide her hands away. He could only aim for her head. Her body was protected by the chainmail and he had promised himself he would not grab her by the hands because of the "ointment".

But how could I be so unmannerly as to strike her cheeks or pull her hair? he asked himself as he ducked and dodged.

Leaping away from another of Lotus's palm strikes, Gallant Ouyang had an idea. He tore his sleeves and took the short respite his retreat had given him to wind the fabric around his hands. Then he flipped his palms down, hooked his fingers and grabbed at her wrists with the grappling technique.

"That's not Flaccid Snake Fist! You've lost!" Lotus tapped the ground with one hand to propel herself away.

"Ah, I apologise for my lapse."

"Your Flaccid Snake Fist is as common as the rest of your kung fu. It can't subdue a disciple of Count Seven Hong. You agree with me, don't you? Remember the last time we sparred? At the Jin Prince's palace? You had Greybeard Liang, Hector Sha, Tiger Peng, Lama Supreme Wisdom and that man with horns on his head – Browbeater Hou – to help you. Six grown men against one girl. I admitted defeat because none of you was worth my energy. Since you and I have each won once, shall we fight another round to determine the winner?"

Vigour Li and the other beggars admired the intricacy of Lotus's kung fu, but it was clear that Gallant Ouyang was the superior martial artist. They doubted her claim of defeating masters like Tiger Peng and Hector Sha. If she had, it was probably through trickery, just as she had cornered Gallant Ouyang, a moment ago.

But why would she want to fight again? They simply could not understand it. They also found their Chief's indifference baffling. Count Seven Hong was munching what was left of the chicken with a smile, licking and sucking the bones clean with relish. He made no move to interfere.

"It would be my pleasure to entertain the lady, should she wish to fight. I'm equally happy, whoever wins."

"When we were at the Prince of Zhao's residence, we were surrounded by your friends," Lotus rattled on, ignoring Gallant Ouyang's reply. "If I had won, they would most certainly have come to your aid, which was why I didn't show you my real kung fu. But, today, you have your friends –" she pointed to the women dressed in white – "and I have mine, too. You have a greater number, but I will overlook this advantage. Why don't you draw another circle on the floor? We will honour the same rules: whoever gets thrown out first is the loser. Now that I'm a disciple of the renowned Count Seven, I shall grant you another advantage: there's no need to bind your hands."

As usual, Lotus was twisting logic and inverting facts, but she spoke with such grace and reason that Gallant Ouyang did not know how to reply. He could not summon enough indignation to refuse her. So, obediently, he extended his right foot three feet from his body and, using his left leg as a pivot, drew a perfect circle, an inch deep and six feet in diameter, in the floor tiles. It was hard not to be impressed by the libertine's kung fu.

Lotus stepped inside the circle and asked, "Are we doing this the civil way or the martial way?"

"Would you mind elaborating?"

"If we do it the civil way, we take turns. The first person launches three moves and their opponent is not allowed to make any counterattack. With the martial way, you do what you want, whenever you want. You can use your Dead Snake Fist, your Live Rat Fist, anything you fancy. Whoever's pushed out of the circle first is the loser."

"But, of course, we shall do it the civil way."

"Good choice. You won't be able to keep up if we do it the martial way. At least, now, you have some hope. Well, shall I be magnanimous today and grant you yet another advantage? Who makes the first move? You or me?"

"Of course, it should be my lady."

"You are sly." Lotus smiled coyly. "You always pick what's best for you." She thrust her palm at Gallant Ouyang before he could take back his gentlemanly offer.

He noticed the air glisten and a shimmering cloud, wider than the circle, flew towards him. She must have thrown some secret weapon!

He could have swept them away easily with his fan or his sleeves. But the former had been destroyed by Count Seven Hong and he had torn the latter off in a bid to win the last fight. He could also dodge them comfortably by lurching sideways, but then he would land outside the circle – and lose.

He only had one option. He tapped his foot and leapt half a dozen feet off the ground. A deluge of needles shot past, underneath his feet.

When Gallant Ouyang's upward momentum was spent and he started to descend, Lotus shouted, "Second move!"

This time, she waved both hands, letting fly more than a hundred needles – the Skyful of Petals technique Count Seven had invented to counter Gallant Ouyang's snakes. She flung them far and wide, and with as much force as possible. Everywhere the libertine looked, needles glinted in the air.

Gallant Ouyang's kung fu could not help him defy gravity.

This is it! What a savage wench! Silently cursing Lotus's cruelty, he steeled himself to meet his end.

Suddenly, he felt his collar tighten and his body soaring upwards instead of plunging down. He sensed the rush of air as the swarm of needles whizzed past below. He heard the metallic clinking of the needles as they rained down on the floor tiles. He had been saved, but, before he could rejoice, he realised he was hurtling across the room.

Once more, his martial training failed him. The force that propelled him was so powerful that he could not latch onto its momentum to flip himself upright. He landed heavily on his left shoulder. It was clear that only Count Seven Hong would have the internal strength to make such a throw.

Avoiding all eye contact, Gallant Ouyang jumped back onto his feet and stormed out of the ancestral temple, his cheeks hot with anger and shame. His women rushed after him in panic.

Lotus Huang went up to Miss Cheng and cut the binds around her wrists. The young woman took Lotus by the hand and whispered her thanks, but remained shyly in a corner, with her head hung low.

Lotus turned to Count Seven Hong. "*Shifu*, why did you help him?"

"The lad deserves to die for the loathsome things he's done, but his uncle and I go back a long way. The Venom would be offended if I let you injure his nephew." Count Seven then put his hand on Lotus's shoulder. "But you preserved your *shifu*'s face today and that should be rewarded. Is there anything you would like?"

"Not your bamboo stick, that's for sure!" Lotus stuck out her tongue.

"I couldn't give you that, even if you asked for it. There are some moves I'd like to teach you, but I've been feeling rather lazy of late."

"I'll make a few nice dishes to get you going!"

Count Seven's eyebrows flew up in excitement, then he sighed. "Alas, time is not on our side." He gestured at Vigour Li and the beggars. "I have so many Clan affairs to attend to."

By now, the beggars had gathered around to thank Guo Jing and Lotus for their help, and congratulated them on becoming Count Seven Hong's disciples. They were all envious of the young couple's good fortune. Their chieftain's refusal to train protégés was well known in the Beggar Clan – even his favourite Clan members were only granted a move or two, and only when he was in an exceptionally good mood. How had they gained such favour with the Chief?

"We would like to organise a banquet, here, at this temple, tomorrow, to celebrate this joyous occasion," Vigour Li proposed.

"I fear they'll find our vagrant ways too disgusting and be put off their food!" Count Seven teased.

"It would be our pleasure to feast with you." Guo Jing accepted the invitation readily. "I would love to get to know Brother Li better. You are a true hero."

Vigour Li was touched by Guo Jing's modesty and warmth. *This young man is the reason why I still have my eyes.* He was full of gratitude.

"Hey, don't talk my disciple into becoming a beggar!" Count Seven wagged a finger at Vigour Li, then turned to Lotus. "Why did you say you're my last disciple? Are you saying I can't take on another?"

"*Shifu* must disregard my ramblings if he wishes to share his knowledge with others." Lotus smiled. "Though, as the saying goes, 'When a thing is rare, it is precious' – if there are too many of us, then we won't be special."

"You think you're so special?" Count Seven snorted. "See Miss Cheng home safely. We beggars will steal a few chickens for tomorrow."

Once the beggars were on their way, Lotus led Miss Cheng out of the temple, with Guo Jing trailing behind.

"Your martial uncle, Elder Ma, taught Guo Jing. Elder Qiu and Elder Wang like him a lot too." Lotus tried to make the young woman feel more at ease. "You are of the same martial family."

Miss Cheng stole a glance at Guo Jing and her face immediately turned crimson, but she managed to murmur a "Brother Guo" in greeting. She gradually opened up to Lotus as they walked. Though still speaking in hesitant whispers, she told Lotus that her given name was Emerald, and explained how she had come to receive martial training from the Sage of Tranquillity, Sun Bu'er. However, bound as she was by the traditional etiquette that came hand in hand with a privileged and sheltered upbringing, her words were directed at Lotus alone and her eyes were firmly fixed on her feet. She dared not speak a word to Guo Jing. Whenever she lifted her eyes and caught sight of him, her cheeks flushed bright red once more. Emerald Cheng's manner was in every respect the opposite of Lotus's forthright confidence and ease.

CHAPTER SEVEN

THE NINE YIN
MANUAL

I

IT WAS PAST MIDNIGHT. AFTER A NIGHT OF ADVENTURE, GUO
Jing and Lotus Huang were ready to head back to the inn – until the
pounding of hooves piqued their interest.

Who was hurrying north, this late at night? Silence reigned again.
Why had the rider stopped? They picked up their pace and were
surprised to find Yang Kang standing by the road, reins in hand,
speaking to Gallant Ouyang. There was a furtive look about him.

They were too far away to hear much of the men's exchange, but
they did not want to move closer lest they be discovered.

From Gallant Ouyang's hushed whispers, Lotus could only make
out the words "Yue Fei" – the patriotic Song general – and "Lin'an"
– the Song Empire capital. Meanwhile, Yang Kang kept muttering
about "my papa". A short time later, Gallant Ouyang put his palm
over his fist, in a gesture of farewell, and went east with his entourage
of women.

She had heard too little to make head or tail of their conversation,
but it was enough to gnaw away at the little faith she had in Yang

Kang. She watched him closely. He seemed dazed. He stared into space for a good while before mounting his horse with a sigh.

"Brother!" Guo Jing called.

Visibly surprised, Yang Kang leapt down from his mount. "I thought you would be halfway to Zhongdu by now, brother?"

"I'm sorry, I've been delayed. I found Lotus here and we've just fought with Gallant Ouyang."

Yang Kang hoped his burning cheeks were cloaked by the night. Did they hear what I said to him? He scrutinised Guo Jing for clues and, to his relief, found nothing to suggest they had.

He wouldn't be this friendly if he knew what we were talking about, and he's too simple to hide it from his face, thought Yang Kang. "Brother," he said in his sweetest voice, "shall we find a place to rest for the night, or press on?"

Once they crossed the River Chu and then the River Huai, north of Baoying, they would be in Jin territory – the only home he had known.

Yang Kang then turned to Lotus with a smile. "Are you coming with us, Miss Huang?"

"No, I'm not coming with you. You are coming with us," Lotus corrected him.

"What's the difference?" Guo Jing laughed. "Why don't we stop at the ancestral temple tonight and set off after the banquet tomorrow?"

"Pretend we saw nothing. Don't ask him about Gallant Ouyang," Lotus reminded Guo Jing quietly.

They walked back to the ancestral temple together in silence. When they arrived, they lit the candles left behind by Gallant Ouyang and prepared a place to sleep. It was the height of summer, so the boys took down the doors of the main hall and set them up as makeshift beds in the cloister, in the courtyard. Lotus, meanwhile, stayed inside the main hall and gathered from the floor the needles she had flung in the fight.

They fell asleep as soon as they lay down, but, before long, the dull thud of hooves invaded their dreams. The noise grew louder and closer.

Eventually, Lotus could take it no more and rushed out into the courtyard.

"Three riders being pursued by . . . maybe a dozen?" Lotus Huang guessed.

"Sixteen." Guo Jing grew up on horseback in Mongolia and could tell the size of a herd by ear. "The first three are Mongolian horses. What are they doing so far from home?"

Lotus took Guo Jing's hand, eager to see what was going on.

Just as they stepped through the temple's main gate – *whoosh!* – an arrow zoomed past, inches above their heads.

The three Mongolian horses were charging straight at the temple.

Another arrow. It hit the rearmost horse in the thigh.

The steed buckled, whinnying in pain. The rider leapt off in one smooth motion, with the agility of a martial man, but his feet landed with a thump.

Not trained in lightness kung fu, then. The same thought flashed through the minds of both Lotus and Guo Jing.

"Keep going! I'll hold them back," the man shouted in Mongolian.

His companions halted their horses and one of them said, "I'll help you. Fourth Prince, you should go!"

"I won't leave without you both!"

Guo Jing could not believe his ears. Tolui, Jebe and Boroqul! What are they doing here? But there was no time to make himself known. The men hunting the Mongolians had arranged themselves in a semi-circular formation and were closing in.

The Mongols quickly let loose a series of arrows. These shafts tore the air with exceptional power, forcing their pursuers to check their advance and fire back from a distance.

"Up there!" One of the Mongols pointed at the ceremonial flag-pole just outside the temple. They scaled it with ease and prepared to defend themselves from the podium at the summit. The high vantage point helped to even the odds against them.

The pursuing soldiers dismounted and surrounded the pole, but they kept out of range of the Mongols' arrows. Once they were in position, an order was shouted. Four men stepped forward and raised their shields high. They crept under cover, close to the ground, and, once in position, began to hack at the flagpole with their sabres.

"You're wrong." Lotus turned to Guo Jing. "There are only fifteen of them."

"The last one was shot."

A horse trotted close to the temple entrance, dragging a man along beside it. The soldier's left foot was stuck in the stirrup and an arrow protruded from his chest.

Guo Jing crawled to the body. He pulled out the arrow and felt along the shaft. As expected, he found an iron ring branded with the image of a leopard's head. This was the stiff arrow that Jebe preferred, heavier than a standard one by two *jin*.

"Brother Tolui, General Jebe and General Boroqul? It is I, Guo Jing," Guo Jing called in Mongolian.

"What brings you here?" The men replied in unison, surprised by the chance encounter.

"Who are they?"

"Jin soldiers!" Tolui replied.

Guo Jing picked up the corpse and hurled it at the bottom of the flagpole as he strode forward. Two of the soldiers were knocked out instantly and the remaining two scuttled back to take shelter among their comrades.

The air stirred and Guo Jing looked up. Two spots of white swirled in the night sky. The white condors he had raised with Khojin in Mongolia!

Catching sight of their master in the dark, the pair of condors swooped down next to Guo Jing, croaking with excitement.

Lotus Huang remembered Guo Jing telling her about these condors when they first met. He had tried to defend them against attack, and adopted the condors' orphaned chicks. These must be the orphans. She had hoped, one day, she might get a pair of condors for herself. Now she had a chance to meet these fabled creatures, the fight no longer held any interest.

"Can I play with them?" She reached out to pat the bird closest to her. It pecked at her defensively. If her reactions had been a fraction slower, she would have had a nasty wound on her hand.

"Oh, you naughty beast!" Giggling, she watched them with her head tilted. She decided she liked these magnificent predators very much.

"Lotus, watch out!"

She could hear two arrows flying straight at her, but she paid no heed to Guo Jing's warning. No weapon could pierce her Hedgehog Chainmail. The arrows simply bounced off her chest. Right now, she had a more important task at hand. The dead soldier must have some food stashed away in his pockets. At last, she found what she was looking for, and threw morsels of dried meat to the condors.

"Lotus, stay with the condors. I'll take care of the Jin soldiers."

Guo Jing darted forward and caught, barehanded, an arrow aimed straight for him. Then he thrust his palm into the shoulder of the soldier next to him.

Crack! The bone snapped on contact.

"Who are you, dog?" The question boomed out of the night, in Chinese.

I know that voice . . . Yet, before Guo Jing could place who it belonged to, he felt the air parting and the chill of a blade.

An axe – no, two axes – hacking down towards his chest and abdomen.

He knew such savage blows could not have come from a common soldier.

Stooping low to avoid them, Guo Jing swung his arm back in a Dragon Whips Tail. He could feel a shoulder blade fracturing into several pieces under his palm as a howl of pain tore at his ears.

Now he remembered: the Reaper Axe, Qian Qingjian, one of the Four Daemons of the Yellow River.

Guo Jing's counter sent Qian Qingjian flying back several paces. The man slammed to the ground, where he stayed, unable to stand up. Though Guo Jing was aware of the improvement in his martial skills since he fought the Daemons in Mongolia, back in the winter, he was astonished by his own prowess. He was not allowed the time to reflect, however, as he felt a metallic chill in the air once more. Then a sabre sliced down at his left side and a spear thrust at his right.

Flipping his right hand palm down and curling his fingers into a hook, Guo Jing latched on to the spearhead, inches from his ribs, and tugged.

The Dispatcher, Wu Qinglie, lost his footing and tumbled forward.

Guo Jing then leaned backwards, out of the sabre's reach. As Wu Qinglie tried to regain his footing, his head strayed right into the path of his martial brother Shen Qinggang's falling Spirit Cleaver.

Guo Jing kicked at Shen Qinggang's sword-wielding wrist. A glimmer of light arced up into the air – Shen's sabre. He then pushed Wu Qinglie in the back. *Pang!* The two Daemons smacked into each other and collapsed in an unconscious heap.

In a couple of moves, Guo Jing had subdued three of the Daemons. The fourth, Soul Snatcher Whip, Ma Qingxiong, had lost his life not long ago, on Lake Tai, defeated by Laurel Lu and his pirates.

Now, only ordinary Jin soldiers remained. Oblivious that their best fighters were already out of action, they were still firing arrows at the Mongolians.

"Are you still fighting?" Guo Jing cried as he lunged. Fists and feet flying, he hurled aside every soldier that crossed his path.

In the blink of an eye, the soldiers had scattered to the four winds.

Shen Qinggang and Wu Qinglie were coming to, stars flashing in their eyes. The two Daemons cared not who had defeated them. Their heads were splitting with pain and all they wanted was to get as far away as possible. They ran in opposite directions, while Qian Qingjian fled in a third, whimpering as he massaged his shoulder.

Jebe and Boroqul, both exceptional marksmen, shot three of the retreating soldiers. Tolui watched as Guo Jing broke up the rest of the pursuing force, in awe of his sworn brother's martial skills.

"*Anda*, my brother, how have you been?" he asked as he slid down the flagpole. The two young men regarded each other with joy, their hands grasped tight. The unexpected reunion had rendered them speechless.

"If it weren't for you, we would have never tasted the sweet water of Onon River again," Jebe said to Guo Jing, after his descent.

"This is Lotus." Guo Jing took Lotus's hand and introduced her to the Mongols.

"Would you grant me the condors, Prince?" Lotus asked sweetly. Tolui understood no Chinese, but he was very taken by Lotus's sonorous voice.

"What brings you, *anda*? Why are the condors here?"

"Papa sent me to the Song Emperor to propose a joint military action against the Jin. We strike from the north and the Song attack from the south. Sister made me take the condors along, in case we met. And she was right! Here you are!"

Guo Jing was struck dumb by the mention of Khojin. He had barely given his betrothal to the Mongolian Princess a second thought since he had met and fallen in love with Lotus. He did not feel right about the arrangement, but he did not know what to do, especially since he had never desired the honour conferred by the Great Khan. He had just pushed the whole affair out of his mind.

Now Tolui had reminded him of her, he was at a loss how to respond. Then he remembered he had promised to go to Peach Blossom Island: I'm sure I will pay for Hurricane Chen's death with my life. None of this will matter then.

He turned to Lotus. "The condors are mine. Now they are yours." Happy to get her way, Lotus turned her attention back to the birds, throwing more dried meat at them.

Tolui told Guo Jing more about why he was so far south. In the past months, Genghis Khan had had great success in his campaign against the Jurchens, but the Jin Empire was vast and their reserves of soldiers ran deep. The Jin had managed to hold on to several strongholds that halted the Mongolian's advance, even though they had lost most of the battles. That was why his father the Great Khan sent him to the Song Empire for help to break this impasse. But the Jin army ambushed them before they could cross into Song territory. Only the three of them, out of the large entourage of guards and followers, escaped the slaughter.

Everything began to fall into place for Guo Jing. That was why Yang Kang had wanted Mercy Mu to go to Lin'an to see the Song Chancellor, when he was held at Roaming Cloud Manor. The Jin had received intelligence of Tolui's mission and sent Yang Kang to forestall the alliance.

"The Jurchens were determined to get rid of me to prevent our alliance with the Song," Tolui continued. "Their Sixth Prince personally led the attack."

"Wanyan Honglie?" Guo Jing asked.

"Yes, he wore a golden helmet. I saw him clearly. I fired three arrows at him, but his guards blocked them with their shields."

Guo Jing turned to Lotus. "Wanyan Honglie is here!"

"Let's get him!" Lotus turned, expecting to find Yang Kang nearby, but he was nowhere to be seen.

"I'll look on the east side; you search to the west." Guo Jing then raced off with his lightness *qinggong*.

Several *li* from the temple, he caught up with a couple of Jin soldiers fleeing from the fight. They confirmed that the Sixth Prince Wanyan Honglie led the mission, but insisted that they had no idea of his whereabouts.

"We deserted the Prince," one of them began. "Our heads will roll for it. Our only option now is to hide in the countryside and pretend to be ordinary Han Chinese."

The sky was growing light. Wanyan Honglie must still be in the vicinity, but Guo Jing could find no trace of his father's murderer. He started to run, fuelled by frustration. Then he saw a shadow moving through the woods and raced ahead. It was Lotus. One look at her face and he knew she had had no luck either. They headed back to the temple, dejected.

"Wanyan Honglie left his main force to pursue us with his fastest horses," Tolui said when Guo Jing and Lotus were back at the temple. "He must have turned back for reinforcements. *Anda*, I have further orders from Father; I must not tarry. Forgive me for this hasty departure. Khojin bade me to say this to you – come back soon."

Guo Jing hugged his friends one by one, knowing this was likely to be their final farewell. He watched as the yellow dust kicked up by their horses engulfed their silhouettes. He stayed standing in the road until he could no longer hear the sound of their hooves.

"Let's wait for Wanyan Honglie's return," Lotus said. "If he comes back with lots of soldiers, we can keep out of sight until it's dark. Then we'll kill him."

"I'll hide the horses in the woods." Guo Jing noticed something glittering in the grass as he led their mounts through the temple's rear courtyard.

A golden helmet, crowned by three spectacular gemstones, each as large as a longan fruit. He picked it up and showed it to Lotus.

"Wanyan Honglie's helmet?" she asked.

"It must be!" Guo Jing lowered his voice. "He's probably inside the temple!"

Lotus tapped a foot against the temple wall, flipped up and landed quietly on the roof. "I'll look from up here. You search on the ground."

Just as Guo Jing was about to dart inside the temple, he heard Lotus's voice: "How was my *qinggong* just now?"

He stopped, unsure why she asked. "Wonderful! Why?"

"Then why didn't you say so?"

"Oh, but I tell myself how wonderful you are all the time!"

Chuckling, Lotus waved and sprinted across the roofs towards the rear garden.

2

WHILE THE MONGOLIANS WERE BEING HARD PRESSED ATOP the flagpole, Yang Kang had caught sight of Wanyan Honglie among

the soldiers, directing the onslaught. Even though he now understood that he was no blood relation of the Sixth Prince, he had
always been treated as his own; he was raised as son and heir. This
man was the only father Yang Kang had ever known, and his for-
tunes would always be bound up with his.

If Guo Jing sees Wanyan Honglie, the man is as good as dead,
Yang Kang told himself. If he did nothing now, he would be letting Guo Jing rob him of the life of wealth and power he had been
groomed to inherit.

No, he was not ready to give that up.

Just then, a soldier thrown by Guo Jing slammed into Wanyan
Honglie. The Sixth Prince of the Jin could not turn his horse fast
enough and was knocked off his mount. Yang Kang darted over and
scooped up the fallen man.

"Sire, don't make a noise," he whispered, and, under the cover
of darkness, he carried Wanyan Honglie to the rear courtyard of the
temple.

Neither Guo Jing nor Lotus noticed what Yang Kang had done.

Yang Kang opened the door to a side chamber and set the Prince
down. The clamour of the fight was dying down. He could hear
footsteps fading into the distance, followed by a conversation in a
language he could not understand, though he recognised one of the
voices as Guo Jing's.

"Kang?" Wanyan Honglie was not sure if this was a dream. "How
come you are here?"

"By sheer chance," Yang Kang said quietly. He sighed. "That Guo
Jing has ruined everything."

Guo Jing was speaking in Chinese again. They could just about
make out his words. He was telling Lotus to head west to look for
Wanyan Honglie.

Wanyan Honglie had seen how Guo Jing had dispatched three
of the Daemons of the Yellow River with his bare hands. If the boy
turns those hands on me, he thought with a shiver, I won't stand a
chance.

"I don't think they'll look this way, sire. Let's wait for them to go further before we make our way out."

"Of course . . . Why are you calling me sire, Kang? You've always called me Pa."

No answer.

Yang Kang was thinking of his mother, and his heart churned.

"Your mother . . ." Wanyan Honglie took his son's hand. It was ice cold, but clammy with sweat.

Yang Kang pulled away. "Stay away from Zhongdu for the next six months. Guo Jing is determined to avenge his father's death. His kung fu is strong and he knows a lot of martial masters. You won't be able to defend yourself."

The memory of Ox Village eighteen years ago washed over Wanyan Honglie along with a wave of grief, both then chased away by a surge of guilt. He did not trust himself to speak.

"Understood. I will keep away from the capital," he eventually muttered. "How was Lin'an? What did Chancellor Shi say?"

"I never got there."

Wanyan Honglie surmised that the coolness shown by his son must have been due to him learning of his true parentage. But, if so, why had he helped him just now? They had been close for eighteen years, doting father and filial son. Now, sitting in the dark in this small chamber, their bodies close, he could feel the bad blood between them.

A battle had been raging inside Yang Kang since they had taken refuge in this room. He realised this was his chance to avenge his parents. He could easily kill the man responsible for the death of his birth parents with a flip of his palm, but he was haunted by doubts.

Can I muster the resolve to kill him right now? Ironheart Yang might be my birth father, but what did he ever do for me? Ma was always kind to Father; if I kill him now, surely it won't please Ma's spirit in the underworld. Do I want to give up all that I've enjoyed since birth? Am I ready to renounce my privileges as a prince and wander around as a thief and a bandit with Guo Jing?

"Kang, my son, you will always be my true-born heir. No matter what."

Wanyan Honglie's words caused Yang Kang's heart to thump against his ribcage.

"Within ten years, our Great Jin Empire will finish the Song. The realm and its infinite wealth will be in my grasp, and one day they will be yours."

He means to usurp the throne! This new insight delivered Yang Kang from his dilemma. Now he could appraise his situation from a different perspective.

The Jin army will destroy the Song easily. The Mongols are a nuisance, but those savages on horseback will never amount to much more than a marauding horde. Not even our Emperor can match Father's wit and abilities. So, once he gets his way, I too will ascend to greatness.

Yang Kang took his father's hand. "Your child will stand by your side, Pa. Always."

His hand isn't cold anymore, Wanyan Honglie noted with joy. "We shall found a great dynasty and you will bring glory to our name."

A crack came from behind, cutting short Yang Kang's reply. The two men whipped around, their hearts gripped by fear.

Faint rays of light were now shining through the window lattice, heralding the break of dawn. They had been leaning against a stack of half a dozen coffins! This chamber must be where they stored unused coffins and placed their deceased before burial. The sound seemed to have come from inside one of the wooden caskets.

"What was that?" Wanyan Honglie was spooked.

"A rat?"

More alarming sounds followed.

Footsteps, voices. Coming their way.

Guo Jing and Lotus Huang.

We dropped the helmet outside, Yang Kang realised with horror.

"I'll create a diversion," he whispered. He opened the door as quietly as he could and leapt onto the roof.

"There!" Lotus raced after the fleeting shadow, but it turned a corner and disappeared.

"He must be in that bush!" As Lotus moved closer, the vegetation rustled and parted.

"Brother! Have you seen Wanyan Honglie?" Guo Jing asked.

"Why would he be here?" Yang Kang asked, feigning surprise.

"He led the soldiers. This is his helmet."

"Oh, really?"

Lotus could tell something was not quite right. Yang Kang's furtive conversation with Gallant Ouyang came back to her.

"Where did you go?" she asked, with an accusatory tone. "We looked everywhere for you."

"Something I ate earlier disagreed with me." He pointed at the bush.

Lotus did not believe him, but she had no desire to be confronted by the proof, should he be telling the truth.

"Let's find Wanyan Honglie!" Guo Jing urged.

"What great news that he has come to us to meet his fate," Yang Kang said, trying to keep his face blank. He hoped he had given his father enough time to escape. "Why don't you and Miss Huang search the east side? I'll take the west."

Guo Jing was already through the eastern entrance, the Gate of Filial Integrity, before Yang Kang had finished his sentence, but the ploy did not work on Lotus.

"Brother Yang, I'll come with you."

"Well, we must make haste. We can't let him slip away!" Yang Kang prayed Lotus would not see through his show of enthusiasm.

The Liu clan was once a wealthy and important family in Baoying. However, as the town was close to the Jin border, the region had suffered numerous incursions from roaming troops. Buildings were torched and fields were trampled. The skirmishes brought about the Liu family's decline and their ancestral temple had fallen into disrepair.

Lotus watched Yang Kang as he searched. Though he kept

stressing the urgency, he was moving with deliberate sloth through each room. The doors he opened were also long-sealed by dust and cobwebs.

She spotted a mess of footsteps stamped into the dust outside the westernmost chamber. As she approached, she saw a fresh handprint pressed into the grime on the door.

Her suspicions were confirmed.

"He's hiding in here!" Lotus cried as she kicked the door down.

Yang Kang rushed over, followed by Guo Jing. Barging ahead of Lotus, Yang Kang raised his voice. "Wanyan Honglie, where are you? Come out, villain!"

"Brother Yang, he heard our approach long ago. There is no need to be his messenger."

"This is no laughing matter!" he snarled back, but the shame of being found out had stained Yang Kang's face crimson.

"Please don't take offence, brother; Lotus loves to tease." Guo Jing smiled. He had never once suspected Yang Kang of wavering in his allegiance. "Look, someone was sitting here not long ago. He really was here."

"What are we waiting for?" The coffins were making Lotus jittery. As she turned to leave, a muffled crack sounded.

It can't be!

She paused and cast her eye over the coffins. One of them appeared to be rocking from side to side. Yelping, she latched on to Guo Jing's arm.

"That . . . that villain must be inside." Fear had yet to cloud her wits.

"Over there!" Yang Kang pointed in another direction and gave chase.

Yet, before he had managed to step outside, Lotus grabbed his wrist and locked onto his pulse. "Enough of your games!"

"What are you doing?" Yang Kang felt his arm become numb.

Guo Jing approached the coffin – "He must be in here!" – and wrenched at its lid.

"Careful, brother. It could be one of the undead!" Yang Kang called.

"Stop it!" Lotus tightened her hold and yanked. She did not need Yang Kang stoking her fears.

"Press down on the lid." Her voice trembled. "Don't let that . . . thing come out."

"The undead don't exist," Guo Jing said, and sat on the coffin. "He can't come out now."

Lotus did not look convinced. "I'll hit the coffin with the Splitting Sky Palm. We'll be able to hear whether it's the cry of a man or the wail of a ghost."

She let go of Yang Kang and took two steps forward. She channelled strength into her hand and got ready to strike at the coffin.

But, of course, Yang Kang had no idea that Lotus had not mastered the technique and could do no damage to the coffin or its contents. She only intended to slap loudly on the wooden board to frighten whatever was within.

"Stop! What if you smash through the wood and it bites you on the hand?" he cried.

Aaaahh . . . yeeeee . . .

A woman's wail.

"A ghost!" Lotus screamed and ran outside.

The supernatural did not frighten Guo Jing. "Brother Yang, let's take a look."

Yang Kang was ready to defend his father, even though he knew he stood no chance. But Wanyan Honglie could not have made that noise. His relief was palpable, and so he went to help Guo Jing.

The lid lifted with ease. It was not nailed down.

Guo Jing summoned his strength and raised his arm as he peered inside, just in case. The coffin contained no creature of death. Only a beautiful young woman looked back at him, wide eyed. Mercy Mu!

Yang Kang could not believe his good fortune as he reached in to pull Mercy out of the coffin.

"Lotus, look who we found!" Guo Jing called. Lotus turned, but kept her eyes screwed shut. "It's Sister Mu!"

Lotus let her right eye open into a slit and saw Yang Kang's arm around a woman that looked very much like Mercy Mu. Gingerly, she approached.

Why does Mercy look so stiff? she wondered, before recognising that her friend's limbs were locked by her acupressure points. Two streams of tears were running down Mercy's cheeks.

With a few taps, Lotus freed Mercy from the bind. "Sister, who put you in there?"

Mercy Mu had been immobile for some time. Even though she was now free, she felt sore and numb all over. She focused on regulating her breathing, while Lotus massaged her joints. After the time it takes to finish a pot of tea, she eventually spoke. "I was captured by a villain."

"Gallant Ouyang?" Lotus asked quietly. She noticed Mercy's movement had been locked via the Gushing Spring pressure point in the arch of the foot. It was not one commonly used in the *wulin* of the Central Plains.

Mercy nodded, reliving the night of her capture. She shuddered at the memory of how Gallant Ouyang had locked her acupressure points beside the stack of skulls made by Yang Kang's *shifu*. When Gallant Ouyang ambushed the blind woman with his snakes, a stranger in a green robe had appeared from nowhere and played a seductive tune on the *xiao* flute, sending Gallant Ouyang's women and snake herders into a frenzy, and the awful lecher himself running for his life. When Gallant Ouyang's followers came to, the next day, they found her still bound by her pressure points on the ground and brought her back to their Master.

After that, things got worse for Mercy. Gallant Ouyang made several advances, but she insisted she would rather die than compromise her chastity. Fortunately, the Master of White Camel Mount felt forcing himself on her was beneath him. He believed his looks, his charm and his martial knowledge were sufficient to melt the coldest of hearts. His conceit preserved Mercy's virtue.

When Gallant Ouyang and his retinue arrived in Baoying, they set up base in the ancestral temple of the Liu clan and placed Mercy in a coffin, for safekeeping. His disciples went around the town, seeking out its beauties, but their abduction of Miss Cheng brought the Beggar Clan out in force, along with Guo Jing and Lotus Huang. Once more, Gallant Ouyang had to run for his life, and everyone forgot about Mercy. The libertine did not much care about leaving one or two of his prizes behind. After all, he had captured many women in his life and knew there would always be more.

If Guo Jing had not searched the temple for Wanyan Honglie, Mercy would have starved to death in this empty coffin, forgotten by the world.

Thrilled by this unexpected encounter with his sweetheart, Yang Kang's face was a picture of loving tenderness. "My dear, do rest a bit. Let me boil some hot water for you."

"Have you ever boiled water?" Lotus grinned. "I'll do it. Guo Jing, come with me." She wanted to give the lovers some privacy.

Stern and without the merest hint of a smile, Mercy's face shared none of the excitement visible on Yang Kang's. Once they were alone, she spoke quietly. "Congratulations, Yang Kang." She spat out his last name with frosty disdain. "I hear you shall come into infinite wealth one day."

She heard my exchange with Father! Yang Kang felt his spine turn to ice and his face sear with embarrassment. He was at a loss how to respond.

Seeing his discomfort, Mercy's heart softened. If they find out he helped Wanyan Honglie escape, they might . . . She decided to keep his secret and vented her annoyance another way. "But why did you suddenly start calling him sire instead of Pa?"

Yang Kang stared at the ground in awkward silence.

Though, by now, Lotus had moved too far away to make out what Mercy was saying to Yang Kang, she could tell the tone between them was cold. She assumed it was a lovers' tiff, that her friend was angry with Yang Kang for not coming to her rescue sooner.

"Let's go." She tugged on Guo Jing's sleeve. "I'm sure they'll make up in no time." Guo Jing smiled and followed quietly.

Yet, once they were in the courtyard, Lotus said, "Let's spy on them."

"Don't be silly, I'm not doing that."

"Fine! But I won't tell you what I find out!" She hopped onto the roof and tiptoed back towards the westernmost chamber.

". . . you called that villain Father. Perhaps you can't quite let go of the past yet, your heart hasn't quite adjusted to reality. But harbouring treacherous thoughts, talking about bringing ruin to the land of your birth, this . . . this . . ." Lotus could tell Mercy was very angry — so worked up that she could not finish her sentence.

"Sweetheart, I—"

"Who are you calling sweetheart? Don't touch me!"

Smack!

She must have slapped him! I need to do something. Lotus flipped down from the roof and entered through the window.

"My, my! Surely, whatever it is, there is no need for violence? We can talk it through, can't we?" Lotus said.

Mercy's cheeks flushed crimson, while the blood had drained from Yang Kang's face.

Before Lotus could say another word, Yang Kang said loudly, "Well, clearly you have met another and I am to be discarded. That's why you're treating me like this!"

"What . . . ? What do you mean?"

"You've been with that Gallant Ouyang. We all know he's ten times the man I am in every way — his kung fu, his learning — I can't compare. After him, why would you still keep me in your heart?"

It was now Mercy's turn to go pale. Her hands and feet had turned ice cold. She almost fainted.

"Brother Yang, you mustn't make up lies," Lotus said. "Why would the villain lock Sister Mu's acupressure points and keep her in the coffin, if she liked him?"

"I don't care whether she really likes him or just pretends to. She's been with that man for days. She is no longer pure. What is there left for me?" Yang Kang's shame at having his true allegiance revealed had turned into blind rage at Mercy.

"I . . . I . . . am no longer pure? What do you mean?"

"You've been in his power for days. He must have held you in his arms and who knows what else! Can you deny it?"

Mercy had suffered enough already. A rush of pure anger flooded her heart. A heart-wrenching wail escaped her body. She spat out a mouthful of blood and collapsed.

Yang Kang regretted his harsh words. He wanted nothing more than to whisper sweet nothings and comfort Mercy. But, as he reached out, he remembered the conversation Mercy had overheard – she knew his secret – and Lotus's obvious doubts about him. If Mercy let on what she knew, not only would she endanger his own life, she would also thwart his father's escape, jeopardising his grand plans.

Steeling his heart, Yang Kang ran out of the room and across the courtyard, vaulted the wall and disappeared.

3

LOTUS CAUGHT MERCY AS SHE FELL AND TRIED TO REVIVE HER by rubbing her chest, over the heart. Gradually, Mercy came to. She collected herself and looked around, as if nothing had happened. Her eyes were now dry.

"Sister, may I borrow the dagger I gave you?"

"Guo Jing, can you come here?" He ran over at Lotus's call. "Give Brother Yang's dagger to Sister Mu."

He pulled out the dagger Zhu Cong had retrieved from Cyclone Mei at Roaming Cloud Manor. The name Yang Kang was carved into the hilt.

"I have Guo Jing's dagger here with me." Lotus reached for the short sword she kept inside her shirt. "And Brother Yang's blade is yours now."

She felt more secure about her future, as well as Mercy's, now they each held the tokens Skyfury Guo and Ironheart Yang had exchanged when they made the pact to join their yet-to-be-born children in brotherhood or matrimony. "Sister, your union is predestined. Don't worry about the fight just now. Don't let it hurt you. Papa and I argue all the time! Why don't you come with us to the Jin capital? We're going to find Wanyan Honglie, and I'm sure Yang Kang will come along too."

"Where's Brother Yang?" Guo Jing asked.

Lotus stuck her tongue out. "He upset Sister Mu and received a slap. Then he ran away. Sister, you know he loves you dearly. Why else would he stand there and let you strike him? He's the stronger martial artist, as we all know from the Duel . . ."

Lotus was going to make a joke about how they had met in the Duel for a Maiden and were used to getting physical. But one look at Mercy made her check her tongue.

"I'm not going to Zhongdu and there's no reason for you to go there either. You won't find the villain there for the next six months at least. He knows you're coming after him and he's afraid. Brother Guo, sister – you two are perfect for each other and fortune smiles on you . . ." Mercy was overcome by sobs. She buried her face in her hands and ran outside. Then, with a tap of her foot, she leapt onto the roof.

Lotus looked down at the splatter of blood Mercy had spat onto the floor, and then turned to run after her friend. She spotted her in the distance, under a large willow tree. There was a flash of light – the sun dancing on metal!

"No!" But she was too far away to do anything.

Mercy Mu raised the dagger Lotus had given her high over her head and pulled back her hair. Then she swung the blade down.

"Sister!"

Paying no attention to Lotus, Mercy let her hair fall to the ground and walked away without looking back.

As Lotus watched the strands of black silk dance in the air, a strange new sensation rose inside her.

Her eyes followed the threads of Mercy's hair as they flew over fields and streams, settled on roads, grazed treetops, fell amid dust and earth, and drifted on the water.

A spoilt child who had grown up without companions, Lotus never felt the need to hide her emotions. She had always laughed when she was happy, cried when she was upset. But this scene has caused a kind of grief, anxiety, loss – something she had never felt before – to well up in her heart. For the first time, she tasted the bitterness of life. Pondering this new feeling, she walked back to the temple.

She told Guo Jing what she had seen, and the young man could not understand Mercy's reaction either. "Why would Sister Mu do such a thing? She's too hot tempered."

Of course, neither knew the true reason behind the quarrel.

Troubled by Mercy's actions, Lotus's thoughts turned to Yang Kang's parting words, and questions swirled in her mind.

Can a woman lose her chastity because a man embraces her? Is that why her sweetheart, who once loved and respected her, now looks down on her? Is that why he doesn't want to have anything more to do with her?

Lotus wandered through the temple's rear garden and sat down against a pillar, haunted by these ideas. She could not fathom the logic behind Yang Kang's response, but she soon fell asleep, accepting this as the way of the world.

4

THAT EVENING, VIGOUR LI RETURNED TO THE TEMPLE TO SET up the banquet. Knowing Lotus Huang would be fastidious about cleanliness, he made sure the cups and plates and everything else were presentable enough for their guests.

Miss Cheng arrived with several dishes she had prepared personally, while her servants carried four large urns of vintage wine. She raised a toast to thank her rescuers, but did not stay for the meal. Guo Jing and Lotus drank and talked merrily with their hosts, but

Count Seven Hong did not make an appearance. The beggars knew their Chief's temperament and paid little attention, continuing their feasting and their conversations with the young couple.

After the banquet, Guo Jing and Lotus discussed what they should do next. Wanyan Honglie was in hiding and there would not be enough time to seek him out before the rendezvous on Peach Blossom Island. Guo Jing suggested they go to Jiaxing to meet with his *shifus* to work out a plan before crossing the sea together.

"Actually, it's probably for the best if your *shifus* don't come," Lotus said. "I doubt any good will come of it. You won't mind kowtowing to Papa to apologise? I'll make it up to you. However many bows you have to make, I'll return twice the amount."

"You're right. And you don't need to bow to me. For you, I'll do anything."

IT WAS now the first half of the sixth lunar month. The people south of the Yangtze used to say, "On the sixth day of the sixth month, duck eggs cook under the sun."

A firmament of fire seared the earth. The young couple travelled early in the morning and after sunset to avoid the scorching heat.

Before long, they had arrived in Jiaxing. Guo Jing left a letter for his *shifus* with the manager of the Garden of the Eight Drunken Immortals. He explained that he had met with Lotus Huang on his way to Yanjing and they were now heading to Peach Blossom Island together.

Since I am travelling with Apothecary Huang's daughter, he wrote, *rest assured that no harm shall come to me. Please do not concern yourselves with travelling to Peach Blossom Island on my behalf.*

Though he sounded confident in the letter, he knew his prospects were grim, faced with a man as unpredictable as Apothecary Huang. He kept his concerns from Lotus, as he did not wish to worry her. He simply comforted himself that he was keeping his *shifus* from a dangerous encounter. He knew, if he had told them personally, they would all have insisted on coming with him.

The young couple travelled east from Jiaxing and reached the coast by Zhoushan. Lotus hired a boat for Xiazhi Island, as she knew the local people feared Peach Blossom Island as much as venomous snakes and scorpions. No amount of money could tempt any boatman to venture even within forty *li* of its shore.

Once they had come out of the bay and sailed into open waters, Lotus commanded the helmsman to steer north, revealing their true destination. Before the frightened man could refuse, Lotus jabbed her dagger into the deck with a casual flick of her hand, and then plucked it out, turning it on the helmsman. With the chill of the blade against his chest and the gleaming metal dazzling his eyes, the sailor bemoaned his misfortune and complied meekly.

Soon, they were approaching Peach Blossom Island and an overwhelming fragrance washed over Guo Jing. Lush and verdant, the island was colourful like a swatch of silk brocade – clusters of green, dashes of red, dots of yellow and streaks of white.

"It's beautiful, isn't it?" Lotus asked.

"I've never seen so many flowers in my life. Nor such beautiful ones!"

"It's already summer, the flowers now are nothing compared to the spring peach blossoms. Though *Shifu* won't say Papa's kung fu is the greatest under the heavens, I'm sure he'd admit that Papa is unrivalled when it comes to horticulture. But our *shifu* cares only for food and drink; he probably knows nothing about what makes a flower or a tree exceptional. He's really awfully common."

"You can't speak so rudely about *Shifu.*"

Lotus stuck her tongue out and pulled a face. She then explained to Guo Jing the story behind the island's name. Once upon a time, a master known as Ge Hong practised Taoism on the island, and, when he departed for the next realm, he splashed ink on the shore, leaving deep marks, shaped like peach blossoms, in the rocks. When her papa moved in, he planted peach trees to match the name.

The boatman, having long heard that the murderous Lord of the Peach Blossom Island took pleasure in disembowelling his victims, steered close to the shore without anchoring. Lotus leapt onto land, followed by Guo Jing and their Fergana horse, Ulaan.

The moment his unwelcome passengers had disembarked, the man shifted the tiller, keen to put as much distance as he could between himself and the dreaded island. Then he heard a thud as something landed on the deck.

"We've got to go back to the mainland. You'll be rewarded handsomely!"

A piece of silver, worth ten *taels*, glimmered from the bow. He promised the generous lady he would return, as he sailed away as fast as he could.

"Papa! Papa! I'm home!" Lotus cried happily, excited to be back on the island.

She beckoned Guo Jing and zigzagged through the jungle of flowers. Guo Jing only had to blink to lose sight of her. He ran along the path, calling her name, but before long he was hopelessly lost.

There were tracks leading east, west, north, south. Which way did Lotus go?

He picked a path and soon noticed that the surroundings looked awfully familiar. He had gone round in a circle and now he was back where he had started! He remembered Lotus telling him that Peach Blossom Island's layout was far more complex than the labyrinthine Roaming Cloud Manor. If he barged ahead blindly, he would only find himself more tangled up in the maze, and probably further and further away from Lotus. So he sat beneath a peach tree and waited.

An hour passed, then two, but there was still no sign of Lotus. Only silence to keep him company. Not a soul in sight.

Guo Jing was getting anxious. He climbed up to the top of a nearby tree to get a better view. To the south was the sea, to the west nothing but rocks, and to the east and north an ocean of flowers of every hue, as far as the eye could see. Their vibrant colours sent his head spinning.

No whitewashed walls, no black tiles, no smoke from the chimney, no dogs barking. No sound at all. It was uncanny.

The silence was beginning to unnerve him. He leapt from branch to branch, plunging deeper into the woods. *What if I've gone so far off track that not even Lotus can find me?* He decided to retrace his steps, but the harder he tried, the less familiar his surroundings became.

The light was failing, so he sat down once more, hoping Lotus would locate him before nightfall. Thankfully, the ground was covered by a soft blanket of grass. It was quite comfortable to sit on, but soon his stomach started to rumble and his mind wandered to all the delicacies Lotus had cooked for Count Seven. The hunger was becoming unbearable.

What if Lotus has been locked up by her papa? Guo Jing's thoughts grew dark, in step with the sky. *I'm going starve to death here!*

And he had not avenged his father's death yet. Nor had he repaid the kindness his *shifus* had shown him. What about his mother? All alone in the Mongolian desert. Who would look after her, if he died?

Despite these worries, he was soon asleep.

He was back in Zhongdu. Lotus was there too. They were on the lake, sharing a meal. She hummed a song. A *xiao* flute answered. Guo Jing opened his eyes with a jolt.

The moon was high. The fragrances of the island's lush vegetation were more intense at night. Flute song drifted from afar on the breeze. He was not dreaming anymore.

Re-energised, Guo Jing decided to head towards the source of the music. Sometimes the path disappeared, but he could still hear the *xiao* ahead of him. He remembered treading similar meandering and interrupted paths in Roaming Cloud Manor, and he decided to ignore the landscape and layout. He followed the flute song resolutely, climbing into the treetops to push forward whenever he reached a dead end.

Soon, the music grew clearer. He sprinted after it and followed it round a bend in the path. A vista opened up suddenly. A lake of white flowers shimmered in the moonlight. Then he spotted a man-made structure peeking from behind the vegetation.

Now the music grew louder, now it softened. Sometimes it sounded ahead of Guo Jing, sometimes it whispered from behind. He listened. It was coming from the east! But, when he started to follow it, the music suddenly seemed to originate from the west. When he dashed north after it, it would suddenly call from the south. Could there be a dozen musicians signalling each other and toying with him? He grew dizzy from running in circles and decided to ignore the music for now and investigate the mound.

Here lies Madam Feng, Mistress of Peach Blossom Island. The characters were carved into a stone slab over the tomb.

Lotus's mother, Guo Jing thought. It must have been so hard on Lotus to lose her mother so young.

He fell to his knees and bowed reverentially four times, his forehead touching the ground. It was an earnest gesture of respect borne out of his love for Lotus.

The music stopped. But the moment Guo Jing was back on his feet, it resumed. Once again, it was ahead of him.

Be it good or evil, I'll follow it.

The flute song led Guo Jing back into the woods. The tune shifted key. It was now smiling at him, murmuring into his ears. Softly, gently, seductively. His heart fluttered, his mind swirled.

Why does this melody sound so good? he asked himself.

The tempo now quickened, urging him to dance. Somehow, the music was causing his blood to rush through his veins, his face was flushed and his ears burned. He sat down and began to regulate his breathing with the *neigong* formula Ma Yu had taught him, but he so wanted to jump up, wave his hands and kick his feet about to the tune. Eventually, he managed to gather his mind, uniting his thoughts and spirit. All concerns and desires were swept from his being, leaving only a bright hollowness within.

The music had lost its allure suddenly. It had become no more beguiling than lapping waves or whispering branches. The Elixir Field below his navel glowed warmly; his body was energised and relaxed at the same time. He did not even feel hungry anymore. He knew he was in a state in which nothing external could trouble his mind, and he opened his eyes slowly.

A pair of glowing green orbs stared at him from the darkness, several paces away.

Guo Jing leapt to his feet and backed away.

What kind of beast is that? he asked himself, frightened.

The eyes vanished.

Not even a creature as fast as a leopard or a raccoon could disappear in the blink of an eye like that!

Then he heard heavy breathing. It sounded human.

Silly me – the man just closed his eyes! That's why they disappeared! He didn't go anywhere! Guo Jing laughed inwardly at his stupidity, but remained vigilant, as he could not tell if the stranger was friend or foe.

Now the tone of the flute fluttered, cooing into his ears, beguiling like a woman's sigh. Now a moan, now whispering sweetly, now beckoning gently. The tune had grown more bewitching, but it had little effect on Guo Jing – he had yet to be acquainted with the music made by a man and a woman between the sheets. However, the stranger was desperately resisting the temptations of the flute, panting harder and faster.

Concerned by the man's painful gasps, Guo Jing crept forward. The night was clear, but the lush canopy of vegetation blocked out the moon.

Only a few steps away, Guo Jing was finally able to discern the outline of the stranger's features. His wild hair tumbled down to the ground. His unusually long eyebrows and overgrown beard obscured most of his face. Sitting cross-legged, the man held his left hand over his chest and his right hand on his back.

Guo Jing recognised the stance. He had learned it from Scarlet Sun Ma Yu atop the cliff in Mongolia. This position kept heart and spirit contained, so no sight or sound could disturb one's internal peace – not the crashing waves, the crumbling mountain, the booming thunder or the flashing lightning.

This man knows orthodox Taoist internal kung fu. Why can't he resist the flute song? Guo Jing could not fathom the reason for his own immunity.

The music now swelled with renewed urgency, causing the stranger to shudder and jump. He leapt up several times, rising more than a foot from the ground. Then he managed to force himself down again, with great mental effort.

Watching the stranger flit between serenity and agitation, Guo Jing grew worried. The man's internal state was growing more precarious as moments of peace were increasingly shortlived. The flute made two coloratura twirls and the stranger sighed, "Let it be . . ." Muscles tensed, he was ready to leap to his feet.

There was no time to think. Guo Jing pressed firmly on the man's right shoulder, pushing him down, then slapped his other hand onto the Great Hammer acupressure point at the back of the man's neck.

Two years ago, when Guo Jing first started training under Ma Yu, the Taoist would gently massage this pressure point, channelling warmth through his palm, when Guo Jing's mind strayed and his spirit grew restless. It prevented the young man's *qi* from misfiring into the demonic way and causing damage to his mind and body.

Guo Jing tried to do the same. His internal kung fu was not sufficiently cultivated to help the stranger resist the music, but he had managed to light upon the very spot that would allow the bearded man to quash the noise within. The agitation was gone. The stranger propelled his energy around his body in peace, with his eyes closed. His breathing grew even and smooth.

Happy with the result of his intervention, Guo Jing then heard "Little bastard!" muttered behind him. The flute song had come to a sudden halt.

He turned. The voice sounded like Apothecary Huang's. But, of course, he could not make out so much as a shadow.

Helping the man must have angered Lotus's papa further. *What if he is evil? I really have made a big mess.*

And, with that thought, his mood sank.

5

SINCE HE HAD NOWHERE TO GO AND NOTHING TO DO, GUO Jing sat down facing the bearded man and started to work on his own internal energy. He closed his eyes and turned his sight inwards. Before long, all worries were purged from his mind and he entered a state where neither he nor the world existed. By the time he opened his eyes again, the morning dew had formed on his clothes and stars were fading in the dawn twilight.

The sun shone through the canopy of flowers and leaves, painting the stranger's face with blossom-shaped shadows. Guo Jing could finally get a good look at him.

It must have been years since the man had groomed his hair and beard. They were long and straggly, and bristled, like a wild creature. Curiously, they were jet black, without a speck of grey.

"Which of the Seven Disciples of Quanzhen is your *shifu*?" The stranger smiled, his eyes twinkling brightly.

Startled, Guo Jing shot to his feet. But the man seemed kindly enough, so he bowed. "Your student Guo Jing pays respect to the Elder. The Seven Heroes of the South are my teachers."

"The Seven Heroes of the South? Ke Zhen'e and his gang? How could they teach you Quanzhen *neigong*?"

"Elder Ma Yu the Scarlet Sun instructed me on internal kung fu techniques for two years, but I was not initiated into the Quanzhen Sect officially."

The man roared with laughter and made a face — the kind of expression a child would make after pulling a prank. "Aha! What brings you to Peach Blossom Island?"

"I came here at the command of the Lord of Peach Blossom Island."

"Why?" His countenance darkened.

"I offended Lord Huang and now I am here to receive my death."

"You're not pulling my leg, are you?"

"I wouldn't dare."

"Good!" The bearded man nodded. "There's no need for you to die, really. Sit down."

Guo Jing obeyed, perching on a rock. He now realised the man was sitting in a cave in a hillside.

"Who else has taught you?"

"The Divine Vagrant Nine Fingers—"

"Count Seven Hong?" The man flashed a half-smile.

"Yes, Master Hong taught me the Dragon-Subduing Palm."

"Wow! You know that? It's an amazing technique!" Envy and enthusiasm poured forth. "Teach me! I'll kowtow and call you *Shifu*." Then he shook his head, vigorously. "No! That won't work! That Old Beggar and I are the same age. I wonder if I'm older or he . . . ? I can't be his martial grandson. That wouldn't be right!"

He turned once more to Guo Jing. "Did the Beggar teach you *neigong*?"

"No, sir."

"Even if he started training in his mother's belly," the man mumbled to the clouds, "he'd still only have been doing it eighteen or nineteen years. Why can he resist the flute song, when I can't?"

He scrutinised Guo Jing from head to toe and back again, before holding up his right hand. "Push against my palm. Show me your kung fu."

Obediently, Guo Jing touched his palm against the man's.

"Let your *qi* sink to the Elixir Field, then channel your energy."

Guo Jing did as he was told.

"Good! Now, watch out!"

The man drew back slightly, then thrust. A potent force gushed forth.

Guo Jing could not hold his ground. His left hand darted up instinctively to swat at the bearded man's arm, hoping to break the palms' contact. Yet the man twirled his hand, and stopped the strike, placing four fingers on the back of Guo Jing's wrist. He followed up with a casual backhand flick. Immediately, Guo Jing's footing was lost.

He stumbled back seven or eight steps, until his back smacked into a tree. Luckily, he had followed Count Seven Hong's training and held back some of his strength. With the reserved energy, he was able to stand firm again.

"Not bad, but nothing special either. How did he resist the 'Ode to the Billowing Tide'?" The man was talking out loud to himself again.

Guo Jing inhaled deeply to calm the blood and energy rushing around his torso.

This man's martial skill is on the same level as Count Seven and Apothecary Huang. Could he be . . . ?

The idea that this man could be the Venom of the West sent a chill through Guo Jing. He lifted his hand towards the light to check for signs of poison – no angry swelling, no black streaks – and heaved a sigh of relief.

The bearded stranger grinned. "Do you know who I am?"

"I have heard that there are five supreme martial masters in the world. Immortal Wang, the Leader of the Quanzhen Sect, has already passed on. I've had the honour of meeting Count Seven Hong, the Divine Vagrant Nine Fingers, as well as the Lord of Peach Blossom Island. Could the Elder be Master Ouyang or His Majesty the King of the South?"

"You think I'm a match for the Heretic of the East and the Beggar of the North?"

"Your student is a novice and has seen very little of the martial world. Yet, of the martial masters I have had the honour of meeting, other than Count Seven and Lord Huang, I cannot think of any who could have equalled the Master a moment ago."

The man was extremely pleased. A childlike joy radiated from his unkempt face.

"No, no, I'm not the old Viper and I'm not a king. Try again."

"I have also met a man called Qiu Qianren. He had us believe he was on the same level as Count Seven, but his claims were without substance, his kung fu average. I'm afraid I am very thick and cannot even guess at the Master's great name."

"I'll give you a hint." He chuckled. "My last name is Zhou."

"Zhou Botong!" Guo Jing blurted out. He bowed deeply in embarrassment. "Your student begs the Elder's pardon."

"Correct! That's me, Zhou Botong." The man was still chuckling. "Zhou Botong is my name, and you called me by my name. What's there to pardon? Double Sun Wang Chongyang was my elder martial brother, and Ma Yu, Qiu Chuji and the rest are my martial nephews. But you're not in the Quanzhen Sect, so there's no need to be so long-winded with all these elders and masters and what not – just call me by my name."

Was he suggesting they throw all the social hierarchies and codes of behaviour of the age out of the window? Flabbergasted, Guo Jing took some time to mumble a limp, "I wouldn't dare," in reply.

Meanwhile, an even more outlandish idea had hatched in Zhou Botong's brain. He had been bored senseless living in isolation on Peach Blossom Island all these years. The young man's sudden appearance meant that, at long last, he had someone to talk to, someone to amuse him!

"Little one, what do you say if we become sworn brothers?"

Guo Jing's jaw dropped at the proposal. He did not mean it, surely! But the man looked very serious, nothing in his demeanour suggested that it was a joke.

After a stunned silence, Guo Jing answered weakly, "Your student is a junior to Elder Ma and Elder Qiu. I should address you as Grandmaster."

Zhou Botong swatted the answer away with both hands. "Why do we need to make such a fuss between generations? My martial brother taught me all my kung fu, and I'm not that much older than Ma Yu and Qiu Chuji. They don't treat me as an elder, anyway, because I don't act like one. I know that you are most likely not my son, and I fear I am not your child, so—"

Footsteps cut him short. An aged servant approached with a tiffin.

"Food!" Zhou Botong announced, visibly excited.

The servant laid out the meal on a rock before Zhou Botong – four dishes, two flasks of wine and a wooden bucket of rice – and stood meekly in waiting.

"Where is Miss Huang? Why hasn't she come to visit?" Guo Jing asked.

The servant shook his head, pointed at his ears, then his mouth.

"Apothecary Huang pierced his eardrums," Zhou Botong explained. "Tell him to open his mouth."

Guo Jing signalled and the man opened his mouth. Half of his tongue was missing!

"All the servants here are the same. Now that you're here, on Peach Blossom Island, if you survive, you'll probably end up like him!"

How could Lotus's father be so barbaric? Guo Jing was in shock.

"The Heretic tortures me every night with that song, but I refuse to admit defeat. And yet, if it hadn't been for you, last night, he'd have broken me." Zhou Botong rambled on without stopping to draw breath. "Ten years of resolve, gone in a puff of smoke! Come, come, come, little brother, we've got food and drink, here. Let's pledge to the heavens and become brothers. From this moment on, we shall share our blessings and bear each other's troubles.

"I remember Wang Chongyang found all kinds of excuses to refuse my invitation, back then, too . . . What? You really don't want to? My brother didn't want to swear brotherhood because his kung fu was much stronger. Are you stronger than me? I don't think so!"

"My skill is too insignificant for me to be your sworn brother."

"If only people with the same level of kung fu can swear brotherhood, are you saying I should be brothers with the Heretic or the Venom? They're nasty, nasty people – I won't do it! Are you saying I should be brothers with that deaf-mute fellow?" He waved his left hand and sent the servant flying in a somersault. Then he started pulling at his beard, yanking his hair and stamping his feet on the ground. Just like a toddler having a tantrum.

Guo Jing tried to explain. "Your student is two generations the Master's junior. If I do as the Elder instructs, I shall be laughed out of the martial world. And when I meet Elder Ma, Elder Qiu and Elder Wang again, would it not be very awkward for me?"

"Only you have so many qualms! I know you don't want to be my brother because you think I'm too old. My beard is long, but actually, in age, I am not so old . . ." Zhou Botong wailed into his hands. "I'll pluck out my beard, then I will look younger!" He yanked out a fistful of facial hair.

"Your student shall do as the Elder commands."

"Nay!" Zhou Botong shouted through his tears. "You're still calling me Elder! You're only saying yes because I've made you do it! If people ask, you'll blame me. No, no, no. I know you don't want me as your sworn brother."

Zhou Botong picked up a plate of food and hurled it to the ground. He sank further into the tantrum, refusing to eat. The servant picked up the debris in evident panic, unable to fathom the older man's mood swing.

Amused by the absurdity of the situation, Guo Jing realised he must play along.

"It was rude of me to refuse this honour from Brother," he said with as much gravity as he could muster. "Shall we make our pledge of brotherhood here and now?"

"The Heretic and I have a pact. I can't leave this cave until I've beaten him. Except when nature calls, of course!" Zhou Botong giggled merrily, but his beard was still glistening with tears. "I'll kowtow from inside and you do it out there."

Guo Jing got down on his knees, wondering if this eccentric man would end up living in the cave his whole life. But, in the short time he had known Zhou Botong, he had already learned that some questions should never be asked.

Zhou Botong, too, sank to his knees. "I, Zhou Botong the Hoary Urchin, pledge to be a brother to Guo Jing from this day forward, to share all my blessings and to bear all his troubles. If I break my word, may I lose all my martial skills, leaving me incapable of fighting a puppy or a kitten."

Guo Jing could not help chuckling at the man's strange title and bizarre vows.

"What are you laughing at? Your turn!"

Guo Jing solemnly promised to be a brother to Zhou Botong the Hoary Urchin. If he broke his word, he would not be able to fight a baby mouse or an infant turtle. They poured wine on the ground and Guo Jing kowtowed to his elder brother.

"On your feet!" Zhou laughed heartily and poured himself a cup of wine. "The Old Heretic is such a miser. His wine tastes like water. A pretty girl came here once, and she brought a delicious vintage. Such a shame she hasn't been back since."

Guo Jing remembered Lotus telling him of this encounter and its aftermath, how her father's reprimand had led her to run away from the island in a fit of anger. Looks like Brother knows nothing about that, he told himself, and the thought of Lotus consumed him as he wolfed down five bowls of rice. After all, it had been a whole day since he last ate.

6

AFTER THE SERVANT HAD PACKED UP THE LEFTOVERS AND DIS-appeared into the forest, Zhou Botong said, "How did you offend the Heretic?"

Guo Jing began to explain his childhood encounter with Hurricane Chen, how he had accidentally killed this feared man of the *wulin* in Mongolia, before moving on to his encounter with Apothecary Huang at Roaming Cloud Manor. He also described the fight with Cyclone Mei, and Apothecary Huang's determination to intimidate his *shifus*, the Six Freaks of the South. Then he described how he had offered to come to Peach Blossom Island to meet his death.

Zhou Botong was engrossed. He loved nothing more than a good story. He listened with his eyes half closed, his head cocked to one side. When he felt Guo Jing had been sparing with the details, he would probe him further, until his curiosity was satisfied.

After Guo Jing had described how he arrived on the island, Zhou Botong asked, "And then what happened?"

"Then I came here."

"So the pretty girl was the Heretic's daughter," Zhou Botong said, after a pause. "Why did she disappear after you arrived on the island? There must be a reason. The Old Heretic must have locked her up."

"Your student thinks so too . . ." Guo Jing frowned, sick with worry.

"What did you just call yourself?" Zhou Botong barked.

"Brother, it was a slip of the tongue. Please forgive me."

"You must never make that mistake again. It's unforgiveable! If we were in a play, it would be terribly confusing, like calling me wife when I'm in fact your mama or daughter!"

Eventually, Zhou Botong was satisfied with Guo Jing's apologies. "Now, guess why I'm here?" He began his tale before Guo Jing could answer: "Well, it's a long story. You know about the martial contest at the summit of Mount Hua? Between the Five Greats – the Heretic of the East, the Venom of the West, the King of the South, the Beggar of the North and Central Divinity."

"I have heard it mentioned." Guo Jing nodded.

"It was the depths of winter – at the year's rump – and snow lay everywhere. Indeed, there was so much snow that all roads up and down the mountain were inaccessible. The five men sparred and debated for seven days and seven nights in the blizzard. In the end, everyone agreed my martial brother Wang Chongyang was the Greatest Martial Master Under the Heavens. Do you know why there was a contest?"

"No, I don't."

"It was for a martial manual—"

"The Nine Yin Manual?" Guo Jing was thinking aloud.

"That's right! Little brother, you may be young, but you have heard rather a lot about the martial world. Do you know the Manual's history?"

"Not at all . . ."

Zhou Botong tugged at a lock of hair by his ear, looking rather pleased with himself. "Well, you told me a rather exciting story just now—"

"It wasn't a story! It's all true!"

"As long as they're amusing, what's the difference between real events and good stories? A lot of people spend their whole life eating, sleeping, defecating and doing nothing else. If you told me every little thing they did, every chicken feather or garlic peel in their pointless, boring lives, every vegetable and chunk of tofu, their every pee and poo, you'd bore the Hoary Urchin to death."

Guo Jing nodded, knowing his brother would always have the last word on any matter. "You're right, brother. Please tell me the story of the Nine Yin Manual."

"Our Great Song once had an Emperor called Huizong. He reigned about a hundred years ago. A devout believer of Taoism. During the Zhenghe regnal era, he collected every single Taoist tract in existence and had them carved into woodblocks, then printed as *The Taoist Canon of Ten Thousand Longevities*. There were, altogether, five thousand, four hundred and eighty-one volumes. A man called Huang Shang was appointed by the Emperor to carve—"

"His name is Huang too," Guo Jing said, under his breath.

"Pah! What do you mean? That man has nothing to do with Apothecary Huang! Don't get funny ideas! There are plenty of things named Huang in the world. The yellow dog is named Huang. So is the yellow cow!"

Guo Jing knew the character "Huang" meant "yellow", but he doubted that dogs and cows had last names. Nonetheless, he was well aware of the consequences of arguing with his brother, the Hoary Urchin.

"So, this Huang Shang, who had nothing to do with Old Heretic Huang," Zhou Botong continued, "was incredibly clever."

Guo Jing nearly blurted out, "He was incredibly clever too?" Luckily, he managed to hold his tongue.

"He was terrified of making mistakes. Because, if he carved a single character wrong and the Emperor found out, his head would not long remain attached to his neck. So he checked each volume carefully. After a few years, he became an expert in Taoist ideas and sorcery, and, from there, absorbed profound martial theories as if they were part of his being. He didn't have a *shifu*. He learned it all by himself, cultivating exceptional skills internally as well as externally. A true martial master. I know I am definitely not as smart as Huang Shang, and I'm sure he's much cleverer than you."

"Of course — for me, it'd take more than a lifetime to read that many books. There would be so many words I wouldn't recognise. I wouldn't gain any martial insights."

"There are some exceptionally clever people in this world. But, I can tell you, nothing good — no, indeed, only the very rotten — comes of running into one of their kind." Zhou Botong gave a sad sigh.

Lotus is exceptionally clever, Guo Jing said to himself, but meeting her is the best thing that's ever happened to me.

"Huang Shang was now a martial master, but he still worked as a government official. One year, a very odd religion appeared in his jurisdiction. Some people called it Manichaeism, others the Religion of Light. Apparently, it was brought over by the Persians in the west. They worship neither the Grand Supreme Elderly Lord, nor the Great Sage, the First Teacher Confucius, nor the Tathagata Buddha. Their deity was an ancient demon from abroad. And they don't eat meat — only vegetables!

"I told you the Huizong Emperor was a devout Taoist, didn't I? When he found out about the Manichaeans, he sent an imperial edict ordering Huang Shang to lead an army and get rid of these apostates and infidels.

"Who would have thought that there were so many martial

masters among the hearers and elects of the Religion of Light? Or that they fought without fear of death? They were more than a match for the useless imperial army. After a few battles, they completely crushed the soldiers led by Huang Shang. But he refused to give up. He challenged his enemies to single combat and he killed a handful of their legates as well as a smattering of their protectors.

"Some of the people he killed were disciples of major martial schools. Suddenly, their martial uncles, aunties, brothers, sisters, god-fathers and godmothers – you name it – came out of the woodwork, bringing friends from other kung fu branches to demand revenge. All of them cursing him for violating the moral code of the *wulin*.

"Huang Shang tried to explain. 'I am a government official. I'm not part of your martial world; how would I know your rules?' But these aunties and uncles with their many mouths cried, 'How could you have learned kung fu without being part of the *wulin*?' 'Did your *shifu* teach you how to fight, but not the code that governs us?' To which Huang Shang replied, 'I have no *shifu*.' Of course, they swore on their lives that he was lying and kept on bickering. What do you think happened next?"

"They fought?"

"Indeed! They started exchanging blows, but Huang Shang's moves were very odd. It was like nothing anyone had ever seen before. In no time at all, he killed a few more aunties and uncles. But, although Huang Shang's kung fu was exceptional, one man cannot prevail against a mob. Eventually, he was injured and ran for his life. They were so angry, they sought out his family and took it out on them, killing his parents, his wife, his children. Every last one of them."

Guo Jing sighed at the needless loss of life. A voice within told him, *Death haunts the martial arts. If Huang Shang had gained no martial knowledge, tragedy would not have befallen his family.*

"Huang Shang ran away to a wild, desolate place, far, far away, and kept himself hidden. He had memorised every single martial move his enemies used on him, and spent every waking moment devising countermeasures – so he could kill them and avenge his family.

"After who knows how long, he finally cracked them all. He was so very happy, because, even if they now all attacked at once, he could deal with them on his own! He left his hideout to seek revenge, yet each and every one of his adversaries had disappeared. Do you know why?"

"Did they hear about his new kung fu? Were they hiding in fear?"

"No, no. My martial brother asked me to guess, when he told me the story, too. But I couldn't get it, even after seven or eight tries. Now, it's your turn. Try again."

"I won't get it, even if I try seventy or eighty times," Guo Jing said sheepishly.

"Don't be so useless, boy! You can't admit defeat already!" Zhou Botong chuckled. "Well, I'll spare you the agony. They were all dead."

"Huh? How? Did Huang Shang's disciples kill them? Maybe his friends?"

"No! You're ten thousand *li* off the mark!" Zhou Botong shook his head wildly. "He never had any disciples. Remember he was a civil servant? His friends were all scholars. You know, reciting poetry and writing prose. They couldn't kill a thing!"

"Was there a plague?" Guo Jing scratched his head. "A disease that wiped out all his enemies?"

"No, no, no, you're still very wrong. His enemies were all over the country, from Shandong in the north-east, to Huguang in the south, in Hebei, in the two Zhes. How could they die of the same plague? Hang on, actually, there is one plague every one of us will fall victim to eventually. You can run to the ends of the earth and you still won't escape it. Can you tell me what it is?"

Guo Jing started listing every illness he knew: typhoid, smallpox, measles, malaria . . . Zhou Botong kept shaking his head.

"Foot and mouth!" Guo Jing slapped a hand over his mouth in a fit of giggles, then knocked himself on the head. "I am so silly. It only affects cattle – not us!"

"You're getting further from the answer!" Zhou Botong laughed at Guo Jing's wild guesses and felt very smug that he knew the answer. "Huang Shang journeyed to far-flung corners of the country, and at last he tracked down one of his foes. When they had first fought, she was a girl of sixteen or so. Now, she was an old grandma of nearly sixty . . ."

"How? Did she disguise herself? Pretend to be an old lady so Huang Shang wouldn't recognise her?"

"No, she really was that old. Huang Shang had scores of enemies. Each one a martial master. Their kung fu came from different schools and branches. Imagine the complexity, the variety! How much time and effort do you think it would take to break down each of their most deadly moves? He spent day and night alone, deep in the mountains, thinking about kung fu. He even dreamed about kung fu. He thought of nothing else, and, meanwhile, a good forty years flew by!"

"Forty years?"

"Yes, if you put your heart and soul into the martial arts, forty years will disappear very quickly indeed. I've been here for fifteen, and it doesn't feel more than a day.

"The girl Huang Shang fought was now a wrinkly old woman, sickly and infirm. She lay in bed, gasping for breath. She'd be dead in a few days, without him lifting a finger. All the hatred and grievances Huang Shang had been harbouring all those decades vanished in an instant. Instead, he looked after her, spoon-fed her congee and medicine.

"Brother, everyone dies one day – this is the plague none of us can hide from. When death comes to you, there's no escape."

Guo Jing nodded solemnly.

"My martial brother and his disciples talked about cultivating nature and nurturing life, day in, day out, but can they really become immortal? I don't believe in that longevity business. That's why I refused to be a rotten monk.

"Huang Shang's enemies were in their forties, fifties and sixties the first time they fought," Zhou Botong continued, after a pause. "Of course no-one was left alive, forty years later. Actually, he needn't have wasted his energy coming up with countermoves. He could have just competed with them to see who could live the longest. He managed to stay in the game for forty years, so the Lord of the Heavens took care of his foes for him!"

Guo Jing began to question whether it was right to seek out Wanyan Honglie to avenge his father's death, but Zhou Botong would not give him a moment's peace to think.

"Kung fu is a store of infinite fun. What else in life is worth doing? Even fun things get boring and flavourless after a while. Only the martial arts grow more interesting the more time you spend with them. Don't you agree?"

Guo Jing gave a non-committal grunt. He never saw kung fu learning as fun. How he had suffered, acquiring martial knowledge in the past decade, forcing himself onwards, head down, teeth clenched. It was his stubbornness that pushed him through. There was nothing fun about any of it.

"Hey, why aren't you asking me what happened next?" Zhou Botong noticed his audience had grown reflective.

"Oh, so . . . then what?"

"You have to ask, or it's no fun for me!"

"Yes, brother, do tell me what happened next!"

"Well, Huang Shang thought to himself, I too have grown old, I don't have many years left. All the amazing martial discoveries he had made over those forty years would die with him. He knew he too would fall prey to that inevitable plague in a few years' time. He couldn't let his efforts just go to waste like that, could he? So he wrote down everything he knew in two volumes. Do you know the name he gave the book?"

"What?"

"Guess!"

After a lengthy silence, Guo Jing asked, "Is it the Nine Yin Manual?"

"Isn't that the stupidest question you've ever heard? Have we talked about anything else today?"

Guo Jing grinned. "I don't want to be wrong."

7

"HUANG SHANG EXPLAINED EVERYTHING I'VE JUST TOLD YOU in the Manual's preface, that's how my martial brother came to know of it, and he told me. Huang Shang hid the book very well. For decades, no-one knew about it. But, one day, it surfaced. Of course, every martial artist under the heavens wanted a peek. They would do anything to get their hands on it. It was chaos.

"My martial brother said that at least a hundred *wulin* masters have died trying to get hold of the Manual over the years. And, when they did, it didn't matter how well they hid themselves; once they started learning the Manual's kung fu, it only took a year or two before they were discovered. Then hordes of martial men would hound them for the text. This kept happening, so no-one who got hold of the Manual ever lived long enough to learn much. So much bloodshed, all because of one book."

Guo Jing was horrified by the death and destruction the Manual had caused. "If Hurricane Chen hadn't taken the Manual, he could have easily lived a quiet, happy life with Cyclone Mei in a village somewhere," he said. "Even Apothecary Huang might not have found them. If Cyclone Mei hadn't got hold of it, she wouldn't be alone and blind. The Manual has only brought harm to the world."

"What? No, no, no, you're wrong! The Nine Yin Manual contains the most wondrous, mystical kung fu. Just one glimpse can ensnare a martial man for life. It may bring death, but so what? Everyone dies eventually! Didn't we just agree on that?"

"Brother, perhaps you're a little obsessed with the martial arts."

"Of course I am. Nothing is as enriching and fascinating as learning kung fu. Most people are stupid. They worship books because they are the means to becoming a government official, or they love gold and jade, or beautiful women – those are the stupidest. None of these things can give you a sliver of the enjoyment you get from martial training."

"I've learned a little, but I've never experienced any enjoyment practising kung fu."

"What? Why do you learn, then?"

"*Shifu* says I should—"

"You really are hopelessly stupid!" Zhou Botong shook his head with dramatic disapproval. "Skipping meals is of no import; sacrifices, I can make many. But I would never give up on learning kung fu!"

Guo Jing pretended to agree. He suspected his brother's single-minded focus on the martial arts had left him a little unhinged. "I've seen Twice Foul Dark Wind practising the kung fu from the Nine Yin Manual. The moves were truly evil and malicious. They should never have been written down."

"That can't be! The Manual comes from an honourable orthodox tradition. Twice Foul Dark Wind must have got it wrong."

Nothing Zhou Botong said could persuade Guo Jing. After all, he had been at the receiving end of Cyclone Mei's infernal talons and had seen her take lives without a crumb of remorse.

"Oh, I know what you mean! Huang Shang did write down some nasty moves used by his enemies. You've got to master the really bad moves before you can overcome them. So, he set down the training methods for both – the moves and the countermoves – but the purpose of the Manual was to subdue malevolent kung fu, not to spread it. I'm sure the Heretic's wicked little apostates learned the vicious skills, instead of the ways to vanquish them."

Zhou Botong did not realise that Hurricane Chen had only managed to steal the second volume of the Manual, and that, without the foundation of internal strength explained in the first volume, it was impossible to learn the countermeasures. That was why Twice Foul Dark Wind only acquired relatively basic techniques, like Nine Yin

Skeleton Claw, Heartbreaker Palm and White Python Whip, and had to give up on the ways to overpower them.

The Hoary Urchin took a moment to bask in his own glory for having uncovered the twisted truth behind Twice Foul Dark Wind's kung fu, then he turned back to Guo Jing. "Where did we get to?"

"You were telling me how the heroes of the *wulin* fought over the Manual."

"Oh, yes . . . So, more and more people got embroiled. In the end, my martial brother Wang Chongyang, Lord of Peach Blossom Island Apothecary Huang and Chief Hong of the Beggar Clan all got involved. Together – with two others, as you know – they decided to hold a contest at the summit of Mount Hua, and the greatest among them would be accepted as the custodian of the Manual."

"So that was how the Manual ended up in Immortal Wang's possession?"

"Indeed!" Zhou Botong grew visibly excited as he approached his favourite part of the tale. "I told you that my brother taught me all the kung fu I know, didn't I? He and I were close friends before he became a monk. He used to say that I was too obsessed with the martial arts and had no grasp of the Taoist way – attaining peace through inaction and all that. And he said again and again that I should not become a monk, even though I belong to the Quanzhen Sect. I couldn't agree more! Who in their right mind wants to be a monk?

"You know, of my seven martial nephews, Qiu Chuji is the best fighter, but my brother liked him the least. He thought Qiu placed too much emphasis on his kung fu and neglected his Taoist self-cultivation.

"Brother loved talking about how martial learning is about practice, hard work and improvement, yet the search for *Tao* – the Way – isn't about fame or fortune, it's about looking for a path to return to the natural self. So kung fu and the Taoist practice are, in actual fact, antagonistic. Ma Yu inherited my brother's philosophical side, but his kung fu can't measure up to Qiu Chuji's or Wang Chuyi's."

"How did Immortal Wang balance the two opposites, being a Taoist and a martial master?"

"He was so naturally endowed. He could understand martial theories and ideas, just like that, whereas I have to work so hard to get there . . . Where did we get to? Why did you distract me, asking all these irrelevant questions?"

"You were telling me how Immortal Wang got the Nine Yin Manual." Guo Jing chuckled, amused by Zhou Botong's childlike mood swings.

"That's right! So, Brother brought the Manual back. He put it in a wooden casket and placed it under a flagstone. Under his prayer cushion. The spot he always sat in when he meditated. He didn't look at it. He wasn't interested in the instructions contained within. It was all very strange, and I kept asking him why. But he just smiled and said nothing. But I didn't give up, and eventually he told me to work it out for myself. Now, why do you think he put it there?"

"Was he worried people would steal it? Or take it by force?"

"No, no! You're way off the mark!" Zhou Botong kept shaking his head. "Who'd be so stupid? To steal from the leader of the Quanzhen Sect would be asking for death!"

Guo Jing thought long and hard. "Actually, perhaps it should be hidden away. No, in fact, it would be better to burn it."

Zhou Botong looked at Guo Jing sharply. "Brother said exactly the same thing! How did you get it, this time? You haven't got anything right all day! Brother told me he tried to destroy the Manual a few times, but he couldn't summon the resolve to go through with it."

"Well, Immortal Wang was already the Greatest Martial Master Under the Heavens," Guo Jing mumbled, his face flushed with embarrassment. He wasn't used to being praised. "He'd be the greatest whether he learned the kung fu in the Manual or not. I don't think he went to Mount Hua to prove his martial prowess. He was there for the Manual. But not for what it contains. He just wanted it for the sake of the heroes of the *wulin*. So it couldn't cause more senseless killing."

Zhou Botong looked up at the sky and said nothing for a long time.

Did my words offend him? Guo Jing was unnerved by his sworn brother's silence.

At last, Zhou Botong sighed and turned his eyes to the ground. "How did you come to that conclusion?"

"I don't know how to put it." Guo Jing scratched his head. "So many lives were lost because of the Manual. It doesn't matter how valuable the content is, it should still be destroyed . . ."

"What you said makes good sense, but somehow I just can't see it that way. My martial brother also said that, though I'm naturally gifted and very interested in martial learning, I'm too obsessed with it and I don't have any real urge to help people or make the world a better place. Because of this, he said, however hard I work, my martial skills will never reach beyond a certain level. Of course, I didn't believe him. I used to think he was wrong.

"Tell me plainly, what does learning to fight, to wield weapons, to swing fists and launch kicks have to do with the size of one's heart? What does it have to do with personality and magnanimity? Yet, in my fifteen years on this island, I've begun to understand . . .

"Too bad he passed away; he would have liked you so very much, little brother. You're kind, honest and forgiving. He'd have been able to pass on all his knowledge to you. Everything."

Tears began to roll down Zhou Botong's face. "How I wish he were still alive! But even he, with all his martial might, still couldn't escape from the plague that is death."

He buried his face in his hands and began to sob loudly.

Guo Jing had not quite grasped Zhou Botong's point, but his grief was infectious.

Suddenly, the Hoary Urchin stopped crying and looked up. "Hey, we haven't finished the story yet! I can cry later. Where were we? Why didn't you stop me crying?"

Guo Jing was amazed by how quickly his brother's moods could flip. He answered, with a smile, "You were telling me how Immortal

Wang hid the Manual under a flagstone and sat over it, on his prayer cushion."

"Ah, yes, that's where we got to!" Zhou Botong slapped his thigh. "Of course, I asked Brother if I could take a peek. He fixed me with a really stern stare and gave me a proper scolding. He had never snubbed me like that and I knew better than to ask again. Anyway, the *wulin* got to enjoy a bit of peace and quiet after Mount Hua, but things began to stir up again in Brother's last days."

Zhou Botong was speaking louder and faster, his emotions running high in anticipation of the drama to follow.

"He knew the end was nigh, the plague that none of us can escape was knocking at his door. So, after he had made arrangements to settle the Sect's affairs, he commanded me to bring him the Nine Yin Manual. When I got there, a fire was already burning. I knew what he was thinking. I handed him both volumes and he held them for a long time. I heard him mumble to himself, 'Can I be the one to destroy the life's work of our Elder?' Then he sighed and declared, 'Water can carry a boat, but it can also capsize it. Let the world decide how it will use the Nine Yin Manual. However, disciples of the Quanzhen Sect are forbidden to learn the kung fu within, lest we are accused of taking the Manual for selfish reasons.' When he had finished speaking, he closed his eyes and left us. We let his body rest in the temple, and placed the Manual on the altar as an offering. And, that very night, trouble broke out, even before the third watch was sounded.

"I was standing vigil with my brother's seven disciples when we were attacked by a group of martial masters. My martial nephews drew the fight beyond the temple so no harm would come to Brother's body. I was left behind to guard him. Once they were gone, I heard a voice saying, 'Hand over the Nine Yin Manual, or I'll raze this place to the ground.'

"I peeped outside and my chest tightened. A man stood at the very tip of a branch, swaying and bobbing in the wind. Such amazing lightness kung fu, I told myself. If he would teach me, I'd gladly call him *Shifu* – no, no, I can't – he's here to take the Nine Yin Manual; he's not worthy of the name.

"Obviously, I knew I was no match for him, but I had to try to protect the Manual. I charged outside and leapt up into the tree. There, balanced on its branches, we exchanged thirty or forty moves. I got more and more scared as we fought. We were about the same age, but my kung fu was just that little bit less accomplished than his. Every move he made was so brutal and merciless. I couldn't really block them, but I had to, for Brother. Then he struck me on the shoulder and I fell out of the tree."

"Your kung fu is so strong and yet you couldn't beat him? Who is this man?"

"Guess!"

When Guo Jing finally spoke, for once, it was with utmost certainty. "Venom of the West."

"Yes! How did you know?"

"There are only five people whose kung fu is stronger than yours and they all took part in the Contest of Mount Hua. My *shifu* Count Seven is righteous and just. He wouldn't do a thing like that. The King of the South is the head of a state. I imagine his actions must befit his status. Lord Huang has a dignified air and an elegant bearing. I doubt he would stoop so low as to take advantage of another's misfortune."

"This knave is more perceptive than he seems." The words echoed among the trees.

Guo Jing sprinted to where he thought the voice had come from, but he only found swaying trees and drifting petals.

"Come back, brother. The Heretic is gone – far, far away."

"Old Heretic Huang knows the rules of the Mysterious Gates and the Five Elements inside out," Zhou Botong explained when Guo Jing returned to the cave. "He planted these trees according to the Eight Tactical Formations devised by the military strategist Zhuge Liang. Once among these trees, all he has to do is dart to the left, or make a few leaps right, and no-one can find him.

"The Heretic is exceptionally gifted, you know. He's not just a martial great, he's also a master of the four scholarly arts – zither, chess, calligraphy and painting. And he's an expert in medicine, divination, astrology, physiognomy, agriculture, irrigation, economics and military strategy. It's a shame he has to torment the Hoary Urchin, and an even greater shame that I can't beat him. But you're right. The Heretic may be eccentric and unpredictable, but he is no villain."

Guo Jing stood for a moment in awe of Apothecary Huang's vast knowledge, and then he remembered Zhou Botong's tale. "What happened after you fell from the tree?"

"Ha! You finally think of asking me to continue the story!" Zhou Botong slapped his thigh merrily. "That palm strike from Viper Ouyang took the wind out of me. The pain was unbearable. For a moment, I thought I was paralysed. But, when I saw him march inside the temple, I made myself run after him in spite of my injury. He was already standing at the altar, his hand reaching over my brother's coffin for the Manual. It was so frustrating. I was already hurt, and I couldn't beat him anyway. My martial nephews were still dealing with the other attackers. Suddenly – *pang!* – slivers of wood flew from the casket. The lid splintered—"

"Viper Ouyang smashed—?"

"No! It was my brother!"

Guo Jing's eyes widened and he gaped at Zhou Botong, unsure if his ears were deceiving him.

CHAPTER EIGHT

COMPETING HANDS

I

"NO, NO, NO, NO, HE DIDN'T RISE FROM THE DEAD, IT WASN'T his ghost – he wasn't actually dead."

"He faked his death?"

"Yes. You see, my martial brother got wind that the Venom of the West was lurking around our temple. He knew he was waiting for him to die so he could grab the Nine Yin Manual. Brother used a *neigong* technique to conceal his breathing, and kept his plan from us, in case our grief didn't seem genuine. The Venom is cunning. He'd probably have seen through the ploy and then have found another way to ambush us.

"Viper Ouyang saw my martial brother die with his own eyes. You can imagine his horror when the dead man burst out of the coffin – very much alive. The Venom was paralysed with shock. Brother jabbed him right between the eyebrows with a Yang in Ascendance mixed with the power of Cosmos *neigong*.

"The Venom had always been wary of my brother. And he was so stunned by the resurrection that he couldn't react fast enough to defend himself. Brother managed to negate his Exploding Toad kung fu with ease. Viper Ouyang had put many years of hard work into this ultimate series of moves. But all he could do now was run, with his tail between his legs.

"With the Venom gone, my martial brother sat cross-legged on the altar table, laughing. The Yang in Ascendance really drains one's internal energy, so I left him alone to channel his *qi* around his body, and ran off to find my martial nephews. They were thrilled to hear their *shifu* was alive, but we came back to a terrible sight.

"Brother had slumped to one side. There was a strange look on his face. I rushed over to him. He was ice cold to the touch. This time, he really had left us. He had beaten off Viper Ouyang for the time being, but we all knew the Venom would be back when he had recovered his strength. We were no match for him, so I took the Manual and headed south.

"My plan was to hide it in a cave in Yandang Mountain. Who would have guessed I'd bump into the Heretic along the way? He has a high opinion of himself. He would never try to take the Manual by force, like that shameless Viper Ouyang. But his young wife was with him and everything went wrong from there."

This must have been Lotus's mother! Guo Jing wondered how she had got involved with the Nine Yin Manual.

"The Heretic was looking very pleased with himself. He told me he was newly wed. She was beautiful. But I've never understood why anyone would want to get married. You know, keep a woman at home all the time. Why? I mean, even someone as clever as Apothecary Huang had fallen for this trap! Naturally, I teased him about it. He was in very good spirits, he wasn't offended at all. He even invited me to their celebrations.

"It was very nice of him, but you will remember that I was on my way to Yandang Mountain. I knew I mustn't tarry and so I made my excuses. And I ended up telling them about how my martial brother had died after striking Viper Ouyang.

"When I finished my story, the young madam begged me to show her the Manual. She was very persistent. She kept saying she didn't know any martial arts. She just wanted to understand how a book could have caused the deaths of so many martial masters.

"Of course, I refused, but the Heretic never said no to his beloved wife. So, he said to me, 'I can vouch that she has no martial knowledge – she just loves anything out of the ordinary. It won't do any harm, letting her take a look. If I, Apothecary Huang, so much as glance at it, I will gouge out my own two eyes and present them to you.'

"I kept shaking my head. I knew a master like Old Heretic Huang would for certain be a man of his word, but the Manual was too important. He was getting impatient. 'I know you're in a difficult position. If you do this for my wife, I promise to repay the Quanzhen Sect's kindness. But, if you continue to refuse me, well . . . I won't do anything to you – after all, we are acquainted – but I don't have any such relationship with your Quanzhen disciples.'

"I understood his meaning. He wouldn't pick a fight with me over the Manual, because it wouldn't be gentlemanly. But, if I didn't comply, he would take it out on my martial nephews. I'd bring trouble on everyone if I crossed him."

"Elder Ma and Elder Qiu couldn't beat Apothecary Huang," Guo Jing said.

"So, I said, 'Heretic, if you have a problem with the Hoary Urchin, take it out on the Hoary Urchin. Why involve my martial nephews? Surely that would be seen as picking on your juniors?'

"His wife giggled at my nickname. 'Brother Zhou,' she said, 'we're just joking with you – don't get upset! I don't need to see your precious Manual.' Then she turned to her husband. 'It sounds like this Viper Ouyang has taken the Manual. I don't think Brother Zhou has it with him. Don't press him any further. It will only make him lose face. After all, he can't show me what he hasn't got.' The Heretic laughed and said to me, 'Hoary Urchin, I'll help you find the Venom. You can't beat him alone.'"

"They were trying to rile you!" Now Guo Jing understood where Lotus got her temperament.

"I knew what they were trying to do, of course, but I couldn't let it go like that, so I replied, 'The Manual is here with me and I don't mind letting Madam take a peek. But I can't have you saying the Hoary Urchin can't keep the Manual safe. We'll have to fight that one out first.'

"Apothecary Huang was in an incredibly good mood. 'Fighting causes bad blood. Let's test our mettle with childhood games.' His wife clapped and cheered before I could even answer. 'That's a great idea! What about marbles?' That game was my speciality, so I agreed immediately. Then she added, 'Brother Zhou, if you lose, you'll have to let me look at the Manual. If you win, what would you like?'

"Apothecary Huang spoke before I could answer her: 'The Quanzhen Sect has its treasures and so does Peach Blossom Island.' He pulled a black shirt covered in little spikes from his bag. Can you guess what it was?"

"Hedgehog Chainmail," Guo Jing replied instantly.

"Correct! So you know about it too? Old Heretic Huang held the steel shirt up and said, 'You don't need this to protect you, but, one day, when you find your lady urchin and give birth to a little baby urchin, this might come in very handy. No-one would pick on them. If you win, this most treasured object from Peach Blossom Island is yours.' And I said to him, 'Nothing can persuade me to marry and I definitely don't want any little urchins. But I'd be delighted to wear your Hedgehog Chainmail over my clothes, so everyone will know that the Lord of Peach Blossom Island lost to the Hoary Urch—' Madam Huang cut me off and said, 'Enough talking! Show us your skills!'

"So, we agreed on the rules. Nine marbles each, eighteen holes; whoever pots all nine marbles first, wins."

Guo Jing smiled. He had played the same game when he was little, against his *anda* Tolui, on the Mongolian steppe.

"I never go anywhere without my lucky marbles. It didn't take us long to find a spot for our contest. It gave me a chance to observe Madam Huang, too. I could tell she had never had a day's martial training, from the way she moved and held herself.

"Anyway, I dug the holes in the ground and let Apothecary Huang choose his marbles. He grabbed them without looking. He must have thought he'd win for sure, with his skill with secret weapons and Divine Flick kung fu. But the holes I dug were a little different. If you don't use a particular blend of force and spin, the marble will pop right out after it's gone in. You have to pull back your strength just before you send the marble flying, to dampen the force of the rebound."

Guo Jing was impressed. These techniques were certainly not familiar to the Mongolian children he knew, and he could hear the pride in Zhou Botong's voice as he relived the game.

"The Heretic flicked three marbles, but they all bounced out again. By the time he understood the trick, I had scored five times. He learned fast, though. He started flicking my marbles into tough spots as he fired his towards the holes. He managed to get three points. But I already had such a lead, how could he catch up? We tussled for a good while, and eventually I scored again. I was so far ahead now, even if the gods descended right at that moment, they couldn't have turned the game around for him. Apothecary Huang had lost! I was jubilant. Then he started to play dirty . . ."

"Did he lock your pressure points?" Guo Jing asked.

"Of course not! He's nasty, but not a brute! He knew he couldn't win, so he started putting greater strength into his flicks. He sent his three remaining marbles into mine. I also had only three left. Somehow, he managed to shatter all of mine into tiny bits and yet not a scratch appeared on his!"

"What? So you didn't have any marbles left!"

"Exactly. I had to watch him slowly flick his marbles into the holes, one by one . . ."

"But that's cheating!"

"I protested too, but the Heretic said, 'My dear Hoary Urchin, we did say whoever bags all nine marbles first wins, didn't we? You can't deny that, can you? Let's not get upset about your smashed marbles right now. After all, I could have taken them by force.'

"He played dirty, but I had no-one but myself to blame, since I agreed to the rules. I had to admit defeat. So, I said to Madam Huang, 'I will lend you the Manual, my lady, but you must return it to me today. Before nightfall.'

"I had learned my lesson. If I didn't specify a time, she could have easily told me, 'We didn't say how long you'd lend it to me.' You know, ten years, a hundred years – it's still a loan!"

"Brother is very clever to have thought of that! I would have fallen for their tricks again."

Zhou Botong shook his head. "There are very few people in the world as smart and quick-witted as the Heretic. I've no idea where he found this wife of his. She was just as clever, if not more so. But I can't understand how such a clever man still fell for the whole stupid trap of marriage!

"Anyway, Madam Huang gave me a smile and said, 'Brother Zhou, you might be known as the Hoary Urchin, but your mind is very sharp! Don't worry, I'll sit right here and give it back to you as soon as I'm done. I promise it will be before sunset. You're welcome to sit with me.'

"So I took the Manual from inside my shirt and handed both volumes to her. She sat down on a rock under a tree and started to thumb through it. Apothecary Huang could tell I was worried. 'Hoary Urchin,' he said, 'how many people under the heavens could hope to defeat us?' 'You?' I replied. 'Perhaps none. But at least four or five can beat me, and you're one of them.'

"He laughed, then said, 'You're too kind. The four of us – the Venom, the King, the Beggar and myself – each have our strengths, but we are more or less evenly matched. You said your martial brother sent Viper Ouyang fleeing back to the west. Iron Palm Water Glider wasn't at the contest, and, however wonderful his kung fu might be, I doubt he's better than us. Hoary Urchin, I dare say you're next in line among the Greats. If we were on the same side, we'd be invincible. So why are you so nervous? Who could steal your precious Manual with us standing guard over it?'

"I nodded and relaxed a little. Madam Huang pored over each page, mouthing the words silently. It was absurd. She was reading the most advanced and intricate martial tract ever written, yet she didn't know any kung fu. She might recognise every character, but she wouldn't be able to make out the meaning of half a sentence.

"She read it slowly, from cover to cover. It took more than two hours. I was getting impatient. You couldn't imagine my excitement when she reached the final page. At last, I thought, she's done. Then she started all over again. But it was much quicker, this time; it only took her the time it takes to drink a pot of tea to finish it.

"She handed the Manual back to me with a smile and said, 'You were tricked by the Venom of the West. This is not the Nine Yin Manual!' I couldn't believe my ears, so I asked her, 'How could that be? It was in my martial brother's possession at all times. The covers look the same!' She replied with absolute certainty, 'Viper Ouyang swapped it for a common book about fortune telling and divination.'"

"Viper Ouyang switched it for another book, just before Immortal Wang burst out from the coffin?" Guo Jing could not believe his ears.

"That was what she was implying, but I knew the Heretic was full of tricks and I reckoned she was the same. She must have noticed my disbelief. 'Have you read the Nine Yin Manual?' she asked, and I could only tell her the truth. 'No-one has set eyes on its contents since my late brother took possession of it. He fought for the right to guard the Manual, to stop it from causing more havoc in the *wulin*. He didn't want it for personal gain. He forbade Quanzhen disciples from learning the kung fu within.'

"Then she said, 'Immortal Wang's selfless benevolence is most admirable, but it is also the reason why you were tricked. Look, Brother Zhou, see for yourself.' She showed me the Manual. I kept my eyes averted. My brother's last words were fresh in my mind.

"Seeing my reaction, she continued, 'This is a popular divination book in the south – it's worth not half a *candareen*. Even if this is the Nine Yin Manual, surely there's no harm in reading the text, as long as you don't put the words into practice? Your martial brother said you couldn't learn, but he didn't say you couldn't look, did he?'

"She was very persuasive. I turned to the first page. There, before my eyes, were descriptions of the most advanced martial skills. It certainly wasn't a book about fortune telling or divination.

"Madam Huang watched me read a few pages before she spoke again. 'I read this book when I was five. I know it inside out. Nine out of ten children in the south know the whole text. I'll recite it for you, if you don't believe me.' She started from the beginning. It flowed from her like water. I checked against the Manual in my hands. Every word she uttered was the same as what was written down. I felt like I'd been plunged into a cave of ice.

"She recounted the first few pages, word for word, then said, 'I can probably remember what it says on any page you choose. Just give me the first line.' So I did as she asked, and, like she said, she knew it inside out. She could recite any page, without a moment's hesitation.

"Old Heretic Huang laughed and laughed. A rage burned in my heart. I ripped the cover off and tore it to shreds. Just as I was about to tear the pages too, I noticed an odd look on the Heretic's face. I realised something wasn't quite right and stopped.

"Then the Heretic spoke: 'There's no need to throw a tantrum, Hoary Urchin. The Hedgehog Chainmail is yours.' I didn't know, then, what an utter fool I'd been. I thought maybe he felt bad that his wife had discovered the Manual had been switched, and he wanted to offer me a consolation. I'd never been so distressed in my life, but I still knew I couldn't take the most treasured object of Peach Blossom Island for nothing.

"So I thanked him and returned to my hometown. I decided to shut my door and focus on my kung fu. I believed Madam Huang. I really thought Viper Ouyang had switched the Manual, but I still didn't believe I could defeat him. Perhaps, if I cut myself off from the world for five years to work on some really powerful kung fu, I could go west in search of him. By then, I'd be able to give the Venom such a beating, he'd never walk again. And he'd have no choice but to give me back the Manual. My brother left it in my care. It was my duty to look after it."

"How could you let the Venom get away with it! You could have taken Elder Ma and Elder Qiu with you. That would have given you the upper hand, surely?" Guo Jing suggested.

Zhou Botong looked at Guo Jing and sighed. "If only I wasn't so intent on winning . . . then I would have realised I'd been fooled a lot sooner. If I had talked to Ma Yu, he would have probably noticed the signs I was oblivious to."

2

"A YEAR OR SO LATER, RUMOURS BEGAN TO FLY AROUND THAT Twice Foul Dark Wind had acquired the Nine Yin Manual," Zhou Botong continued. "People were saying that the disciples of Peach Blossom Island had learned the kung fu contained within its pages and were behaving savagely. I didn't believe it at first, but the story kept circling round and round the *wulin*.

"Another year passed. Qiu Chuji came to my home. He told me he had been investigating the rumours and he had confirmation that the second volume of the Nine Yin Manual was in their hands. I was furious. I muttered out loud to myself, 'Apothecary Huang is a terrible friend!' Qiu Chuji overheard me and asked, 'What do you mean, martial uncle?' So I told him, 'He went to Viper Ouyang for the Manual and he didn't tell me about it! Now he's got the book. Even if he isn't going to return it to me, he should at least have the courtesy to tell me!'"

"Maybe he intended to return it to you, but his unfilial disciples stole it before he had the chance?" Guo Jing said. "He seemed very angry about it. He broke the legs of his four other disciples and banished them. And they didn't have anything to do with the Manual."

Zhou Botong shook his head sadly. "You're a simple, honest

fellow, like me. You wouldn't have realised you'd been tricked, if you were in my place. Qiu Chuji stayed with me for a few days and we worked on some moves together. Two months later, he came back to tell me Hurricane Chen and Cyclone Mei had indeed stolen the Manual and were practising some unspeakable techniques: the Nine Yin Skeleton Claw and Heartbreaker Palm. He took a great risk listening in on them and eventually he heard them say that Apothecary Huang had stolen the Manual from me. He hadn't taken it from Viper Ouyang!"

"Did Madam Huang switch the Manual?"

"As I told you, she wasn't trained in the martial arts. Still, I made sure not to take my eyes off her, even for a second. She didn't switch it – she swallowed it whole. She memorised the whole thing!"

"How is that possible?"

"How many times do you have to read something before you can remember it?"

"If it's a simple text, maybe thirty or forty times. Long and difficult ones, perhaps seventy or eighty, even a hundred. Some texts I just can't learn, however hard I try."

"Exactly, but, well, you aren't particularly smart."

"I know I'm slow – both in kung fu and in reading."

"Forget about reading, for now; let's stick to something we know. So, when your *shifu* teaches you a new martial move, he has to demonstrate it dozens of times before you get it?"

"Yes . . ." Guo Jing answered sheepishly. "Sometimes I get the gist, but can't remember the details. Sometimes the details are there, but I don't know how to put it all together."

"But you do know that there are people who can learn a whole set of kung fu from watching it once?"

"Definitely! Lotus, Lord Huang's daughter, can do that. Count Seven never had to repeat a move more than twice when he taught her."

"If she's that smart, I hope she isn't like her mother." Zhou Botong said with a sigh. "The poor woman contracted the plague of death at such a young age. She read the Manual twice that day and remembered every single word. She wrote it down for her husband the moment I left."

Guo Jing said, after a long pause, "So Madam Huang didn't understand the text, but she was able to memorise it from the first line to the last. It's hard to believe anyone could be so clever."

"You've heard the phrase, 'Through the eyes, into the mind', right? Your girlfriend can probably do it too. I was so frightened and ashamed when I heard Qiu Chuji's report. I immediately summoned all seven martial nephews and we decided we must take the Manual back.

"Qiu Chuji said to me, 'Martial uncle, you don't need to attend to the matter personally. You are their senior, we wouldn't want the masters of the *jianghu* to claim that you pick on the young. However strong Twice Foul Dark Wind may be, I doubt they're on the same level as the disciples of the Quanzhen Sect.'

"So I sent Qiu Chuji and Wang Chuyi to track them down. The rest remained in reserve, keeping their ears to the ground, to make sure Huang's disciples didn't slip through our fingers."

"They wouldn't have been able to beat the Seven Immortals of the Quanzhen Sect." Guo Jing remembered that night on the cliff in Mongolia, when the Six Freaks pretended to be Ma Yu's martial siblings.

"Yet, by the time Chuji and Chuyi arrived in Henan, Twice Foul Dark Wind had left. They had taken too many innocent lives practising their infernal kung fu, and the heroes of the Central Plains had banded together to stop them. Outnumbered, they had to retreat, but no-one knew where to. They killed a few more men of the *wulin* as they made their getaway."

"What did you do after you lost Twice Foul Dark Wind?" Guo Jing asked.

"I went to confront Old Heretic Huang. I didn't wait for Qiu Chuji and his brethren to come back. I went to Peach Blossom Island alone to find answers. The Heretic said to me, in his twisted logic,

'Brother Bottom, Apothecary Huang never broke his word. I said I would not glance at your Manual – and I did not. The Nine Yin Manual I read was set down by my wife. It wasn't yours.'

"I was furious and demanded to see her. He said, with a wry smile, 'My wife is dead.' I didn't expect that and my few words of condolence set him off further. 'Brother Bottom, no more pretence. If you hadn't gone around boasting about your cursed Manual, my wife wouldn't have left me behind.' I asked him, 'What do you mean?' He just glared at me with rage. Then a tear rolled from the corner of his eye and he broke down and wept.

"In the end, he told me everything. Madam Huang knew her husband was interested in the Nine Yin Manual and memorised it for him. But, though the Heretic now had the Manual, his pride kept him from practising any of its kung fu. He said that, as my martial brother had never sought to learn from it, if Apothecary Huang chose to study its contents, then he would be inferior to Double Sun Wang Chongyang. He just wanted to make sense of one strange passage at the very end, which was contained in the volume stolen by Hurricane Chen and Cyclone Mei.

"Madam Huang tried to recreate the text to comfort her husband, but it had been months since she had crammed it into her mind without comprehending a word of it. Needless to say, she'd read many other books and poetry since. How could she still remember it, word for word? She was eight months with child at the time, but she stayed up for several days and nights, racking her brains for any remnants of the Manual. She did manage to set down seven or eight thousand words, but much of the second volume was beyond her, and she could barely remember anything of the gibberish at the end.

"By the end, she was so physically and mentally exhausted, she gave birth prematurely. She was burnt out in every way. There was nothing Apothecary Huang could do to revive her, even with his vast medical knowledge.

"The Heretic has always directed his rage at others, shifting the blame. You can imagine how the grief rocked him. He rambled on and on as tears streamed down his face. With his Zhejiang accent, he kept calling me 'Bottom' instead of 'Botong'. I let it pass. It wasn't the time to debate pronunciation.

"Eventually, I said to him, 'You're a martial man. Does it not bother you that you're a figure of fun in the martial world because you place so much value on your relationship with your wife?' He answered proudly, 'My wife stood head and shoulders above anyone else.' I've always found this 'one man, one woman' thing ridiculous, so I said, 'You can focus on your martial skills, now that she's dead. I'd rejoice, if I were you. I'd have been willing it to happen. You know, it's great – it's brilliant that she's gone. The sooner, the better. Congratulations! Many congratulations!'"

"How could you say that?"

Zhou Botong rolled his eyes. "Why can't I say what I truly believe? Anyway, once I said those words, rage consumed the Heretic and he thrust his palm at me. That was how our fight started."

"Did you lose?"

"Do you think I'd be here if I'd won?" Zhou Botong laughed. "He broke both my legs. It was his way of forcing me to give him my copy of the second volume of the Manual. He said he wanted to burn it as an offering for his wife. So I hid the Manual in this cave and placed myself at the entrance. I told him, if you try to take it by force, I'll destroy it. And he said, 'I'll find a way to make you step aside.' And I told him, 'We'll see about that.'

"That was five and ten years ago. I told you he's conceited. He won't sink so low as to starve me or poison me. He's tried a thousand ways to lure me away. Oh, but he refuses to take advantage when I leave the cave to answer the call of nature. Sometimes, I take two hours. I know how tempting it is for him, but he's managed to resist, so far."

Zhou Botong chuckled and Guo Jing also laughed, yet was secretly astonished that a martial master could bring a quarrel down to such a base level.

3

"FOR FIFTEEN YEARS, THE HERETIC TRIED EVERYTHING, AND failed." It had taken Zhou Botong a long time to stop laughing and regain his composure. "But, if it weren't for you, the Manual would be in his hands right now. He has played the 'Ode to the Billowing Tide' many times, but it's never bothered me that much. Who'd have thought he'd put in all those new flourishes? Last night, he almost caught me off guard. My dear brother, thank you."

"What are you going to do now?" Guo Jing was still flummoxed by how a book could cause so much havoc and ruin so many lives.

"We'll see who lives longer." Zhou Botong dissolved into laughter again. "Remember Huang Shang? He won by outliving all his enemies."

Guo Jing was not convinced that hoping to outlive Apothecary Huang was the best way out. Then he remembered he too was stuck on this island, in this cave, with no word from Lotus. "Why didn't Elder Ma and the others try to rescue you?"

"They probably don't know I'm here. Even if they do, every tree, rock and hill here is enchanted; they won't be able to get anywhere unless the Heretic lets them in. And, besides, I won't leave until this fight has a winner."

Guo Jing had greatly enjoyed the company of his new sworn brother. Despite his age, he had an endearing childlike frankness. Now, Guo Jing's mind wandered back to Lotus. He wished he knew where to find her.

The sun was blazing in the sky. The mute servant returned with their midday meal.

When they had finished the food, Zhou Botong said, "I may have been stuck here for fifteen years and counting, but my time has not been wasted. I know my kung fu has improved a great deal. There are no distractions in this cave. It would have taken me at least twenty-five years to get the same results elsewhere. My biggest problem is not having a sparring partner. I have to get my hands to fight each other."

"How does that work?"

"Let's say my right hand is the Heretic and my left is the Hoary Urchin," Zhou Botong said, raising his hands to demonstrate. "Now, the right throws a palm strike, like this. My left deflects it and returns the favour with a punch. And now I'm fighting." The blows grew faster and more intense, the left hand attacking, while the right defended.

Guo Jing watched with a smile: yet another of Zhou Botong's eccentricities. But, before long, he was transfixed. He was witnessing a unique and complex brand of kung fu.

As every student of the martial arts knew, when throwing a punch, striking with the palm, wielding a sword or thrusting a spear, the different motions of the hands worked together towards the same goal: to attack or to defend. Yet Zhou Botong's hands were attacking each other's vital points – the wrist, the back of the hand, the palm – and responding to the other's offensive with countermoves. Each hand employed a completely different kung fu!

"You didn't make the full move with your right hand just now. Why?" Guo Jing asked suddenly.

Zhou Botong stopped and appraised his sworn brother with a satisfied smile. "Your eyes are sharp. You're right. Come, spar with me. I'll show you."

Guo Jing put his hand against his brother's outstretched palm.

"Careful, now. I'll push you to the left."

Energy flowed from Zhou Botong's hand. Guo Jing answered with a move from the Dragon-Subduing Palm. The two internal forces clashed, propelling Guo Jing half a dozen steps back. His arm felt weak and numb.

"I just unleashed my full force on you. Now I'm going to let loose only a portion of it."

Their palms clashed once more. The moment Guo Jing sensed

Zhou Botong's strength, it vanished. The energy kept appearing and disappearing, rocking his balance.

Thud! Guo Jing hit the ground, his face in the dust. He climbed back to his feet quickly, but the fall seemed to have plunged him into a daze.

"Do you see?" Zhou Botong asked.

Guo Jing shook his head.

"Well, it took me ten years stuck in this cave to work it out. My martial brother always told me how 'the immaterial beats the material and absence trumps excess'. I thought he was droning on about Taoist philosophy and shut my ears.

"But, five years ago, I had a moment of clarity as my hands were fighting each other. I can't really explain it, but I feel it and understand it now. Yet, without a sparring partner, I still couldn't quite believe it. Now you're here, it's just perfect. It'll hurt a bit, but you'll know what I mean once I've sent you flying a few more times."

Guo Jing looked reluctant and Zhou Botong changed tack. "My good brother, I've been here for fifteen years. All I've ever wanted is someone to exchange a few moves with. When the Heretic's daughter was here, a few months ago, I was going to get her to spar with me, but her palm kung fu wasn't strong enough. And she never came back. I promise I won't make you fall too hard, my dear brother." His hands were poised to strike before he had even finished speaking.

Seeing how eager Zhou Botong was, Guo Jing relented. "I can handle a few falls."

After exchanging several moves, all the tension suddenly disappeared from Zhou Botong's palm. Guo Jing could not retrieve his strength fast enough and tipped forward again.

He swung his left arm out, hoping to change the momentum of the fall and find his equilibrium again. But nothing he could do was powerful enough to overcome the force that was flipping his body around in a somersault. He crashed down on his left shoulder.

"My good brother, I won't let you fall for nothing. Let me explain how I did it." Zhou Botong looked somewhat apologetic.

Guo Jing crawled to his feet and limped over.

"Do you know these lines from Laozi's *Classic of the Way and Virtue*? 'When clay is moulded, from its hollowness a vessel finds its use. When openings are made in a wall, from its hollowness a room finds its space.'"

Guo Jing blinked and shook his head, thoroughly confused.

Zhou Botong picked up a bowl. "If this was a solid piece of clay, could it hold any rice?"

Guo Jing shook his head again, amazed how he had never noticed such a simple and obvious truth.

"Think how you'd build a house. If there's no door or window, if wood and bricks are just piled up in a great big heap, is it a room? Has it got any use?"

Guo Jing shook his head once more, with a further spark of comprehension.

"Hollowness and suppleness are two fundamental concepts of the Quanzhen Sect's most advanced kung fu. 'When wholeness appears incomplete, fail it shall not; when abundance appears short, deplete it shall not.'"

Zhou Botong explained how these lines from *Classic of the Way and Virtue* related to the martial arts. Guo Jing listened with his whole being, trying to grasp their significance.

"Your *shifu* Count Seven Hong's kung fu represents the very best of external martial arts. Even though I know some internal skills from the Quanzhen Sect, I don't think I can beat him. But he's probably reached its apex. There isn't anywhere further to go with this type of martial knowledge.

"However, with Quanzhen *neigong*, there's no end to the learning. I've only just peeked through the doorway. My martial brother didn't win the title of the Greatest Martial Master Under the Heavens through sheer luck. If he was still alive today, he could beat the Heretic, the Venom and the others in half a day. He wouldn't have to fight them again for seven days and seven nights."

"I wish I could've seen Immortal Wang's martial magic. I know the Dragon-Subduing Palm is the most firm kind of strength. Does it mean my brother's kung fu is the most supple?"

"Yes, you've got it! The supple can overcome the firm. However, I wouldn't be able to send you flying if you were as good as Count Seven. Watch carefully, now."

Zhou Botong described the move he had just performed and explained how he controlled his energy, going into great detail, since he knew Guo Jing would be slow on the uptake.

With his solid grounding in Quanzhen *neigong*, Guo Jing began to get to grips with the basics after repeating it several dozen times.

"Are you still in pain? If not, can I throw you again?" Zhou Botong burned with anticipation.

"My body's fine, but I haven't perfected the move yet." Guo Jing played the motion over and over in his head, trying to carve it into his memory.

A moment passed. Zhou Botong's patience was stretched to breaking point.

"What about now? Have you learned it yet? Come on! Are you ready now?"

His interruption meant that it took even longer for Guo Jing to memorise the technique. But, after the time it takes to finish a meal, Guo Jing was finally ready to face Zhou Botong again.

At last, he understood how Apothecary Huang had dislocated his wrist by simply pulling in his stomach. It was the same kind of hollow strength that sent him flying this very moment.

4

ZHOU BOTONG WOULD HAVE HAPPILY FORGONE SLEEP TO SPAR all day and all night, but Guo Jing needed a few hours' rest to function properly. But, over the next few days, they practised every waking hour.

By now, poor Guo Jing had been sent sprawling at least seven or eight hundred times. Battered and bruised from head to toe, he finally grasped the underlying concept of Zhou Botong's technique.

Guo Jing withstood the falls with the same steely determination that had helped him acquire his kung fu. Enduring the pain through gritted teeth, he had now learned the whole Luminous Hollow Fist repertoire: seventy-two moves that Zhou Botong invented in the cave.

In no time at all, Guo Jing was able to manipulate his strength in the same hollow and supple way. Zhou Botong could no longer rock the young man's footing and send him flying.

A couple of days later, everything came together for Guo Jing. "When Master Hong taught me the Dragon-Subduing Palm, he kept stressing that I should reserve more energy than I propel. So it wasn't just about being fierce and firm."

"Indeed! That combination of suppleness and strength is what makes Count Seven Hong's kung fu so potent. I probably couldn't beat him, even when using Luminous Hollow Fist."

Time was passing much faster now. The days flew by. Guo Jing was growing ever more anxious about Lotus, but he had no way to find her or contact her. He came close to asking the mute servant who brought their meals on several occasions, yet, each time, Zhou Botong pulled him back.

One day, after lunch, Zhou Botong said, "You have now mastered the Luminous Hollow Fist. I can't throw you off your feet anymore. Let's play a new game."

"Of course! What have you got in mind?"

"A four-way fight!"

"Four-way?"

"That's right. Four. My left hand is one person; my right is another. You've got two hands, too. So, four altogether. No hand is allowed to help another hand. A four-hand melee. It'll be so fun!"

"It sounds great, but I can't fight separately with my hands."

"I'll teach you later. Let's try a three-way brawl first!" Zhou Botong launched two different kung fu moves, one with each hand.

Guo Jing was amazed. How did he retain the full power of the moves when he only performed them with one side of his body?

Soon, he was hard pressed by two strong opponents. Then, one of Zhou Botong's hands switched sides and came to his rescue. Now fighting two against one, Guo Jing found himself in the dominant position. But that did not last long; the helping hand withdrew and Zhou Botong's two hands attacked as a united front once again. Alliances were made and remade, always shifting. No single party could gain the upper hand.

Fighting was a tiring business. They paused to catch their breath and Guo Jing's mind turned to Lotus once more.

She'd love this! We could wage a six-handed battle.

The moment Guo Jing's pulse slowed to the resting rate, Zhou Botong began regaling him with ways of mastering this technique, which he named Competing Hands.

Wise men had said, "To do two things at once is to do neither," and they had also warned, "If the hands in unison draw a square and a circle each, neither would look angular or round."

Yet, the key to this very kung fu was to do two things at once and to do them well. So the first task Guo Jing was given was to draw, simultaneously, a square with one hand and a circle with the other.

At first, Guo Jing could only draw two circles or two squares, or shapes that were neither angular nor curved. Eventually, he realised the action was not unlike eating: bowl in the left hand, chopsticks in the right. The hands moved in different ways and performed separate tasks, yet, together, they put food in the mouth. Holding that idea in his head, he was able to draw the shapes as required.

Pleased that Guo Jing had grasped the underlying theory of the technique so quickly, Zhou Botong said, "You know, it'd take a lot longer if you didn't know the Quanzhen Sect's internal kung fu. Without your *neigong* training, you wouldn't be able to split your focus like that. Now, launch some moves from the Southern Mountain Fists with your left hand and the Yue Maiden Sword with your right."

These martial skills Guo Jing had learned from Woodcutter Nan and Jade Han were so ingrained that he could perform either kung fu, on its own, without thinking. Yet he now struggled to control his arms to create any semblance of the moves he had known so well since childhood.

Desperate to pass on his technique, Zhou Botong bombarded the young man with every trick and tip he could think of.

After several days of intensive training, Guo Jing could just about use different moves with each hand.

"Come! Your right hand and my left hand will be a team, and these two –" Zhou Botong grabbed Guo Jing's left hand with his right – "are their enemies."

Then he roared, "Let the battle commence!"

How could a young man not like a game like this? Following Zhou Botong's instructions, he plunged in, willing his right hand to fight his left. Guo Jing had never seen, nor heard, nor imagined such a wild combat. He could scarcely believe that it was happening and he was part of it.

Zhou Botong shouted prompts to sharpen the attack and tighten the defence. For the Hoary Urchin, this was a game, a little fun to alleviate his solitude. He had no idea he was teaching Guo Jing a peculiar and powerful kung fu that had no precedent.

One day, an idea came to Guo Jing. We can train our legs the same way and have an eight-way battle! Yet, he did not share the thought with his wayward brother. He dreaded to think of the consequences of making such a suggestion.

Days flew by quickly, thanks to this new diversion. One morning, they battled as four individuals. No alliances, no fixed opponents. Zhou Botong was in a more buoyant mood than usual, chuckling as he fired off his attacks.

Before long, Guo Jing found himself unable to stand his ground. His right hand buckled under the onslaught. Naturally, his left hand came to its aid.

But Zhou Botong kept the torrent of moves raining hard. Guo

Jing could no longer split his moves between his hands, so the Hoary Urchin folded one arm behind his back to keep the fight fair.

With two hands working in unison, Guo Jing managed to push back Zhou Botong's single-handed offensive.

Zhou Botong laughed in triumph. "You lose! Your hands are using the same kung fu!"

Guo Jing hopped back. A sudden thought had struck him. Eventually, he spoke. "You fight with two separate forms of kung fu, one from each hand. That's like two persons firing off moves individually, is it not? If you were to use Competing Hands in an actual battle, your opponent would have to fend off two attackers – your two hands – at the same time. Doesn't that make it a very useful skill in combat? You can't double your strength, but you've got a great advantage, all the same!"

For Zhou Botong, Competing Hands was simply a game with which to amuse himself, a way to stop himself wilting from boredom as he whiled away the hours he spent stuck in his tiny cave. He had never considered its martial implications.

He digested Guo Jing's words for a moment and then sprinted out of the cave. He paced and paced, shrieking with laughter.

"Brother?" Guo Jing was worried. "Brother?"

Ignoring Guo Jing, he kept laughing.

Suddenly, he stopped. "I'm leaving, brother. Not to answer the call of nature. I'm leaving! I've become the Greatest Martial Master Under the Heavens. Apothecary Huang doesn't scare me anymore. Why can't he come here now? I'll send him flying, like petals on the wind!"

"Are you certain you can beat him?"

"My kung fu may still be a little inferior, but I can split myself in two. I'll be fighting two against one. No-one under the heavens can beat me again! It matters not how fancy Apothecary Huang, Count Seven Hong or Viper Ouyang's kung fu skills are. Can they beat two of Zhou Botong the Hoary Urchin?"

Pleased for his sworn brother, Guo Jing agreed that two Zhou Botongs would be rather a handful.

"Little brother, you have a good understanding of the principle behind Competing Hands. You know how to split your attack simultaneously. Keep up your practice. Give the technique time to mature inside you. In a few years, your kung fu will double too. It's a shame it can't increase internal strength by even a *candareen*. We'll have to split our energy between our hands, but no-one needs to know. We'll hit them quick and hit them hard, with different moves from each hand. We'll make their heads spin so fast that they can't spot the flaw."

5

FOR FIFTEEN YEARS, ZHOU BOTONG HAD DREADED THE DAY he would have to fight Apothecary Huang again; now, he wished his adversary would appear that instant. He would have sought the Heretic out, if he knew his way around the island's labyrinthine layout.

Full of impatience, the Hoary Urchin scanned the horizon all day, yet the first person he spotted was the servant approaching with their dinner.

He grabbed the man by the shoulders, shouting, "Bring Apothecary Huang here now! I want to show him my kung fu!"

Petrified, the servant said nothing, just kept shaking his head.

"Fie! I forget you can't hear me!" He let the man go and turned his attention to the food. "Let's have a feast tonight!"

The moment Zhou Botong lifted the lid, Guo Jing noticed the aromas were more fragrant than usual. There was a large bowl of his favourite dish, braised chicken with mushrooms. He picked up a spoon and tasted the broth. The delicate hint of salt teased out the sweetness of the chicken. His heart pounded in recognition. Lotus had made this for him.

The servant laid out the dishes. Nothing looked out of the ordinary to Guo Jing, until he clapped eyes on the dozen *mantou* steamed buns still inside the food carrier. On one of them, a very faint outline of a gourd was scratched onto the surface. He grabbed it and found a wax capsule hidden inside. He dropped it into his shirt pocket before Zhou Botong or the servant noticed anything was amiss.

They ate heartily because of their exertions during the day, but food was the last thing on their minds. Guo Jing gobbled down his dinner as quickly as possible, so he could read Lotus's message the moment the servant cleared up and left.

Zhou Botong was still coming to terms with the fact that he had accidentally invented an invincible form of kung fu. Absent-mindedly, he grabbed a *mantou* with his right hand while trying out a few boxing moves with his left. He too wanted to finish the meal quickly, so he could return to his training. He started spooning broth and shoving bun into his mouth, and then stopped and laughed when he realised what he was doing.

"One mouth can't eat from two hands at once!"

From Guo Jing's perspective, Zhou Botong was taking an exceptionally long time with his meal. But, at long last, his sworn brother was finished with the buns and had gulped down all his soup. The servant packed up the plates and took his leave. Guo Jing took the note out and broke the wax casing.

My dear Guo Jing – he was overcome with joy at seeing Lotus's elegant handwriting – *Papa and I have made up. I'll beg him to free you. Don't worry. I can't come to visit you yet, but I think about you every day. Lotus.*

"I'll make sure the Heretic lets you go," Zhou Botong said, after reading the message. "He'll have no choice. And we won't beg him. We'll make him. If he refuses, we'll shut him in this cave for five, no, ten years . . . Actually, no, we won't lock him up. We don't want him to come up with some fantastic martial technique like Competing Hands!" Then he wandered off to practise.

Guo Jing sat cross-legged, with his eyes closed, in the fading light, to work on his internal energy. However, Lotus kept stealing into his mind, disturbing the silence and his peace within. It took him much longer than usual to purge all thoughts and worries. Eventually, he was able to channel his *qi* around his body. Then an idea popped into his head: my internal strength needs to work separately, as two distinct forces, or else the different moves from each hand will contain no substance.

He pressed a finger to one side of his nose and tried breathing with one nostril at a time. He persisted for the duration of one watch. Satisfied with the small improvement he had made, he gradually brought himself back to the present. A gale seemed to be blowing outside. He opened his eyes and saw hair and beard dancing in the night air.

Zhou Botong was practising the seventy-two moves of the Luminous Hollow Fist with his left hand and a Quanzhen Sect palm kung fu with his right hand. Though each move was slow, they parted the air with a whistle, a testament to great strength contained within.

Guo Jing watched in awe. He could sense the instantaneous flow of internal energy through Zhou Botong, switching from his left arm to the right and back again. The actions made by either hand contained his full strength.

Watching the Hoary Urchin practise, he realised his earlier notion of splitting his inner strength into left and right might not work, as the body only contained one set of meridians. But he could try mastering Zhou Botong's energy-transfer technique, between the two sides of the body. If he could propel his strength quickly, at will, from left to right and back again, which should not be too difficult, he could achieve an effect not dissimilar to adjusting the disposition of troops in the heat of battle.

"Argh!"

A cry ripped through Guo Jing's concentration. Then he heard a loud smack and caught sight of a long and floppy thing slapping against a tree trunk. When he looked back at Zhou Botong, he was swaying.

"Brother, are you alright?" Guo Jing rushed over to steady the older man.

"I got bitten by a snake. In the foot. Rot!"

Zhou Botong leaned his weight on Guo Jing's shoulders and hobbled back into the cave. He tore a strip from his shirt and bandaged it tightly around his thigh to slow the venom as it passed up through his veins.

Guo Jing pulled out the flint and tinder from inside his shirt and struck them together for light. His heart skipped a beat. The ruddy, youthful radiance had disappeared from Zhou Botong's face. The bite had already caused his calf to swell to twice its usual size.

"I've never seen any rotten snakes on this island. Where did this viper come from? The little pest wouldn't have caught me out if I hadn't been splitting my concentration to work on two . . ."

The Hoary Urchin's booming voice was beginning to tremble. Guo Jing surmised his sworn brother was still conscious only because his advanced internal kung fu had slowed the poison's progress. He needed to stop it from spreading. He could only think of one way.

He bent over and sucked on the wound.

"No! Don't . . . You'll die." Zhou Botong wanted to struggle, but he could barely feel his body and soon blacked out.

The only thing on Guo Jing's mind right now was saving his sworn brother. After nearly half an hour, he had managed to draw out the majority of the venom and spit it out onto the ground.

An hour later, Zhou Botong came to and croaked out what he thought were his last words: "I won't live to see tomorrow. I'm very happy to have a caring little brother like you."

Tears rolled down Guo Jing's cheeks. He had only known this brother for a matter of days, but he felt they had been best friends for decades. He could not believe the Hoary Urchin was about to die.

"The Nine Yin Manual is buried in a stone casket, just here, where I'm lying. It should be yours, but you won't live through the night after sucking out my poison. Well, we'll travel down to the underworld together. At least we'll never be bored. We can still do our four-man fights. No, four-ghost fights!" He cackled, his grief turning to demented elation. "I bet you the ghosts down there have never seen anything like it!"

Guo Jing was bemused by the talk of his death. He felt absolutely fine. He lit another match. A blackness shrouded Zhou Botong's face, extinguishing the childlike glow.

Noticing the light, Zhou Botong smiled at Guo Jing, then sucked in a mouthful of air in surprise. "How come you aren't affected by the poison at all? What magical panacea have you taken?"

That reminded Guo Jing of Greybeard Liang. "Perhaps it's the python blood I once drank? Maybe it's given me a resistance to snake venom?"

Zhou Botong gave it some thought, but before long he passed out again. Guo Jing massaged and pressed his acupressure points, but he could not elicit any response from his sworn brother. He felt around the wound. It burned like fire and the leg had swollen up even more.

Then Guo Jing heard his brother murmur:

"For the fourth time the loom is ready,
  To weave a pair of lovebirds so they can take flight . . ."

"Brother, what did you say?"

"Pity the hair that grows grey before its time, pity . . ."

The poison had made the Hoary Urchin delirious.

Guo Jing sprinted out of the cave, scaled the tallest tree and shouted into the night, "Lotus! Lotus! Lord Huang! Lord Huang! Help, please! Help!"

But his voice reached no-one. Peach Blossom Island covered several dozen *li*, and Apothecary Huang's quarters were a long way away.

Hearing no response, Guo Jing rushed back to the cave with a desperate idea.

I'm not affected. Maybe my blood can repel the poison.

He groped around in the dark and found Zhou Botong's celadon drinking bowl on the ground. With the golden dagger given to him by Genghis Khan, he cut his left arm and held it over the bowl. The wound soon congealed and he made another cut.

Once the bowl was filled, Guo Jing shifted Zhou Botong, resting his sworn brother's head on his knees. He wrenched open his jaw and poured the blood into his mouth.

Weakened by the loss of so much blood, Guo Jing slumped against the wall of the cave and soon dozed off. He was woken by a slight pain on his arm, with no idea of how long he had been asleep.

Someone was dressing the wound.

He opened his eyes to a mass of dark hair.

"You – you're alive!" Guo Jing blinked.

"Yes! I'm fine now! You gave your life to save mine. The Ghosts of Impermanence were most annoyed. I reckon they won't be back for my soul for a good while," Zhou Botong said, as he showed off his swollen leg, no longer blackened by the poison.

6

THIS BROTHER OF MINE IS A SELFLESS SOUL. HE SUCKED THE poison from my wound knowing that it could kill him. For some reason, he didn't die and neither did I! How do I repay this gift of life? I haven't got any more kung fu to teach him.

This conundrum troubled Zhou Botong all day, until he went to bed.

When Double Sun Wang Chongyang took the Nine Yin Manual, it was not to benefit himself, but to curb its destructive influence on the *wulin*. As such, he declared that no disciple of the Quanzhen Sect should ever practise the kung fu within. Of course, Zhou Botong lived firmly by his martial brother's instruction, but he also could not forget Madam Huang's words: "Your martial brother said you couldn't learn, but he didn't say you couldn't look, did he?"

Over the fifteen years of captivity inside the cave on Peach Blossom Island, Zhou Botong had no other books with him and nothing to do. Flicking through the Manual was one way to pass the time, so, having read it countless times, he now knew it back to front.

The first volume detailed key Taoist theories about cultivating internal strength, as well as principles of fist and sword kung fu. The second volume contained all kinds of strange and wonderful martial skills. Everything from methods of training for them to the ways to defeat them. He knew that Madam Huang had been lying to him when she called it a book of divination and fortune telling.

Obsessed with the martial arts as he was, Zhou Botong was desperate to learn the kung fu within. He had no ambition to be hailed as the greatest martial artist in the world or to use the skills to avenge the wrongs he had suffered. He was purely driven by a curiosity and a passion for all things martial. He wanted to feel with his body how powerful the kung fu in the Manual was.

He knew the moves within must be magical. After all, Huang Shang read the whole of *The Taoist Canon of Ten Thousand Longevities* – a total of five thousand, four hundred and eighty-one volumes – and spent forty years thinking through ways to overpower all the kung fu he had encountered. He had also heard how Twice Foul Dark Wind terrorised the *jianghu* with just two sets of martial arts from the second volume. Imagine if he were to learn everything recorded within its pages!

Though he had read and thought about the Manual every day over the past decade and a half, he had never tried ro replicate the moves described, out of respect for his martial brother.

And yet, he longed to see the Manual in action.

The next morning, a brainwave came to Zhou Botong as he awoke: Guo Jing isn't officially a disciple of the Quanzhen Sect – I can teach him the Nine Yin Manual! Once he's learned everything, he can show them to me, one by one. He will have acquired the most powerful kung fu known to the martial world, and I will at last satisfy my curiosity without disobeying my martial brother's last wish!

Congratulating himself, he chuckled out loud. "Yes! This is the perfect plan!"

"What plan?"

Zhou Botong grinned, ready to reveal his grand idea. Then he remembered how Guo Jing had denounced the Manual as evil, because of Twice Foul Dark Wind.

I can teach him without telling him! Another moment of inspiration struck the Hoary Urchin. He hates the Manual because he's only seen the lowly moves Twice Foul Dark Wind learned from the second volume. He doesn't know that the cultivation of *qi* is described in the first volume. He doesn't know the Manual is about proper, honourable martial practice. I'll only tell him once he's learned it all. Then, he can throw as many tantrums as he wants, but he can't make his body forget the moves he's acquired!

Zhou Botong cared little if people loved him or hated him, insulted him or praised him. Nothing made him as happy as a good prank – and learning kung fu. He put on a serious face and set his scheme into motion.

"Brother, I've invented many other kung fu techniques during these years stuck in this cave. What do you say, shall I share a little more? We haven't got much else to do, anyway."

"It's so kind of you to offer, but Lotus said she's thinking of a way to free us."

"Well, has she freed us yet?"

"Er . . . no."

"Can't you learn a few more moves while you wait?"

"Of course!"

Don't be so eager! You've fallen straight into my trap! Zhou Botong was crying with laughter inside. He reassured himself repeatedly: his victim would benefit enormously and no-one would be hurt in the process.

Putting on his most solemn face, the Hoary Urchin began with the first volume of the Nine Yin Manual, selecting a few Taoist theories to share with Guo Jing. Naturally, the young man struggled to comprehend them, but Zhou Botong found within him a well of patience he did not realise he possessed, and he explained everything in slow and painful detail.

Once the basics were covered, Zhou Botong moved on to the second volume, which detailed training methods and countermeasures for a variety of kung fu. Before each lesson, he would step aside to look over the Manual to refresh his memory, but he made sure he kept well out of sight, in case Guo Jing grew suspicious.

Martial arts had never been taught in such a way before – or since. The instructor himself did not know the moves. He would only illustrate them verbally, and never once lifted a hand to demonstrate.

Once Guo Jing had grasped a few moves from the Manual, Zhou Botong would spar with him using Quanzhen kung fu. It was giddying to experience its power. The Hoary Urchin noted that the techniques recorded in the Manual were often superior to his own Quanzhen skills.

Even after Guo Jing had been learning the kung fu from the Nine Yin Manual for several days, he never once suspected the source of the martial knowledge. Delighted with how everything was going, Zhou Botong had taken to chuckling in his sleep.

At meal times, there was always one of Guo Jing's favourite dishes, lovingly prepared by Lotus. Though she had yet to visit him, the gesture was reassuring. He could devote himself wholeheartedly to learning kung fu.

Things got interesting when Zhou Botong had Guo Jing try out the All-Shattering Grip. The young man was told to focus his spirit, channel his *qi*, then tear at the rock face with his fingers.

After several attempts, Guo Jing turned to Zhou Botong. "Brother, is this from the Nine Yin Manual? I've seen Cyclone Mei doing something similar. She did it on a living person, plunging her fingers into the skull – it was savage!"

"How can you compare Cyclone Mei's infernal move with my orthodox invention? There are often similar forms in kung fu, but their roots differ. That's what truly matters!"

Zhou Botong made a mental note to stay away from this move. At the same time, he pitied Cyclone Mei for her misunderstanding and ignorance of the Manual's gifts.

What a silly woman! he thought. Yes, the text does say, *Strength courses through the fingers, no matter can stand in their way. Shattering the skull of the enemy, as if clawing through rotten earth.* It's a metaphor rather than a literal instruction! You're not meant to plunge your fingers through your enemy's skull!

The first volume of the Nine Yin Manual clearly explained that it was founded on the Taoist concepts of harmony, selflessness and union with nature, and that the kung fu within was supposed to expel evil and nourish life.

Some brutal moves were recorded within its pages because, in order to learn the countermeasures, it was important to first gain a thorough knowledge of their dark intricacies. Of course, as Cyclone Mei had never seen the first volume, she did not realise she had spent her life learning something twisted and mistaken.

"Let's try some internal kung fu exercises." Zhou Botong knew this would take Guo Jing's mind off Cyclone Mei, for now. He quoted the opening lines of the Manual and got the young man to repeat after him until he had learned them by heart. Once Guo Jing had a firm grasp on the first volume, it would give him a foundation that would make the kung fu from the second volume a natural progression. He would not associate anything with Cyclone Mei again.

Guo Jing had little understanding of the meaning of the passage he had just committed to memory. Each sentence was so complex and each character imbued with so much resonance. In his incomprehension, he told Zhou Botong how Count Seven Hong had instructed him to learn the theories behind the Dragon-Subduing Palm by heart and not worry about their meanings or applications yet – as they were also too complicated for his understanding.

This method was perfect for Zhou Botong's purposes. So, over the next few days, he read the Manual to Guo Jing, line by line. The young man parroted the words over and over again, several dozen times, until they were engraved on his mind. Soon, Guo Jing could recite a good portion of the martial tract, though he could fathom only a fraction of it.

They reached the final part of the Manual, a section of incomprehensible incantation-like sounds, over a thousand characters long. Zhou Botong had read it hundreds of times, but could not make head nor tail of it. Still, he was going to make Guo Jing learn the gibberish by heart. Perhaps, by then, he would have worked out how to explain the passage to the young man.

Zhou Botong patiently fed his little brother the text in bite-sized chunks. If he pushed a few extra characters, the young man would forget what he had already learned. Guo Jing swallowed it whole, without comment, but even his docile mind began to wonder at its meaning.

"The intent of the heavens shall not yet be revealed," Zhou Botong replied cryptically. "You just need to learn it."

Memorising this cluster of meaningless characters was a hundred times harder than getting to grips with any of the moves or martial theories. But Guo Jing always met challenges head on. Everything he had learned, he had learned through hard graft, without questioning its meaning or purpose. It was the only way he knew. Though there was no semantic anchor to latch on to, he read the passage out loud – *mahaparas gatekras hahoramanpayas* – a thousand times, until the sounds became an inseparable part of him.

Once Guo Jing had learned the whole Manual by heart, Zhou Botong guided him through the cultivation of internal strength, according to the methods described in the first volume. As the Hoary Urchin predicted, nothing reminded Guo Jing of Cyclone Mei's Nine Yin Manual again.

To Guo Jing, this new training was in the same vein as what he had been taught by Ma Yu, only more complex and harder to grasp. Somehow, it made sense to him. After all, Zhou Botong was Ma Yu's martial uncle, so naturally his martial knowledge would be more advanced. Also, in the back of his mind, he remembered Cyclone Mei's questions about Taoist *neigong* secrets as she rode on his shoulders while they fought together at the Prince of Zhao's residence. Because of her ignorance of all matters Taoist, there was nothing to link what Zhou Botong was making him recite with the Nine Yin Manual as he had seen it in action.

Guo Jing did notice a twinkle in his sworn brother's eye during the lessons, but he dismissed it as the Hoary Urchin being his mischievous self. Little did he know he was the victim of an elaborate prank.

When Guo Jing had finished his morning's training, he opened the tiffin and found a *mantou* bun lightly marked with a gourd. He grabbed it and headed into the woods.

Guo Jing, the Venom of the West has asked Papa for my hand, on behalf of his nephew. Papa gave his con— The note broke off. It had been scrunched up hastily into the wax pellet.

It was clear to Guo Jing that the incomplete word was "consent". He showed the message to Zhou Botong, once the servant was gone, but his brother was not remotely interested.

"It's no business of ours if the Heretic decides to marry her off, or to whom."

"But she only wants to be with me! She must be devastated."

"Once you are in thrall to a woman, you are barred from a whole world of wonderful martial discoveries." For once, Zhou Botong hesitated over his next words. "I . . . I've always regretted it. My good brother, trust me, it's far better to stay away."

Guo Jing was exasperated. His sworn brother would not offer any help. He just kept droning on. "If I still had my virginity, I'd have learned some really amazing kung fu from my martial brother. The Heretic wouldn't have been able to hold me on this rotten island.

"Look at yourself now, the thought of that girl has driven you to distraction. You won't achieve anything with your practice today. If you really end up marrying the Heretic's daughter . . ." He sighed dramatically.

"Pity. What a pity! Back then, I just . . . There's no point talking about it. Just believe me, if a woman gets her claws into you, you won't get far with your kung fu. And, if that's not bad enough, you'll also end up double-crossing your friends . . .

"And offending my brother. They wouldn't kill me. They wanted to give her to me. Of course, I couldn't take her. But, having refused her, I couldn't get her out of my mind . . . I wonder how she's . . .

"Trust me. Don't look at a woman's face. And don't ever touch a woman's body. Never teach them about acupressure points. Never let them touch yours. It's a trap . . .

"Never ever take a wife. Never, never, never . . ."

Guo Jing was fed up with Zhou Botong's rambling. "Whether or not we get married, that's another matter. But you have to help me rescue her first!"

"The Venom of the West is a nasty piece of work. I suspect his nephew is cut from the same cloth. The Heretic's daughter is pretty, but I bet she's like her old man. The Venom's nephew is going to have a tough time if he marries her. And he'll never be able to practise any kung fu that requires a pure body. It'll kill two birds with one stone. He'll end up with the worst of both worlds!" Zhou Botong said with relish.

Groaning with frustration, Guo Jing stalked into the woods.

I will find her, he promised himself. I don't care if I die along the way, I will find her.

A screech echoed in the trees. Two white dots swooped from the sky. The condors! Guo Jing waved at them.

When they landed, he noticed a bamboo tube was tied to one of the condors' talons.

Untying it quickly, he opened the container to find another note from Lotus, written in haste.

The Venom of the West would soon arrive with his nephew, and her papa was keeping a close eye on her, forbidding her to cook for Guo Jing or to leave her quarters. If she could not find a way out of this predicament, she would take her life to stay true to her love.

Please do not come looking for me, she entreated in the end, *there are many dangers and traps scattered all over Peach Blossom Island.*

Guo Jing stared at the note, then, using his golden dagger, he carved *live together, die together* onto the bamboo tube. Once he had secured his message to the condor again, the magnificent creatures unfurled their wings and took flight, circling over him several times before flying north.

He sat down to practise his internal energy. Now that he had written back to Lotus with his decision to live and die by their love, the anxiety and frustration he had felt earlier eased. After a while, he sought out Zhou Botong for his daily lesson. He spent the next few days consolidating the words he had memorised, and listening to Zhou Botong's explanations. His brother kept insisting it was not time to put the words into practice yet – lest he arouse Guo Jing's suspicion.

The young man docilely accepted the instructions. For anyone else studying the martial arts, it would have been next to impossible to learn the method of training without applying it in practice, but Guo Jing had always been an honest soul. Even when he was learning from the Six Freaks of the South, he had followed what he was told to the letter, without ever questioning his teachers' decisions. He was now showing the same obedience to Zhou Botong, reciting the text he was taught, over and over again, hundreds of times, including that passage of nonsense, with its *mahaparas*, *gatekras* and *hahoramanpayas*. Before long, Guo Jing could repeat it without making a single mistake. Zhou Botong had to admit that *he* could not have learned it. He was impressed by the boy's dogged determination.

Night fell. The sky was exceptionally clear. The sea glowed brilliantly in the moonlight. Guo Jing had just finished sparring with Zhou Botong and they were now resting on the ground, chatting about nothing in particular.

He had not realised how much his kung fu had improved over the past days, but Zhou Botong was keeping a close eye on it. The Hoary Urchin guessed that he would not be able to beat his little brother once the younger man had absorbed all the kung fu from the Manual. Even Apothecary Huang and Count Seven Hong would probably struggle to overcome him.

Without warning, a swishing sound rose from the undergrowth

and the shrubs started to twitch. Zhou Botong leapt up and screamed, "Snakes!"

Now, the noise grew into waves of hissing. Zhou Botong ran into the cave in fear, his wits scattered to the four winds. The sight of so many snakes drained the blood from his face.

"Stay inside, I'll take a look," Guo Jing said, and he started to block the mouth of the cave with large rocks.

"Be careful! Come back quickly!" Zhou Botong had composed himself a little, but a tremor was evident in his voice. "Actually, what's there to see? How come there are so many snakes? I haven't seen a single one in fifteen years. The Heretic may think he's omnipotent, but, in truth, he can't even keep these horrid things from infesting his little island. Are we going to find turtles, terrapins, adders and scorpions crawling all over the place next? Something deeply rotten is afoot."

CHAPTER NINE

THE THREE TRIALS

I

FOLLOWING THE SOUND FOR SEVERAL DOZEN PACES, GUO Jing came upon a slithering mass of green snakes. Several thousand of them. Their scales gleamed in the moonlight.

Among them walked ten men, dressed head to toe in white, flicking straying serpents back to the group and herding them forward with their staffs.

Does this mean the Venom of the West has arrived? What are they planning with the snakes? Guo Jing was awed and sickened by the sight.

The snake column cleaved north through the woods, guided by Apothecary Huang's mute servants. Luckily, the trees provided good cover and the herders appeared to have no martial training. Guo Jing was able to creep along undetected.

Several *li* later, they took a turn around a hill and arrived at a large grassy clearing. At a whistle, the snakes stopped and settled into coils, their triangular heads raised towards the bamboo forest to the north.

Guo Jing could not risk being spotted, so he stayed in the woods and skirted over to the east and around, before hurrying north. He paused at the edge of the bamboo thicket to listen – nothing but silence – before squeezing through the dense vegetation on his tiptoes.

Soon, he glimpsed a pavilion fashioned from the same type of bamboo growing around him. Over one of the arches was a horizontal plaque with three characters glistening in the moonlight: *Sword Trial Pavilion*. Below this sign, a couplet hung on the supporting pillars, framing the entrance.

> *Ghosts of peach blossom cascade as the sword flies,*
> *Tides of the green sea billow as the jade flute sings.*

Inside, he could make out a table flanked by matching chairs, also made of bamboo. They had a glossy patina, gained over years of use, glowing warmly in the moonlight. Ancient pine trees stood either side of the pavilion. Their branches, twisted and gnarled through the centuries, reached several *zhang* high into the sky.

Facing this serene pastoral sight were the bobbing heads and dancing tongues of thousands of snakes. They had now been arranged into two columns, leaving a path in the middle, which scores of women, also dressed in pure white, were walking, lighting the way with red silk lanterns. Strolling a dozen paces behind them were two men. The first, with a folding fan in his hand, wore a white silk robe embroidered with threads of gold.

Guo Jing recognised him immediately.

Gallant Ouyang!

As the Master of White Camel Mount approached the bamboo grove, he announced, "Master Ouyang of the West greets the Lord of Peach Blossom Island."

So this grand entrance was put on for the Venom of the West, Guo Jing said to himself, turning his eyes to the last man in the procession.

He too was dressed in white. While the moon outlined his tall and broad frame, his face was shrouded in darkness. Every two steps he took were punctuated by the sound of his staff striking the ground.

Two people emerged from the bamboo the moment the visitors had taken position among their entourage.

Guo Jing fought hard to suppress a yelp.

Lotus, walking hand in hand with her father, towards their guests.

Viper Ouyang stepped forward, put his hands together and bowed, a gesture of respect that Apothecary Huang immediately returned.

Gallant Ouyang meanwhile was on his knees, touching his head to the ground four times as he spoke. "Gallant Ouyang kowtows to Father and wishes him golden peace."

"There is no need for such ceremony." Apothecary Huang reached out to help Gallant Ouyang back to his feet.

Their exchange made Guo Jing sick to his stomach.

Apothecary Huang placed his right hand on Gallant Ouyang's left arm. They both knew this outwardly cordial gesture was a test of the younger man's kung fu.

Gallant Ouyang was prepared, and kept his *qi* reined in to steady his body. He hoped he could stand up on his feet without mishap, but his body convulsed involuntarily the moment Apothecary Huang lifted him.

"Ah!" A cry escaped from his lips as he plunged head first into the ground, his legs kicking in the air.

In the blink of an eye, Viper Ouyang spun his staff horizontally, touching it lightly on his nephew's back. It gave the younger man leverage to flip over. He landed firmly on his feet.

"My, my, Brother Apothecary, are you trying to make your son-in-law give you a somersault as his first greeting?" Viper Ouyang cackled.

His words tore with metallic sharpness into Guo Jing's ears.

"I'd like to gauge his skill. I've heard that he ganged up with a party of martial masters against my blind disciple and also used his snakes against my daughter."

Viper Ouyang let out another laugh. "Children's games they were, dear brother; please don't take it to heart." He paused before asking, "Do you think this child of mine is worthy of your precious daughter?" And, without waiting for a reply, he said, "Brother Apothecary, I have to give you credit for raising such a beauty."

The Venom turned his eyes to Lotus Huang, appraising her with his head cocked. Then he took out a brocade box from his robe. He lifted the lid to reveal an orb of dull yellow, the size of a pigeon's egg, nestled on a bed of silk.

"This amulet is made of rhinoceros horn and earth dragon." He showed the unassuming object to Lotus. "If you carry it on your person, no poison can ever harm you. It is made from the rarest beasts in the west, tempered with fire in the presence of precious medicinal herbs. This is the only specimen in the world. With this, you need not fear our serpents and insects when you come to live with us." He offered the box to Lotus. "Your father is no doubt sneering at this country bumpkin's gift. It cannot compare to the treasures he has seen and acquired on his travels, but this amulet has its uses."

For a man whose speciality was all creatures venomous, this betrothal gift was intended to quell any suspicions Apothecary Huang might harbour about the motive behind the match.

When Viper Ouyang presented the gift, he also stepped out of the shadows. Guo Jing could at last see the face of the man he had heard so much about.

His nose was proud and flanked by deep-set eyes. His gaze was as sharp as lightning and a knife's edge. Hair framed his face, and his beard appeared a brownish yellow, quite unlike the darker shades common among the people of the Central Plains.

Guo Jing could see the resemblance between uncle and nephew. Gallant Ouyang's face was a refined echo of the older man's roughly hewn, but still handsome, features.

Throughout Viper Ouyang's speech, Guo Jing kept telling himself, Lotus will never err. She will never accept your gift . . .

But, cruelly, she defied his expectations by reaching out with a jovial "Thank you!" and offering the Venom her most beguiling smile.

Setting eyes on Lotus's snow-white skin and blossom-like beauty again, Gallant Ouyang was dazed. The sight of her lips sent him floating to the heavens.

Now that we are betrothed, her attitude has changed completely, he observed with pleasure.

Then Gallant Ouyang saw a smattering of golden glitter in the air.

"Oh no!" he muttered under his breath, and he bent over backwards in an Iron Bridge, his shortlived joy brutally punctured.

"What are you doing?" Apothecary Huang barked. He flicked his left sleeve, swatting away the gilded steel needles Lotus had flung. His other hand slapped down at her shoulder.

"Yes, kill me, Papa!" She burst into tears. "I'd rather die than marry this rake."

Viper Ouyang stuffed the amulet into her hand and blocked Apothecary Huang's strike with a smile. "Your lovely daughter was merely testing my nephew's martial skills." His hollow laughter rang out again.

Of course, Apothecary Huang had no intention of hurting his daughter. Viper Ouyang let his arm glide past him without summoning internal strength.

Gallant Ouyang felt a dull throbbing pain on the left side of his chest as he straightened up.

A few needles must have found their way through, he realised. I must act as if nothing has happened, even though she is refusing to marry me.

He focused on hiding the pain and banishing the taint of embarrassment from his countenance.

"Brother Apothecary, I am honoured you still hold me in high enough regard so many years after we parted ways at Mount Hua." The mirthless smile had not left Viper Ouyang's face. "You don't know how much it pleased me that you agreed to my nephew's proposal. If there is any way your brother, here, can be of service, you know we should not refuse you."

"Nobody would dare to trouble the Venom." Apothecary Huang

answered in the same exaggerated politeness. "Come, do show us the exceptional martial skills you have acquired in the Western Regions these past years."

Intrigued, Lotus stopped crying and leaned closer to her father. She was fascinated by the gnarled staff Viper Ouyang carried.

Black as the darkest night, the iron-wrought weapon was of unusually hefty girth. A grinning man crowned the staff, bearing his sharpened teeth. The white fangs gleamed in the moonlight.

"My martial knowledge has always been lesser than yours and I have not trained for years. I must be far inferior now," Viper Ouyang said. "Nonetheless, since we are family, I would love the chance to stay a few days, to spar and learn from you."

The false modesty irritated Apothecary Huang. He doubted the Venom of the West would have fundamentally changed in the intervening years. His words were known to be honey-coated barbs. Such a proud man would never admit he was less able than another.

Apothecary Huang had been flattered when he received Viper Ouyang's emissary asking for Lotus's hand on behalf of his nephew. It pleased him that one of his few martial equals had written him so humble a message. He assumed his prospective son-in-law must be a formidable figure among younger martial artists, since Viper Ouyang had trained him himself.

He also knew his daughter well. She was used to getting her way. If her husband was of lesser martial skill, she would be domineering and difficult.

Though he had taken the emissary's praise of the young man's literary learning with a pinch of salt, Apothecary Huang was confident that anyone would be smarter and less hateful than the boy his daughter preferred.

The thought of Guo Jing riled the Heretic. He had always imagined his son-in-law would be a brilliant mind like himself or his daughter.

How could Apothecary Huang, the most learned man in the *jianghu*, be lumbered with an ignoramus like Guo Jing for a son? He would not invite mockery and derision from the martial world.

Moreover, the boy had killed Hurricane Chen.

Yes, stealing the Nine Yin Manual was unforgiveable, but a martial man should not die at the hand of an untrained child. All the anger he felt towards his dead disciple was redoubled and redirected at Guo Jing.

Apothecary Huang considered himself above convention, but his pride was not ready to let go of reputation and pedigree. He believed a man of Gallant Ouyang's martial, social and intellectual standing would be a good match for his daughter and appropriate to his own status.

For the first time, he had overruled Lotus's preference, giving his consent to Viper Ouyang's man on the spot.

But being in Viper Ouyang's presence once more roused Apothecary Huang's suspicions. He was reminded of the Venom's cunning. He did not believe this martial master would have abandoned his Exploding Toad kung fu completely, after Double Sun Wang Chongyang injured him.

"Our honoured guests have travelled a long way to be here. I should like to play a song to welcome you," Apothecary Huang said, as he retrieved the jade *xiao* flute from his sleeve.

Viper Ouyang cracked a smile – *You want to gauge my kung fu?* – and waved his left hand almost imperceptibly.

The women in white strolled forward and prostrated themselves before Apothecary Huang. They were all pale and unusually tall. Some were blonde with green eyes, others had brown hair and grey eyes. Their features were quite different from those of the women of the Central Plains, but no-one could deny that they were all exceptional beauties of voluptuous charm.

"I present thirty-two virgins to you, my dear friend. I sent men to gather them from all over the west and invited renowned instructors to guide them in the arts of singing and dancing. They can now put on a passable performance. Please accept this humble gift from an old friend. Though, of course, the wenches from the Western Regions cannot measure up to the beauties of the south," Viper Ouyang said.

"I must say I have never been fond of such diversions. Since my wife passed away, beautiful women of this world mean little to me. I cannot accept such a lavish gift from Brother Viper."

"Surely there is no harm in keeping them? To while away the days, to entertain the eyes and the ears?" Viper Ouyang clapped three times.

Eight women took out their musical instruments and started to play. Their music sounded foreign to southern ears.

The remaining twenty-four began to dance. The dancers at the front stooped low, while those at the back stood tall. Some spun to the left, others swirled to the right, each body supple to the extreme, each perfectly synchronised with the next. Extending their arms, a rippling movement spread from the left fingertips to the right. The effect mimicked the undulating movement of a slithering snake.

The dance reminded Lotus of Gallant Ouyang's Sacred Snake Fist. She glanced over and found him staring at her. He was without doubt the most loathsome man she knew. The anger she felt towards her father surged through her once more.

How dare he block her needles! She wondered what she could do to undo this arranged marriage. The ancient strategy, "Remove the firewood to cool a boiling cauldron," came to mind.

This would be a drastic resort . . . But, if she could be rid of him for good, then even if her father forced her, Ouyang would not be around to honour the match!

She felt less hopeless now. The scowl on her face was replaced by a smile. Gallant Ouyang caught the change and decided she was warming to him. For a moment, he forgot the pain in his chest.

The dance had grown more urgent and seductive. Hands now hovered sensually over bosoms and hips. The women swayed and thrust as if they were disrobing and engaging in acts of intimacy.

Apothecary Huang watched with a half-smile and raised the flute to his lips. The first notes sent a shudder through the dancers, jolting their steps out of sync. Another few twirls of the flute song and the women were dancing to Apothecary Huang's tune.

The musicians too had abandoned their music, and started playing along with Apothecary Huang. The snake herders were also affected, running and jumping among their flock. Even Gallant Ouyang felt a stirring in his heart.

Displeased by the disruption, Viper Ouyang clapped loudly, snapping the woman closest to him out of the music's ensnarement. She handed him an iron *zheng* zither. He strummed a few times – harsh twangs over the flute's airy whispers. It sounded like warriors on horseback crossing swords.

"Come, let's play together," Apothecary Huang said. The moment the *xiao* flute moved away from his lips, the compulsive dancing slowed.

"Cover your ears. Lord Huang and I shall play a duet," Viper Ouyang announced.

Gallant Ouyang had come prepared, and had stuffed cotton wool into his ears. His entourage tore strips of fabric from their clothes to make earplugs. They wound several layers of fabric around their heads to prevent any scrap of sound from finding its way into their ears.

"It's a real honour that my father plays for you. How dare you insult him thus!" Lotus snarled at Gallant Ouyang.

"He is not being rude," Apothecary Huang said to his daughter. "He has heard my song once; he is showing his self-awareness. And I am afraid you haven't got the ability to appreciate Uncle Ouyang's exceptional zither either." He took a silk handkerchief from inside his shirt, tore it in two and covered her ears.

Guo Jing, his curiosity piqued, tiptoed closer, eager to hear Viper Ouyang's playing.

"Your snakes cannot protect themselves," Apothecary Huang said, as he gestured at a servant.

The man waved at the lead snake herder, indicating that they should follow him. With a nod from Viper Ouyang, the herders whistled and drove the snakes after the serving man, relieved to be moving out of earshot.

"I do hope dear Brother Apothecary will be understanding if my performance is not up to scratch." Viper Ouyang sat cross-legged on a nearby boulder. He balanced the zither on his knees and closed his eyes to gather his *qi*. Then he plucked and strummed the first notes with his right hand.

The *zheng* was known for its melancholic twang, and this variety from the Western Regions was particularly mournful. Guo Jing had no ear for music, yet he noticed that each time a string rattled, his heart pulsed. As Viper Ouyang played faster, his heart throbbed along uncomfortably, as if it were about to burst out of his chest.

Realising he could die if the tempo increased further, he sat down to gather his spirit and still his thoughts in the Quanzhen way. As he channelled his internal energy around his body, his heartbeat slowed and soon he found he was no longer ensnared by the music.

Viper Ouyang's playing had accelerated to the point where it was impossible to distinguish between individual notes. A wall of sound pressed into Guo Jing, as if ten thousand horses were galloping towards him or hundreds of battle drums were being beaten.

Now and again, a gentle crooning rose above the twang of the zither, growing more confident and persistent. It brought a flush to Guo Jing's face and a flutter in his chest, prompting him to turn his focus back to controlling his senses.

However loud the *zheng* was, it failed to drown out the murmur of the *xiao*. Each Master held firm to his own tune. Together, they produced a raucous discordance.

The iron zither was the call of monkeys and apes in a remote mountain range, the hoot of owls in a dark wood. The jade flute was songs under the spring sun, whispers in a maiden's chamber. Fierce grief against the softly sensual.

When one tune rose in pitch, the other descended. When one reached a crescendo, the other fell all but silent. Neither succeeded in dominating the other.

With the silk handkerchief in her ears, Lotus Huang watched the silent display with amusement. Then she saw her father paced in the coordinates of the Eight Trigrams. He only did that while he was working on advanced internal kung fu. Now, she understood the music making was an intense contest and Viper Ouyang a formidable opponent.

She turned her eyes to the Venom. It seemed he was also putting everything he had into the music. Wisps of vapour rose from the crown of his head, like a steamer on the boil. His sleeves flapped in the wind as he pressed and plucked the zither's strings with both hands.

Guo Jing also sensed the competition between the two Masters, but he could not work out how music related to the martial arts, nor what made these tunes so seductive. Focusing on guarding his heart and spirit, soon he felt he had regained full control of himself. He turned his attention to the tone and colour of the musical instruments. After a while, he decided that one embodied the qualities of yin and the other those of yang, as they ebbed and flowed between attack and defence. As if two martial masters were sparring . . .

It's a contest of internal kung fu!

With that realisation, the opposing pull of the *zheng* and the *xiao* no longer bothered Guo Jing. The music could not take hold of his senses or emotions. He closed his eyes and let the finer details of the duel come to his ears.

He felt a bright sense of detachment forming within. The twist and turn of each note now appeared clear and distinct. Somehow, he was applying the essence of the Luminous Hollow Fist as he listened, putting its mantra, "From hollowness, luminosity glows," into practice.

He could not compete with the two Masters, because they had decades of internal-strength training over him. But what he had learned from Zhou Botong was enough to keep him removed from the clamour and help him understand this fight from a position of heightened mental clarity. He was living out the saying, "Looking on from the sidelines," with his ears.

Nonetheless, he still could not fathom why Zhou Botong, with his far superior kung fu, was so affected by the flute song. He did not know that his sworn brother had been haunted by a romantic entanglement most of his adult life. It was that very demon that the music was feeding. For it was not the level of his kung fu, but the purity of a heart unburdened by desires and regrets that helped Guo Jing resist the music.

Guo Jing had at first thought that the thunderous strumming of the *zheng* would obscure the airy whistle of the *xiao*. The flute darted up and down its registers, struggling to find its place. Gradually, it began to pick out gaps between each pluck of the strings. Its sound began to shine through and grew bright, projecting heroic grace, while the zither seemed to flag and fade. But, when the flute reached the ascending *qingyu* half tone – *clang!* – the zither reclaimed its might with a metallic rattle.

"The firm cannot endure, the supple cannot defend."

A line from the mnemonic verse explaining the Luminous Hollow Fist came to Guo Jing. The words no longer seemed so cryptic.

As he listened to the greatest martial artists of the age duel with music, he noticed that their tactics matched the theory behind Zhou Botong's invented kung fu. Guo Jing was delighted with this new-found understanding. After all, he could barely comprehend one-tenth of all the martial sayings he had crammed into his head, and verbalising abstract concepts was not the Hoary Urchin's forte.

Guo Jing also sensed that the new text he had just learned bore some relation to this musical contest. However, his sworn brother had yet to explain those complicated theories. And, when Guo Jing dwelled on them now, the pressure of the music began to weigh heavy on him. He shut his mind from that line of thinking. If he let his concentration lapse for even a split second, he would be caught in the music's snare.

Guo Jing felt Apothecary Huang was close to winning on several occasions. He just needed a few extra coloratura flourishes. He also noticed the opportunities Viper Ouyang failed to seize. These misses confused him. Perhaps the Masters were holding back out of politeness?

By now, they had been playing for more than an hour. He had come to understand their tactics and could discern a curious pattern. Whenever the Masters' choice diverged from the concepts underlying the Luminous Hollow Fist, they missed the chance to deal the winning blow.

Could Zhou Botong's invention be superior to these two Masters' kung fu?

Guo Jing dismissed this idea as improbable. His sworn brother would not still be stuck in his cave if he could beat Apothecary Huang.

Presently, the flute began to creep higher and higher up its register, bringing Guo Jing's attention back to the contest.

If he plays just a little higher, Viper Ouyang will lose! He began to will the flute to climb higher, but it seemed to be stuck at this one particular note.

Why doesn't he go higher? Guo Jing laughed at his stupidity as the answer flashed across his mind. He's reached the flute's limit. He can't go any higher! If I could pack the force of ten thousand *jin* into a punch, I could smash anything with my fist. But can I muster such strength? Clearly not! Fourth *Shifu* used to tell me that people made carrying heavy parcels with a shoulder pole look effortless. Yet, if I tried to do the same, my back would snap in an instant. A lot of things are easier said than done. And that's especially true when it comes to advanced kung fu!

2

THE MUSICAL DUEL WAS NOW MORE INTENSE THAN EVER. THE Venom and the Heretic were fighting blade-on-flesh in this metaphorical hand-to-hand combat. A winner was bound to emerge soon.

At this decisive point, a whistle wafted in from the sea.

It sent a shockwave through the two Masters and their music faltered for a moment. The whistler must be on a boat nearing the island.

Viper Ouyang struck the *zheng* twice, sending forth a tremolo so violent that it could tear cloth. The newcomer accepted the challenge by skipping effortlessly to a very high note.

Apothecary Huang joined in. His flute flitted between grappling with the whistle and contending with the zither. The contest was now a fierce melee, much like the Competing Hands games Zhou Botong staged.

A third martial great had arrived.

Now the whistle came from the woods. Dipping and soaring, it roared with the might of tigers and lions, it neighed and brayed like a horse or a donkey. It was like the wind blowing through a forest, or a drizzle caressing petals. There was infinite variety to its tones.

The flute answered in a clear and gentle voice. The zither rattled and rasped with melancholic menace. Each Master stood firm. No-one could gain the upper hand.

"Wow!"

All music stopped.

It dawned on Guo Jing that he had cheered out loud. Just then, a whirl of green materialised before him.

"Come with me, lad."

Guo Jing mumbled, "Lord Huang," and trailed after his host, shamefaced.

Lotus burst into tears of joy at Guo Jing's sudden appearance. She did not realise that he had interrupted the music making.

Pulling out her makeshift earplugs, she rushed towards him, grasped his hands and hugged him tightly.

"You're here, at last . . ." Her voice betrayed a streak of sorrow that tainted her joy at their reunion.

Jealous rage burned in Gallant Ouyang at the sight of Guo Jing, and Lotus's reaction fanned its fires. He lunged, his fist poised to strike. He was confident that he would give the odious whelp a black eye, perhaps even a broken nose. That would make him feel a lot better. He was the superior martial artist, with the element of surprise on his side. Little did he know that the boy's kung fu was already so very different from the one he defeated at the Liu clan's ancestral temple, just a few weeks before.

Though Lotus had Guo Jing's full attention, he caught a glimpse of the punch from the corner of his eye.

Guo Jing turned slightly and evaded the blow with ease. He replied with two moves from the Dragon-Subduing Palm simultaneously: Wild Goose Approaches Land with his left hand and Haughty Dragon Repents with his right.

One of Count Seven Hong's powerful palm strikes was hard enough to withstand. Now, Gallant Ouyang faced two simultaneously, thanks to Zhou Botong's outlandish Competing Hands technique.

Apothecary Huang and Viper Ouyang were both proud of the breadth of their martial knowledge, yet neither had seen quick-fire attacks launched like this. Even the martial greats were taken aback by this unusual kung fu.

Gallant Ouyang felt Guo Jing's left palm pressing close to his right flank.

Dragon-Subduing Palm – I can't block this head on, he told himself.

So he swerved to the left. Yet this very act of self-preservation threw his body into the powerful move from Guo Jing's right.

Thwack! A sickening crunch. A rib snapped.

Gallant Ouyang leapt back, then up onto the roof of the bamboo pavilion, riding the momentum of the blow. He did not care that it looked like a retreat.

If he stood his ground, his heart and lungs would suffer irreparable damage. Preserving his life was more important than saving face, right now.

He stumbled several steps before finding his footing. Then he jumped down and staggered over to his uncle, humiliated and hunched in pain.

Lotus cheered and clapped, but Guo Jing remained cautious. He kept his eyes trained on Gallant Ouyang, then took two steps back to put more distance between them, in case of a counter-attack.

Guo Jing thought his success was a fluke. Gallant Ouyang must have let his guard down. He did not realise how much his kung fu had improved since he had met Zhou Botong.

"Such a formidable disciple, Beggar Hong. My hearty congratulations!" Viper Ouyang projected his voice as he gave Guo Jing a sideways glare.

"*Shifu!*" Lotus ran into the bamboo thicket. The heavens had at last sent her someone to deliver her from this terrible bond!

Soon, the Beggar of the North emerged. His left hand held Lotus's, and his right, a jade-green bamboo cane. On his back was slung his trusty red gourd.

Apothecary Huang extended his welcome to Count Seven Hong and exchanged the customary pleasantries, all the while desperate to ask his daughter one question: "What did you call Count Seven just now?"

"Count Seven has taken me as a disciple," she explained. "I remember you often talked fondly of his martial ability and upright character. When I had the chance to call a man you have praised *Shifu*, I took it. I know I should've asked your permission, Papa, but I knew you'd be very happy for me. You don't mind, do you, Papa?"

"I am most grateful that Brother Seven has deemed my daughter worthy. She is naughty and disobedient; I hope you will help me discipline her." Apothecary Huang was genuinely pleased and he bowed deeply.

Honoured by the generous response, the Beggar said, "It would take her more than a lifetime to absorb Brother Apothecary's knowledge. I must confess, I took her on for purely selfish reasons, so she would always lavish her culinary magic on me. There is no need to thank me." The two martial greats broke out into hearty laughter.

"Papa, if Count Seven hadn't saved me from that villain —" Lotus jabbed a finger at Gallant Ouyang — "you'd have never seen your Lotus again."

"Nonsense! Why would he want to hurt you?"

"I'll get him to tell you." Lotus turned to Gallant Ouyang. "Swear you will speak the truth, or else . . . your uncle's strange snakes will be your death."

Her words drained the blood from the faces of the Ouyangs. As masters of poisonous creatures, Lotus's casual words had hit upon their greatest fear.

Two such snakes were housed at that very moment in Viper Ouyang's staff. The tip of this weapon could be flipped open to reveal two small cavities. In there dwelled two small serpents.

Viper Ouyang had spent more than a decade breeding these vipers by crossing many varieties of the most deadly species. He used these snakes on his opponents during combat, as well as to punish anyone who dared to cross him. The poison began as an intense itch all over the body, swiftly resulting in death.

Though Viper Ouyang had developed an antidote, the venom was so strong and fast-acting that it would still cause great suffering and prevent the victim from practising the martial arts again.

"I would never dream of lying to my father-in-law," Gallant Ouyang said through gritted teeth.

"I'll box your ears if you call him that again! We first met at the Prince of Zhao's palace in the Jin capital, did we not?"

Gallant Ouyang nodded. Beads of sweat had appeared on his forehead. He had managed to suppress the pain from his injuries with internal kung fu. But, the moment he opened his mouth, his attention was split and a savage onslaught of pain all but floored him. He knew, if he uttered another word, his suffering would be plain for all to see. He could not live with such a serious loss of face.

"That night, you allied yourself with Hector Sha, Tiger Peng, Greybeard Liang and Lama Supreme Wisdom to attack me, did you not?"

"No . . . I did not . . ." He started to defend himself, but the pain choked off the words in his throat.

"You don't need to speak. Just nod or shake your head. I'll ask you again: Hector Sha, Tiger Peng, Greybeard Liang and Lama Supreme Wisdom were picking on me, were they not?"

He nodded.

"They tried to capture me, but they failed. And you were on their side, were you not?"

He could not deny it. Feebly, he moved his head up and down.

"I was all alone in the banqueting hall at the Prince of Zhao's residence. No-one was there to help me. Papa didn't know where I was, so he couldn't help me, even if he'd wanted to. Is this not true?"

Gallant Ouyang knew she was trying to turn her father against him. But he could not deny what had actually happened and so he nodded again.

Lotus reached out for her father's hand. "Pa, see! You wouldn't treat me like this if Mama were still around . . ."

Apothecary Huang's heart tightened at the thought of his late wife, and he put his arm protectively around Lotus.

"Miss Huang, these established martial artists failed to detain you because you inherited your father's extraordinary kung fu. Is it not so?"

Lotus nodded with a grin. Apothecary Huang smiled at Viper Ouyang's praise.

The Venom continued, "Brother Apothecary, that was when my nephew saw your daughter's great talent and came fervently to admire her. It was under the spell of such passion that he sent word by the fastest pigeon to White Camel Mount, begging me to traverse thousands of miles to ask for your daughter's hand on his behalf. No-one else in the world could induce me to make such a long journey."

"I am most obliged." Apothecary Huang was indeed flattered by Viper Ouyang's presence.

"Brother Seven, I wonder why our admiration for Peach Blossom Island has seemed so unpalatable to you that you would physically confront a junior. My nephew would have perished under your Skyful of Petals technique had he not been blessed with such resilience."

Laughing at the absurdity of Viper Ouyang's accusation, Count Seven Hong unplugged his gourd and took a long gulp of wine.

Whether the Venom was distorting facts or Gallant Ouyang had lied to him, it was not worth a response.

But Guo Jing could not let such unfounded nonsense go unchallenged. "Count Seven saved your nephew!"

"Who has given you permission to speak, boy?" Apothecary Huang barked.

"Tell everyone how he . . . abducted Miss Cheng." Guo Jing turned to Lotus for help.

Lotus knew her father had always disregarded moral codes to stay true to his nature. He would probably side with Gallant Ouyang, just to show his disdain for Guo Jing. He would most likely consider that awful man romantic rather than lecherous.

Noticing the sneer on her father's lips, she decided to change the subject completely.

She turned to Gallant Ouyang once more. "I haven't finished! When we fought at the Prince of Zhao's residence, you claimed you could defeat me without using your hands or any kung fu moves, did you not?"

Gallant Ouyang nodded.

"When we duelled again in Baoying, you said this one technique from your uncle could defeat me. It mattered not whether I fought back with Papa's kung fu or my *shifu* Count Seven's. Did you not?"

You set that rule, not me! Gallant Ouyang wanted to argue back.

But Lotus gave him no chance to retort. "You drew a circle on the ground with your foot and said that if I pushed you out with Papa's kung fu, then I would win. Did you not?"

Gallant Ouyang nodded.

"Pa, see, he holds you and Count Seven in contempt. He says so himself, the combination of your kung fu is still inferior to that of his uncle. He thinks the two of you together can't beat the Venom."

"What would you know, little girl?" Apothecary Huang was beginning to find Gallant Ouyang irritating. "It is known throughout the martial world that the Heretic, the Venom, the King and the Beggar are equals in martial learning."

He turned away from Gallant Ouyang and changed the subject. "Brother Seven, might I ask to what I owe the pleasure of your visit?"

3

"THERE IS SOMETHING I WOULD LIKE TO ASK OF YOU," COUNT Seven Hong answered.

"We've been friends for decades. If dear Brother Seven has a request, how could I refuse?"

It pleased Apothecary Huang that such a martial great should turn to him for help. He knew that the Beggar never asked anything of outsiders, always handling everything personally or with the assistance of the Beggar Clan.

"Don't be so hasty. I fear it is rather a delicate matter."

"I doubt you would come all the way if it was a mere trifle."

"You know me well!" Count Seven clapped his hands together and laughed. "So you will agree?"

"I give you my word! Into fire or over water, I shall go along with you."

Apothecary Huang was happy to give his consent, certain that a man as honourable and just as Count Seven Hong would not compromise him by asking for anything untoward.

Viper Ouyang raised his staff. "Brother Apothecary, there is no need for such haste. We should perhaps ask Brother Seven to explain his business first."

"Old Venom, it has got nothing to do with you." Count Seven chuckled. "Just get ready to toast the bride and groom."

"A wedding?"

"Yes, indeed." Count Seven gestured at Guo Jing and Lotus. "I have promised my disciples to seek Brother Apothecary's consent for their betrothal, and he has just agreed to it."

Guo Jing and Lotus looked at each other with joy and surprise, but shock and dismay marred the faces of the Ouyangs.

"Brother Seven, I fear you are mistaken. Brother Apothecary has given his daughter's hand to my nephew. We are here today to perform the engagement ritual and deliver betrothal gifts."

"Is that true, Brother Apothecary?" Count Seven asked.

"Yes, Brother Viper speaks the truth. I hope Brother Seven isn't playing a prank at my expense," Apothecary Huang replied.

"Who has time for pranks?" Count Seven's face darkened. "So your daughter is engaged to two men, both with your consent. I am the matchmaker for the Guo family. Where is your matchmaker?"

Viper Ouyang was floored by the question. Eventually, he said, "Why do we need a matchmaker when Brother Apothecary and I have both agreed to the match?"

"But there is still one person who hasn't given his consent," Count Seven said.

"Who?"

"Your humble beggar!" Count Seven laughed.

Viper Ouyang understood that Count Seven had just issued a challenge. He kept his face expressionless and made no reply.

"Your nephew's character is wanting. How could he be good enough for this blossom-like maiden?" Count Seven continued. "You two can force them to marry, but you can't make them like each other. They will be waving swords and thrusting spears, day in, day out. What would be the point of such a union?"

Of course, Apothecary Huang wanted Lotus to be happily married. He turned to his beloved daughter and caught her looking tenderly at Guo Jing. A swell of repugnance surged through him, chasing away the doubt that Count Seven Hong's words had stirred.

This boy was beyond hateful.

Apothecary Huang took great pride in his mental acumen and his mastery of every literary and martial pursuit. Literature, military strategy, music, chess, calligraphy, painting – he was an expert in all these fields. All his associates were cultured, refined individuals, worthy of his intellect. Lotus was exceptionally clever, just like her mother. He refused to plant a sprig of blossoms in a pile of cow dung; he would not give his only daughter to this blockhead, this cretin, this dolt. No, no, no!

He looked at the other young man. Handsome, dashing, elegant, learned. In every aspect, a hundred times better.

His mind was made up. His resolve firmer than ever.

Lotus will marry Gallant Ouyang, but I won't spit in Count Seven's face and refuse outright.

An idea came to Apothecary Huang.

"Brother Viper, why don't you look to your nephew first? We shall discuss this at length afterwards," he said.

Gallant Ouyang's injury had been weighing on Viper Ouyang's mind. Without another word, he gestured at the young man and the two of them disappeared into the bamboo forest.

Apothecary Huang and Count Seven Hong remained by the pavilion and exchanged further pleasantries, studiously avoiding the subject at hand.

When the Ouyangs returned, Gallant Ouyang's rib had been reset and the needles removed from his chest.

Apothecary Huang then announced, "I am deeply honoured that both Brother Seven and Brother Viper hold me in such high esteem, coming all the way here to seek the hand of my wayward, headstrong daughter. She was already promised to Gallant Ouyang, but it would be churlish of me to refuse Brother Seven's request. I have an idea that perhaps may help us find a happy solution."

"Spit it out; this beggar hasn't got the patience for your flowery words."

Apothecary Huang smiled. "My daughter has neither looks nor ability, but I have always hoped that she would settle down with a good man. Now, Master Ouyang is Brother Viper's nephew and Master Guo is Brother Seven's disciple, so both have benefitted from an impeccable upbringing. It is impossible for me to choose one over the other. I have no choice but to set up three trials to test our young masters. The more learned and talented young man will win my daughter's hand. I promise I shall show no bias and I invite my two friends to help me decide the winner of each trial."

"Excellent!" Viper Ouyang applauded. "However, if we were to do martial trials, we would have to wait until my nephew recovers."

Gallant Ouyang's injury was the perfect excuse to avoid any combat – the Venom knew his nephew would not stand a chance against Guo Jing.

"Indeed, we most certainly would not want to sow discord by proposing a physical fight." Apothecary Huang shared the Venom's concerns.

You've clearly chosen your son-in-law, you old Heretic, Count Seven Hong grumbled silently to himself. We're all *wulin* men, yet you won't have martial trials! Why don't you marry your precious daughter to the Top Scholar? If you test this idiot disciple of mine on his knowledge of poetry and literature, he is sure to lose, in this lifetime and the next. You say you're not biased, but I know what you're really thinking. You want Guo Jing to fail. Well, well, I'll have to challenge the Venom to a fight myself.

"All of us standing here today are martial men. Are you saying we should compete on eating and shitting instead of kung fu? The one thing we are all trained in?" Count Seven Hong cackled. He glared at Viper Ouyang. "Your nephew may be injured, but you're not. We'll fight on their behalf."

Count Seven Hong launched his palm at Viper Ouyang's shoulder.

Lowering his shoulder and rolling back his arm, the Venom stepped back several paces.

"Fight back!" Count Seven set his cane down on a bamboo side table and launched seven moves at an incredible speed.

Viper Ouyang swerved left and right, evading them with ease. Then, in the short time it took to plant his staff between the tiles of the floor of the pavilion, his left hand had thrown seven strikes.

Apothecary Huang made no move to restrain his guests – rather, he cheered at the display. He wanted to see how much these two Masters had improved since they last crossed paths atop Mount Hua, more than two decades ago. Each had been honing their skills for the next encounter, pushing their already formidable knowledge to ever greater heights.

Count Seven Hong and Viper Ouyang tossed out rapid-fire moves, but pulled back just before hitting the target. They had to gauge how the other's kung fu had changed first.

Fists and palms darted and danced among bamboo leaves, each movement intricate and complex.

Guo Jing was mesmerised by the innovative and the unexpected in each move. He could not have imagined such kung fu, even in his wildest dreams. Soon, he began to notice similarities between the action and the text Zhou Botong had taught him. He tried to compare the two. Though the swift attacks barely left a shadow on Guo Jing's mind, it was more illustrative than the musical contest of internal kung fu earlier.

In no time at all, more than three hundred moves had been exchanged. The two Masters were impressed by each other's improvement.

Apothecary Huang, meanwhile, was a little dispirited. He had fondly imagined, after Double Sun Wang Chongyang's death, that he would become the world's greatest martial artist. Seeing how the Beggar and the Venom had developed in the intervening years, he realised with frustration and grudging respect that the three of them remained on an equal plane.

Gallant Ouyang and Lotus Huang were simply rooting for the fight to go their way, too invested in its outcome to recognise the virtuosity on display. Then Lotus noticed Guo Jing kicking his legs and waving his arms, with a strange glint in his eyes. She called to him, quietly. But he was so engrossed in the fight, he heard nothing. Concerned, she watched him and smiled at his attempt to emulate the moves of Count Seven and Viper Ouyang.

Lotus turned to her father. Like Guo Jing, he too was entranced by the duel. An odd expression graced his face and he appeared entirely disconnected from his surroundings. She glanced across at

Gallant Ouyang, who was trying to make eyes at her, waving his fan languidly under the delusion that he cut a dashing figure.

By now, the tempo of the fight had slowed. Moves were launched intermittently, each strike prefaced by a lengthy pause. Once the opponent had evaded an attack, both would sit down to rest and regroup before returning to their feet to deliver another sally. The pace of the duel was reduced to that of a training session in which a disciple is grappling with new kung fu. However, from the concentration on their faces, this sluggish phase of the fight was more consuming and intense than the brisk exchange that had preceded it.

Spellbound, Guo Jing cheered whenever a great move was made.

"Stop that racket!" Gallant Ouyang snapped. "How could an oaf like you appreciate such complex martial arts?"

"Speak for yourself!" Lotus retorted. "Just because you don't know what's going on, it doesn't mean he can't understand."

"He's obviously trying to appear clever. He's far too green to recognise the intricacy of my uncle's kung fu."

"How do you know what he can or can't understand?"

Their bickering continued, but neither Apothecary Huang nor Guo Jing heard a word of it.

Now, both Count Seven Hong and Viper Ouyang had taken to squatting on their haunches. One flicked himself between the eyebrows with the middle finger of his left hand. The other held his head in his hands, shielding his ears and squeezing his eyes shut. Both of them were thinking hard.

Suddenly, a howl. They leapt up at the same time. A punch or a kick. Then they settled back into their crouching positions, flicking themselves between the eyebrows or holding their head in their hands.

The two Masters had such a thorough knowledge of each other's kung fu, they could deflect even the deadliest move with ease. There would be no winner until one of them could invent a new and unexpected move on the spot.

In the two decades since the Contest of Mount Hua, Count Seven Hong and Viper Ouyang had not kept in touch. The distance between the Central Plains and the Western Regions also meant they were each cut off from news of the other. They would not have known how each other's kung fu might have developed.

Now, in spite of the improvements each had made, they were still equals, each with their own strengths and shortcomings. Neither could prevail.

The moon had grown pale and the blushing sun began to steal in from the east. The two Masters were physically and mentally exhausted. They had invented countless new moves and variations in the past hours, yet they were still stuck in the same rut.

Fascination and confusion tugged Guo Jing's mind in different directions. Some of the kung fu echoed the new theory from Zhou Botong. So he tried to emulate it, but, before he could grasp it, a new and innovative move would chase what little he had committed to his memory clean out of his head.

Lotus Huang could not make head nor tail of the fight, but it was obvious Guo Jing was relishing every move. Had he received divine instruction in the weeks they were apart? she wondered. Perhaps he missed me so much that he's no longer right in the head? I know that's how I'm feeling, right now. I shouldn't have run so fast when we got to the island. I was so desperate to see Papa. When I turned to look for him, he'd disappeared. I'm sure he's been just as worried as I have.

Lotus reached out to take Guo Jing's hand, just as he was copying one of Viper Ouyang's palm strikes. He spun as he pushed his palm out. His movement looked harmless enough, but the moment they touched, she felt a great force pulsing through her, so strong that it sent her flying into the air.

Oh no! Guo Jing noticed her presence too late and leapt over to catch her.

But Lotus managed to twist from her waist while she was airborne, and landed softly on the pavilion roof.

Guo Jing jumped with a tap of his foot and grabbed a corner of the flying eave. Then he swung himself up in a somersault.

Sitting shoulder to shoulder, the young couple watched the fight together.

The mood had shifted once more. Though Viper Ouyang was still squatting, his arms were now folded and he held them raised at his shoulders, like a giant frog about to leap. He bellowed and grunted fitfully, like a bull.

"What do you think he is doing?" Lotus asked, and smiled.

"I have no idea." Then he remembered Zhou Botong's description of Wang Chongyang's death. "It must be his most powerful kung fu, the Exploding Toad."

"He does indeed look like a mangy toad!"

Viper Ouyang's peculiar technique drew on the toad's sudden burst of energy as it emerged from winter hibernation. Over the years, he had practised different ways to store strength within his body, which could be unleashed in one wave, upon attack. He also took inspiration from the moon toad myth, cultivating the kung fu at night while facing the dark spots of the moon, where the lunar spirit was believed to dwell.

Gallant Ouyang was consumed by jealousy yet again at the familiar way Guo Jing chatted with Lotus Huang. He was desperate to fight the boy, but his chest was still hurting. He also knew he could no longer beat Guo Jing, even when fully recovered.

Just then, he heard the words "mangy toad".

How dare they call me that!

In a fit of rage, he took three silver Swallow Shuttles and tiptoed to the back of the pavilion. Tightening his jaw, he flicked his wrist and sent the secret weapons hurtling into Guo Jing's back.

Count Seven Hong was now circling Viper Ouyang, striking at the hunched figure from different directions with the Dragon-Subduing Palm. The two martial greats were competing with their most famed kung fu, drawing on their potent internal strength, acquired over decades of practice. They were now gambling everything they had — including their lives — to win.

Watching as his *shifu* improvised complex variations of the simple actions from the Eighteen Dragon-Subduing Palms, Guo Jing realised he had barely scratched the surface of the repertoire. He was intoxicated by the superb display, blind to the danger that was flying at him from behind.

The fight had now reached a decisive moment. But Lotus did not have the martial insight to read the situation. As she was chattering away, she noticed suddenly that Gallant Ouyang had disappeared. Then she heard a faint swishing noise from behind.

She glanced at Guo Jing and threw herself sideways onto his back.

Pop, pop, pop! All three darts bounced off her Hedgehog Chainmail. He was so focused on the fight, he did not notice what had happened.

Aching a little where she was hit, Lotus reached behind and scooped up the Swallow Shuttles.

"How did you know I needed to scratch my back? Here you go." She smiled at Gallant Ouyang and offered him the weapons.

Her action fanned Gallant Ouyang's jealousy further. He thought she was going to throw the shuttles down. But her hand remained outstretched as she waited for him to fetch them himself. So he tapped the ground lightly with the tip of his left foot and leapt up, perching elegantly on an upturned corner of the roof.

With his white robe fluttering in the wind, even Lotus had to admit that he cut rather a dashing figure at that moment.

"Wow, fantastic *qinggong*!" Lotus cheered at his ascent and took a step closer. She held the shuttles out in her hand.

Gallant Ouyang saw the exposed skin on her wrist, white as virgin snow, and he swooned. He reached out gleefully, grateful for a chance to caress her skin. But a golden cloud dispelled his wishful thinking.

Having suffered these needles twice already, he flipped over in a somersault and landed back on the ground, waving his sleeves to flick away the needles.

Giggling, Lotus hurled the shuttles at Viper Ouyang's head.

"Don't!" Guo Jing grabbed Lotus by the waist and they jumped down together.

"Brother Viper!" Apothecary Huang exclaimed.

A billow of energy rushed at Guo Jing just as his feet touched the ground. He set Lotus down and immediately launched a Dragon in the Field with each hand. Pushing back with every ounce of his strength, he kept nothing in reserve.

Pang!

A turbulence of *qi* ripped through his chest, throwing him back by half a dozen steps. He had never felt so awful, but he thrust his feet down in a effort to stand his ground.

What mattered was shielding Lotus from this destructive force.

He took a deep breath and held his palms out, one in front of the other, ready for the next wave of the onslaught.

Both Count Seven Hong and Apothecary Huang were now standing between him and the still-crouching Viper Ouyang.

The Venom straightened up and said, offhandedly, "My mistake, my mistake. I wasn't able to pull back fast enough. I didn't hurt the young lady, did I?"

Though frightened, Lotus would not let him have the last word. "You can't hurt me with Papa here."

Apothecary Huang took her hand and spoke with genuine concern: "Take a deep breath. How do you feel?"

Lotus inhaled slowly, then exhaled quickly. She could not feel anything unusual. She smiled and shook her head.

"Your uncles were comparing martial knowledge. It was no place for a little girl to interfere. Uncle Ouyang's Exploding Toad is unlike any other kung fu. If it wasn't for his mercy, you would have lost your life." A note of relief was evident in Apothecary Huang's voice.

The true power of the Exploding Toad came from inertia. Viper Ouyang simply gathered strength and waited for his opponent to strike. The force of that blow, when it came, would bounce back at the attacker, compounded with the blast of energy stored up in the Venom's body.

Although Double Sun Wang Chongyang had set him back in his pursuit of this kung fu by tapping Viper Ouyang with a Yang in Ascendance, the Venom had worked hard in the intervening years to recover lost ground.

Just now, Viper Ouyang had summoned all his might against Count Seven Hong. He was as taut as a fully drawn bow when Lotus threw the shuttles.

When he heard Apothecary Huang's shout, his energy had already been unleashed. Though he did try to pull back, there was little he could do once his power had burst forth.

Such a shame this beautiful girl will die by my hand!

As the thought had crossed Viper Ouyang's mind, a gust of energy was thrown back at him, and he had taken the chance to retrieve as much of his own strength as he could, surprised to find it was Guo Jing. He could only be impressed that the Beggar had trained such a powerful disciple.

Apothecary Huang assumed that Viper Ouyang had held his energy back as a courtesy to him. The Guo Jing he met at Roaming Cloud Manor could not have withstood the Exploding Toad. He sneered at the young man's stupidity. Was he really foolish enough to raise his hand against Viper Ouyang's ultimate kung fu? He had no idea that Guo had saved his daughter's life. Even so, he could not deny that Guo Jing had just thrown himself in death's way to protect Lotus.

I shall give him a gift worthy of his devotion to Lotus, Apothecary Huang decided.

Though he still could not countenance Guo Jing as a suitor, he was reminded of the time when he had harboured such single-minded passion for a woman. He found the boy a little less repulsive now.

"We aren't done yet, Old Venom!" Count Seven Hong said, and stepped forward for another round.

Apothecary Huang raised his left arm to hold Viper Ouyang back. "Brother Seven, Brother Viper, you are both guests of Peach Blossom Island. Should we not sit down and share a few cups of the wine I brew? You have already exchanged more than a thousand moves and still we have no winner. The second Contest of Mount Hua is soon upon us. I shall be there, and so will Duan, the King of the South. We can finish the fight then. What do you say?"

"I shall most certainly have to concede, if we continue today." Viper Ouyang smirked.

Count Seven chuckled. "Since our dear Venom, here, is well known for speaking in opposites, I take it you mean you will most certainly gain the upper hand. Well, we shall see."

"I am very happy to learn more from Brother Seven."

"Excellent." Count Seven flicked his sleeve, raring to go.

"Ah, so this is the real reason why our two Masters grace Peach Blossom Island today. To show off your martial skills," Apothecary Huang said, with a smile.

"Brother Apothecary is right." Count Seven roared with laughter. "We are here for the lady's hand, not to fight."

4

"AS I WAS SAYING BEFORE, I WOULD LIKE TO SET UP THREE trials so our two young masters can show us their knowledge," Apothecary Huang said, returning to the matter of Lotus's betrothal. "I will welcome the young master who passes the tests as my son-in-law, but I shan't let the other young man leave empty-handed."

"Eh? Have you got another daughter?" Count Seven asked.

"I am afraid not, and I doubt I can find a new wife to make another one fast enough. However, I have acquired a little knowledge through the years. The three religions, the nine schools of thought, as well as medicine, divination and astrology. If our young master is willing, he may choose a subject and I will be happy to share all I know. He would not have come to Peach Blossom Island in vain."

Count Seven Hong weighed up Apothecary Huang's words. The Heretic has clearly made up his mind; whatever tasks he comes up with will definitely put Guo Jing at a disadvantage. But if this simpleton learns kung fu from the Heretic, the benefits will be for life . . .

Noticing Count Seven Hong's deliberation, Viper Ouyang agreed immediately. "This really is an excellent suggestion. Though Brother Apothecary had already consented to my nephew's proposal, we shall put our two young men to the test, out of respect for Brother Seven."

He then turned to Gallant Ouyang. "If Master Guo, here, proves more knowledgeable, you mustn't blame anybody for your shortcomings. We shall gladly drink to his happiness. If you try anything, not only will the two Masters, here, not abide it, I won't let it pass either."

Count Seven Hong guffawed into the sky. "Those words are for our ears, aren't they?"

"Who can predict the result? One thing is certain, though: people of our stature always accept our defeat gracefully. Don't we?" Viper Ouyang grinned. "Brother Apothecary, please name your first trial."

Though Apothecary Huang was determined to marry Lotus to Gallant Ouyang, it would not befit his status as a martial great to be seen as biased. He also wished to avoid offending Count Seven Hong.

While Apothecary Huang deliberated over the tests he could set that would guarantee his preferred suitor would win, Count Seven Hong said, "We are all men who live by our fists, Brother Apothecary. Your trials must be about the martial arts. If you test them on poetry, songs, chants, talismans, or some other rot like that, then we might as well admit our ignorance now, dust our behinds and go. We have not come here to make fools of ourselves."

"Of course, the first trial will test their martial skills," Apothecary Huang replied.

"That won't do," Viper Ouyang protested. "My nephew is injured."

"I am aware of that and I have no intention of sowing discord by letting the two young masters duel, here, on Peach Blossom Island."

"They will not fight each other?" Viper Ouyang asked.

"Indeed."

"Are you going to test them yourself?" the Venom pursued.

"No, it would be impossible to demonstrate my impartiality if I played an active role," Apothecary Huang said. "We have just seen that your kung fu and Brother Seven's are not only at the very pinnacle of martial excellence, but also truly on the same level. I propose that you be the judge of Master Guo's skills and that Brother Seven should test Master Ouyang."

Count Seven Hong had to bow to Apothecary Huang's quick thinking. I couldn't come up with a solution as clever or as fair.

"Not a bad idea." Then he beckoned Gallant Ouyang. "Come, let's begin."

"We haven't set the rules yet," Apothecary Huang said. "First, Master Ouyang is injured; he can't summon his internal strength. So we are only judging moves, not the level of internal kung fu. Second, the trial shall take place on these two pine trees – whoever falls first, loses. Third, if one of you strikes too hard and hurts your young opponent, then your side must concede this trial."

"I lose if I injure him?" Count Seven Hong asked.

"That's right. Do you think either of them could fight one of our martial greats and come away unscathed? So, Brother Seven, for example, if you so much as scratch Master Ouyang, then your side loses. Same for Brother Viper, here. One of the young masters will be my son-in-law. How can I let him come to harm?"

"That's a rule unheard of in the martial world." Count Seven Hong scratched his head with a laugh. "Our Heretic is living up to his eccentric reputation. But if it's fairly judged, I'll play along."

Apothecary Huang invited the four men to take their positions. Count Seven Hong and Gallant Ouyang leapt to the top of the tree on the right, while Viper Ouyang and Guo Jing took the one on the left. Count Seven was giggly and giddy, the other three solemn and grave.

Lotus Huang was desperate to help Guo Jing, but what could she do against a master like Viper Ouyang? Moreover, injured as he was,

Gallant Ouyang was still the superior martial artist and his lightness *qinggong* kung fu was exceptional.

"The trial begins on the count of three," she heard her father announce. "Master Ouyang, Master Guo, whoever touches the ground first loses this round. Ready? Three, two, one!"

A blur of shadows danced up and down the trees. In the twinkling of an eye, Guo Jing had exchanged more than a dozen moves with Viper Ouyang.

Lotus could hardly believe her eyes. When had his kung fu improved so much? He's not struggling at all!

Her father was equally surprised.

Growing irate, Viper Ouyang let his strength seep back into his strikes, hoping to send Guo Jing tumbling down quickly. Yet, the fear of injuring the young man held his aggression somewhat in check.

Leaping up, he charged at Guo Jing with a series of kicks, fast and relentless, like the wheels of a speeding chariot. Guo Jing fought back with a Dragon Soars in the Sky, jumping higher and higher as he sliced and hewed at Viper Ouyang's legs with his palms.

Lotus's heart was pounding. She could not bear to watch, so she glanced over at the other side.

Gallant Ouyang flitted around, darting up and down the branches, dodging Count Seven Hong's attacks with his lightness kung fu.

Annoyed by Gallant Ouyang's refusal to engage, Count Seven Hong looked over to check on Guo Jing.

My silly boy's matching the Venom, blow to blow, while this coward scurries around to kill time, Count Seven thought angrily. If you think you can defeat the Beggar with your little tricks, well, well . . .

He sprang high into the air, then swooped, his fingers extended like talons, aimed towards the crown of Gallant Ouyang's head.

This is not a sparring move. He's striking to kill!

Fearing for his life, Gallant Ouyang swerved to the right.

The fearsome dive turned out to be a feint and Gallant Ouyang reacted just as Count Seven Hong had anticipated.

With a twist of his waist, the Beggar changed course and landed at the tip of the branch beside Gallant Ouyang.

"I don't mind losing. Let's see if a ghost can find a bride!" He raised his hands to deliver the knockout blow.

Gallant Ouyang was already petrified by Count Seven Hong's physically impossible act of changing direction mid-air. Now, the Beggar had made his intentions clear with his words and his moves.

All the fight went out of the Master of White Camel Mount. He just wanted to run. He shrank back, forgetting he was standing on a tree branch – and plunged.

I've lost!

As that thought flashed across his mind, he sensed another weight rushing through the air.

Guo Jing had actually managed to resist Viper Ouyang's on-slaught for quite some time. Then a voice screamed in the Venom's mind: *You're no martial great if it takes you fifty moves to send a boy down a tree!*

Quick as lightning, Viper Ouyang darted forward and snatched at Guo Jing's collar.

"Down you go!"

Ducking, Guo Jing flung a backhand to block. A great strength rushed at him. "You—"

Before he could accuse the Venom, the energy was replaced by a smirk.

"Yes?"

Guo Jing had channelled everything he had into his defence. He thought Viper Ouyang was going to use the Exploding Toad kung fu and turn his inner organs into pulp.

Now, he pushed back at nothing, and he had yet to master the skill of pulling back his internal-energy flow at will.

Luckily, the Luminous Hollow Fist had given him a better grasp of the concept of "repent", of reserving strength. He narrowly avoided repeating his fate against Apothecary Huang at Roaming Cloud Manor. Only, this time, his shoulder, rather than his wrist, would have been dislocated. Even so, he was rocked off balance. He tipped forward and plunged, head first.

The two young men plummeted, side by side. One was about to land on his feet; the other seemed certain to crash on his head.

Gallant Ouyang congratulated himself on his luck, flung his arms out and pushed down on Guo Jing's airborne feet, both to send his rival down even faster and to leverage the moment of contact to slow his own fall.

"*Aiya!*" It was clear to Lotus that Guo Jing had lost.

Yet, somehow, with a heartbeat to spare, Guo Jing shot upwards, before her attention was caught by a loud thud.

Gallant Ouyang lay sprawled on the ground, while Guo Jing bobbed serenely on a branch.

How did Guo Jing do it? He was inches from crashing head first into the ground! She let out a very different *aiya!*

Count Seven Hong jumped down from his tree, roaring with laughter.

With a look as dark as cast iron, Viper Ouyang turned to Count Seven Hong and said, in a voice sharp and frosty, "Your disciple's mongrel kung fu is quite something. He's even well versed in Mongolian wrestling tricks!"

"Don't look at me!" Count Seven could barely speak through his chuckles. "That's not a martial skill I'm familiar with. I didn't teach him that."

When Gallant Ouyang had tried to break his fall by pushing down on Guo Jing's feet, he had left his own legs dangling in Guo Jing's face. Guo Jing had wrapped his arms around Gallant Ouyang's calves instinctively, yanking hard to hoist himself up.

A classic throwing technique in Mongolian wrestling, and one Guo Jing was familiar with long before he met the Six Freaks of the South, tumbling around the Mongolian steppe with his sworn brother, Tolui. And, in his teens, he had honed his skills under Genghis Khan's generals and master wrestlers, Jebe and Boroqul. These moves came as naturally to him as walking and eating.

And, because of this, even Guo Jing himself did not understand how he had won.

5

APOTHECARY HUANG SHOOK HIS HEAD IMPERCEPTIBLY AT THE result, certain that only a cruel twist of fate had allowed the dim-witted Guo Jing to emerge victorious.

"Master Guo wins the first trial. Brother Viper, be not troubled. With your nephew's solid learning, there is a chance to catch up in the second and third trials."

"We look forward to the next task," Viper Ouyang said.

"We will now move on to cultural subjects—"

"Pa, you're clearly biased," Lotus interrupted her father. "You promised it would be martial trials. Why are we doing cultural subjects now? What's the point of making Guo Jing go through this?" Her face settled into a sullen pout.

"What do you know? When martial skills reach an exceptional level, do you think we'll still be throwing punches and brawling like commoners? Do you think we would lower ourselves to stage demeaning spectacles, like a Duel for a Maiden?"

Lotus and Guo Jing exchanged a glance, remembering the snowy day when Mercy Mu and Yang Kang met at such a fight.

"For the second trial, I would like to invite our young masters to critique a tune that I will play."

Gallant Ouyang eyed Guo Jing with satisfaction. This country bumpkin clearly has no understanding of the harmonies created by silk and bamboo. This round is mine, for sure.

Viper Ouyang, however, suspected it would prove a trial of internal kung fu, and he knew how deep Guo Jing's inner strength ran, from their fight just moments ago.

If it came down to internal control, his nephew might not perform better than Guo Jing. The music might even aggravate his chest injury . . .

So, he said, "I fear our young men, here, aren't learned enough to appreciate your music. May I ask—?"

"There is nothing to worry about, Brother Viper. The tune is very ordinary; I am not testing their internal strength." He turned to Guo Jing and Gallant Ouyang. "Please take a switch of bamboo and beat time to the music I play. Whoever does better shall win this trial."

Guo Jing stepped forward and bowed deeply. "Lord Huang, I am completely ignorant in matters of music and rhythm. Allow me to admit defeat now."

Count Seven Hong jumped in before Apothecary Huang could reply. "Hey, not so hasty! If you're going to lose anyway, what harm is there in trying? Are you afraid of being laughed at?"

Guo Jing would not dream of disagreeing with his *shifu*, so he copied Gallant Ouyang and plucked a bamboo branch.

"Brother Viper and Brother Seven, forgive my rusty playing." Apothecary Huang put the jade *xiao* to his lips. A mellow, graceful sound wafted forth. Ordinary flute song, as if played by an ordinary person without internal kung fu training.

Gallant Ouyang grasped the metre instantly, striking each beat perfectly in time.

Guo Jing's switch simply hovered in the air. He gazed skywards at nothing in particular.

Apothecary Huang kept on playing. If they were drinking tea, by now they would have savoured one whole pot. Still Guo Jing had not figured out what to do.

The Ouyangs were growing confident that they would win this round, and probably the next too, if it was on a cultural subject as Apothecary Huang had promised.

Lotus tapped her left wrist anxiously, hoping Guo Jing would notice and follow her lead. But he continued to stare blankly into the sky, oblivious to everything happening around him.

At last, Guo Jing lifted his arm.

Tak! He struck right in between two beats.

Gallant Ouyang sniggered audibly – His first beat and it's already horribly off! – but it did not deter Guo Jing.

Tak! Once again, the bamboo branch marked the quaver instead of the beat.

Tak, tak, tak, tak!

Four more attempts. All hitting that awkward in-between point. All of them wrong.

It's really unfair of Papa to make Guo Jing do this! He doesn't know a thing about music, Lotus grumbled to herself.

If she could not help Guo Jing win, maybe she could do something to disrupt the trial? Papa would have to accept a draw then.

As she turned over ideas in her head, she noticed a look of surprise on her father's face, and she thought she heard the flute song falter, almost imperceptibly.

Guo Jing continued to thrash his bamboo twig. Each time, he was off the mark. First he pre-empted the beat, then he lagged behind. Sometimes he would strike too fast, sometimes too slow.

In his musical ignorance, he had decided he was supposed to unsettle and disrupt the *xiao*, thinking of the musical melee earlier, between the flute, the zither and the whistle.

With the tactics he had gleaned from the previous sonic tussle, Guo Jing gradually grasped the song's pulse as he beat the branch against a dry bamboo stalk.

Tak, tak, tak!

A hollow, rasping dissonance.

So persistent and unmusical was the noise, it managed to pierce Apothecary Huang's concentration. Several times, Guo Jing almost succeeded in dragging the melody off track to follow the racket he was making. Count Seven Hong and Viper Ouyang looked on in amazement.

Impressed, Apothecary Huang took on the challenge. He dropped his tempo, and the tune became sensual and alluring.

By now, Gallant Ouyang had lost the ability to beat time. Losing control of his body, he waved his bamboo switch as he danced to the flute song. Viper Ouyang gripped his nephew's wrist with a sigh and blocked his ears with a silk handkerchief. He waited until the young man's pulse had slowed before letting him go.

Lotus had grown up listening to her father playing the "Ode to the Billowing Tide". He had also explained its complexities and variations. That understanding allowed her to be on the same plane as him, so the music had no effect on her. But she knew its power and she was worried for Guo Jing.

The song began as a perfectly calm sea, undisturbed by even the gentlest ripple. Then, the tide crept closer, the water moved faster, churning and frothing. The once gleaming mirror now splintered into white spray and snowy crests.

Fish leapt, gulls swooped, the wind howled. Water sprites and sea monsters stole forth as the tide swelled. Icebergs drifted by. The sea boiled, bubbling and steaming.

Mermen and mermaids frolicked in the undertow, intermingling, embracing, their lovemaking more arousing and sensual than it could ever be on land.

As the tide receded, a dark current prowled unseen beneath the calm surface, tugging, pulling with each ebb and flow, ensnaring its heedless listeners.

Guo Jing sat cross-legged on the ground. He summoned his Quanzhen-trained internal kung fu to resist the music. It also helped him keep his arm moving, bashing the bamboo branch crudely in his arrhythmical way, to disrupt the flute song.

When Apothecary Huang, Viper Ouyang and Count Seven Hong competed, they were able to attack and defend at the same time. They could keep their minds and hearts at peace and in focus while still searching for cracks and fissures in their opponents' composure.

Needless to say, Guo Jing was a novice. He was not skilled enough to hold his spirit still and keep his senses open to scan for flaws in the Heretic's musical attack. He simply kept guard and his defence strong, while causing enough chaos to hold Apothecary Huang back.

The Heretic, by now, had shifted the tone of his flute song several times. Still, he could not force Guo Jing into submission. Once more, he changed tack, playing so softly that the tune was barely audible.

Guo Jing strained to hear the notes. Soon, the branch began to fall in time to the music. The song was most alluring when it was played softly.

Fearful he would fall prey to the music's snare, Guo Jing split his concentration in two, using the Competing Hands technique. With his left hand, he whipped off his shoe and slapped it against the bamboo stalk.

Dok, dok, dok!

Most martial masters would be hopelessly caught by now. There's more to this boy than meets the eye, Apothecary Huang thought, as he began to pace in the formation of the Eight Trigrams.

Thanks to the noise made by his shoe, Guo Jing managed to wrench his right hand back under his control. Now, it sounded as if two masters had joined forces against Apothecary Huang, as each hand beat its own rhythm.

Tak, tak, tak!

Dok, dok, dok!

Tak, tak, tak!

Dok, dok, dok!

The din Guo Jing was ratcheting up grinded abrasively against the metre of the *xiao* music.

Both Count Seven Hong and Viper Ouyang had secretly increased their *neigong* engagement to maintain their focus. It would be deeply embarrassing if they showed any outward sign of trying to resist the music, and their reputations would be tarnished beyond repair if they were actually affected by it.

The flute darted from one extreme of its register to the other, the tune growing ever more unpredictable. Guo Jing soldiered on stubbornly.

Somehow, he felt the music as a gust of cold wind, plunging his body into a blizzard. He could not help but shiver and shake.

The *xiao*'s supple, sensual tone had tightened into a sharp, grating shrill. The sound made Guo Jing feel as if his bones had turned into ice. He immediately split his concentration further, bringing to mind the hot summer sun, a blistering forge in the midsummer heat, red hot coals in his hands, diving into a burning furnace. Soon, the chill retreated somewhat.

Now, the left half of Guo Jing trembled under the wintry sound and his right side sweated profusely under the heat he had conjured in his mind.

Apothecary Huang watched in astonishment and let the music take a new turn, a glorious summer dispelling the bleak winter. Guo Jing was once again seduced by the flute song and forced into tapping in time.

He can probably resist my music a little longer, but it will make him very ill. With that thought, Apothecary Huang held on to one note and let it dissipate into the bamboo forest.

Guo Jing exhaled in relief. He stood up, and his legs wobbled and almost buckled under his own weight. Once he had regulated his breathing, he approached Apothecary Huang and bowed low. "Lord Huang, I am most grateful for your forbearance." He knew the music was cut short out of consideration for his well-being.

"Put your shoe back on!" Lotus giggled.

"Oh! Yes." Only then did he realise he was still clutching his shoe in his left hand.

As Guo Jing struggled with his shoe, Apothecary Huang was beginning to question his decision. *Could the boy's stupidity be an act? He can't have attained such a level of kung fu at his age without an extraordinary intellectual capacity. Perhaps letting Lotus marry him wouldn't be such a bad idea?*

"Why do you still call me Lord Huang?" he said, with a smile.

It was his way of saying that Guo Jing had won two trials out of three, and could now call him father-in-law.

Guo Jing stammered, "I . . . I . . ."

Unsure how to respond, he looked to Lotus for help.

Beaming, she raised her right thumb and bent it up and down. Guo Jing fell to his knees and kowtowed four times.

Apothecary Huang chuckled. "What are you doing that for?"

"Lotus told me to."

He is a blockhead, after all! Apothecary Huang sighed and gestured at Gallant Ouyang to remove the silk handkerchief from his ears.

"In terms of internal kung fu, Master Guo is stronger. But we were testing musical knowledge and Master Ouyang's is far superior . . . I shall declare this trial a draw. The final trial shall determine who will win my daughter's hand."

"Yes, let's move on to the last test," Viper Ouyang said. He knew his nephew had lost twice, but Apothecary Huang was giving him a final chance.

She's your daughter, you can marry her to that cad if you want; it's nobody else's business, Count Seven Hong thought, seething at the unfair treatment. I can't fight the two of you alone, but I'm not going to let this rest. I'll get King Duan to help.

6

"MY WIFE AND I ONLY HAD THIS ONE DAUGHTER BEFORE SHE tragically passed away during labour. I am honoured that both Brother Viper and Brother Seven are here, seeking her hand. If my wife were still with us, I have no doubt she would be overjoyed."

Lotus Huang wiped her eyes at the mention of her mother.

Apothecary Huang then carefully retrieved a hand-bound volume with a tattered cover from inside his shirt.

"This book was written in my wife's hand. She put her lifeblood into it. It was lost for a long time, but it found its way back to me recently. This is the most valuable object I possess. I now ask our young masters to read it once, together. I shall give my daughter's hand to the one who can remember the most and recite the text with the fewest mistakes."

He paused and glanced at Count Seven Hong. "It is true that Master Guo is one round ahead, but this volume has played an important role in my life. My wife died for it. I am hoping her soul in the heavens will select her son-in-law and help her chosen one win."

"Enough of your hogwash, Heretic! You know full well that my disciple, here, isn't the brightest and he knows nothing about books and poetry. Yet you want him to memorise a book, even dragging your dead wife out as an excuse! Have you no shame?" Count Seven Hong flicked his sleeve and stormed off.

"Brother Seven, if you came here to show your temper, I fear you are in need of a few more years of learning," Apothecary Huang sneered.

Count Seven turned, with his eyebrows raised. "What do you mean? Are you threatening to hold me captive?"

"You have no knowledge of the arts of the Mysterious Gates and the Five Elements. You will never find your way out without my permission."

"I'll raze your stinking island to the ground."

"You can try!"

I can't let *Shifu* come to harm or be stuck here because of me! Guo Jing stepped boldly forward. "Lord Huang, *Shifu*, I shall take part in this final trial. I am not bright and I will most likely lose. So be it."

In Guo Jing's mind, once he had helped Count Seven Hong get away, he could turn to the sea. He and Lotus could trust their fates to the waves and swim until they had no strength left.

"Fine! If you want to be humiliated, be my guest!"

Count Seven was quibbling with the Heretic on purpose, to create an opportunity for the three of them to make a break for the shore. They could deal with the ramifications once they had sailed away. But his calculations had not factored in how stubbornly honourable his disciple would prove to be. And now there really was nothing to be done.

"Sit down properly. No more tricks," Apothecary Huang said to Lotus.

Still sulking, she ignored him. She could tell from the way he had brought up her mother, this last trial would be decisive. He clearly intended to disregard Guo Jing's two wins. Even if he decided to take all three tests into account, when this next one was done, it would mean both Guo Jing and Gallant Ouyang had won one trial each. Then he no doubt would invent another test, and another, until that loathsome man came out on top. If only she could find a way to escape from the island with Guo Jing . . .

By now, Apothecary Huang had Gallant Ouyang and Guo Jing sitting side by side on a boulder. He sat down opposite them and held out the book.

It was worn and weathered from years of use and rough handling. The once-white paper had yellowed, its corners and edges were dog-eared and creased. The words were obscured by smudges from hands and spots of water damage. Was it tears or tea? And the blots of purplish black – were they blood?

Gallant Ouyang saw the cover and his heart leapt with excitement. The Nine Yin Manual! Father-in-Law clearly cares for me; why else would he offer me a glimpse of this most coveted book?

Who can read these tadpole scribbles? Guo Jing stared at the title calligraphy written in curvilinear seal script. I know he wants me to lose. I'll admit defeat, anyway.

Apothecary Huang turned to the first page. The paper showed signs of having been recently repaired. The handwriting, in the much more legible regular script, was slender and elegant. The penmanship of a woman.

Guo Jing's heart hammered as he read the opening line:

It is the heavens' Way to take away from excess and to supplement when in absence, such is how the immaterial beats the material and how absence trumps excess.

This is one of Brother Zhou's phrases! He cast his eyes over the rest of the page. Every sentence matched exactly with words he had recently learned by heart.

After a moment, Apothecary Huang turned the page. Guo Jing was once more greeted by words Zhou Botong had instructed him to memorise:

The weak overcomes the strong, the supple conquers the firm. Everyone under the heavens knows it, though no-one can put it into practice.

He read on.

The most supple under the heavens can gallop through the toughest.

There were several characters he did not know on this page, but those he recognised corresponded exactly with his sworn brother's words.

Did Brother Zhou teach me this book? It had never occurred to Guo Jing that the Hoary Urchin's martial theory could be someone else's invention. How come Lord Huang has a copy? How would Madam Huang choose her son-in-law through it? He stared blankly at the familiar words, perplexed by these questions.

Apothecary Huang assumed the complicated content had set Guo Jing's head spinning. Ignoring Guo Jing's dazed inattention, the Lord of Peach Blossom Island turned the leaves at his own pace, slowly and steadily.

In the beginning, Gallant Ouyang had felt rather pleased by what he could remember, but soon he was utterly lost. The text was steeped in Taoist jargons and *neigong* theory, and he knew nothing about the religion, its philosophy or its martial concepts. He recognised every character on the page, but, strung together, they made no sense. He could not even commit half a phrase to memory.

Strength courses through the fingers, no matter can stand in their way. Shattering the skull of the enemy, as if clawing through rotten earth.

He paused at this line in despair. What on earth does that mean? The Nine Yin Manual is incomprehensible!

He looked over at the dumbstruck Guo Jing. Still, I'll remember more than that halfwit. I'm going to win this trial, for sure!

Reassured, he turned to his future bride in triumph.

Lotus stuck her tongue out and pulled a face. "Do you remember Mercy? My friend you abducted? You left her in a coffin in that ancestral temple. Did you know she suffocated? She came to me in a dream last night, her hair unkempt, her face bloody. She's coming for you."

"I forgot to let her out!" Gallant Ouyang muttered. Such a shame, she was a pretty young thing. Then, seeing Lotus's grin, he grew suspicious. "How do you know? You freed her, didn't you?"

"Focus!" Viper Ouyang growled. It was obvious that Lotus was trying to distract his nephew.

"Yes, Uncle." Gallant Ouyang turned back to the text.

Guo Jing had stopped reading. Every sentence he had seen so far corresponded, word for word, with Zhou Botong's theory, which he knew by heart. He stared at the trees instead, trying and failing to work out why.

Unable to decipher the script on the title page, Guo Jing had no idea he was reading the second volume of the Nine Yin Manual – the very same copy Cyclone Mei had returned to Apothecary Huang at Roaming Cloud Manor.

The Lord of Peach Blossom Island chose it because, without the internal-energy foundation explained in the first volume, it was impossible to understand the martial skills described. He did not mind Count Seven Hong gaining a few insights, but he did not wish to share anything that would allow Viper Ouyang to improve his kung fu.

Moreover, the second volume ended with a long, incomprehensible passage. After their encounter with Zhou Botong, his wife had transcribed this section the moment they returned to their room. He remembered how confident she was of her memory of the main text of the Manual, but she had revised this meaningless incantation again and again, doubting herself each time she looked at it. It was unlikely Gallant Ouyang would remember much after reading the Manual once through, and the little he could retain would surely deviate in important ways from what his wife had set down. So, even if he had one-tenth of her memory, whatever he repeated to his uncle in the future was unlikely to expand their martial knowledge.

Apothecary Huang kept turning the pages at a steady pace. Many of them were marred by smudges and fingerprints, which sometimes obscured the words entirely.

When they reached the final pages, Gallant Ouyang said, after glancing at the first line, "Uncle Huang, what is this '*mahaparas gatekras*' business? I can't make any sense of this page and there's no chance I can learn this."

"Do what you can. It is difficult for a reason – so your talent can shine through."

Hearing this exchange, Guo Jing looked at the page. It was that nonsensical passage that had robbed him of sleep and appetite for at least three days when he tried to learn it. And then he had persisted for another ten days, and eventually these one thousand or so characters became a part of him.

They reached the last page of the book. A final paragraph of meaningless characters, quotes from poems written in another hand. Apothecary Huang knew those words and the handwriting well. He had once copied those poems many times and he was the one who had shaped the calligraphy of the young woman who had recorded them here.

> *Our encounter was lodged in my heart then,*
> *And ever more so now.*

Then she wrote:

> *Waking after drinking, my gentle friend is gone.*
> *A thousand times,*
> *Whether wind or water, the current carries you away.*

Which was followed by:

> *Men aged, things changed.*
> *No desire to drink amid flowers as tears stain my clothes.*
> *Now I but wish for sleep with the door shut,*
> *Let the plum blossoms fly like snow.*

Then, at the very bottom, in characters lopsided and ill-formed: Shifu*, please kill me. I have wronged you. I want to die by your hand,* Shifu. Shifu!

Apothecary Huang had noticed how spotted with blood and tears the Nine Yin Manual was when Cyclone Mei returned it to him. A swell of pity swept away all the bitterness he had felt at her betrayal. Her writing brought back memories of how she used to take his hand and swing it lightly, left and right, calling, "*Shifu! Shifu!*"

Sighing, he remembered copying those lines by Ouyang Xiu and Zhu Xizhen. Then his eldest disciple, Tempest Qu had shared them with Cyclone Mei after finding them in his study.

She must have held these words close to her heart all these years. The brushwork was straight and powerful. She must have been able to see, back then.

Apothecary Huang was reminded of how he had stopped speaking to her after his marriage. Soon afterwards, her illicit romance with Hurricane Chen was discovered by Tempest Qu. His two eldest disciples had fought a bitter fight over their martial sister.

The rage and pain he felt was still fresh in his mind. He had cast Tempest off the island and ostracised Hurricane and Cyclone, refusing to teach them. He realised, now, that he had played a part in driving them to steal the Nine Yin Manual. Sympathy, tinged with guilt, nestled in his heart.

Apothecary Huang turned his eyes back to the present – Gallant Ouyang was still grappling with the *mahaparas* passage – and closed the volume. He did not want to show them Cyclone Mei's writing.

"Let's finish here. That strange passage is too hard." He studied the bewildered young men. "Who would like to go first?"

"I should like to give it a try," Gallant Ouyang answered immediately, knowing his best chance would be while his memory was fresh.

Nodding, Apothecary Huang turned to Guo Jing. "Head into the bamboo forest until you are out of earshot."

Guo Jing obediently put close to a hundred paces between himself and Gallant Ouyang. Lotus trailed after him quietly, thinking that this could be their chance to run away. Then she heard her father's voice.

"Lotus, sit here with me, so you can see I'm not biased."

"You are biased, and you know it."

"Where are your manners?" he replied in good humour. "Come, sit with me."

"I don't want to."

She knew that, with his eyes on her, they would not be able to run far. She walked slowly towards Gallant Ouyang and then asked, with a smile, "Master Ouyang, why do you like me so much?"

Dumbstruck, the normally eloquent young man broke into giggles and only managed to stammer, "My lady, you . . . you . . ."

"You mustn't hurry back to the Western Regions. Do stay on Peach Blossom Island for a few days. Is it very cold, out there?"

"The west is huge. Of course it is cold in many parts, but others are warm and sunny. Just like here, in the south."

"I don't believe you! You do love to trick people."

Before Gallant Ouyang could explain himself, Viper Ouyang intervened. "Save your prattle for later, child," he said, sharply.

Lotus's little interruption had caused Gallant Ouyang to forget a sizeable chunk of the text he had crammed into his head. He gathered his thoughts and began slowly. "'It is the heavens' Way to take away from excess and to supplement when in absence, such is how the immaterial beats the material and how absence trumps excess.'"

Gallant Ouyang's memory was impressive. He recited the opening lines precisely as they were written down, but once he got to the main content – complex Taoist internal-energy theories, to channel *qi* and balance yin and ying – he could only recall about a tenth of what he had read.

Whenever his memory faltered, Lotus would loudly proclaim, "No, you've got that wrong!"

Soon, her interjections were so frequent that he could barely get a word out. He gave up as he reached the final nonsensical passage, unable to remember a single character.

"Well done for remembering so much." Apothecary Huang smiled, then let his voice boom over the bamboo forest. "Master Guo, it's your turn."

Guo Jing surmised from Gallant Ouyang's grin that he must be pleased with his performance.

He must be extremely clever to remember so much. I'll just recite the text I learned from Brother Zhou, he told himself as he walked back. It's bound to be wrong, but what else can I do?

"We might as well admit defeat now," Count Seven said. "Why make a fool of yourself, my silly boy?"

At the same time, Lotus tapped her foot and leapt up onto the roof of the pavilion. She flicked her wrist, flashing a dagger, which she pressed tight against her chest.

"Pa, if you force me to go with that lecher to the west, then I will die here today."

"Do put that away – we can talk," Apothecary Huang said, knowing she might go through with it.

Viper Ouyang touched his staff on the ground and – *whoosh!* – a dart of an unusual shape flew from its head.

Before Lotus could make out what was flying at her, the dagger was knocked from her hand.

Apothecary Huang leapt onto the roof and said, softly, "If you don't want to get married, I don't mind at all." He put his arm around her shoulders. "You know I'd love nothing more than to have your company on Peach Blossom Island always."

"You don't love me! You don't love me!" she cried, stamping her feet.

Count Seven Hong was shaking with laughter. Apothecary Huang – the martial great who dominated the lakes and the seas, the murderous monster who killed without remorse – had been gagged and bound by his young daughter's tantrum.

Viper Ouyang watched with interest Apothecary Huang's futile efforts to appease Lotus. *Once we've won her hand and sent the Beggar and that boy on their way, we can deal with her moods easily enough. What's the point of fussing over a little girl's tears?*

Deciding to take matters into his own hands, he said, "Our young master Guo has superb kung fu and exceptional internal energy. An example for the younger generation. I am sure his memory is outstanding. Shall we invite him to demonstrate?"

"Indeed, Master Ouyang," Apothecary Huang replied. Then he turned back to Lotus. "You do realise your temper is spoiling young Master Guo's concentration."

Lotus at once quietened down.

"Young Master Guo, please do begin. We are beside ourselves with anticipation." Viper Ouyang was eager to see him shamed.

I suppose I don't have a choice, Guo Jing thought, bright red with embarrassment. *I'll just recite what Brother has taught me.*

So he began. The words poured out, without pause or hesitation.

"'It is the heavens' Way to take away from excess and to supplement when in absence . . .'"

After all, he had repeated these very words out loud several hundred times under Zhou Botong's instruction.

A few lines in, everyone was flabbergasted. The same thought flashed across the minds of both Apothecary Huang and the Ouyangs: they'd been fooled! The boy was not as he seemed!

Lotus and Count Seven knew Guo Jing could not have memorised the text just now, but they were too happy to question how he had ended up learning the Nine Yin Manual by heart.

In one breath, Guo Jing had reached the fourth page of the

Manual. Apothecary Huang checked against his copy and was astounded to find that he had got every word right. Even those lines smudged by blood, water and sweat, scratched by sand and disfigured by rough handling when Hurricane Chen and Cyclone Mei had struggled with their training.

More remarkable still was that the words rolling off Guo Jing's tongue were connected, logical and complete. The young man even filled in the missing characters from the quotes from Laozi's *Classic of the Way and Virtue* and Zhuangzi's *Classic of Southern Florescence*, which his wife had not set down in full.

Apothecary Huang could feel his heart skip a beat and a cold sweat dampen his robe.

Are you speaking to me through this youth, my dear? Did you remember every word of the Manual once you reached the next world and somehow pass it on to him?

Guo Jing's voice rang in his ears, enunciating clearly every word in the Manual. Even the garbled nonsense in the last section flowed like running water.

"I know you are sharing the Manual with me through this boy, Astra. Will you let me see you? I play the flute for you every night. Can you hear it?" Apothecary Huang spoke quietly into the sky. He was convinced that his wife had made her choice.

Now, everyone's eyes were fixed on the Lord of Peach Blossom Island, perplexed by the change in his countenance. They could see that he was mumbling, his eyes glinting with tears, but they did not realise he was talking to his late wife.

The vacant look on Apothecary Huang's face was eventually replaced by a fierce and frosty glare.

"You studied the Nine Yin Manual when it was in Cyclone Mei's possession, did you not?" He barked the accusation in Guo Jing's face.

"I was captured by her . . . She was going to strangle me to avenge her husband, but she needed me. She couldn't walk and so she made me carry her around. I acted as her legs so she could fight that night at the Jin Prince's residence. She didn't show me the Manual and I've never set eyes on it," Guo Jing said, alarmed by the malice in Apothecary Huang's eyes.

From the young man's panicked expression, it was clear to Apothecary Huang that Guo Jing was telling the truth. He also knew that Guo Jing's version was more complete than the volume he held, especially when it came to the strange concluding passage. His wife must have recovered her memory of the Manual, now that she had passed into the spirit realm.

Under normal circumstances, the rational and learned Apothecary Huang would not have believed something so outlandish as the deceased sharing knowledge with the living. But so in love was the Heretic and so devastated had he been by her premature death, he persuaded himself that his wife had spoken, that she had chosen her son-in-law.

Torn between joy and grief, he declared, "Brother Seven and Brother Viper, my late wife has made her choice and I will not dispute her decision. Son, I am giving you my daughter's hand. Please look after her. I have spoiled Lotus, and I hope you will indulge her whims."

"Hey, I'm not spoiled!" Lotus said with a giggle, ecstatic that she had her way at last.

This time without prompting, Guo Jing fell to his knees and kowtowed.

"Thank you, Father!"

CHAPTER TEN

INTO
THE WAVES

I

"WAIT!" GALLANT OUYANG STEPPED FORWARD.

"What do you want now? You think you lost unfairly?" Though exasperated by this interruption, Count Seven Hong was still grinning from ear to ear at Guo Jing's bookish talent. He could never have predicted the result of the third trial. Even if his silly disciple sent the Venom's nephew tumbling another dozen times, he would not be as shocked as he was now.

"Brother Guo recalled more than what was recorded in the book," Gallant Ouyang explained. "He must have set eyes on the original Nine Yin Manual. Forgive my impertinence, but I should like to search him."

"Don't you remember what your uncle said about losing?" Count Seven retorted. "Lord Huang has chosen his son-in-law. Why are you making trouble?"

Viper Ouyang rolled his eyes. "The Ouyangs won't be played for fools!"

To the Venom, the Nine Yin Manual was far more important than any marriage. If his nephew suspected Guo Jing had the original Manual, then he must get to the bottom of it.

Back on his feet again, Guo Jing undid the belt fastening his shirt and pulled it open. "Master Ouyang, you are welcome to search me."

He removed every object on his person and laid them on a boulder. A handful of silver pieces, a handkerchief, flint and tinder, and some other personal items.

Snorting with contempt, Viper Ouyang reached out to pat Guo Jing down. He was planning to strike Guo Jing in the abdomen with his Exploding Toad kung fu, leaving an injury that would lie dormant for three years before it claimed his life.

But, before he laid his hands on the young man, he heard Apothecary Huang cough, and saw that the Heretic's left hand was hovering over the back of Gallant Ouyang's neck. If Viper Ouyang went ahead with his attack, Apothecary Huang could retaliate by crushing his nephew's spine.

Count Seven Hong could barely suppress a giggle at Apothecary Huang's reaction. *Now my silly disciple is his son-in-law, the Heretic goes out of his way to protect him. Well, I guess I can't call him silly, with a memory like that.*

After a thorough search, Viper Ouyang could find nothing on Guo Jing other than the clothes on his back. He did not for one moment believe Apothecary Huang's superstitious hogwash about his dead wife choosing her son-in-law, however. His nephew's explanation made much more sense.

Pinning the young man down with his glare, Viper Ouyang throttled his staff once more. Golden rings jangled at its head and a metal covering flipped up to reveal two small holes, from which two serpents slithered out and curled themselves around the shaft.

Lotus and Guo Jing both took a step back.

"Guo Jing." Viper Ouyang's voice had taken on a higher pitch. "Where did you learn the contents of the Nine Yin Manual?"

"I've never set eyes on the Nine Yin Manual. Brother Zhou Botong told me—"

"You call Zhou Botong 'brother'? Have you met him?" Count Seven interrupted.

"He is my sworn brother."

Count Seven burst out laughing. "That's absurd! He's decades older than you."

Viper Ouyang continued his line of questioning. "Twice Foul Dark Wind stole the second volume of the Nine Yin Manual and Hurricane Chen died by your hand. You took the Manual from him, did you not?"

"I beg your pardon, sir – I was only six years of age at the time and had not learned how to read. I knew nothing of the Manual and took nothing from him."

"You claim to have never set eyes on the Manual, but you just recited the text in full. Explain yourself!" There was an edge of impatience to Viper Ouyang's voice.

"I didn't recite the Nine Yin Manual. It was a text I learned from Brother Zhou. A martial theory he invented. He told me no disciple of the Quanzhen Sect is allowed to learn the Manual's kung fu. His martial brother Double Sun Wang Chongyang gave that decree before he passed away."

Apothecary Huang sighed. *How silly of me not to have thought of Zhou Botong! After all, he is the custodian of the Manual and he's been stuck in his little cave all these years. What was there to do but read the Manual, over and over again? I should have known it wasn't a power beyond this world that taught it to the boy. Perhaps this coincidence is a sign that Lotus and this boy are fated to be married?*

"Where is Zhou Botong now?"

Viper Ouyang's question brought Apothecary Huang back to the present. "Brother Viper, Brother Seven, we haven't seen each other for many years. I propose we drink and feast together for the next three days."

"*Shifu*, I'll cook for you," Lotus added. "Our lotuses are exceptional. I'll make you steamed chicken with lotus petals, as well as water caltrop and lotus leaf soup – you'll love them."

"Look how happy you are, now that you've got your way," Count Seven replied, with a teasing glint in his eyes.

It was true. Now that her wish had come true, she felt a warmth towards the whole world. Even Gallant Ouyang seemed a little less repulsive.

"*Shifu*," she said, with a radiant smile, "Uncle Ouyang and Brother Ouyang, please follow us."

Viper Ouyang put his hands together and bowed. "Brother Apothecary, I thank you for your hospitality, but it is time for us to leave."

It was the Nine Yin Manual that had enticed Viper Ouyang into travelling thousands of *li* to Peach Blossom Island. When he received Gallant Ouyang's letter about Lotus Huang, in which he also mentioned that the Manual was in the hands of a blind woman who was a former disciple of Apothecary Huang, he reasoned that, if their families were joined, he would be gifted a chance to take the Manual for himself. But now their suit had failed, with all hope of obtaining the Manual in this way extinguished, there was no point in staying any longer.

"Brother Viper, you have come such a long way; do allow me to play the host for a few days."

"Uncle, I am sorry I failed to win the lady's hand, but Uncle Huang did say that he would teach me some kung fu," Gallant Ouyang said.

Viper Ouyang sighed. He should have known the lad would not give up so easily. No doubt he was looking for an excuse to spend more time with the girl in order to seduce her.

Feeling a little sorry for Gallant Ouyang, Apothecary Huang said, "Young Master Ouyang, your uncle's kung fu is peerless. Few of us can even dream of attaining such heights. You don't need to look to outsiders for martial guidance. However, I have managed to acquire a smattering of wayward knowledge. If you don't find them too lowly, pick a subject. I shall teach you everything I know."

Gallant Ouyang considered his offer. I should ask for something that will take the longest to learn, so I get to spend more time with Lotus . . .

He bowed deeply and said, "I have long admired Uncle Huang's insights into the Five Elements and the Mysterious Gates. I would be most honoured if Uncle were willing to share his knowledge."

Now, it was Apothecary Huang's turn to pause. Gallant Ouyang coveted the secrets of his proudest scholarly achievement. Not only was he well versed in the literature of the field, Apothecary Huang had also developed his own interpretations and made his own discoveries. He had shared but a morsel of his knowledge with his daughter; how could he pass it on to a stranger? Yet, he had given his word, and his word was his bond.

At last he spoke: "There is much to impart concerning the Mysterious Gates. Which area interests you?"

"I am awed by the intricacy of Peach Blossom Island's layout. I hope Uncle will grant me permission to stay here for a few months to study and experience the immense wisdom behind its planning," Gallant Ouyang said, thrilled at the thought of spending so much time with Lotus.

Apothecary Huang glanced at Viper Ouyang. Is this the Venom's doing? What is he planning?

Viper Ouyang noticed this flicker of concern and turned to his nephew. "You ask too much. The topography of Peach Blossom Island is Brother Apothecary's life's work and the key to its defences. How can he share such secrets?"

"No-one could cause me harm, even if this island were a slab of bare rock," Apothecary Huang sneered.

"Of course, I let my tongue run away with me. My apologies," Viper Ouyang said, though his words carried little conviction.

Count Seven Hong chuckled. "Old Venom, I don't think your goading has had the desired effect."

Apothecary Huang stuffed the *xiao* flute down the back of his shirt. "Please follow me to my study," he said tersely.

Alarmed, Gallant Ouyang looked to his uncle, unsure what to do. Receiving the slightest nod of affirmation, he trailed after his host.

The group meandered through the bamboo grove for some time,

until, suddenly, a vista opened up onto a lotus pond. Large white blossoms stood tall and proud over rippling green leaves. Floating on the surface of the water, they suffused the air with a light fragrance.

They followed Apothecary Huang across the pool on a narrow stone causeway and arrived at a handsome, rustic hut. It was constructed from unpeeled pine logs and entangled in vines, and the sight of it alone seemed to cool the midsummer air. Once they entered the study, mute servants came forward with tea that was jade green in colour, ice cold to the touch and refreshing to the core.

Count Seven Hong admired the surroundings and said, with a smile, "We all know the saying, 'Three years a beggar, you yearn no more for rank.' If I lived here in your magical world for three years, Brother Apothecary, I bet I would yearn no more for my beggar's life!"

"Brother Seven, I would love nothing more than to have you on the island. We can drink and talk!"

"That would be agreeable indeed." Count Seven Hong was touched by the earnest invitation. "Sadly, I am born to toil, though I wish I could live in such peace and tranquillity, like you, Brother Apothecary."

"I am certain you two would create some extraordinary martial techniques, if you managed to spend a month or two together without falling out," Viper Ouyang added.

"Are you jealous?" Count Seven laughed.

"No, not at all. There is nothing more wonderful than serving and bringing glory to the martial arts," Viper Ouyang said.

"Well, well, are we speaking in opposites again?" Count Seven replied.

Viper Ouyang smiled. He would remain on good terms with the Beggar and the Heretic until he was confident he had the ability to defeat them with just one move.

Apothecary Huang pressed his hand against the edge of his desk and an ink-wash landscape painting on the western wall lifted, revealing a hidden cupboard, from which he reverently removed a scroll. He stroked it gently before turning to Gallant Ouyang. "This scroll contains the plans to Peach Blossom Island. Every single build-ing, path, trap, gateway and door is marked on here, with notes on how they relate to the Five Elements, yin and yang, and the Eight Trigrams. Take it and learn from it."

Bowing, Gallant Ouyang reached out to accept the map with both hands as disappointment spread through him. His hopes of staying on Peach Blossom Island – staying close to Lotus – had been dashed.

"Wait!" Apothecary Huang barked.

Gallant Ouyang jerked his hands back.

"You must stay in Lin'an while this map is in your possession. Three months from now, I will send someone to retrieve it. You may only learn the content by heart. You must not copy any portion of the map or let anyone else set eyes on it."

I'm only interested in your trifling knowledge so I can be near your daughter, Gallant Ouyang grumbled to himself. Now, you want me to hang on to this scroll for three months and vouch for its safety? This is a rotten deal!

As Gallant Ouyang deliberated over how to refuse, it occurred to him that Apothecary Huang would most likely send his daughter to collect the map.

Now, that would be a chance to get close to her! Eagerly, he reached out again and thanked Apothecary Huang for his generosity.

Lotus Huang held out the amulet of rhinoceros horn and earth dragon. "Uncle Ouyang, I don't think I should keep this treasure."

Viper Ouyang hesitated for a moment – It's miserly to take back a gift, but I can't let the Heretic keep an antidote to my poisons – then grabbed it. Then he raised his hands to bid them farewell.

Apothecary Huang did not entreat him to stay, as was the custom of the age. He simply accompanied the Ouyangs out of the study.

Count Seven Hong followed them to the door. "Brother Viper, remember we agreed to meet again at the summit of Mount Hua in twenty-five years? That date is soon upon us. Look after yourself. We shall fight to our heart's content, this time."

"I don't think any of us need compete." Viper Ouyang smiled faintly. "The title of the Greatest Martial Master Under the Heavens has been taken."

"Has my Brother Viper invented some indomitable technique?"

"I know my skills are paltry. I could not hope to gain such a title." The curious smile was still painted on Viper Ouyang's face. "I am talking about the Master who taught our Master Guo."

"Well, this Beggar does dream about winning the title, I won't deny it. But, with our Brother Apothecary's ever improving skills and your sprightly old age – and I'm sure King Duan hasn't been idling away the years in his palace – I doubt I'd stand a chance."

"Of all the masters who have taught our Master Guo, I fear Brother Seven might not be the most accomplished one."

"What—?"

"You mean Zhou Botong the Hoary Urchin?" Apothecary Huang cut in.

"Indeed! The Urchin clearly knows the Nine Yin Manual inside out. I fear none of us – not the Heretic, not the Venom, not the King, not the Beggar – will ever be his match."

"I would not be so sure," Apothecary Huang said. "The Manual is but words on paper. Martial arts live in the body."

2

VIPER OUYANG HAD NOTICED THAT APOTHECARY HUANG quickly changed the subject away from Zhou Botong's whereabouts when he was questioning Guo Jing. The Heretic must be hiding something to do with this wayward member of the Quanzhen Sect. He was determined to find all there was to know.

Thanks to Count Seven Hong's dry, arched comments, he had been able to turn their parting conversation back to the Hoary Urchin. And, as predicted, Apothecary Huang's pride led him to take the bait.

"The Quanzhen Sect's kung fu is exceptional and we have all

experienced it first hand," Viper Ouyang said, seizing the chance to push Apothecary Huang further. "Now, the Hoary Urchin can combine what he already knows with the kung fu set down in the Nine Yin Manual. I dare say, even if Wang Chongyang came back to life, he wouldn't be able to defeat his little martial brother. As for us? Even less likely."

He threw the last few words out casually, then paused to let them sink in.

"Well, perhaps it is the Quanzhen Sect's turn to prosper."

Another pause, then a sigh.

"We three toil all our lives. Yet, in the end, we lose out by failing to foresee this turn of events."

Apothecary Huang said immediately, "Even if the Hoary Urchin's kung fu was better than mine, he still could not surpass our Brother Viper and Brother Seven, here. This I know for a fact."

"You are too modest, Brother Apothecary. We have always been equals. You speak as though you know, without a doubt, that Zhou Botong cannot defeat you. This, I fear . . ."

Viper Ouyang shook his head and let his words hang in the air.

"You shall find out at the Contest of Mount Hua," Apothecary Huang said.

"Thinking of it, it has been years since I last heard about the Urchin. Perhaps news of his antics did not reach the remote corner I call home. Do you happen to know his whereabouts these days?" Viper Ouyang paused and then added, "And, Brother Huang, you know I have always had the greatest admiration for your kung fu. And yet – if I may be blunt – when you say he is not your match, I must admit I am not entirely convinced. I don't think we should take anything for granted."

Apothecary Huang knew Viper Ouyang was goading him into revealing more about Zhou Botong, but his pride would not let such a slight pass.

"The Hoary Urchin is on Peach Blossom Island. He has been my prisoner for fifteen years."

Count Seven Hong raised his eyebrows in surprise, but Viper Ouyang just laughed. "Don't pull our legs, Brother Huang."

Beckoning everyone to follow him, Apothecary Huang flew into the bamboo grove as if he were airborne, so light and quick were his steps. Count Seven Hong raced along with equally remarkable *qing-gong*, carrying Guo Jing with his left arm and Lotus with his right. Viper Ouyang, taking his nephew by the arm, brought up the rear.

Though Zhou Botong's cave was a fair distance from the study and the way was full of twists and turns, it only took a moment for them to reach it.

"Hmm?" Apothecary Huang muttered under his breath, surprised to find the cave empty. He tapped the ground lightly, gliding up and floating forward, as if he were weightless. A few more similar leaps brought him to the mouth of the cave.

He touched down with his left foot. The ground gave way beneath him.

A right kick, mid-air. It changed his downward motion into a forward thrust, propelling him into the cave.

He landed on his left foot once more. Another hollow.

There was no momentum left in his body to counter gravity. So, in a fluid backhand move, he drew the jade flute from the back of his collar. Holding it horizontal, he touched its end lightly against the cave wall.

Out he shot. Fast as an arrow.

In the blink of an eye, Apothecary Huang had slipped in and out of the cave.

Count Seven Hong and Viper Ouyang cheered his elegant, lightning-fast reflexes, but at that very moment – *plop!* – the martial Master plunged. Yet another hole. This time, outside the cave.

Apothecary Huang stepped on something a little moist and soft. But the ground was at last solid. He tapped with the tip of his toes and leapt once more into the air.

By now, everyone had gathered in front of the cave. He landed next to his daughter and an awful stench attacked his nostrils.

He looked down. His shoes were caked with faeces.

How could a martial master as quick-witted and agile as Apothecary Huang have fallen prey to such a prank?

Apothecary Huang snapped a branch from a nearby tree and prodded the ground. Only the three points he had stepped on had been dug out. He had to give Zhou Botong credit for predicting his movements so accurately. Only in the last trap had the Hoary Urchin emptied his bowels.

Apothecary Huang re-entered the cave. It was empty but for a few clay jars and bowls. Then he noticed a faint message written on the wall.

Laughing silently at Apothecary Huang's misfortune, Viper Ouyang rushed inside to see what he was studying so intently. To the Venom's mind, the contents of this cave, even something as minor as a needle or a thread, could determine whether he would at last be able to lay his hands on the Nine Yin Manual. Time was of the essence and he could not afford to be complacent.

Tiny words were carved on the cave wall:

Old Heretic Huang, you shattered both my legs and held me captive here for fifteen years. I should have done the same to you; that would have made me feel better. But, when I thought about it, I decided to let it go. I am presenting you with a fragrant reminder of the Hoary Urchin instead. Please, please—

The rest of the text was obscured by a leaf.

Apothecary Huang peeled it off and immediately realised his mistake. It was attached to a thread. He heard it – and leapt to the left.

Seeing Apothecary Huang flinch, Viper Ouyang jumped to the right.

Bing bong! Bing bong! Several clay jars tumbled down from above, splashing urine onto the two men.

Count Seven Hong let out a belly laugh. "What an aroma!"

Apothecary Huang swore loudly at the indignity of it all, but Viper Ouyang just pulled a wry smile. Lotus ran back to the house for clean clothes, returning with an extra robe for Viper Ouyang.

Once he had changed into fresh clothes, Apothecary Huang examined the cave from top to bottom and left to right. No further ambushes. Where the leaf had been affixed, there were two lines of extremely small writing:

Never must this leaf be removed, or stinky piss shall pour forth from up high. Please heed this warning. Ignore at your peril.

Though angry, Apothecary Huang could not deny the humour of the set-up. Then it struck him.

The urine was still warm!

He rushed out of the cave.

"The Urchin can't have gone far. We'll find him."

It will be an intense fight when we do, Guo Jing thought.

But, before he could raise any objection, Count Seven grabbed him and pulled him along after Apothecary Huang, who was speeding towards the east of the island, with Viper Ouyang following close behind.

Soon, they spotted Zhou Botong strolling along at a leisurely pace.

Apothecary Huang raced ahead. In an instant, he was right behind Zhou Botong, aiming a palm at the Hoary Urchin's neck.

Zhou Botong sidestepped it with a nonchalant turn of his body, then spun to face Apothecary Huang. "You smell lovely!"

Apothecary Huang was shocked. The strike, swift and lethal, had contained the full force of his internal strength, accrued over a lifetime of martial practice. It was also fuelled by the humiliating treatment he had suffered in front of two of the world's most esteemed martial greats. The Hoary Urchin he knew could not have evaded it with such ease. He paused to appraise his opponent.

For no discernible reason, the Hoary Urchin had bound his hands over his chest. He seemed very pleased with himself and gave Apothecary Huang a big smile.

Guo Jing ran up to greet him. "Brother, Lord Huang is my father-in-law. We are all family now." He hoped the news would defuse the tension.

"Father-in-law? Why did you not listen to me? I told you the Heretic was cunning. And most eccentric. Do you think his daughter will be easy to live with? You're going to suffer until your dying day.

"My dear brother, I've told you before. You can do anything you want in this world, so long as you never take a wife. I warned you already.

"You haven't completed the marriage ceremony, have you? Well, what are you waiting for? Run for your life! Now! Hide! Far, far away! Somewhere so remote that she'll never find you, even if she searches for a lifetime . . ." Zhou Botong rambled on without realising Lotus had tiptoed up behind him.

"Brother Zhou, guess who's behind you?" she said.

He turned. No-one. Then he caught a glimpse of something hurtling towards him. Once again, he leaned sideways.

Pak! The soiled clothes hit the ground. A foul stench choked the air.

"Heretic, you broke my legs and kept me here for fifteen years. In return, I made you step in poo and poured some piss on your head. That's it. I've done right by you, haven't I?" Zhou Botong rocked back and forth, convulsing with laughter.

Apothecary Huang considered the Hoary Urchin's words. It was true that the ambush in the cave was insignificant compared to the suffering he had inflicted on Zhou Botong. He put his hands together in a gesture of respect. "Thank you, Brother Botong, for your generosity. I have wronged you all these years and I apologise. May I ask why your hands are tied?"

"The hermit has his reasons. The heavens' mysteries must not be revealed." Zhou Botong shook his head in dejection.

3

OVER THE YEARS, ZHOU BOTONG WAS TEMPTED MANY TIMES to leave the cave and challenge Apothecary Huang. But, each time, after careful consideration, he stopped himself.

His kung fu was not strong enough to defeat his gaoler. He would probably die in combat, or have his movement locked by his pressure points, leaving the cave – and the Nine Yin Manual – undefended. He could not let the Manual fall into that man's hands.

Though he had been held on Peach Blossom Island for fifteen years, Zhou Botong's disappearance did not cause alarm among his martial nephews, the Seven Immortals of the Quanzhen Sect. Familiar with their martial uncle's temperament, they assumed he was enjoying himself in some far-flung, secluded place. They knew, if he did not want to be found, no-one – mortal or immortal – would be able to locate him. It never occurred to them he could have been captured. The idea of mounting a search effort never crossed their minds.

Zhou Botong had only recognised the martial potential of the Competing Hands, a game he devised to alleviate the boredom of captivity, after Guo Jing had pointed it out. Now, he need not fear Apothecary Huang anymore. After all, who could deal with two Zhou Botongs at the same time? He could at last make the Heretic pay for the suffering he had endured since arriving on Peach Blossom Island. The only problem was, he had yet to settle on a plan.

When Guo Jing had left to investigate the snake formation, the night before, he was once more left alone in the cave. As usual, Apothecary Huang's flute song wreaked havoc in his mind, dredging up his past entanglements. This time, he was all the more disturbed by the competing tugs of the zither and the whistling. Then a thought intruded upon his struggle.

Why is Guo Jing not affected by the flute? His kung fu is far inferior!

Zhou Botong had asked himself that question the first night he met Guo Jing. Now, having spent some weeks with him, he knew the answer.

He has a childlike simplicity and openness. He's yet to learn all the strange, wonderful and troublesome emotions that bind men and women. "Strength grows when desire is weak." Why am I still obsessed with revenge? It's laughable to be so petty, at my age!

The Hoary Urchin was not a Taoist monk, but he had spent the majority of his life with the Quanzhen Sect, and their veneration of peace and tranquillity undisturbed by desires and worries had rubbed off on him.

Coming to terms at last with his inner burdens, Zhou Botong stood up and stepped outside, laughing.

The sky was a deep blue, dotted with a few white clouds.

The heavens were as clear and light as his heart. The torments Apothecary Huang had subjected him to seemed as trivial and commonplace as a flock of chickens foraging for bugs.

He simply did not care.

Still, I should leave a little memento for the Heretic. I'll probably never set foot on this island again. With that thought, Zhou Botong put the Nine Yin Manual inside his shirt and gleefully set about preparing his traps.

Several steps away from the cave, it struck him. This place is a maze! How am I going to find my way out? And I can't leave Brother Guo stranded here either; he'll certainly come to harm. I'll take him with me. Let the Heretic try to stop us! One Heretic cannot beat two Hoary Urchins!

Chuckling, he waved his arms and flicked his wrists in merriment.

Crack! A small tree snapped in two.

When did my strength improve so much? he asked himself, taken aback. This has nothing to do with the Competing Hands.

He rested his hand on the tree stump and tried to ascertain what had just happened.

He flung both arms out.

Crack, crack, crack, crack!

Half a dozen trees. Felled in an instant.

This is kung fu from the Nine Yin Manual! When . . . ? When did I learn that? A cold sweat broke out all over Zhou Botong's body, soaking him from head to toe.

He ran, screaming, "Ghosts! Ghosts!"

Though Zhou Botong had read the Nine Yin Manual many times over the years, he had faithfully followed his martial brother's dying decree and never put into practice the martial skills within.

However, in order to teach Guo Jing, he had read the text out and explained it, over and over again. Without conscious effort on his part, the contents had wormed its way into Zhou Botong's mind and seeped into his being as he slept.

After all, the Hoary Urchin was a quick and intuitive learner, with a deep understanding of the martial arts, and the Manual's kung fu was rooted purely in the Taoist tradition, just like his.

Now, his every move was informed by the theories laid out in the Nine Yin Manual. Its teachings were firmly implanted within him.

"Rot!" he squealed, realising what had happened. "I pulled a prank on Guo Jing and it rebounded on me!"

Zhou Botong slapped himself across the head, again and again, overwhelmed and full of regrets. Then another idea struck him. He tore a few strips of tree bark and fashioned them into a rough rope. With the help of his teeth, he tied his hands together.

"If I can't get the Manual's kung fu out of my head, then I'll never be able to fight again. Not even against the Heretic. I will not disobey my martial brother," he promised himself, sighing dramatically. "Urchin, oh, Urchin, you've brought this on yourself. Your little prank backfired spectacularly. You are the butt of the joke now!"

NEEDLESS TO say, Zhou Botong's answer left Apothecary Huang none the wiser as to why his hands were tied. He assumed it was yet another of the Hoary Urchin's games.

"Hoary Urchin, you have met Brother Ouyang before, and this is—"

"This must be Count Seven Hong," Zhou Botong said. He had already circled the group several times, sniffing theatrically. "He's a good man. As the saying goes, 'The celestial net of justice catches all who err.' My piss only drenched the Heretic and the Venom. You injured me with your palm strike once, Viper Ouyang, and I've just returned the favour. Now, we're equal."

With a disdainful curl of his lip, Viper Ouyang whispered into Apothecary Huang's ear, "Look how fast he moves! His kung fu – both internal and external – is clearly superior to ours. It's best not to upset him."

You haven't seen my kung fu for twenty years. How do you know it isn't as good as his? Apothecary Huang thought, before turning to Zhou Botong. "I shall repeat what I've said many times before. Hand over the Nine Yin Manual and you are free to leave the island."

Even now that Cyclone Mei had returned his wife's copy, Apothecary Huang still wanted Zhou Botong to surrender the original, so he could burn it as an offering, and his wife could read it in the underworld.

"I'm bored of this island. It's time for me to leave," Zhou Botong said.

"Then give me the Manual." Apothecary Huang held out his palm.

"I've given it to you already."

"Nonsense. When did that happen?"

Zhou Botong chuckled. "Guo Jing is your son-in-law, isn't he? So what belongs to him, belongs to you. I've taught him the whole Nine Yin Manual. From cover to cover. Have I not given it to you, then, in a way?"

"Is . . . Is that really what you taught me? The Nine Yin Manual?"

"Do you think I can make up something so complex?" Zhou Botong doubled over with laughter.

The truth left Guo Jing reeling, wide-eyed and dumbstruck.

The Hoary Urchin was delirious with joy. This look was worth all the hours, days and weeks he had put in. All the hard work. Even the predicament he faced at that very moment.

"You didn't tell me it was the Nine Yin Manual."

Zhou Botong loved nothing more than toying with his sworn brother's honest nature. "Huh? Don't you remember me saying that, because you're not part of the Quanzhen Sect, you wouldn't be defying my martial brother's final decree by learning from it?"

Apothecary Huang glared at Guo Jing before turning to Zhou Botong. "I would like to burn the original Nine Yin Manual as an offering to my late wife."

"Brother, could you do the honours?"

Guo Jing walked up to his sworn brother, reached inside his shirt and pulled out two thread-bound volumes, half an inch thick.

With his hands still tied together at the wrists, Zhou Botong clapped his palms over the books and said, "Here are the two volumes of the Nine Yin Manual. Take them – if you've got the skill."

"What do you mean?"

Zhou Botong tilted his head and pondered the question.

"The skill of binding and mounting," he said, with a giggle.

"Huh?"

The Hoary Urchin raised his hands over his head and thrust them skywards. Thousands of pieces of paper fluttered above him like a swarm of butterflies, dancing in the sea breeze, drifting east and flying west, impossible to catch.

An exceptional feat of internal kung fu. I could not tear such a thick pile of paper into so many small pieces in the blink of an eye, Apothecary Huang said to himself, stunned to find Zhou Botong suddenly so skilled. It took him a moment to collect himself. His mind slipped back to thoughts of his wife, fuelling his outrage at the Hoary Urchin's act of defiance.

"Hoary Urchin, you presume to mock me, do you? You will not leave this island today!" Apothecary Huang lunged, striking his palm at Zhou Botong's face.

Zhou Botong swerved a fraction to dodge the blow, his hands still tied together. He swivelled left and right as Apothecary Huang's palms sliced noisily around him, and neither so much as grazed his person.

The Cascading Peach Blossom Palm was Apothecary Huang's signature martial invention, but, twenty moves in, he had yet to force the Hoary Urchin to fight back.

The Heretic was about to channel more strength into his attack when he realised in horror what he was doing. How can I fight a man whose hands are tied? he thought, and he leapt back three paces.

"Untie your hands. Show me the might of the Nine Yin Manual. If you don't, I fear I may cause you harm again."

Zhou Botong shook his head, his face a mask of misery. "My hands are bound for a reason, and I will not break these bonds, no matter what."

"Then I'll break them for you!" Apothecary Huang shouted, grabbing at his wrists.

"Argh! Help! Help!" Zhou Botong threw himself to the ground and began to roll from side to side.

"Father!" Guo Jing rushed forward, curbed by a hand on his arm, pulling him back.

"Don't be silly," Count Seven Hong muttered, under his breath. "Just watch."

Zhou Botong was writhing on the ground with extreme agility. Not one of Apothecary Huang's strikes or kicks landed.

Guo Jing, transfixed by his display, recognised the Slithering Snake Pouncing Fox technique from the Nine Yin Manual, and cheered when Zhou Botong performed a particularly nimble dodge.

This only enraged Apothecary Huang further. His palm strikes were like sharp blades, slicing strips from Zhou Botong's sleeves and the hem of his robe. Even the tips of his hair and beard were trimmed by the searing force of Apothecary Huang's internal strength.

Zhou Botong knew he could not dodge Apothecary Huang much longer. If he were hit, it would be the end of him – or result in grievous injury, at the very least.

The Heretic now launched a renewed flurry of attacks. His left palm swept sideways. His right hand sliced down diagonally. Each blow contained three sly and lethal twists.

Caught between the two attacking hands, Zhou Botong realised now was the time to act. He summoned strength to his shoulders and – *pang!* – the ropes snapped. He raised his left arm to block, and at the same time twisted his right arm around to scratch his back.

"Ah, I can't ignore this itch any longer!"

Apothecary Huang was flabbergasted. How could anyone take the time to scratch an itch in such an intense fight? He let fly another three ferocious attacks, each containing the full force of a lifetime of martial training.

Zhou Botong sighed. "I can't overpower you with just one hand. But there's no other way. I will never disobey my martial brother."

He channelled all his energy into his right arm and let his left hang limp by his side. He was fully aware that his own kung fu was no match for Apothecary Huang's. The moment they connected, a great force pushed him back. He staggered and stumbled as he fought to keep his footing.

Palms raised, Apothecary Huang pounced. Zhou Botong was still reeling from his last attack.

"Fight with both hands! You can't block with just one arm!"

"No! I will only use one!"

"As you wish."

He struck down at Zhou Botong's lone arm with both hands and let his internal energy pour forth.

Thump!

Zhou Botong collapsed on his backside, his eyes closed. Blood shot out of his mouth, followed by a strangled gurgling sound. His face was now as white as paper.

Apothecary Huang stepped back. No-one could fathom why Zhou Botong had refused to fight back properly with both hands. Even if he could not win, he would not have lost within a handful of moves.

Zhou Botong opened his eyes, stood up slowly and said, "The Hoary Urchin fell for his own prank. Without realising it, I learned the kung fu from the Nine Yin Manual, against my martial brother's dying wish. If I'd used both hands, you would not have been able to subdue me."

Full of remorse, Apothecary Huang fell silent. Zhou Botong had not bound his hands and fought at a disadvantage just to spite him. He realised he had imprisoned this man for fifteen years for no real reason, and had now injured him once more in an irrational fit of rage. He reached into his shirt and took out a jade casket. He lifted its lid, counted out six pills and handed them to Zhou Botong.

"These Dew of Nine Flowers are made from rare and precious herbs. Take one every seven days. They will reduce the pain and aid the healing process. Brother Botong, I am very sorry for injuring you again. I, Apothecary Huang, humbly apologise. The injury you have suffered today will heal quickly, thanks to your deep *neigong*. I will see you off the island myself."

Nodding in gratitude, Zhou Botong took one of the pills and channelled his *qi* to heal his body. A moment later, he spat out a mouthful of darkened blood.

"Heretic, no wonder they call you Apothecary. This pill of yours is most effective. Hmm . . . What does my name, Botong, mean?"

It sounds just like "bottom"! Lotus thought, giggling silently, but, wary of her father's grave expression, she knew better than to make such a joke.

Zhou Botong pondered his question for a moment, then shook his head and said, "Heretic, I'm leaving now. Do you want to make me stay?"

"You are free to come and go as you please, Brother Botong. Should you wish to visit the island again, I shall welcome your return with all my heart, as my best friend and an honoured guest. I will send for a boat now."

4

GUO JING CARRIED ZHOU BOTONG ON HIS BACK, FOLLOWING Apothecary Huang to the shore, where half a dozen boats were moored in the bay.

"Brother Apothecary, there is no need to arrange another boat; Brother Zhou can sail with us," Viper Ouyang said.

"How very kind of you," Apothecary Huang replied, gesturing at a servant. The man disappeared into one of the larger boats and returned with a tray of gold ingots.

"Brother Botong, please accept this gift to fund your antics. Your kung fu is most certainly stronger than mine and I am full of admiration. If you decide to take part in the next Contest of Mount Hua, then I shall withdraw. The Heretic concedes that you are the Greatest Martial Master Under the Heavens."

Zhou Botong blinked and pulled a silly face, plainly delighted. But, the moment he looked over at Viper Ouyang's ship, he frowned and shook his head in disapproval.

Hoisted at the stern of the grand vessel was a large white flag embroidered with a double-headed snake, two forked tongues protruding from its open mouths.

Viper Ouyang made a rasping tone with a wooden flute and the vegetation seemed to come alive. Led by two servants, the snake herders of White Camel Mount guided their flock down to the bay. They slithered up the gangplanks in tidy rows and disappeared below deck.

"I hate snakes! I'm not setting foot on the Venom's boat!" Zhou Botong said.

"Of course. You are very welcome to use my boat." Apothecary Huang smiled and gestured towards a smaller vessel nearby.

Zhou Botong shook his head. "I want that big one!"

Apothecary Huang's face darkened as he saw where Zhou Botong was pointing. "I am afraid I cannot let you use that boat," he said in a queer voice. "It's being repaired."

The ship was impressive. Ornate, clean lines, the paintwork new, glistening like gold and jade. There was no visible sign of damage. It looked like it had never been used.

"I want the new boat! Why are you being so mean, Heretic?"

"Ill fortune sails with that vessel. Its passengers succumb to sickness or meet with disaster. That is why it is docked here and never used. I am not being mean. If you don't believe me, I will reduce it to ashes this instant." At Apothecary Huang's command, four servants ran towards the boat, each holding a flaming torch.

Zhou Botong flopped to the ground, pulling on his beard and crying loudly. Everyone was at a loss what to do – all except for Guo Jing. He was used to his sworn brother's tantrums and he was smiling on the inside.

"I want the new boat! I want the new boat!" the Hoary Urchin insisted, bawling like a newborn baby.

Lotus Huang raced ahead to stop the servants, returning a few moments later.

"Brother Apothecary, I will keep the Hoary Urchin company on this ill-starred vessel," Count Seven Hong said. "This old beggar is no stranger to ill luck. We shall fight fire with fire. Let's see if my dark cloud is blacker than your boat's curse."

"Brother Seven, do stay on the island for a few more days. Surely there is no need to leave so soon?"

"Beggars great and small are gathering in the city of Yueyang in Hunan soon, to hear this aged one appoint my successor. If I meet my fate without naming the next in line, the beggars of this world will be left without a chieftain. When the matter is settled, it would be my pleasure to visit you."

"You are a generous man, Brother Seven, devoting your life to the service of others, perpetually galloping back and forth."

"Beggars don't ride. It's my feet that do all the galloping! Wait, are you slyly insulting me? If I gallop, then I must be a horse!" he said, in good humour.

Lotus chuckled. "*Shifu*, you said it – not my pa."

"The martial father is never as close as a real father. I'd better find myself a beggar woman and get her to give us a beggar girl."

Lotus cheered and clapped. "I'd love a little martial sister. I'd cuddle her all day!"

All the while, Gallant Ouyang's eyes were fixed on Lotus. The sunlight gently brushed her cheeks, radiant as spring blossom, beautiful as a dawn sky. She gazed at Guo Jing so tenderly, so full of feeling, her affection so plain to see. One day, I will kill that wretched lad, he promised himself in a fit of jealousy.

Count Seven Hong held his hand out to help Zhou Botong to his feet. "I'll travel on the new boat with you. We know the Heretic is full of schemes, but we won't let him trick us."

Zhou Botong was overjoyed. "Old Beggar, you're so kind," he said. "We should be brothers."

"Brother, wouldn't it be odd to swear brotherhood with my *shifu*?" Guo Jing asked, before Count Seven Hong could reply.

"Who cares?" Zhou Botong laughed. "Your father-in-law is letting me sail in the new boat. I'm happy and I want us to be brothers."

Lotus giggled. "What about me?"

"I don't believe anything a lass says. One look at a beautiful woman is guaranteed to bring bad luck." Zhou Botong glared at her, then linked arms with Count Seven. Together, they marched towards the boat.

Apothecary Huang threw his arms wide to block their path. "I am not deceiving you. No journey in that boat will end well. There is no need for either of you to put yourself in such danger. And yet, forgive me – I would prefer not to say any more on the matter."

"You have made yourself very clear. I will praise your friendship, even as I die from seasickness."

Despite his jovial tone, Count Seven knew Apothecary Huang's warning was genuine. But he also knew nothing could change the Hoary Urchin's mind, and he could not let an injured man sail into danger alone.

"Perhaps I worry too much. Your extraordinary kung fu should see you safe." Apothecary Huang turned away from them and glared at Guo Jing. "Go with them, lad. Tell me, did Zhou Botong reveal to you that you were learning the Nine Yin Manual?"

"He never said so." Guo Jing shook his head. "I saw Cyclone Mei practise the Nine Yin Skeleton Claw. It was inhuman. I would have refused to learn, if I'd known it was—"

"Oh, you knew!" Zhou Botong cut Guo Jing off. There was no better time to pull a prank than when everyone else was deadly serious. "I only taught you the first volume! You told me you tricked Cyclone Mei into lending you her copy of the Manual. You made your own and learned it by heart. I remember you saying that Twice Foul Dark Wind's kung fu was too brutal and you weren't interested in it. But I told you Cyclone Mei had got it all wrong because Apothecary Huang didn't understand the text. He taught her the wrong method. And then I said I could show you how to correctly interpret the Manual."

"You . . . You never said any of that . . ." Guo Jing trembled uncertainly.

Zhou Botong blinked, a picture of sober sincerity. "I did. And you were delighted to hear it!"

It was hard for Apothecary Huang to believe Guo Jing could have learned the Nine Yin Manual by heart without knowing what it was he was committing to memory. Surely, Zhou Botong, with his child-like honesty, must have blurted out the truth. He did not imagine a martial master would joke about something so serious. Guo Jing was a lying, conniving cheat, who deceived people by playing dumb.

What's more, Zhou Botong's suggestion that it was Apothecary Huang who had led Hurricane Chen and Cyclone Mei's training down the wrong path was a mortal blow to his pride. They had misinterpreted the Manual, but not because of his instructions. He had already experienced enough upheaval and disillusion in one day. His wife had not chosen her son-in-law from beyond the grave. He had conceded the martial title he coveted to his prisoner of fifteen years. The man his daughter had given her heart to had turned out to be a treacherous knave. He could no longer hold back the tide of fury.

"Father . . ." Guo Jing said fearfully.

"I am not your father-in-law, you devious boy! If you set foot on Peach Blossom Island again, I will show no mercy!"

Apothecary Huang struck a servant from behind with the back of his hand. "This will be your fate!"

A low groan escaped from the servant's tongueless mouth as his body hurtled into the sea. The strike had ruptured his five internal organs, and he vanished beneath the waves. The other serving men fell to their knees in unison, fearing for their lives.

All of Apothecary Huang's servants had once been rogues and vagabonds. He had investigated each of their crimes before bringing them to the island, where he pierced their eardrums and cut out their tongues.

"I, Apothecary Huang, known as Heretic of the East across the *jianghu*, am not an upright gentleman," he had once said. "Naturally, I have no interest in keeping the company of upright gentlemen. As for my servants, the more evil and villainous they are, the more they are to my liking."

Weighed against the crimes he had committed, the servant's death was not to be pitied. But the senseless way in which he had been dispatched brought forth the same thought in everyone's mind: No wonder he's known as the Heretic! That servant took the brunt of his anger for no reason.

Unsure how he could have caused such offence, Guo Jing fell to his knees.

Apothecary Huang knew he was in danger of killing Guo Jing on the spot, he was so furious, but such an act would be unworthy of a martial master of his stature. Putting his hands together in a gesture of respect, he turned to Zhou Botong, Count Seven Hong and Viper Ouyang and, through gritted teeth, said, "Please."

"Guo—" Before Lotus could say any more, her father grabbed her hand and dragged her away.

Zhou Botong was struggling to contain his laughter, even as Apothecary Huang disappeared into the woods, and the merry convulsions were making his injury worse.

"The Heretic is so gullible. He's fallen for my prank again. He believed everything I said! I made it all up! This is so much fun!" He gave in to his mirth.

"So Guo Jing knew nothing?" Count Seven Hong had not been expecting such a revelation.

"Of course he knew nothing. Guo Jing believes with his whole being that the Nine Yin Manual is infernally wicked. Do you think he would have learned a word of it, if he knew? But, now that you've memorised it, brother, there's no way you can get it out of your head, is there?" Zhou Botong dissolved once more into laughter, the pain gripping his chest.

"This is a joke we can ill afford, Hoary Urchin. I will find Brother Apothecary to set things right."

Count Seven Hong ran into the forest, but it was criss-crossed with paths and trails, impossible to guess which one Apothecary Huang had taken. The servants had dispersed as soon as their master left the shore, so, unable to find anyone to guide him, Count Seven Hong gave up and returned to the others. Then he remembered. "Nephew Ouyang, could you lend me the map of Peach Blossom Island?"

"Please don't take offence, Uncle Hong, but, without Uncle Huang's permission, I am not at liberty to show the map to anyone."

Count Seven Hong sighed at his own stupidity. Of course he won't help – he wants the Heretic to hate my silly disciple!

Flashes of white appeared among the trees as the thirty-two dancers and musicians presented to Apothecary Huang emerged from the forest. The woman in front curtseyed to Viper Ouyang. "Master Huang asked us to return with my lord."

With barely a glance in their direction, Viper Ouyang waved them onto the ship and turned to Zhou Botong. "I will sail behind you. Should there be any trouble, I will gladly offer you assistance."

"Spare me your fawning! I want to find out what strange contraptions the Heretic has hidden on that ship. We won't come across any dangers if you sail behind us. Where's the fun in that? If you spoil my fun, I'll pour another jar of pee over your head!"

"Very well," Viper Ouyang said. He put his fist against his palm in a gesture of farewell and boarded his ship with his nephew.

5

GUO JING WAS STILL STARING AT THE SPOT WHERE LOTUS HAD vanished into the woods.

"Brother, come aboard. Let's see what this inanimate ship will do to us three living, breathing men!" Zhou Botong took Count Seven Hong's arm in his left hand and Guo Jing's in his right, pulling both of them up the gangplank at a sprint.

The crew of half a dozen men were waiting silently on board.

The Hoary Urchin took one look at the mute servants and said gleefully, "If one day the Heretic truly lives up to his wicked name and cuts out his darling daughter's tongue, then I'll say he's earned his title." Guo Jing shuddered at the thought.

Zhou Botong chuckled at his sworn brother's reaction. "Did I frighten you?" He gestured at the crew to get them underway. They lifted the anchor and unfurled the sails without a word. The south wind guided the boat gently into the sea.

"Let's find out what's so odd about this ship," Count Seven Hong said.

The three of them examined it carefully from the bow to the stern and from the deck down to the hold. Nothing seemed unusual or out of place. In fact, every spar and surface glistened with fresh paint. The galley was well stocked with water, rice, wine, meat and vegetables.

"The Heretic lied!" The Hoary Urchin felt cheated. "He said something wasn't right, but it all looks fine! Spoilsport!"

But Count Seven Hong still had his suspicions. He leapt onto the mast and rocked it a few times, before turning his attention to the sails, giving them a good tug. Everything appeared to be in perfect working order.

He watched as the gulls swooped and soared over the blue expanse, where sea and sky blended into one. The three sails pulled taut by the wind and took them northwards. His sleeves flapped in the sea breeze, and a carefree joy lifted his heart. Then he noticed Viper Ouyang was tailing them, keeping a distance of some two *li*.

He jumped down onto the deck and gestured for the crew to sail north-west. A few moments later, the Venom's vessel also changed course.

Why is he following us? Count Seven Hong was certain Viper Ouyang could not be keeping them company out of concern for their safety. If the Venom had grown a heart, then the sun would henceforth rise from the west.

The Beggar kept the discovery to himself, lest the Hoary Urchin throw another tantrum. He signalled the helmsman to head east. The sails all turned at once, and, as they were no longer catching the wind in full, the ship began to slow down. Once again, Viper Ouyang also changed course, still stubbornly tailing them.

Perhaps they'll try to board, Count Seven Hong thought, and he returned to the cabin. There sat Guo Jing, downcast and in a daze.

"I'll teach you a trick," Count Seven Hong said, to boost his disciple's spirits. "This is how we beggars wrangle for food. If they won't give you anything, you harry them outside their house for three days and three nights."

Zhou Botong giggled. "What if they've got nasty dogs and they set them on you?"

"Since they're so rich and yet know no kindness, sneak in at night and steal their treasures. Such a deed hurts no-one."

"Do you understand what your *shifu* is saying?" Zhou Botong turned to Guo Jing. "He's telling you to pester your father-in-law until you get what you want. If he still won't give you his daughter and he threatens to beat you up, go back at night and spirit her away. The best thing is, you're stealing a living treasure. You just need to say, 'Come, precious!' and she'll follow you! Easy!"

Guo Jing could not help but smile. Watching Zhou Botong pace up and down the cabin, he was reminded of someone. "Brother, where will you go now?"

"I don't know. I'll wander around — wherever takes my fancy. I've been on that little island for too long, the boredom was killing me."

"May I ask you for a favour?"

"If you're asking me to go back to help you steal your woman, then no!" Zhou Botong waved frantically to bat the idea away.

"No, not that . . ." Guo Jing flushed bright red. "I was hoping Brother would visit Roaming Cloud Manor, near Yixing, on the shore of Lake Tai."

"What for?"

"The lord of the manor, Zephyr Lu, is a great man and true hero. He was a disciple of Peach Blossom Island. Thanks to Twice Foul Dark Wind, his legs were broken by my father-in-law and he has been crippled ever since. Since Brother found a way to recover fully, I was hoping you might share your method."

"Oh, yes, that's simple. And, if the Heretic breaks my legs again, I'll know how to mend them once more. Break them now, if you don't believe me!" Zhou Botong sat down and extended his legs, goading Guo Jing with an impudent stare.

Guo Jing smiled. "I'm confident of your skills."

The cabin door crashed open and the helmsman tumbled through, his face ashen. He waved his arms and stamped his feet in panic, but he could utter no words to explain his fear. They leapt up and rushed after the man. Had the danger Apothecary Huang prophesied come true?

6

LOTUS HUANG CRIED ALL THE WAY BACK TO THE HOUSE, FURI- ous that her father had dragged her away before she could bid Guo Jing farewell. She ran into her room and slammed the door.

Now his rage had subsided somewhat, Apothecary Huang began to wonder if he had done his daughter wrong by condemning Guo Jing to death. He wanted to say a few words of comfort, but when he went to her room, his knocks were ignored. The door remained shut at supper time. He ordered a servant to bring her dinner, but the poor man was sent sprawling out of the doorway, along with the food he had brought for her.

Papa always keeps his word – he'll kill Guo Jing if he comes back to Peach Blossom Island. But, if I go looking for him, Papa will be left on his own. There'll be no-one here to keep him company.

For once, Lotus was at a loss what to do. Some months ago, after her father had said a few stern words to her, she had run away without a second thought. But when she was reunited with him at Roaming Cloud Manor, the first thing she had noticed was how grey he was at the temples. In the short time she was gone, he seemed to have aged ten years. The sight had weighed on her heart. She swore never to cause him to worry again, yet now . . .

She buried her face in her bed and sobbed.

If Mama were alive, she'd know what to do, she wouldn't let me suffer like this.

At the thought of her mother, she got out of bed and headed to the main hall.

Once outside, Lotus was greeted by a glittering heaven, full of stars. The summer air was heavy with the scent of flowers.

Guo Jing must be dozens of *li* from the island, now. Would they ever see each other again? She dried her tears on her sleeve and walked into a knot of blossoming trees.

Following a path carpeted by fallen petals and leaves, she was soon at her mother's tomb. In this part of the island, the trees were always lush and rare flowers bloomed all year. Her father had personally selected each of the plants that surrounded her mother's grave, collecting the most famous and unique flora under the heavens. Fragrance and beauty vied with each other under the moonlight.

Lotus put her hand on the tombstone, pressing down on the left and right side several times, before giving it a shove. The stone slab shifted to reveal a tunnel. She stepped into the unlit passage and followed it deeper underground. After the third turn, she triggered another mechanism to open a second stone gate. Once she had entered the burial chamber, she took out some tinder and a flint to light the coloured-glaze lamps on the altar.

Emotions swirled within her at the sight of her mother's portrait.

Mama, when I die, will I finally get to meet you? Is this how you look? So gentle and beautiful. Where are you now? Are you up there, in the heavens? Or down there, in the underworld? Maybe you're here, in this chamber, with me? Mama, perhaps I should stay in this room forever, so I can be with you always.

Not only had Apothecary Huang painted his wife's portrait and hung it in the burial chamber, he had also filled the space with many precious objects – antiques, jewellery and scrolls of paintings and calligraphy. A keen connoisseur, he had built up an impressive collection when he roamed the lakes and the seas, using his martial prowess to commandeer treasures from royal palaces, wealthy families and notorious bandits. When his wife passed away, he had interred everything with her body to keep her company.

Lotus looked from her mother's likeness to the jewels laid out around her. Warmed by the glow of the lamp, the pearls, jades and ambers glistened.

These treasures have no feelings, yet they are unchanging for hundreds and thousands of years. Lotus's sorrow was reflected in

their sheen. I shall turn to dust and earth, yet, on that day, these pretty things will still be here, as perfect as they are now. Is it because we have become aware that our lives must be fleeting? Was it because she was so clever that Mama was only allowed to live to twenty?

As she gazed at the portrait, she lost all sense of time. Eventually, she blew out the lamps and parted the woollen drapes to reveal her mother's jade sarcophagus. Feeling its coolness, she leaned against it and curled up on the ground. Sadness filled her heart, but she found some comfort in being there, as if she were pressing close to Mama.

The swing between extremes of joy and grief in this one day had exhausted Lotus, and soon she fell into a deep sleep.

She was back in Zhongdu, the Jin capital, in the Prince of Zhao's residence, fighting a group of martial men alone. Then she was on the northern border road, where she came across Guo Jing. Just as they got talking to each other, she thought she saw her mother. She wanted to see Mama's face, but it would not come into focus. She tried to get a good look at her, but suddenly Mama flew upwards into the sky. She ran and ran, earthbound, while Mama ascended higher and higher. Now, she could hear Papa's voice, calling Mama's name. His cries grew clearer and clearer.

Her father was calling from the other side of the drapes. She was not dreaming anymore. He was here, in the burial chamber.

Papa used to take her down here to see Mama all the time. He would carry her in his arms and report to his wife in great detail all the little things they had done that day. In recent years, these trips had become few and far between.

Hearing her father's voice right now did not surprise Lotus, but she was still angry with him and preferred not to make herself known. She decided to stay hidden behind the drapes until he had left.

"I made you a promise. I promised to find the Nine Yin Manual and burn it as an offering to you, so your spirit up there can learn its full contents again. You tried so hard to remember it. For fifteen years, I failed you. Today, I can at last fulfil my word."

Did Papa get the Nine Yin Manual today? Lotus was confused.

"I do not intend to kill your son-in-law. They insisted on taking that boat."

Does he mean Guo Jing? Why is he talking about the boat again? Lotus was worried, but her father said nothing further on the matter. Instead, he launched into a repetitive soliloquy detailing the solitude he had endured since her mother's passing. She had never heard him open up like this, and she realised how much pain she would heap upon him if she were to run away again.

We have years ahead of us, Guo Jing and I, she told herself. One day, we will meet again. We're not even twenty yet.

"The Hoary Urchin's kung fu is now superior to mine; I will not be able to send his soul to you. He destroyed the Manual today, the copy he lent you, all those years ago. I thought he had made me break my word to you. Who knows what higher powers induced him to insist on sailing out in the pageant boat I had built for our reunion?"

Papa has always forbidden me to play on that boat . . . but how can a boat bring Papa to Mama?

Lotus did not know that, when her mother died, her father planned to take his life, as the ultimate act of devotion. For a man of his martial skills, killing himself by hanging or poison would take a long time. His lifeless body would be left undefended from the abuse of his servants, too. So he decided to turn to the sea. He travelled to the mainland to capture the most skilled shipwrights. He had them build a very particular boat: the wooden hull was held together with glue and ropes, instead of being nailed tight with iron. In the bay, it was the most lavish of vessels, but, in open waters, as waves lapped and crashed, it would quickly come apart and sink.

Apothecary Huang's plan was to sail out with his wife's remains. He would play the "Ode to the Billowing Tide" as the ship disintegrated, and together they would find their final resting place beneath the waves. Such a death would be worthy of his status as a martial great and a fitting end to his life. Yet, each time he built up his resolve to take to the seas, he found he could not bear to take his infant daughter along or leave her behind. In the end, he built a tomb to inter his wife's body temporarily. At the same time, he continued to maintain and repaint the boat every year, to keep it in the best possible state of repair. He would set sail once his daughter had grown up and found a suitable home, when no earthly worries could hold him back.

Since Lotus did not know the story behind the boat, she had no idea of the danger Guo Jing was in, until she heard her father say, "Cyclone did return the Manual she took. But I know that you weren't able to set down that final strange passage accurately. Even with your extraordinary memory, how could it be possible to remember something you couldn't comprehend?

"Now sailing to you on the boat I made for us are the Hoary Urchin, who knows the Manual inside out, and the lad, Guo Jing, who can recite the text without a single mistake. When the sea takes them, I will have fulfilled my promise to you.

"I have sent as offerings two sets of the Nine Yin Manual – living flesh, instead of dead paper. Your spirit above must have the memory of heavenly creatures. Your mental abilities now must far exceed those of your mortal self, all those years ago. You can check the Manual in their minds against your memory, so you can at last rest in peace. Though, it's perhaps a little unfair on Old Beggar Hong, making him give his life for no reason.

"In one day, I will kill three supreme martial artists to keep the promise I made to you. When we meet again, you can proudly proclaim, 'My husband lives by his word – he carries out every vow he makes to his beloved wife!'"

A bitter laugh echoed in the stone chamber.

"Guo Jing didn't lie. He couldn't have taken the Manual from Cyclone, as the Hoary Urchin claimed. The passage of nonsense that came out of Guo Jing's mouth was structured, and longer than our incomplete, garbled version. Cyclone also wrote down a few lines of poetry, before she lost her sight. Knowing that lad's intellect, he'd have taken them to be part of the Manual and recited them out loud. But he didn't. The Hoary Urchin was pulling my leg. No doubt he lied when he said Guo Jing knew he was learning the Nine Yin Manual, too. It's not plausible, with his history with Cyclone and Hurricane.

"Lotus is so very fond of this honest fool. Her heart will hurt so much when she finds out he died at sea. But who in this world goes through life without a broken heart? Joy is limited, sorrow plentiful, the soul breaks, always! I never intended to kill Guo Jing! Lotus, Lotus, I have not done you wrong!"

The last words were spoken directly to Lotus, as if Apothecary Huang had sensed her presence in the burial chamber.

The boat must be fitted with some horrible, deadly contraptions! The thought made Lotus's hair stand on end and sent a chill to her heart, freezing her whole being. Given her father's precision and rigour, his design would not fail. Guo Jing, her *shifu* and Zhou Botong might have already fallen victim.

She wanted to rush out and beg her father to save them, but fear and shock had made her legs weak and she could not even stand. She tried to cry out, but her voice would not obey her. Slumped against her mother's coffin, all she could do was listen to his departing footsteps and the fading echoes of his melancholy laugh, ringing like a song and a sob.

Lotus tried to gather her wits. I must find Guo Jing. If I can't rescue him, then I'll die with him! Knowing her father's temperament and his obsessive love for her mother, there was no point asking him for help, especially after what he had said about offering the Manual to her spirit.

When she recovered her strength, she sprinted from the entrance of the tomb, all the way down to the shore, and leapt onto the first boat she could find. She shook the sleeping crew awake and ordered them to set sail immediately. As they emerged from the bay, she heard the sound of thundering hooves and her father's flute song floating on the breeze.

Lotus looked back to shore and saw Ulaan galloping back and forth along the shoreline, his coat glistening in the moonlight.

Ulaan must feel so sad, so constricted, here, on this island, she said to herself. He might be an exceptional steed, but his strength would be of little use if he boarded the boat with her.

Where do I start to look for Guo Jing on this boundless sea?

APPENDIX I

CHINESE MARTIAL ARTS AND PHILOSOPHY

CHINESE MARTIAL ARTS ARE INTRINSICALLY LINKED TO Chinese philosophy and its worldview, not dissimilar to the way that yoga is rooted in the Hindu tradition.

When practising martial arts, one is searching for a path towards spiritual cultivation through movement. It is an effort to attain focus and clarity of mind, the first step in preparing oneself to face the familiar existential questions: of life and death, and beyond. In a way, it is a form of meditation. Martial prowess is simply a by-product of this process, rather than its goal; becoming the *greatest fighter* would never be the original reason for training.

The exercises in martial-arts training are often a physical manifestation of aspects of the philosophies that underpin particular branches of kung fu. For example, in tai chi, grounded in Taoist beliefs, every stance, posture and movement expresses the circular, continuous interplay of growth and decline between yin and yang – very crudely put, relaxation and strength – in a search for balance through unceasing motion.

So far, in the *Legends of the Condor Heroes*, the theories and ideas behind the moves described do correspond to actual martial practice and classical Chinese writings. That said, the more fanciful ones are fictional, by and large.

For instance, Count Seven Hong's explanation of the underlying concept of the Dragon-Subduing Palm quotes directly from the *I'Ching*, also translated as the *Book of Changes*. This divination text is a cornerstone of Chinese culture and its beliefs, serving as a guide to moral, social and familial decisions, particularly important to Taoist thought. The names of individual moves also come from the *I'Ching*, with several drawn from the description and commentary of the first hexagram, called Dynamic.

Meanwhile, the opening lines of the Nine Yin Manual are taken from another text of the Taoist canon, *Classic of the Way and Virtue*, sometimes known by the Romanisation of its Chinese title, *Tao Te Ching*. The text, written by Laozi, a thinker believed to have lived around the sixth century B.C., is of central importance to the Taoist philosophy and religion, and was also influential in the development of Confucianism and Buddhism. *Classic of the Way and Virtue* is fundamental to the values and principles held by Chinese people over centuries, even to this day.

Quotes from these classic texts in this volume are phrased in the way that best relates to, and explains, a martial skill or a particular concept that is key to the narrative. Any readers interested in exploring these Chinese philosophical writings, and their influence on civilisation in East and South-East Asia, are encouraged to consult full translations of the original works, all of which have been rendered into many different languages.

APPENDIX II

NOTES ON THE TEXT

PAGE NUMBERS DENOTE THE FIRST TIME THESE CONCEPTS OR names are mentioned in the book.

P. 21 OUYANG XIU

Poet, historian and statesman, Ouyang Xiu (1007–72) exerts a lasting influence on Chinese culture. He led the compilation of two major histories, one on the Tang dynasty (618–907) and one on the Five Dynasties period (907–60). His prose and poetry departed from the strict, ornate conventions popular at the time, pioneering a new simpler style, cementing his reputation as a literary master. His works are still studied in Chinese schools to this day.

P. 23 ZHU XIZHEN

Xizhen is the courtesy name – acquired when a man comes of age, at twenty – of Zhu Dunru (1081–1159), a poet and statesman who lived at a time when the Song Empire was losing half its realm to the Jurchen. He is best known for his *ci* poems, whereby he set lyrics to the prosody of standard musical tunes, a literary form that reached its apogee during the Song dynasty.

P. 24   GRIEF FOR THE GREY HAIR REFLECTED IN THE MIRROR

Apothecary Huang quotes Li Bai's (701–62) poem "Bringing in the Wine", also translated as "Drinking Song". This Tang dynasty poet's name is sometimes spelled Li Bo, Li Po or Li Pai. He is regarded as China's greatest poet, alongside Du Fu (712–70).

P. 26   CENSOR-IN-CHIEF

The Censor-in-Chief was one of the highest-ranking officials at court, holding almost as much power as the Chancellor. The Censor was tasked with keeping corrupt and illegal practices in check, with the power to question fellow officials. The Censor's office – often called the Censorate, in English – controlled the lines of communication between officials and the Emperor: petitions and memorials to the throne had to be submitted through it; indeed, imperial edicts had to be countersigned by the Censor before they were passed on to the court. Though the power and remit of the Censor varied somewhat as dynasties rose and fell, this powerful role came into existence as early as the Han dynasty (206 B.C.–A.D. 220) and remained in place until the end of imperial rule in China, in 1911.

P. 26   THE GAOZONG EMPEROR

In 1126, the Jurchen Jin dynasty laid siege to the Song capital, Kaifeng. By 1127, they controlled the northern half of the Song Empire's realm, holding the Song Emperor Qinzong hostage, along with his father, the abdicated Huizong. Qinzong's brother, Gaozong (1107–87), fled south, re-establishing the Empire – subsequently known as the Southern Song dynasty (1127–1279) – in Lin'an. Gaozong was the first Emperor of the Southern Song, reigning from 1127 to 1162.

P. 26 CHANCELLOR QIN HUI AND GENERAL YUE FEI

Chancellor Qin Hui (1090–1155) is regarded as a traitor in Chinese history, due to his role in the death of the beloved patriot General Yue Fei (1103–42).

After the Song Empire lost its capital, Kaifeng, and the northern half of its territory to the Jin, Qin Hui became the leader of a faction in court which favoured maintaining the status quo with the Jin, negotiating treaties and paying tributes. However, Yue Fei, the commander of the Song forces, believed in taking the fight to the enemy and marching north to recover annexed territory; he had already successfully halted the Jin cavalry's advance south.

Chancellor Qin persuaded the Gaozong Emperor that General Yue was a threat: a successful campaign into the Jin-occupied north would likely result in Gaozong himself being dethroned if his captured brother and father were freed. Gaozong recalled Yue Fei from the frontline, sending twelve successive orders to urge the General's return, even though the Song army was on the verge of recapturing the capital, Kaifeng. Yue Fei had no choice but to abandon his campaign. Once he arrived in the southern capital, Lin'an, he was imprisoned and eventually executed.

Nonetheless, Yue Fei's reputation as a loyal subject was rehabilitated just twenty years later, and his name became synonymous with righteous loyalty, appearing frequently in novels, poems, plays and films throughout the centuries.

P. 26 JANG SATAM

Jang Satam is the region of modern-day Lijiang, Yunnan province.

P. 32 SHE POINTED AT TWO VOLUMES ON HER DESK

Bound volumes in Song-dynasty China were structurally very similar to books today. By the ninth century, printed books were already in mass production. Usually, they were made by carving words and pictures into wood. These wooden blocks were then inked and paper was pressed onto them. Placed in order, leaves then had a front and back cover added – often made of a thicker paper, or silk glued to a paper backing – before being stitched together using silk cord. When the binding of a book wore out or was damaged, the cover or stitching could be easily replaced or repaired.

Traditionally, Chinese books were bound on the right-hand edge, with the first word appearing at the top right and characters running down the page vertically; one turned the page from left to right – in the opposite direction to books in the West.

P. 32   MOON FESTIVAL

Moon Festival, also known as Mid-Autumn Festival, is the fifteenth day of the eighth lunar month, when the full moon is closest to the autumn equinox. On this night, it is believed that the moon is at its roundest and brightest. As the full moon appears as a perfect circle to the eyes, it becomes an image in the Chinese language for coming together and reunion. Therefore, it was, and remains, an important day for family and friends to gather and spend time together. The festival is rooted in thanksgiving rituals for the autumn harvest, not unlike similar celebrations in the West. Even today, Moon Festival is celebrated in Chinese communities with family dinners, outdoor strolls to admire the moon, and, in some cases, by making offerings to the moon and to related deities. Sweet or savoury pastries, known as mooncakes, are commonly gifted and eaten, with fillings and fla-vourings differing from region to region across China.

P. 35   SILVER STREAM / WEAVER GIRL AND THE COWHERD

Silver Stream is the Chinese name for the Milky Way; the Weaver Girl refers to the star Vega; similarly, Cowherd is the star Altair. In Chinese mythology, the Silver Stream was created by one of the most important deities of the heavens, Queen Mother of the West. Angry to discover that her daughter, the Weaver Girl, had fallen in love with a Cowherd from the mortal realm, she brandished her hairpin in rage: it became the Silver Stream, forcefully separating the lovers. However, the magpies of the heavens pitied the young couple and formed a bridge to allow the lovers to meet. The Queen Mother eventually relented, allowing Weaver Girl and the Cowherd to meet on the seventh day of the seventh lunar month each year, with the help of the magpies.

P. 35 NORTHERN DIPPER

The Northern Dipper is the constellation known as the Plough or the Big Dipper, formed by the seven brightest stars of the larger constellation Ursa Major. The position of the Northern Dipper was of great importance to the ancient Chinese: the constellation's unique outline meant it was easy to see with the naked eye, so it was a useful way to locate the Polaris and determine where north was; in addition, the Northern Dipper rotates east to west around the Polaris during the year and its position helped to mark seasonal changes. This group of stars also symbolised the imperial carriage trailing after the Emperor, who was represented by the star Polaris. In Taoism, the seven stars are sometimes regarded as a single deity, or separated into seven individual deities, each with unique celestial responsibilities.

P. 39 SPIRIT TABLET

Writing the name of an ancestor or deity on an object imbues it with their spirit. Usually taking the form of a wooden or stone plaque set on a stand, the spirit tablet is placed on a shrine or altar table and offerings are made. They are most commonly found in temples, but also in homes.

P. 73 SCRIBE'S BRUSHES

A weapon similar in shape and size to a Chinese calligraphy brush, with a slender cylindrical body and a pointed tip at one end. The weapon's main purpose is not to cut through the skin and draw blood like a dagger, but to disable opponents when targeted at acupressure points. Sometimes, it has a ring in the middle, or towards the rounded end, so that it can be twirled easily. Scribe's Brushes are usually made of metal or hardwood and most often wielded in pairs.

P. 96   HIS ART IS ROOTED IN THE FIRMNESS OF HIS STRENGTH

"Firmness" is used here as the opposite of "suppleness". Together, the two words form a fundamental concept that first appeared in the *I'Ching*, and are often used interchangeably with yin and yang.

To put it in very generalised terms, firmness is associated with yang (things that are tough, hard and strong), and suppleness with yin (things that are soft and malleable). For example, water can be considered as "supple", as it will change shape to fit any container, yet a trickle, over time, has the ability to bore through rock – something that is solid and unyielding, or "firm".

In this volume, the word "firm" recurs in the discussions of martial arts, especially as a way to characterise the way strength is channelled. It should be noted that the discussion of strength in the novel is not so much about how many kilograms of weight someone can lift or pack into a punch, but rather how the power of a strike has the ability to penetrate beyond the surface of the skin and shake the flesh, bone and organs beneath.

P. 114   *DIZI* FLUTE

A traditional Chinese transverse, side-blown flute, which is held horizontally when played. Usually made of bamboo, though also sometimes from the wood of another tree, or of metal or jade, its airy and bright sound can be found in most genres of Chinese folk music and Chinese opera. Uniquely, the *dizi* has an additional hole between the blowing hole and the finger holes, mounted with a thin membrane of bamboo tissue, creating a distinctive resonance and timbre.

P. 114   TOP SCHOLAR

Imperial China had an elaborate, multi-tiered public examination system to select educated men for state office. First implemented in the Tang dynasty (619–907), it remained in place up until the early twentieth century, towards the end of the Qing dynasty (1644–1911), when the Imperial Court and its system of government was pressured into reform. The Top Scholar, sometimes translated as Principal

Graduate, is the candidate ranked the highest among all those sitting the examination in the Imperial Palace.

P. 114 BOOK OF SONGS

One of the Five Confucian Classics, *Book of Songs*, also called *Classic of Poetry*, is the first anthology of Chinese verse. Containing some three hundred temple, court and folk songs dating back to the Zhou dynasty (*c.* eleventh century – 221 B.C.), the collection was, it is thought, compiled by Confucius (551–479 B.C.), and is studied and recited to this day, by children as well as scholars.

Lotus Huang quotes a line from the first and best-known poem in the *Book of Songs*, which, to Confucius, expressed the balance of "pleasure without being immoral, sorrow without wallowing in misery".

P. 159 *KANG* BED-STOVE

Found in central and northern China even to this day, the bed-stove – *kang*, in Chinese – is an important interior feature that warms homes during freezing winters. A brick or fired-clay platform, often taking up a third of the room, its hollow interior is connected to the cooking fire or stove in the kitchen or in the same room. The latter's hot exhaust heats up the earthen mass of the *kang*. A well-built bed-stove can retain heat for a good portion of the day without requiring much fuel or attention. Its warm surface is the site of social life and household activities throughout the day, and it also provides ample space for restful sleep at night.

P. 161 WINDOW PAPER

China is a relatively late developer when it comes to glass making. The first recorded use of glass panes was on specific portions of a handful of windows in one of the palaces within the Forbidden City in Beijing, at the beginning of the eighteenth century, during the Qing dynasty (1644–1911). Traditionally, Chinese windows consisted of wooden frames with a geometric lattice, which was pasted over with paper – to block out wind and dust, but which would still allow light to come through.

P. 161 SCHOLAR'S ROCKS AND MINIATURE ARTIFICIAL MOUNTAINS

Scholar's rocks and miniature artificial mountains are essential elements in a traditional Chinese garden. They are chosen for their sculptural shapes, distinctive textures and depth of colour, as focal points of the garden; they bring to mind soaring peaks or mountain paradises where immortals and deities dwell. The meticulous placement of these rocks, among ponds and springs, shrubs and miniature trees, pavilions and covered corridors, create the sense of being in the natural world, albeit in an entirely artificial environment. As one moves through a Chinese garden, its scenery shifts according to changing perspectives: be that the time of the day, changing seasons, or the viewing eye. Such a garden expresses the owner's taste, aspirations and personal cultivation – an integral part of the literati culture.

P. 172 ZHANG YUHU

Yuhu, or the Scholar of Yuhu, is the self-styled literary name of poet, statesman and calligrapher Zhang Xiaoxiang (1132–70). Yuhu refers to the city, Wuhu, south of the Yangtze River, where his family eventually settled after retreating south with the Song Empire during the Jin invasion. Zhang Xiaoxiang supported General Yue Fei's military campaign to claim back land lost to the Jin and petitioned to clear Yue Fei's name; as a result, he attracted the ire of Chancellor Qin Hui.

P. 177 THE CAVES OF CELESTIAL MASTER ZHANG AND HERMIT SHAN JUAN THE VIRTUOUS

These caves are well-known sights that have attracted travellers for hundreds of years and can still be visited today. The Cave of Celestial Master Zhang is named after two Taoist figures, Zhang Daoling (A.D. 34–156) and Zhang Guolao (c. mid-seventh to mid-eighth century). Both were believed to have lived in the limestone cave as hermits. The cave of Hermit Shan Juan the Virtuous is also a natural limestone cave, named after the recluse, Shan Juan, who refused legendary leader Emperor Shun's (c. twenty-third century B.C.) offer of the throne, preferring to roam the land instead, travelling to Yixing to live a life distanced from worldly demands. The cave is famous for its stalactites and underground river.

P. 179 MYSTERIOUS GATES / EIGHT TRIGRAMS / FIVE ELEMENTS

The Mysterious Gates are commonly referred to as a method of divination, though the method was most likely first applied on the battlefield as a way to devise formations and military dispositions. It determines the success or failure of any endeavour based on the interaction between time, space, people and divine forces, making predictions through a combination of astrology, geography, and an understanding of the seasons as they relate to the material world. The Mysterious Gates are intricately linked to the system of the Eight Trigrams, as well as the Five Elements, both of which are fundamental to traditional Chinese thought, explaining cosmology through the interrelationships between matter and natural phenomena – how they develop, co-exist and destroy each other.

A trigram is a symbol made up of three lines, each either solid or broken, with, altogether, eight unique combinations – the Eight Trigrams. When two trigrams are paired together, they form a hexagram; in total, there are sixty-four different combinations, here. These symbols are a key concept in the *I'Ching*. The interplay of the Eight Trigrams are held to explain all occurrences in nature and are a cornerstone of Chinese philosophy, touching every aspect of culture and science, including martial arts and music.

The concept of the Five Elements contributes no less to the Chinese understanding of the world: namely, the interaction between metal, wood, water, fire and earth. The existence of each depends on another. Yet, each element can also destroy another. For example, fire requires wood to burn, but, in turn, can be extinguished by water. The Five Elements also correlate to cardinal directions, seasons, colours, musical tones and bodily organs: they underpin explanations of the physical world as well as unseen structures and processes, from medicine to morality, from politics to society.

In Roaming Cloud Manor, these concepts are important to the overall spatial layout, resulting in an unexpected placement of man-made structures and vegetation, so that the whole functions somewhat like a maze. Only those familiar with the underlying philosophy, like Lotus Huang, are able to navigate it without becoming hopelessly lost.

P. 196   THE SONG CHANCELLOR SHI MIYUAN

Shi Miyuan (1164–1233) served as Chancellor of the Song Empire between 1208 and 1233. An advocate of peace with the Jin, he was also instrumental in installing Emperor Lizong, a minor prince outside the line of succession, to the throne (he reigned from 1224 to 1264), allowing him to exert great influence over the Imperial Court.

P. 200   PINGJIANG

Pingjiang is modern-day Suzhou, Jiangsu province.

P. 209   *XIAO* FLUTE

Traditional Chinese end-blown flute, which is held vertically when played. Its tone is more mellow and sombre than the horizontal side-blown *dizi*, and it is an instrument closely associated with the literati – indeed, it is sometimes described as the scholarly gentlemen's voice. It is often played as a solo instrument or paired with another instrument favoured by learned men, the fretless, seven-string zither, or *qin*. Commonly made from bamboo, but sometimes of jade or metal, the modern *xiao* is around seventy to eighty centimetres in length.

P. 218   WANG XIANZHI / WANG XIZHI / MADAM WEI / ZHONG YAO

Four calligraphers whose work shaped Chinese calligraphy. It is believed that Zhong Yao (151–230) contributed to the formation of the tall, rectangular Regular Script, as Chinese writing evolved from a squatter, wider Clerical script, which was first developed around the third century B.C. Regular Script is the forerunner of the "typeface" we see in print and standard handwriting today.

Madam Wei (272–349), whose full name was Wei Shuo, learned from Zhong's work, developing theories of calligraphy and ways of using the brush that remain fundamental to the art.

As a child, Wang Xizhi (303–61) was taught calligraphy by Madam Wei. He remains one of the most celebrated and admired practitioners and his style has been emulated throughout the centuries. However, no work by his own hand has survived, except those carved in stone. All we know of his calligraphy comes from copies made by later calligraphers.

Wang Xianzhi (344–386) was Wang Xizhi's son and studied calligraphy from his father. He is best known for his Cursive Script, a very fast way of writing that blends individual strokes of characters into a continuous flowing line, conveying a great sense of energy and movement. Again, his work only survives through a handful of reproductions made during later dynasties.

P. 277   FLORAL CARVING YELLOW WINE

Yellow wine is one of the oldest alcohols in the world – it is mentioned in written records dating back at least two thousand years. It can be made of rice, sorghum, millet or wheat, depending on the region where the wine is produced. It is not uncommon for the wine to be aged for a decade or two, however, because it is not distilled, its alcohol content is no more than twenty per cent.

Floral Carving yellow wine is made with glutinous rice and is specific to the Zhejiang region. The city of Shaoxing is its most famous producer. The name Floral Carving likely comes from the ceramic container in which the wine is aged. Such vessels are decorated with auspicious patterns and sometimes painted before being buried, leaving the wine to mature. In the past, families would brew such wine after the birth of a child, only unearthing them at the child's marriage, presenting them as a dowry or gifts to be drunk at the celebration.

Yellow wine from Shaoxing tends to be slightly sweet, rather similar to sherry in taste, and is often used in Chinese cooking, for example, drunken chicken is traditionally marinated with a yellow wine of good vintage.

P. 288   DISCIPLE OF EIGHT POUCHES

The number of pouches indicates how senior a member is in the Beggar Clan. There are only nine Disciples of Eight Pouches, who sit close to the top of the hierarchy, just beneath the Chief of the Clan and the Disciples of Nine Pouches, of which there are four; the most junior beggars have no pouches at all. The Beggar Clan is a fictional community that has appeared in martial arts novels by different authors.

P. 323   UNDEAD

The undead, here, refers to "hopping cadavers", one of the many supernatural creatures in Chinese mythology. They are dead bodies that somehow did not decay, and instead became reanimated. They tend to shun the light and prefer darkness, and survive by sucking on the qi, or life energy, of a living person. The common explanation of why these creatures "hop" – instead of being able to move naturally – is that their bodies are stiff from rigor mortis. There are many stories, films and games that feature this kind of supernatural figure, and they may have been inspired by the custom of transporting the dead back to their hometown for burial.

P. 332   GE HONG

Ge Hong (284–364) was a physician and Taoist who left behind writings detailing chemical reactions and his efforts at alchemy – a Taoist attempt to achieve immortality – as well as some of the earliest extant descriptions of and remedies for infectious diseases, including smallpox.

P. 332 HE SPLASHED INK ON THE SHORE, LEAVING DEEP MARKS, SHAPED LIKE PEACH BLOSSOMS, IN THE ROCKS

Jin Yong notes that he has seen floral markings on the rocks when visiting Peach Blossom Island, one of the largest of the Zhoushan Islands, an archipelago of more than a thousand islands at the mouth of Hangzhou Bay, across from Ningbo, in Zhejiang province. The author adds that the patterns were in fact fossilised remains of trilobites and other prehistoric marine life.

P. 346 HUIZONG / ZHENGHE REGNAL ERA

Emperor Huizong (1082–1135) was better known for his calligraphy and paintings than his ability to govern. He invented the Slender Gold style of calligraphy, so called because the form resembles gold filigree work: delicate and full of twists and turns. His paintings, mostly of birds and flowers, were treasured for their meticulous detail, accurate colours and elegant composition, and can still be found in museum collections today. Huizong's pursuit of the arts meant that he left the management of the country – domestic affairs as well as military matters – to the court, resulting in his favourite eunuchs amassing enormous power. Furthermore, the territorial ambitions of the Jurchen Jin Empire were overlooked, to great personal and national cost. When the Jin forces pressed close to the capital, Kaifeng, in 1125, he abdicated and fled to the south-east of the country, and, by 1127, he had been abducted with his son, the Emperor Qinzong, after the Jin sacked the city. He died eight years later, as an exiled captive in Manchuria, in the far north, a decade later.

In China, the custom of an Emperor declaring an era name as they ascended to the throne began around the second century B.C.; the year was named the first year of that era. Some Emperors used only one era name throughout their reign, others changed them according to personal preference or political needs. Era names are often auspicious and sometimes express the ideas that the Emperor held regarding his role or hopes for the realm. Emperor Huizong bestowed six different era names during his reign, from 1100 to 1125;

the Zhenghe era was between 1111 and 1118, and its name means "Harmonious Governance".

P. 346 *TAOIST CANON OF TEN THOUSAND LONGEVITIES*

It is believed that a Taoist canon was first compiled in the fifth century, when around 1,200 scrolls or volumes of Taoist teachings and commentaries were collected by monks. During the Tang dynasty, in the eighth century, Emperor Xuanzong ordered the compilation of another Taoist canon, which eventually became the *Taoist Canon of the Kaiyuan Reign*. This work, of at least 3,700 volumes, was destroyed during wartime, at the end of the dynasty. During the Song dynasty, several Emperors compiled Taoist canons, expanding on their predecessors' work; the first of the era was around 4,300 volumes in length. When it came to Emperor Huizong, not only did he bring the total number to 5,481, he also had the texts carved and printed. However, this version has not survived.

P. 346 HUANG SHANG

A historical figure in charge of the printing of the Taoist canon, who lived between 1044 and 1130. Huang Shang was also Minister of Rites, an important government role overseeing religious rituals, court ceremonies, imperial examinations and foreign relations.

P. 347 MANICHAEISM

A religion founded in Persia in the third century, by Mani (c. 216–74). It is based on a primeval, dualistic struggle between light and darkness – with light seen as spiritual and good, and darkness as material and evil – with salvation possible through knowledge of spiritual truth.

The religion spread quickly through the Roman Empire, reaching Spain by the fourth century. However, by the fifth century, it had mostly disappeared from Western Europe and, by the seventh century, from the rest of the Roman Empire.

Manichaeism's spread to the east, especially to China, began in the seventh century, with the opening of trade routes. The religion gained recognition from the Imperial Chinese Court in 732, but, in 843 – still during the Tang dynasty (619–907) – it was proscribed. However, Manichaeism was likely practised in China until at least the fourteenth century, through the Song dynasty (960–1279), the Yuan dynasty (1271–1368) and the early years of the Ming dynasty (1368–1644).

P. 347 GRAND SUPREME ELDERLY LORD / GREAT SAGE AND FIRST TEACHER CONFUCIUS / TATHAGATA BUDDHA

These three figures are crucial to the three main religions or spiritual systems in China: Taoism, Confucianism and Buddhism.

The Grand Supreme Elderly Lord is one of the Three Pure Ones – the highest deities in the hierarchy of the Taoist pantheon. He is believed to be the founder of Taoism and to have been manifested in the human form through Laozi (c. sixth century B.C.), the author of *Classic of the Way and Virtue*, also known by the Romanisation of its Chinese title, *Tao Te Ching* or *Dao De Jing*.

The Great Sage and First Teacher Confucius refers to the philosopher whose ideas are the cornerstone of Chinese morality, ethics and social relationships. His influence touches the cultures of many East Asian countries. Confucius lived between 551 and 479 B.C.

Tathagata is one of the titles assumed by a buddha, often used by the Buddha Siddhartha Gautama to refer to himself.

P. 358 THE EIGHT TACTICAL FORMATIONS DEVISED BY THE MILITARY STRATEGIST ZHUGE LIANG

Zhuge Liang (A.D. 181–234) was an adviser to Liu Bei, founder of the Shu-Han dynasty (221–263) during the Three Kingdoms period (220–280). His name remains a byword for exceptional intelligence and insight, and he was immortalised in the popular imagination by the fourteenth-century historical novel *Romance of Three Kingdoms*, attributed to the author Luo Guanzhong, as well as countless other plays and stories. Zhuge Liang was credited with the invention of the Eight Tactical Formations, based on the directions of the Eight Trigrams laid out on a wheel and the cyclical relationship of creation and destruction of the Five Elements, as noted above in the entry on the Mysterious Gates / Eight Trigrams / Five Elements. However, few details of the Formations are known. They are believed to be strategic combined-arms deployments of cavalry and infantry that encouraged high morale and provided each soldier with sufficient space to wield weapons in combat, along with intelligent use of topography to entrap opposing forces by disrupting their organisation.

P. 388   GHOSTS OF IMPERMANENCE

Two deities in charge of escorting the spirits of the dead to the underworld, sometimes also called Black and White Impermanence.

P. 406   *ZHENG* ZITHER

A traditional Chinese plucked-string musical instrument with moveable bridges. The number of strings varied over time, from twelve strings in the fifth century to the twenty-one strings of the most common version played today. The body – the resonating chamber – tends to be made of wood.

P. 409   *QINGYU* HALF TONE

Traditionally, the Chinese musical scale is pentatonic, with only five notes per octave: *Gong* 宮 (do), *Shang* 商 (re), *Jue* 角 (mi), *Zhi* 徵 (so), *Yu* 羽 (la), with *Yu* being the highest note of the sequence. *Qingyu* is half a tonic note above *Yu*; it is part of the seven-note-per-octave heptatonic scale. For example, if *Gong* is middle C and *Yu* is A, then *Qingyu* is A sharp.

P. 434   SILK AND BAMBOO

Two major families of traditional Chinese musical instruments – stringed instruments, with strings traditionally made of silk, and a variety of flutes and pipes, mostly crafted from bamboo, similar to the category of woodwind in Western orchestras.

P. 484 THE HEAVENS / THE UNDERWORLD

The Chinese cosmos is made up of three realms: the heavens, where gods and celestial beings hold court; earth, where deities and mortals live; and the underworld, where the souls of the deceased go.

Unlike the Christian Hell, which is a place of perpetual punishment, the "life" led by the dead in the Chinese underworld is believed to be similar to their corporeal self, with the same needs for food, money, clothing and housing.

Depending how far one reaches back in history and one's belief, the underworld may differ somewhat. However, there is usually an element of where the soul will be judged or assessed by how virtuous one has lived. This decides where the soul goes next: ascend to the heavens and join the ranks of gods; or face reincarnation, where the soul becomes human again, perhaps, or may become an animal.

During the judgment process, the soul may face punishment – sometimes grisly – for crimes committed when alive. Nevertheless, the majority of souls, at some point, leave the underworld to begin a new life in the earthly realm; only a select few are granted a place with the celestial beings in the heavens and transcend this cycle.

JIN YONG (1924–2018) (pen name of Louis Cha) is a true phenomenon in the Chinese-speaking world. Born in Mainland China, he spent most of his life writing novels and editing newspapers in Hong Kong. His enormously popular martial arts novels, written between the late 1950s and 1972, have become modern classics and remain a must-read for young readers looking for danger and adventure. They have also inspired countless T.V. and video game adaptions. His death in October 2018 was met with tributes from around the globe.

Estimated sales of his books worldwide stand at 300 million, and if bootleg copies are taken into consideration, that figure rises to a staggering one billion. International recognition came in the form of an O.B.E. in 1981, a Chevalier de la Légion d'Honneur (1992), a Chevalier de la Légion d'Honneur (2004), an honorary fellowship at St Antony's College, Oxford, and honorary doctorates from Hong Kong University and Cambridge University, among others.

GIGI CHANG translates from Chinese into English. Her translations include classical Chinese dramas for the Royal Shakespeare Company and contemporary Chinese plays for London's Royal Court Theatre, Hong Kong Arts Festival and Shanghai Dramatic Arts Centre.

THE NEXT TWO VOLUMES OF LEGENDS OF THE CONDOR HEROES

VOLUME III: A SNAKE LIES WAITING

Guo Jing is faced with the evil plotting of Venom of the West Viper Ouyang, who is determined to become the most powerful Master of the *wulin* and win Lotus Huang for his nephew Gallant Ouyang. The full extent of Yang Kang's treachery is also revealed.

VOLUME IV: A HEART DIVIDED

Guo Jing's love for Lotus Huang is tested when he becomes convinced that her father has murdered someone dear to him. Upon his return to Mongolia, he discovers Genghis Khan wants to enlist him to help conquer the Chinese. Guo Jing must prove his loyalty to the country of his birth if he is to be worthy of bearing the name of his patriot father, Skyfury Guo.